Angle of Attack

By
David A. Mallach

FIRST EDITION

Library of Congress Control Number: 2017935111

ISBN 978-0-9860459-0-5

Website: dmallach.com

Penhurst Books

Printed in the United States of America
by Bookmasters

Dedicated

To
Dr. Glenn Hyatt
For helping me and
so many people stay healthy and happy.

From the Author

This book is a work of fiction. Therefore, it should not be assumed by any reader that any specific investment or investment strategy made reference to in this book will be either profitable or equal to historical or anticipated performance levels. It should also not be assumed that the performance of any specific investment style or sector will be either profitable or equal to its corresponding historical index benchmark. Finally, different types of investments involve varying degrees of risk, and there can be no assurance that any specific investment or investment strategy made reference to in this book will be suitable or otherwise appropriate for an individual's investment portfolio. To the extent that readers have any questions regarding the suitability of any specific investment or investment strategy made reference to in this book for their individual investment(s) or financial situation, they are encouraged to consult with the investment professional of their choosing.

About the Author

David Mallach is a Managing Director of Investments for one of the world's largest investment firms where he has spent his entire professional career since 1973. He resides in the greater Philadelphia area. He is the author of *Dancing With The Analysts, Walking With The Analysts, Running With The Analysts, Myth, The Trillion Dollar Sure Thing and Turning Final.*

David is a selected member of *Registered Representative Magazine's* Outstanding Advisor of the Year and *Research Magazine's* Hall of Fame. In 2010, 2011 and 2012, he was selected as one of the top 1,000 advisors in America by *Barron's Magazine*. David serves on the Board of Trustees for Gwynedd Mercy University and the Troy University Foundation. David is the proud father of five children, an accomplished saxophone player, and a registered private pilot.

Preface

This is the third book in a trilogy, following *The Trillion Dollar Sure Thing* and *Turning Final*. *Angle of Attack* is my darkest work to date. This book is the culmination of my exploration into three fundamental questions. First, do the forces of good and evil exist in all of us? Second, how does this shape the human experience? And third, what are the possibilities for meaningful change?

I know these questions have challenged history's greatest thinkers. As a novelist, I must inevitably face them myself. As a novelist, I must aspire to take on the Herculean task of dramatizing the human struggle to make sense of it all. This is where the pen meets the paper, so to speak. This is where the novelist lives—in the space between what is and what could be, the battlefield where the wonderful world of possibility clashes with the dead weight of fate.

When I started this, my second trilogy, I did not know where my characters would take me. They're alive, you know. My characters live all around me, each a pastiche of the world. Some of them live in the shadows; others stand as a beacon of light. When I set out writing *The Trillion Dollar Sure Thing*, I wanted to explore the resonance of different cultures as they interacted on the world stage. From there arose Becket Rosemore, the man who would be president of the

United States. At the time, Beck seemed like a decent guy—a bit egotistical and power hungry but determined to do the right thing. His goals were aligned with a noble cause, and that was enough for me to breathe life into his literary soul.

However, when I paired him with Camille O'Keefe, a vibrant, spiritual, clairvoyant, something intriguing happened. My hero, the great Becket Rosemore, became a different man. A terrible beast emerged in *Turning Final*. What's more, I felt no desire to control the beast. I let him run rampant into his own demise. From the ashes arose the great, redheaded Camille O'Keefe, a woman representing the voice of alternatives and the power of possibility.

As a writer, it's wonderful when one of my characters outgrows me. This is Camille. She fascinates and enthralls me. There is so much mystery about her, so much I don't understand. But as I contemplated this book that you hold in your hands, I realized I must challenge that which I hold most precious. This is, in my opinion, the great art of the novel. As a matter of course, Camille O'Keefe was heading for the greatest challenge of her life. To be honest, I wasn't sure if she was going to survive the ordeal.

Welcome to *Angle of Attack*, the harrowing story of Camille O'Keefe and her fight against *Boko Haram*, the despicable terrorist outfit in Nigeria specializing in raping and murdering women and children. Those whom they do not slay, they sell into sex slavery. *Boko Haram* is a scourge and has a hand in the most vile activities. Rape and murder are just the beginning. The group embodies the dire state of affairs in Africa. Accordingly, Camille O'Keefe needs to go there, to see it for herself, to bear witness for my readers, to relate to you the scope of atrocity and the depth of human depravity.

The Trillion Dollar Sure Thing attracted attention within the United States military establishment. Because the book raises unique geopolitical scenarios, I was extended a personal invitation to participate in a week-long symposium at the prestigious United States Air University, the war college of the United States Air Force. What I experienced there shattered my world view and laid bare a state of affairs in Africa I never knew existed. I left the Air University determined to write a story that too many choose to ignore, a story that cuts to the core of our existence. Unfortunately for Camille, she has to pack her bags, too. What follows is *Angle of Attack*. I have supported worthy projects in Botswana, and I even own a house there. But never have I exposed myself to the rest of the sub-Saharan continent like I do in *Angle of Attack*. This book plunges into the world of shadows—the darknet, sex trafficking, the resource state, terrorism, corruption and espionage. You will hate being dragged there because it will reveal a part of us we don't want to see.

As with my previous books, Todd Napolitano worked beside me to make this story come to life. Todd helps bring my world of ideas to life in magnificent fashion. This story is cutting and harsh. Yet there are moments that give hope and affirm human potential. Todd helps bring this duality to words in a way that conveys the great complexity of human existence.

I am also deeply indebted to the following people:

Jeanette Freudiger, to whom once again I owe special thanks for her long-term work so closely related to this novel and my previous works. She was always ready with her wit, help, and advice to insure that this novel was designed in the most thorough and entertaining fashion;

Sharon Cromwell, my editor who made this manuscript and all my books readable novels;

Stephanie Heckman, for her tireless editing of this novel;

Rhonda Branch, for her support and editing skills;

John Sasso, my longtime friend and editing professional;

Bob Wagner, my Costa Rican advisor whose Internet skills are equal to his generosity;

Lt. Colonel David Warnick USAF, for his accurate battle procedures;

Lieutenant Jeff Webb, Navy SEAL Operator, for sharing his real life experiences;

Lt. Colonel Phil Schrode, for sharing what war really feels like;

Lastly, I thank all the wonderful investors I have known, who in their quest for growth chose to honor me with their trust.

Chapter 1

When did *jihad* become a household word? On September 11, 2001. On that day, the rules we live by, what we find acceptable and abhorrent, shifted. The dust has now settled on a very different world. It is a new dawn.

The sun begins to rise over the horizon, bathing the Nigerian village in a calming pink glow that will soon dissipate. The many homes, built from cinderblock or mud and clay, are still dormant. That, too, will soon change. Stray dogs wend their way from house to house in search of a spare morsel. They must compete with the villagers for survival, for in this Nigerian village in Borno, near Chad, there is never enough to feed the people, let alone feral dogs. Rain would be very welcome, but there will be none. Despite the proximity of Lake Chad to the east, the Borno region is an expanse of arid dirt. A breeze would be nice, but there will be none of that either. Instead, the desiccated earth coughs dust into the air at the slightest provocation, making babies cough and children wheeze, while those old enough to toil through the day will be covered in dust and grit by noon.

These are the children who are strong enough to cough and wheeze. These are the children who haven't yet died, who are living on borrowed time—if you can call existing in a permanent state of hunger, disease and despair "living" at all. 40 out of every 1,000 babies die here. Many children in the village will perish, reclaimed by the harsh realities that govern their lives in a country where millions more die each year from starvation, disease and war. We cannot forget war. It is a way of life and the path to death.

Daraja is the first to awaken in her hut. The rest of her family is still asleep. Her husband, Yabani, lies next to her. He is sprawled on his back, legs spread, so that Daraja barely has room to lie on the filthy, threadbare mat they call a bed. It's okay. It is his home after all. She knows it is his prerogative to take up as much of anything as he sees fit within these walls.

Many of the people in Borno province are Muslim, and have been so for centuries. Identifying themselves as Allah's chosen people, the Muslim families in the village all live next to each other in the middle of the village. They send their children to the local *madrasa*. The boys learn to read and write. They also study the Koran. The girls are not taught to read and write. They study the Koran and the teachings of Mohammed through lecture and memorization. The girls wear the full *hijab*. They are taught by male teachers whom they are forbidden to meet face-to-face.

Daraja and Yabani live along the perimeter of the village along with the rest of the non-Muslim families. Because they are not Muslim, they lack much of what the Muslims have secured for themselves. Their lives are devoid of formal education. Instead, they garner their lessons from life's harsh realities. Like almost all of the other non-Muslim children in the village, Daraja's children will not learn to read, will not learn to write, will not learn the teachings of Mohammed, or Jesus or Buddha. A few children fortunate enough to outlive their parents, "fortunate" enough to be orphans taken in by some Western relief agency, will have a chance at education. The rest learn about life through their constant struggle with death.

Everyone in Africa has a death story. Some have more than others. Death stories originate in places like Borno, Nigeria. The story of Daraja and Yabani is a death story, one among so many others that will never be told but only suffered by a mass of people like them who seem born cursed to an anonymous death in a land nobody cares about, save for the huge deposits of oil and other precious resources. For the very select few, the system also mines and refines immense wealth along the way.

That is the usual story the world hears. And it is true. But the story of Daraja and Yabani is not a story of oil, precious metals and wealth disparity. For them, it doesn't matter what resources lie buried for the taking. It doesn't matter what day of the week it is. Every day is the same for them, so why worry about what day it is? The hours melt into one another. A distinct dreariness infiltrates everything, working its way into the fiber of everyday life. A steady monotony dictates the pace of life.

It's different for the many Muslim families residing in the northeast of Nigeria. For them, the day is graciously divided into five prayer times that bring meaning to the monotony of existence. For the non-Muslim families in the village, keeping the time or keeping a calendar is a pastime of privilege that presupposes there is something important to do. Daraja's day is not organized by the Koran. Her day is governed by the immutable law of survival. In Borno, in this village, staying alive is the primary chore, and a last-minute meeting with death can be made without an appointment.

And so Daraja rolls off the mat and stands up, not knowing that today is her family's appointment with death but assuming it could be all the same. By the time Yabani wakes up, stretches away the stiffness of his life and makes his way into the eating area, the intense heat of the northern dry season begins to make itself known. As the sun works its way upward, scorching rays melt the mellow pink tones that earlier enveloped the village, penetrating the landscape with harsh heat and bright white light. From the perimeter of the village where their house sits, Daraja and Yabani can see for miles out across the barren surroundings. Eventually, when the rains come, crops will rise from that ground. But they will rise unwillingly, for the soil is much less fecund than what the people have in the south of Nigeria. Once again, it comes down to the birth lottery.

When Yabani enters the small room that serves as a kitchen and family area, he is greeted by Daraja first, and then by Bako. Bako, twenty-one, lives with the family. He is not part of the family, but he is part of the household. Like 10 percent of Nigeria's population, Bako's parents died of HIV. He entered Yabani's household agreeing to work the fields during the planting and harvesting seasons and also help protect the family. In exchange Yabani gives him shelter, food and clothing. There are young males like Bako in every village. It is a mode of survival, a throwback to pre-capitalist days where barter and exchange ruled.

Daraja is busy trying to make something interesting out of the same dried maize they've been eating for days. She hands Yabani a cup made from a hollowed-out gourd.

"This is indeed a good morning," says Yabani, swirling the liquid. "I have not had a drink of *Fura de Nono* since . . . yesterday," he adds, making reference to the drink made from pounded millet, a bit of sorghum and some cow's milk.

"Morning?" chirps Daraja with a tone of consternation. If she had a clock, if time actually mattered, she would have motioned to it sardonically. "It is almost time for bed."

Daraja sits down on the dusty woven mat that covers the dirt floor. Seated along with Bako is Daraja and Yabani's only son, Zaki, thirteen. Sitting next to Zaki are the three girls of the family, Tambara, Alkana and Iyawa. Tambara is fourteen; Alkana and Iyawa are ten and nine, respectively.

Yabani is the only one with a cup of *Fura de Nono,* which he sips gently, savoring what little he has. There is not enough for anyone else. Instead, Daraja hands round bowls of white rice with some lentils. She gives Yabani his rice first. He is the man of the house. Next is Zaki, the eldest son. Bako receives the third bowl. Even though he is not related, he is still a male and entitled to certain privileges.

"Yabani is a hard-working man who needs his rest," jokes Bako. They all laugh because there has not been work to do since the dry season started. "I mean to say, he works very hard pleasuring himself."

Daraja balks at the crude joke. "Bako, do not speak that way in front of the children." The household belongs to Yabani, but the children are her purview.

Yabani waves his dry, cracked hand. "Do not mind my wife, Bako. She knows she has cut me off after Iyawa was born." He makes a snipping gesture, implying she castrated him.

"There are many mouths to feed," replies his wife.

Yabani has a sour look. "Eh . . . everybody here has mouths too big."

Daraja is used to this sort of outburst from Yabani. "My husband has a very special mouth. He puts rice and millet in, and strange words come out. You will understand when you have a family of your own, Bako. Wishes and desires are not for people like us. We are people trying to survive. And then we die. What happens in between we call life, but I wonder sometimes."

"And then we die," says Yabani, toasting her with his cup mockingly. "And I am free."

"I'm going to go to Chad to find my wife," says Bako.

"Me, too!" exclaims Zaki. "I want to go to Chad with you, Bako."

Yabani scoffs. "What use is there for you in Chad, boy?"

Bako puts his tongue between his teeth and makes a sucking noise. "What use is there for *me* here? For any of us?"

Yabani laughs. He is rather jovial this morning. "I found my woman right here. Our families arranged it all. Daraja had eyes for another, but she came to see things differently. Isn't that right, my love?"

Daraja purses her lips and mutters something to herself.

Yabani laughs and holds out his hands. "You see, she cannot even find the words to describe her feelings for me."

They all laugh. It's a nice way to start the day. Iyawa, the nine-year-old, is rocking back and forth. It is obvious she has to pee.

Daraja scolds her. "Iyawa, go already. You are making me nervous squirming about like that."

The girl gets up excitedly and heads outside. They do not have the luxury of an indoor bathroom. Not far away is an outhouse made of cinderblock with a thatched roof. They share it with several other families. It is a wretched breeding ground for bacteria and viruses. Iyawa manages to deftly position herself over the hole in the ground just so. She is something of a germophobe, so going to the bathroom is an ordeal for her. That's why she prefers to hold it in. She hates going to the bathroom in what amounts to a boxed-in hole full of feces, a hot box that rises to temperatures above 100 degrees, providing a perfect place for fetid stink and disease to multiply. Some things kids just know.

When she emerges, she is about to start singing one of her favorite songs. *Bobo waro, bobo waro* . . . everybody loves, everybody loves.

Her words are muted abruptly, violently, as a calloused hand with only three fingers covers her mouth from behind. She feels the wide blade of the man's machete against her throat.

"*Boko Haram* is here," he says in a cold, matter-of-fact voice devoid of all feeling. Iyawa is not a Muslim, she does not have Allah's grace, and so she must die.

Iyawa falls to her knees and then flops forward onto the ground. She screams. She tries to warn her family. Her lips are moving, but no words are coming out. There is only a gurgling sound as the blood from her slit throat pools in her mouth and then pours forth, a waterfall of her nine years running forth and soaking into the dry earth which has reclaimed her. The last thing she thinks of, this little girl, is who will help her mother in the home?

And like that, Iyawa is gone forever.

"The infidels live on the perimeter," says the man to the fifty others behind him. "Kill them all. You will find the Muslim females in the middle of the village. Take the girls prisoner. Kill the rest of their families even if they resist. If they do not resist, let them die for Allah."

The fifty-man death squad from Maiduguri, the regional capital of Borno, sets to work. They lock and load their AK-47s, then fan out to deliver their divine justice. This is the same group of men responsible for kidnapping and raping thousands of women and girls in Nigeria, Chad, Niger and Cameroon. Along the way, they have murdered countless men, women and children whom they saw as less than worthy of Allah's grace.

This is *Jama'atu Ahlis Sunna Lidda'Awati Wal-Jihad,* the *Group of the People of Sunnah for Preaching and Jihad.* This is *Boko Haram.* They are African men, Nigerian men mostly, who have sworn solidarity with *ISIS* and vowed to institute Wahhabi and *Sharia Law* among Muslims and non-Muslims alike. They do so by any means necessary. Most often those means involve kidnapping, slavery and murder. It's all in a day's work to them.

Today they have come to bring death and destruction to Yabani's village.

Chapter 2

In seconds, *Boko Haram* infiltrates the village. They wear dirty fatigues reeking of body odor, piss and whatever else. They wear ammo belts slung around them, mostly for effect. They wear sweat-stained scarves, traditional Arab *keffiyehs*, around their heads. Many of the men use their *keffiyeh* to cover their face as well. This is how they envision themselves as good *jihadists* . . . dirty, anonymous, deadly but divine.

When the screaming begins, Yabani knows intuitively that the end has come. He calls out for his daughter, "Iyawa! Iyawa!" in a panic. But the girl has already bled out from the gash in her throat. Her open eyes are glazed, lifeless and soulless. She looks to be staring out into another dimension, perhaps the dimension where her spirit now resides.

Yabani jumps to his feet and runs outside. He is followed by Daraja and Bako. One man grabs a long, scythe-like farming tool, the other picks up a machete. The screams from the neighboring huts rise to a piercing level. Gunfire begins to explode in sporadic intervals, silencing each scream one by one as the terrorists work systematically from hut to hut.

The death squad organizes itself into ten groups of five. If there is a door, the first man kicks it in. Usually there is no door. The gateway into the heart of each family lies wide open. One of the terrorists sprays his AK-47 into the doorway haphazardly. His arms wobble under the power of the semiautomatic discharge. Bullets fly indiscriminately through the shoddy walls of the hut, even those incorporating cinderblock. Inside each hut, the bullets tear into the men, women and children, huddled and screaming.

The lucky ones are killed instantly. Less fortunate are the severely wounded, losing a leg or an arm, but still alive and suffering. They must be finished off one at a time by the other men in the death squad. Not even the non-Muslim females are of any use to *Boko Haram*. Every non-Muslim boy and girl, man and woman, is summarily executed and will be left to rot in the sun . . . human excrement . . . shit.

As Daraja, Bako and Zaki try to take in the horror of what is occurring around them, a team of terrorists begins their assault on a neighboring hut. It is particularly well-built and has a front door. The first man kicks it in. He has no fear. Why should he? He knows the villagers have no guns to protect themselves. He unloads his AK-47 into the front room of the hut, the family area where only minutes before a household of six sat eating cold millet cakes like they did every morning. It will now become their tomb.

The first terrorist empties his clip into the hut. His skinny arms flail wildly, sending bullets spraying from floor to roof, left wall to right. When his clips are emptied, the other *Boko Haram* in his team laugh and call him names like *pikin*, small child.

He yells back, "*Your Fada, ikpu.*" Shove it, white pussies. He thumps his chest. "*Oga.*" I am the boss.

The men start arguing in front of the hut they just strafed. All the while, a body is lying on the ground in the front room. It is Popoola, head of the household. His name means "intelligent people love God" in Yoruba. He is about to find out if his faith amounted to anything. His body is mangled and unrecognizable, piled in a massive pool of blood that is quickly seeping into the dirty floor mats. Popoola's gaunt, chiseled face is gone, blown away along with the other pieces of his body that are splattered against the mud and cinderblock walls. A piece of his brain sits like Jell-O in the glistening pool of blood. The wall behind him looks like a Jackson Pollock painting made with entrails. Popoola's right arm, severed in half, lies a few feet away from his corpse, the hand still grasping a machete, the only defense he could muster to save his family. Two of the fingers are still twitching as random synapses fire their last stores of energy.

When the *Boko Haram* team realizes they have more work to do, they agree to disagree on the first man's ability to wield his weapon like a warrior instead of a child. It is now time for the men to move into the hut. One of the terrorists moves into the hut and finds the remaining family huddled in a corner in a back room. There are two young girls, a boy and the mother, who is clinging to a screaming infant. When the terrorists enter, they become silent except for the baby, who does not understand.

Yelling at the woman, the terrorist thrusts his machete right through the baby, skewering both mother and child. The baby's cries cease instantly, its body nearly severed in half when the terrorist withdraws his blade. At first, the mother looks surprised, as if she was not expecting the massive blade to penetrate her chest, too. She tries to stand up and looks at the remains of her beloved infant seeping into the dirt floor. She sees the murderer standing in front of her. He is smiling at her, his machete still dripping. He considers it highly efficient to take both lives at once. He is proud of himself for coming up with the idea. It makes perfect sense to him. The villagers are not human to him; they are "infidels." This is what he was taught in *madrasa* when he pledged himself to the glorious *jihad* to be waged in the name of Allah, as if he knows anything about the great God.

The mother struggles to her feet, her lifeblood running out faster than her realization that this is the end for her. She looks down and holds her protruding stomach. The man stops, smiling when he sees that she is pregnant. With a second vicious thrust, the life of the woman and her unborn child are over as well.

Another *Boko Haram* terrorist enters the room. He grabs the two girls by their hair and drags them outside. The boy bolts and somehow manages to make it out the door. He starts running toward Daraja, Bako and Zaki. Without thinking, Zaki runs toward him. They are friends. They play soccer together with a ball made of duct tape. One of the terrorists empties half of a clip in their direction. Both boys fly forward as the bullets penetrate their bodies. They are gone.

The fourth man on the team, the "torch man," begins throwing gasoline on the hut. He ignites it. Thick, choking black smoke rises instantly. There are many huts ablaze now and gunfire is heard everywhere. People are shouting. People are screaming. People are dying.

The man with the two girls in his grasp emerges from the hut and starts yelling at the torch man. "*Your fada! Ode oshi!* Are you trying to light me on fire, asshole?"

The torch man laughs. "It would be funny to see you jumping around with your hair on fire." He pretends to throw gasoline on the man and the girls.

The man throws the girls down and begins arguing with the torch man. Having seen enough, one of the other guys unloads his AK-47 into the two girls. They are both gone. "So much for that. *Allahu Akbar!*" he shouts. God is the greatest. He spits on the two girls' bodies. "I have freed them from sin."

Bako is unable to restrain himself. Farm tool in hand, he rushes the gunman, letting loose a primal war cry. The gunman tries to reload quickly, but he is new to the game of mass executions in the name of God. He struggles to get a clip in. It is just enough time for Bako to drive the long blade of his makeshift weapon into the gunman's chest. The gunman has enough life in him to spit in Bako's face. Bako pulls the blade from the man's chest and rips it across the gunman's neck. The terrorist lands facedown as his own blood pools around his face.

For a split second, everything stands still. The power flowing through him as he exacts his revenge is undeniable. It feels good. This is what he will take with him as he is cut down from behind by one of the other men. His head is severed with one quick blow from behind. Seeing the end has come for them all, Yabani runs back into his hut. He wants to see his wife and daughters one last time. They all come together in the front room and embrace.

"I am sorry for failing you," says Yabani. He is angry, bitter. "God has forsaken us."

"This is not God's will," Daraja tells them all, as if trying to impart one last life lesson. "This is the will of man."

The torch man is not one for sentimental goodbyes. He pours gasoline on the hut and lights it. The hut goes up instantly. Another fire burns. From the sky, it would look like a festival. In reality, it is a slaughter. One of the terrorists runs inside and grabs Daraja, yanking her away from her family, who are all crying. One of his cohorts sends a wave of bullets through the front door. Yabani and his two remaining girls are wounded and fall to the floor writhing in pain. There they remain until the flames engulf them. The roar of the fire muffles their anguished screams. The pain is indescribable until the point that death relieves them.

Three of the terrorists pin Daraja to the ground facedown while the gunman circles her like a predator. They force her to watch as her husband and two daughters go up in flames. She wishes to God she had the power to retaliate and strike down every one of her attackers. And although she is consumed with rage, she cannot imagine words appropriate enough for the moment. Instead, she says nothing.

But one of the terrorists speaks. "*Allahu Akbar,*" he says. He bends down to speak in her ear. "Your man died like a dog. Your daughters were infidel whores beneath us taking them. But you should thank me. I have freed them from their life of sin."

He tears the dirty dress from her trembling body, drops his filthy camouflage pants and mounts her. He is filled with rage. He chokes Daraja while he savagely rapes her. As she loses consciousness, he climaxes. That was the thrill for him. Bringing the woman to the point of death with his bare hands, that power . . . that was it for him. He hated all women. Muslim women he could not rape. But women like Daraja were his to take and punish. It was his entitlement as a man. This, he was taught. He liked raping them because it fused his loathing, power and punishment into a single act.

Still pissed off about being called a child by one of the other men, he stands up, tucks himself in and praises himself. "Was that the act of a *pikin*? I am no child." He grabs his protruding crotch. "I am a big man." He spits on Daraja's dead body and kicks it as hard as he can, breaking two of the ribs in her lifeless body. "*Boko mi, ashewo.*"

He grabs his AK-47 and heads for the Muslim huts in the middle of the village. The three other men who were holding Daraja down leave in disgust. The torch man pours gasoline on her dead body and sets her ablaze. She is consumed in flames immediately. Then they follow along to the Muslim huts.

The treatment of the Muslim females is quite different. They are not to be raped or murdered. Instead, they are to be taken prisoner, saved from the sinfulness of their current lives among infidels. The practice of taking conquered females prisoner is a staple of *Boko Haram*'s operations. Many will be sold into slavery or prostitution. It is a cruel double standard to the outsider. But there is no contradiction among the men in *Boko Haram*—it is not their place to beat a Muslim female, but it is a female's place to satisfy her master. Where civil war in Sierra Leone is funded in war diamonds, *jihad* in Nigeria and neighboring Chad is financed with either oil or flesh. This is how *Boko Haram* funds their *jihad,* their holy war.

Women, bound and gagged, are laid out in the middle of the village like an array of wares at a sidewalk sale.

"We are here to save you," the men keep saying. "This is the way of God," they say.

By this time, all ten *Boko Haram* teams have converged on the middle of the village. They have killed over 150 villagers, all "infidels." It's a very good day's work by their standards. The perimeter of the village is on fire. Those bodies that were not burned along with the huts are strewn in groups of ten or twenty. Most of the dead are barefoot and shirtless, including the women. Many of the people killed had their hands tied behind their backs.

They took a bullet to the head execution style. Others, like Zaki, were gunned down in action with machine-gun fire, leaving their bodies severely disfigured.

It is now time to impose a *Sharia* lesson on the Muslim villagers who have been assembled in lines in preparation for their re-edification. One man appears to be the top dog, the leader of the death squad. His name is Aliyu, Aliyu Adelabu. He was the best student in his *madrasa* and found in the Wahhabi ways an ascetic code of conduct that matched well with his sadistic nature. By the time Aliyu Adelabu was ten, he'd killed more small animals then he could remember. He had always been a mean, nasty son of a bitch. Radical Islam simply provided him a justification to act without restraint. He killed his first person at the age of thirteen. It was a girl about his own age. She made a joke about Aliyu being poorly endowed, not that anyone would have known. It was the last joke she would ever tell because Aliyu pounded her head with a rock until her skull finally cracked like an egg, allowing the yolk, a bit of her child's brain, to spill out. That first taste of human death, that first time over a female, eclipsed anything he had ever experienced killing animals.

It was not long after that he took to raping girls when he needed to exercise his will and demonstrate that he did, indeed, possess a "man's tool," as he called it. Nobody cared about these village girls except their families, and nobody cared about them, so what did it matter? From the beginning, he understood the perversity of logic and how to manipulate it to his ends.

"You people," he shouts as he walks down the long line of Muslim villagers his men have assembled. "You are holy people, Allah's people. And yet the way you live your lives is a disgrace to His good name. In doing so, you disgrace yourselves."

He stops in front of a woman named Khadija. It is clear he has singled her out. "I know you, woman, do I not?"

She casts her eyes down. She knows what is coming. She is afraid and says nothing.

Aliyu is not one to be ignored. He grabs hold of Khadija's face and bites her lip until it bleeds. He licks her blood from his lips.

Still, the woman says nothing. Tears run down her face and mix with the blood from her lip.

"Look at me when I talk to you, woman. Don't you know how to show respect to an important man?"

She looks at Aliyu Adelabu. "I am sorry for offending a great warrior like you, *Sidi*. I apologize, but I do not think we have met before." She calls him *Sidi*, "my master," again.

Aliyu laughs. "No, we have not met, woman. But I know who you are. That is the problem. You are Khadija. You sell tobacco, do you not?"

Khadija breathes deeply. She knows she is in trouble. She nods. "I do."

Aliyu motions to one of his men, who then runs into her hut and returns carrying an assortment of tobacco and bottles of *Ogogoro*, a kind of alcoholic homebrew. Aliyu becomes quite grave now. "You sell this to the infidels, don't you?"

Khadija nods in shame. "Yes, but never to a Muslim family, *Sidi*.

"You have no more customers now, you sinful bitch. We have slaughtered every last one of them."

He examines the tobacco. "You fail to live in accordance with Allah's will. I look at you and feel sick because you are sick. Burn their entire hut to the ground," he orders.

Khadija drops to her knees and wraps her arms around Aliyu's legs. "Please, *Sidi*. Have mercy on my family. I was wrong. It will not happen again. I beg you, *Sidi*. Show mercy."

Aliyu kicks her away. "If you lived in the great Saudi Kingdom, you would be put to death for selling alcohol like this. But I . . . I am more forgiving. I will say this—you are right, woman. This will not happen again. I am here now. *Boko Haram* is here now. Allah's will shall be done. There will be no more peddling of sin and depravity."

Aliyu knows that he may not beat a proper Muslim woman who understands her place. He also knows that a sinner like Khadija is not protected under *Sharia Law*. He takes a heavy bottle of *Ogogoro* home brew, turns to Khadija who is still on her knees and brings the bottle cashing down on her skull. She flies backward like she is little more than a twig beneath an axe. Blood spews immediately from her head as she falls on her back unconscious. Her family cries out. Her husband runs toward his wife. Aliyu puts three rounds from his AK-47 into the grieving man, whose dead body collapses atop his wife. Aliyu then puts three more rounds into Khadija. He knows she will eventually return to her depraved ways and corrupt other good Muslims in the process. Killing her is the best way to ensure this sort of thing doesn't happen again.

He yells at one of his torch men. "I said burn that hut!"

Within seconds, Khadija's hut is ablaze.

Aliyu turns to the horrified line of Muslim villagers. "Let this be a lesson for all of you. You will live in accordance with *Sharia Law* or you will not live at all. It is very simple. Even you simple villagers can understand what I am saying."

The people are speechless, everyone afraid to speak . . . except for one man. He dares to make eye contact with Aliyu. It is a challenging gaze that does not sit well with the *Boko Haram* leader.

"What the hell are you looking at, *ewure oshi?*" He gets right in the man's face, but the man doesn't back down. "You think you are brave, yeah, *ode buruku?*"

He turns to the others. "We have a big man here." The other *Boko Haram* men laugh.

Aliyu returns his attention to the defiant man. "What is your name?"

"My name is Zaynabou." He stands tall.

"Do you have a problem with me, Zaynabou?"

Zaynabou does not back down. He is not intimidated by Aliyu. "How do you call yourself a Muslim? You are murdering your brothers and sisters. *You* are the problem. *You* are shameful to the name of Allah."

Aliyu can't believe what he is hearing. His men go silent in the face of this temerity and disrespect. Aliyu knows he has to do something. He raises his AK-47 and discharges a round into the face of the woman standing near the defiant Zaynabou. It is Zaynabou's wife. He then fires two shots into the boy standing on the other side of Zaynabou. It is his son. The boy dies instantly, his open eyes staring off somewhere as his body lies lifeless.

Aliyu Adelabu whistles, and one of his torch men runs to his side. Staring Zaynabou right in the eye, he orders the torch man to set Zaynabou ablaze. Once defiant, Zaynabou now succumbs. His awful screams eventually cease, but the distinct smell of scorched human flesh will linger on for days.

"Let that be a lesson for you all," says Aliyu again. "Change your ways, or I will bring far more suffering with me next time."

Chapter 3

"Can you see anyone?" said one of the men. "Jeez, it must be ugly in there."

"I can't see shit, man. Throw me your flashlight, will ya?" said the second man as he knelt down next to the driver's door.

The second man grabbed a flashlight from the back of his truck and ran over to the wreckage.

"Shine it in there so I can see what the hell's up," said the first man.

Camille was still strapped in her seat. Shards of glass covered her broken body.

"Jeez," said the first man. "It's a woman. She don't look too good, man."

"Holy shit," said the man with the flashlight. "It's Camille O'Keefe. It's the First Lady."

"The president's wife? You're kidding me. Is she dead?"

"Shit if I know." He shined the flashlight on Camille's bloody face. "Wait, wait! I saw her fingers move."

"Are you sure, man?"

"Look! They just moved again."

That was the night they pulled Camille O'Keefe from her mangled car. It was months ago. Still, the memory of that night remained sharp in her mind. She could feel it all viscerally . . . pain, betrayal, vulnerability, confusion. Her body was healing, but her emotional wounds still ran deep.

Camille O'Keefe had good reason to be concerned. When her car suddenly careened off the road a few months before, it was too much of a coincidence not to raise suspicion. From that moment on, worry gripped her and had yet to let go. As her vehicle tumbled and crumpled, time seemed to stand still for her. The last thing she remembered before losing consciousness was a profound sense of relief . . . free from her earthly coil, free from the limitations of life in this dimension, free from Becket Rosemore. When her leg shattered against the steering column, she slipped into darkness.

Death did not frighten her. She was not afraid to die. To the contrary, she felt free. Her sense of angst stemmed from her feeling that she had not fulfilled her life mission, that which she was born to do. It was not yet her time to move on, for her work had yet to be completed. This sense of obligation to something higher, something perhaps unattainable but obligatory nonetheless, manifested as an uneasiness. It was uncharacteristic of her to worry, but it had weighed on her ever since the accident.

She breathed deeply, absorbing the energy of her remarkable achievement. She ran her hands through her mane of fiery red hair. "I feel like I have finally paid off my karmic debt," she had told Johnny Long from her steaming bubble bath shortly after giving her now-famous speech.

It was a speech that shocked the world, a speech that tore away the veil of women's complacency. It was the speech in which the First Lady, Camille O'Keefe, announced to the world that she was throwing her philandering, egomaniacal husband out of the White House. The man she intended to send packing, the man who needed a walk-in closet to hide his skeletons and mistresses alike, was none other than President Becket Rosemore.

That day, the media declared the birth of the Red Dragon First Lady.

"I feel like my work here is done," said Camille. "I feel like I can finally graduate from this dimension. My spiritual boot camp may finally be over."

"I don't know about all that," answered Johnny Long. "Something tells me there are greater things to come for you. After all, you are still the First Lady."

"Just wait until my new book comes out," said Camille. "It's gonna blow the lid off the dumpster where Beck hides his filthy secrets." She was referring to Becket Rosemore, president of the United States and her estranged husband.

Johnny Long laughed. "As if throwing him out of the White House didn't humiliate him enough? I might think twice if I were you."

"Yeah," replied Camille. "I wouldn't put it past Beck to have me killed."

"Don't even put that thought out to the universe," replied Johnny Long. "Isn't that the sort of thing you always say to me?"

"I'm just saying . . . he scares me sometimes."

"He's also the president of the United States."

"Like I said, he scares me sometimes."

Chapter 4

"Do you think I'm a moron?" yelled Becket Rosemore at the group of advisors sitting around the table. "I'm the damned president of the United States. Do you think I became the most powerful man in the world by being a moron?"

The group sat in silence, each afraid to speak.

Beck threw the newspaper across the room. It hit an oil painting of Thomas Jefferson. Luckily, the frame was screwed to the wall. Still, Beck's projectile marred the canvas.

"Get me that damned paper," ordered the president, referring to the one he had just launched across the room.

Three advisors scrambled to pick it up and return it to Beck. He held it up for everyone to see. Taking up most of the front page was a color picture of Camille's car wreck. The headline put into words what the entire world was already thinking: *Washington Deceit.*

"How do you people let this happen? That's what I want to know. How? What do I have you people for? I'll tell you. . . . Your job is to prevent crap like this from happening. And if you can't do that, you can't work for this administration. It's as simple as that."

Vice President Harry Pierson slipped into the room. Beck's rise to fame came after defeating a terrorist organization called Allah's Fortune while simultaneously penning a deal with China that effectively gave them boots-on-the-ground control of the Middle East following a U.S. withdrawal. It was a stroke of genius that won Beck the White House, but not without Pierson's help. Pierson worked his way onto Beck's ticket by tapping his CIA contacts precisely when Beck needed help the most. The Rosemore-Pierson Administration was born, and the country and the world would never be the same again.

Pierson was a seasoned Pentagon guy who lived most of his professional life in the shadow world. What he didn't know he could easily find out. Harry Pierson was a valuable asset. He could get to anyone at any time and had done so for Beck on more than one occasion. From time to time, he had to lean on people for his own good, too. Either way, it was never pretty when Pierson's people came for you. It always ended the same way.

Beck viewed people as assets or liabilities. That's how he parsed the world. Pierson always got what he wanted. Knowing this, Beck had identified him as a critical ally from the beginning. And so the two men, each with their murky past of dirty deeds, strode hand-in-hand into the White House two years earlier.

Pierson listened to Beck's rant and enjoyed watching the staffers quiver. When he felt the time was right, he chimed in. "I've already made calls to some people about that prick of a headline editor. He'll be back doing obits for the *Scarsdale Inquirer* soon enough."

"See that?" Beck barked at his staffers. "That's someone who knows how to get things done, someone who knows how to *protect this house*." He slapped the paper against his hand for emphasis. "That's why he's the vice president and you're a bunch of lame-ass wannabes. And if any of you are offended by that, then quit. You know where the door is, and I'm assuming each of you can at least turn a doorknob, although, frankly, I have to wonder sometimes. But none of you will leave because, like I said, you are a bunch of lame asses."

"It's true," said Pierson. "I'm great in times of crisis because I get things done. Unfortunately, Mr. President, it's equally true that you look like an ass in front of the entire world. First, Camille holds a press conference to reveal to the world your deceitful ways and announce that she's throwing your cheating ass out of the White House. This is the First Lady of the United States, mind you. Not only has she made a fool out of you in front of the entire world, she has also violated the First Lady code of conduct by airing your dirty laundry, thereby diminishing the United States."

"Jackie Kennedy she's not. But you're not John Kennedy either, Mr. President. However, the one thing you do have in common with the Kennedy clan is a knack for the apparently sinister. For only days after your wife trashes you and the grandeur of the presidency along with you, she's found upside down in a car wreck. Really?"

"Everyone's pointing the finger at you, Mr. President. It seems the American people now consider you the type of man who could have his wife knocked off, as if this were some sort of Mafia movie. In short, people, we need to do something about this. We need to lock this shit down right now."

Pierson motioned for Beck to dismiss the staffers so they could have some privacy.

Beck stroked his temples in a futile attempt to quell the migraine that was growing like a brain tumor. "Everybody get out," he ordered in a forlorn monotone.

The room emptied immediately. Beck and Pierson were alone.

"I hate that bitch, Harry. I mean it. I hate her from her red hair down to her red toenails. That bitch. I really wish I could kill her. She has it coming."

Pierson exhaled loudly. "Never . . . I mean never, repeat those words again, do you understand me?"

Beck didn't like being told what to do. He knew Pierson was offering sound advice, but he hated obeying people all the same. He said nothing.

Pierson laughed to himself. "Speaking of red hair, do you know they're calling her the Red Dragon First Lady or some shit like that now? Christ, she's made quite an impact. Who knows what else she has in store? She's just getting started, man. She has the entire world's sympathy in her sails right now. To be quite honest, Beck, you look like a total asshole. Not good."

Beck threw the newspaper again. "This is absurd, Harry. Who the hell does she think she is? The only reason people know her name is because I married her."

"That was your first mistake."

Beck threw his hands up as he sat down at the head of the conference table. "What was I supposed to do? She was pregnant."

"I stand corrected," said Pierson. "*That* was your first mistake."

"Oh, please. She was always a hot piece of ass. Even a salty bastard like you has to admit that, even if you're too old to get it up anymore. And what's with all her bullshit about my moving into the Watergate Hotel? The White House is *my* house, not hers."

"Relax," said Pierson. "She's trolling you. It's part of her campaign to make you look bad. It's working, by the way."

Beck glared at him. "Are you here to help or piss me off some more?"

"Just keeping it real, Boy-O . . . keeping it real. Camille helped you win the election. The American people love her. Along the way, she has a miscarriage, announces to the world that you have been cheating on her repeatedly, and calls for the women of the world to stand up for themselves and stop tolerating awful behavior by powerful men. Did I mention that she has a new tell-all book exploring why men of anger and deceit rise to positions of power . . . naming *you*, by the way, as Exhibit A. And if that weren't enough, she ends up in a suspicious car accident due to some sort of mysterious brake failure? Come on, Beck. This wife of yours has single-handedly destroyed your entire career. At the same time, in case you haven't noticed, she has created one for herself in the process. I'd say she's pretty damned smart. Interpret it how you will."

Beck was dismayed by his vice president's apparent apostasy. "You sound as if you actually admire the bitch."

Pierson smiled. "Oh, I do. Honestly, I could have used a woman like her back in the day. It's much easier to slide a hot woman into a field op. Men drop their guard entirely. They just can't help themselves. I'm quite sure you know what I'm talking about."

"Why do I get the sense you're poking fun at me?"

"Because I am. She got you good by getting pregnant. You're just lucky she lost the baby. All you need is a presidential custody battle for the press to feed on. Good God, that would be something."

Beck sat back and sighed. "Only a month or two ago, I was a media darling. Remember how I had them feeding out of my hand, running with whatever story I fed them? My ass was getting sore from all the kissing."

"Yeah, well . . . things change. They always do. Be prepared," cautioned Pierson, and for good reason. "There's a lot more to come."

Pierson picked up the television remote and turned on the large flat screen hanging on the wall opposite the president. He flipped through various cable-news channels. One after the other . . . it was all the same. Camille O'Keefe Rosemore, the Red Dragon First Lady, was everywhere. Her story had eclipsed all others. There was footage of Camille rehabbing her fractured leg or getting a bite to eat, or planting trees for some cause. There were sound bites of her describing her forthcoming book, *This Soul's Journey through the Eye of the Storm*. She had set off a flurry of opinion pieces about morality and the presidency. One channel went so far as to promote its upcoming special on America's most influential cheaters.

Pierson stopped on the *Rebecca Radmore Show*, a daytime talk show with a predominantly female audience. Radmore was heatedly opining about Beck's alleged history of infidelity. She didn't pull any punches, either.

"The First Lady will be the ex-First Lady soon enough," she declared. "She will be the Red Dragon Lady instead of the Red Dragon First Lady. But we all hope she continues to be a force for change not just here in America but across the globe. And she can. Camille O'Keefe has that power!"

There was tremendous applause from the studio audience.

"I have a feeling Camille O'Keefe will make history," continued Radmore.

"I don't know why. There's just something about her. She has . . . power. Yeah . . . power."

There was another round of applause.

"How many of you in the audience voted for Rosemore? Show of hands . . . how many?"

The camera turned to show almost every hand raised.

"Wow," commented Rebecca. "We need to stop handing power and prestige to men who cheat and lie their way to the top. We need to stop giving Super Bowl rings to men who beat up their wives. We need to stop doing business with countries that keep their women illiterate, disenfranchised, stripped of their rights and covered up from head to toe. Wouldn't it be something if we could all vote for Camille O'Keefe instead?"

The thunderous applause from the audience drove Beck to his limit. "Turn this shit off, Harry. I can't take it anymore. I'm telling you, I'm gonna go ballistic if I hear this bitch pontificate about that other bitch."

"I hate to break the news to you, but the days when you could run around doing and saying anything you want are gone, Beck. Camille's killing you out there. In the court of women's public opinion, you're just another cheating scum. They obviously think you tried to have her killed."

"I did no such thing," cried Beck, as he slammed his hands on the table. "Sure, my life would be a hell of a lot better were Camille to suddenly vanish. But there's no way in hell I would jeopardize everything like some sort of Mafia boss. Come on, Harry. What sort of man do you think I am?"

Pierson stroked his bony chin. "That's what every American is trying to figure out right now, Mr. President."

Harry Pierson was probably the only guy on the Hill who could have gotten away with dressing Beck down like that. Noticeably older and thinner than Beck, his sharp features gave him a somewhat gaunt look compared with Beck's more robust physique and overall appearance. His reputation around the Capitol preceded him always. People on both sides of the aisle knew it was a grave mistake to cross Harry Pierson even before he became vice president. His demeanor complemented Beck's quite well. Where the president wanted to act on public proclamation and ego,

Harry Pierson preferred to do his business in as stealthy a manner as possible.

However different in age, both men were old dogs who chose not to learn new tricks. Things had gone great for them most of their lives, so they figured there was no need to change the way they had lived their lives and gone about their business. But this recent mess with the First Lady posed entirely new challenges for which neither man was prepared.

"I still say she's crazy," said Beck. "If she thinks that people are gonna remember her after I divorce her, she's sadly mistaken. She's nobody without me . . . some past-life medium, or psychic, or whatever the hell she claims she is."

"She had a very prestigious clientele before she met you. Everyone in D.C. knew her," commented Pierson.

"There you go, trying to piss me off again. Let her go back to worrying about people's past lives and star charts. It has nothing to do with me."

Beck stood up and started pacing. Pierson said nothing. "What? I hate when you stand there looking like the Grim Reaper. It makes me nervous."

Pierson smiled. "If you think I'm bad, you should have met my first wife."

Beck stopped pacing and turned to his vice president. "I was, like, five years old when you were married to your first wife. And believe me, I can't get rid of Camille fast enough."

"As long as it's over."

"Oh, it's over," Beck said. "Gone like yesterday's news."

"The problem is that Camille O'Keefe is today's news. Along with everybody else, she probably thinks you tried to have her killed."

Beck threw up his hands and sat down at the opposite end of the table from where he was sitting previously. "There's no precedent for this. What the hell am I supposed to do? How is she able to capture the media like this? This is a load of crap, Harry."

"It's true, Camille made history when she threw you out of the White House. No First Lady has ever done anything like that before."

"Bullshit," spat Beck. "She's not empowered to do that. She was grandstanding."

"Of course," agreed Pierson, taking a seat of his own to Beck's right. "But tell that to the women of the world. She became an overnight hero. Twitter . . . Facebook . . . all that social media stuff. It was instantaneous. I heard this morning that her Twitter page has the largest number of followers in the world, Beck. Think about that for a second. She has the entire world in the palm of her hand, hanging on her every word."

Beck rubbed his face. The fatigue was beginning to show. Everything he'd worked for his entire life was hanging in the balance. Who knew what secrets the pages of *This Soul's Journey through the Eye of the Storm* contained? Camille had him by the balls, and boy was she gonna squeeze. Beck never handled defeat well. In fact, he could barely tolerate even the slightest challenge to his autonomy, nor was he accustomed to being challenged. Despite his role as so-called leader of the free world, there was very little genuinely democratic about him.

Back in the days when he was an Army special ops very few constraints existed. Becket Rosemore lived essentially uncurtailed. His job was clear-cut, unambiguous—seek out and destroy the enemy. Outside of the guys on his direct-action team, there was little else he needed. Beck's world revolved around the mission. When he wasn't on a mission, his world revolved around the guys on his team.

How times changed. Sitting there in the White House suffering a barrage of jabs from his vice president, Beck ran through the myriad ways in which he was, despite a position of power, completely powerless. Looking around the room, he took in the many portraits of previous presidents. The dark, rich oil paints still glistened in the light from the chandelier that hung in the middle of the ceiling. The dentil molding reminded him of George Washington's teeth.

"Did you know George Washington had wooden teeth?"

"What did he brush with?" said Pierson. "Pledge?"

"He was a tough son of a bitch. They all were back then. Marching for miles in the snow with rags on their feet instead of boots and then lining up fifty feet from the enemy and firing at each other."

When Beck took office, there wasn't a wrinkle in his tan face. Now, when he forced himself to look in the mirror, he could see age creeping up, wrinkles beginning to show like weeds popping through the mulch. His colorful army of handmade suits that once hung at attention in his walk-in closet all had succumbed to the sea of presidential blue he was now obliged to sport. He had any woman he wanted without having to date a single one of them. Now, his affairs made him an adulterer and a target for media attack. Where control once meant everything to him, becoming president meant he had to forfeit sovereignty of his thoughts and actions. In what seemed like the blink of an eye, Becket Rosemore fell from grace as America's chosen savior. And now this thing with Camille pushed him to the limits of his own ego.

He breathed deeply, deliberately. "She's really got me good, huh?"

Pierson laughed. "That's an understatement, old boy. When her book comes out, she'll be wearing your balls on a necklace. It'll be very quaint."

The more Beck thought about it, the more alive he became. His ego—a fiery orb of fractured boundaries, performative grandiosities and alienating needs—grew more inflamed in the face of this new challenge to his power and autonomy. It was more than he could take. He had to lash out. His overblown ego that served him so well as a soldier now fueled his descent into disgrace.

Harry Pierson had seen Beck like this before. A few months earlier, Beck had blown up at Senator Everhardt following an interview in which Everhardt referred to Beck as "the giant libido currently occupying the White House." Just the other day, Beck almost threw one of his female staffers out of Limo One when she speculated that Camille's forthcoming book would be "a best seller virtually overnight." Were there not a Secret Service agent sitting in the car with them, Beck might well have pushed her from the moving car. Most recently, of course, Beck went ballistic when Camille announced to the world that she was throwing his cheating ass out of the White House and sending his belongings ahead to the Watergate Hotel. That was the angriest anyone had ever seen Beck.

Pierson sat in quiet observance as the president's face became more crimson, his upper lip twitching ever so slightly. Having known Beck for years, he knew the president's volcanic ego could erupt without warning. Pierson also knew that for the last two years, it was Camille O'Keefe who naturally pushed Beck's buttons. He chalked it up to a personality conflict.

Sartre wrote that Hell is other people. If so, Beck and Camille were a match made in Hades. They were bound together in karmic recompense in which simple conversation was its own torture device. There truly was no exit for these two. Whatever it was, she set off tectonic shifts that wrenched apart Beck's defense mechanisms, exposing his most painful vulnerabilities. Beck would inevitably blow his top, while Camille would inevitably cry, wishing with all her might that a "drop-in from the Fifth Dimension" would simply occupy her body so she could leave earth once and for all.

Pierson saw that old, familiar steam rising. He knew the lava would soon flow forth from the president in the form of scatological tirades, demeaning declarations and, often enough, an executive order that had revenge at its core. Sure enough, Beck had reached his limit. He slammed his hands down on the table and abruptly rose.

"This is bullshit, and I'm not gonna take it anymore, Harry. I want you to put some of your boys on her."

Pierson tried to placate his boss. "I don't know if that's wise, Beck. The last time you asked me to get involved like that was before the election with that Secret Service guy Frank Lonza or whatever his name was."

"He was a good man."

"Yeah, but he's a dead good man. Before that, it was Abdul Al-Alibri."

"He was an asshole."

"Yeah, but he's a dead asshole now. See a trend here?"

Beck gritted his teeth. He was clenching the edge of the table so hard his hands were white. He spoke slowly, methodically. "I don't care. Do you hear me, Harry? I want you to put a guy on that bitch's ass. Yes, I used to be the guy on that bitch's ass. But that's not how

I mean it now. What I mean is I want to know everyplace she goes. If she goes out, I want to know who's with her. If she stays inside, I want to know what programs she watches. If she goes to the freaking bathroom, I want to know how many times she wipes. All the shit you're good at." He waved his hand to suggest so on and so forth.

Pierson said nothing. It was uncomfortable.

"Harry . . . do you understand what I want done?"

Harry Pierson looked the president square in the eye. "Do you?"

"Oh, spare me your ironic counselor bullshit, will ya Harry? Just do what you're told. Remember, you're here because of me, not the other way around."

"Yeah, well . . . I may be out on my ass after one term because of you, too."

Chapter 5

Camille O'Keefe Rosemore—soon to be Camille O'Keefe once again—sat down on a wooden bench to take a breather. She still had a bit of a limp from the accident, and her back could viciously tighten up on her without notice. Her opulent red hair was pulled back. Sweat ran down her face, and her green *Chive On* tank top and gray yoga pants both bore sweat marks. The physical rehab center she was using to recover was kind enough to provide a private room for her sessions. It was a good thing, too, because, as the First Lady thought, pain and high humidity didn't make for very good paparazzi shots.

She wiped her face and tossed the towel aside. "I don't know what's worse, the accident or the physical therapy."

Nicole Gerstlauer, the First Lady's physical therapist and personal trainer, laughed. "I hear ya. At least you were unconscious during the accident. Can't say the same for the rehab. Did you take your Percocet?"

Camille rolled her eyes. "Please, I had to sneak it." She gestured toward the Secret Service agent who was standing watch unseen out in the hallway. "Apparently, the Secret Service prefers I not take opiates, if at all possible. Anyway, I'm getting to the point where I don't need any meds. I'm healing up pretty good."

Nicole bent down and touched her toes with a long, pronounced stretch. "I thought all that bodyguard stuff would have stopped when you separated from Beck?"

"Oh, no. Until we're divorced, I'm still the First Lady. They're with me around the clock. It's like they're keeping an eye on me more than protecting me. I wouldn't put it past Beck."

Nicole switched over to Camille's other leg and brought her head down to her knee. Camille exhaled deeply. "What happens after your divorce is official?"

"I'm sure they'll drop me like a hot potato, which is fine by me. I just want my life back. And to be honest, I don't really want these guys following me around for the rest of my life. It would be creepy. I can just see them mumbling into their cuff every time I take an aspirin, never mind a prescription drug."

Nicole stood up from her stretch. She was tall, maybe 5'10" and brunette. Men liked to make lewd comments about her excessive flexibility and ripped core, but it was her gray eyes that struck people the most. She had a gaze like a cat's. When she engaged people in conversation, it was difficult to tell if she was looking at them or right through them. It could be disconcerting. Camille, however, chose Nicole as her physical therapist because of her eyes.

"Hey, I know," Nicole said. "Maybe we should shatter *his* leg and put twenty-two pins in? See if his opinions toward pharmaceuticals change any."

Camille lifted her bad leg up onto the bench with both hands. She tried to be ginger with it, but she still winced. "It hurts today. Ugh, is that me I'm smelling? You don't even want to know what's going on inside these yoga pants."

"Hey," joked Nicole, "yoga pants are where yeast go for vacation, right? Seriously, though, you're doing great. I'm totally impressed with your progress. You're a fighter. You're Camille O'Keefe, the Red Dragon Lady."

Camille exhaled loudly and blew a wet curl from her face. She stretched out until her forehead touched the knee of her bad leg. "I'm not sure who I am right now. The universe is sending me a message no doubt. I'm just not quite sure what it is. The funny thing is . . . I'm a medium and past-life regressionist. I've written seven books on the subject. I'm supposed to know these things. Not knowing is unsettling. I wish I could open a book and find all the answers . . . or at least the questions. I can figure out the answers if I have the questions."

"That should be your next book, girl."

Nicole sat down on the bench next to Camille's bad leg and started manipulating it a bit. "It'll all make sense to you in due time. Like I always tell my clients, serious accidents like yours are life changers. The important thing is to find the message in it. When you figure out why this happened, your recovery will spring forward. It's like releasing a weight. I know most people don't care about that sort of stuff. Most of my patients like to play the victim. It makes them feel special, getting all the attention and stuff, you know. But you're different. You're famous for being open-minded toward things that other people run from. I'm not worried about you at all. You have what I call *I Am*. You exude *I Am* presence."

"Excuse me," protested Camille. "I wrote that. Nice try. Using my own stuff against me . . . nice try."

Nicole gently lifted Camille's leg up by the heel. "Oh . . . yeah. That's right. Seriously, though, I love that book. Read it three times."

Camille laughed. "Which one? I don't even remember which book I wrote that in."

"For real? The book was titled *I Am*."

Camille buried her face in her hands. "Oh my God, I'm losing it, Nicole. Too many pain meds."

Nicole stretched Camille's bad leg farther. "Your range of motion is really improving."

"It's still sore after these sessions. I can't wait to lose the limp."

Nicole carefully lowered Camille's leg and stood up. "Rest, ice, compression and elevation . . . RICE. That's the ticket. The rest will take care of itself." She tossed Camille a brand-new Ace bandage and winked. "Don't say I never do anything for you."

"Wow, a new Ace bandage. You must have slept your way to the top, huh?"

"Hey, watch what you say. It's bad enough I have an endless line of roiding meatheads trying to get in my yoga pants. They never stop. They're like sharks. What does Jimmy Buffet say? Fins to the left, fins to the right. and you're the only bait in town?"

Camille stood up and stretched her leg. "Gotta love men."

"Right? They're like . . . prehistoric? Is that the right word? I don't know."

"Every time I hear him mentioned, my stomach cringes. I never thought I'd feel that way about a man I chose to be my husband. I guess it's this whole thing with the accident. Trust issues now. . . ."

"So you think he had something to do with it?" whispered Nicole.

Camille shrugged. There was a tinge of sadness in her voice. "Honestly, I don't know. Crazy, right? Not knowing if your husband tried to have you killed? Oh, and it just so happens that your husband is the freaking president."

"Oh . . . my . . . God." mouthed Nicole, too afraid to say it out loud. "Remember the walls have ears wherever you go, Camille. I mean . . . you're, like, the most famous woman in the world right now. Who cares whether you're the First Lady or not? You're, like, a hero for women all over the place. To tell you the truth, I think women around the world will respect you more for leaving that jerk, even if he is the president of the United States."

Camille was undaunted. "I don't trust him anymore. Once that happens, there's no going back. He's disgusting."

"You wouldn't go back to him would you? Once a cheater, always a cheater, right? Wow, what a book this is gonna make," Nicole continued, this time loud enough to be overheard. "This is, like, the best final chapter ever."

"I don't know. This doesn't feel like the final chapter. It feels like a prelude of some sort. I feel like there is something much bigger, something really important for me out there. I'm here on earth for a reason. The universe has a plan for me. It's time for me to figure out what that is. But I'll tell you one thing . . . my destiny does not involve propping up a man. I'm done with all that. This time, it's got to run through me. I think that's the message. I am my own reason for being. My mission in life is not to proclaim some man's greatness. Mine needs to be a whole different story."

Camille paused and thought about what she had said. "No . . . I think the real story is about my own inherent greatness. Does that sound too arrogant?"

The two women headed for the showers. Nicole put her hand on Camille's shoulder. "Not at all. I think men might be turned off, but women will understand what you mean. We all know you should be running the country instead of your ex-husband."

"We're not divorced yet."

"Eh . . . it's all in the intention," quipped Nicole. "Anyway, I don't have to tell you that when big life events like this happen, there's a message. Breaking your leg in five places was the universe's way of getting your attention."

Camille laughed. "Yeah, Twitter would have been better, you know?"

"Hashtag *Red Dragon Lady*. That's you."

Camille pondered the moniker that the press had given her. "Hmm, I'm not so big on the Red Dragon Lady thing. How about hashtag Woman of the World?"

"You're putting me to sleep. Anything but Camille Rosemore. That never really sounded right. So welcome back, Camille O'Keefe. You've got a lot of work to do."

Camille stopped at the door to the women's showers. "Do me a favor, tell Mr. Secret Service out there that I'm hitting the shower. He's welcome to come in and guard me, but he'll need to leave his blue suit on the hook outside. He'll totally freak out. He's such a tight ass. I can't wait to get away."

Nicole chuckled. "Oh my God, I'll hand him a tiny towel and tell him this should cover everything up."

Chapter 6

A battered black Land Rover rolls into the smoldering village, kicking up a cloud of dust in its wake. The fires have all but burned out now. Most of the huts lay in ruins . . . ash, scorched brick and clay. Smoke still rises in thin, black wisps, but it is nothing like the inferno that raged a few days earlier when *Boko Haram* rolled in. The fear and death that enveloped the village have dissipated. The screams have all been silenced. But a careful ear can still hear the anguish wafting in the breeze like a mass of spirits caught between dimensions.

All that is left is the smoldering ruins of innocent lives—men, women and children snatched from existence by a group of men seeking to exercise their deep-seated hatred and resentment for humanity in the form of what they call "divine justice." *Boko Haram* has pledged itself to *ISIS* in the great *jihad*. Their belief is that they are the true chosen ones. Their goal is Pan-Islam, a new world order bringing about the final judgment and the end of days.

But Aliyu and his men—all the operatives of *ISIS* throughout the world—are the furthest thing from divine. They know only the hatred they feel for themselves, and so spew forth their venom upon the weak and helpless. It makes the men of *ISIS*, the men of the "Islamic State" as they now call themselves, feel strong when they humiliate a man by cutting off his penis before killing him in front of his family. It makes them feel powerful when they rape a fifteen-year-old girl, cut off her head and make her father kiss her lips still wet with blood. It makes them feel better about themselves when they shoot a pregnant mother in her belly and then cut the fetus out. And necklacing, the practice of standing a person inside a stack of tires, dousing it in gasoline and lighting it on fire . . . well, that's just a good, old-fashioned tribal tradition unique to the African movement.

Boko Haram . . . ISIS . . . they are all very big men when it comes to murdering unarmed civilians.

The driver's door opens. The legs that emerge are long and muscular. He plants one black combat boot firmly on the ground, then the other. His stance is solid, self-assured. He is wearing camouflage pants in shades of green, and a khaki button-down shirt with pleated breast pockets. The sun, already high in the sky, scintillates off the dark lenses of the man's aviators. He wipes his forehead with his dark-green beret and tosses it back in the truck. He contemplates grabbing his M4 assault rifle but decides against it. For the time being, he feels it's safe enough to carry only his Sig M11 handgun. Both weapons were supplied to him by U.S. forces through his contacts at the United Nations.

This is Kofi Achebe, special envoy to the United Nations Council on Women and Families. He is a huge and foreboding man, 6'3" tall. His size 13 boots seem to flatten the ground where he walks. His skin is very dark, his teeth bright white in contrast, and veins run visibly up his muscular forearms and thick neck. But he is not just a hulking physical specimen. He is also a relative to a great Nigerian author whose first novel, *Worlds Coming Down,* stands firmly in the canon of great world literature. Kofi Achebe is not a writer, but he is a lot like his great-uncle. Both men see Africa as a world divided by religious, cultural and economic agendas that have brought death and destruction in waves as intense as the African heat itself. Both men recognize the immense potential buried beneath the surface of their great continent, for Africa is one of the richest regions in the world in terms of natural resources. Oil, precious metals like gold and platinum, copper, bauxite, coltan, even salt and wood . . . Africa is among the richest in these resources. And yet the African people are among the poorest, continually ravaged by war, starvation and disease. All this plays in the back of Kofi's mind every time he listens to UN diplomats debate what's best for their countries but never for sub-Saharan Africa itself.

Kofi takes a deep breath. His animal senses take over. The sharp odor of smoke hits him first. It is quickly supplanted by the rank, oddly pungent stench of rotting flesh coming from the corpses strewn about. Kofi Achebe knows these smells. Now a man in his fifties, he once knew war from a soldier's perspective. The smells are familiar to him. They bring back memories . . . bad memories. He now dedicates his life to helping people instead of killing them. He has helped a lot of people, but he has killed a lot of people, too. His role as special envoy has given him a way out, a way to personal salvation. As it stands now, he is damned for what he did as a young man.

All Kofi Achebe can do is work to redeem himself, use his position with the United Nations to help however he can. It may not amount to much on a global scale, he may not be able to change things overnight, but it means something in the little part of the world he calls his life now. Always, it seems, women are the primary targets, the easy marks. The men are almost always murdered in as degrading a fashion as possible. But it is women—Muslim and non-Muslim alike, the women who are even lower than the murdered men, who are, themselves, considered the lowest scum—who are condemned to a life of humiliation and suffering before they are finally dispatched.

That's why he has committed himself to the Council on Women and Families. The men suffer and die in a single engagement with the enemy, however inglorious their end may be. And many women are killed alongside their men, but many more are not. Many more are taken as *sibya*, female war captives. *ISIS* is notorious for taking *sibya* and is feared from Nigeria all the way to Iraq. In many ways, it is a fate worse than death, even if that death is painful and degrading.

ISIS men consider *sibya* to be their possessions, their playthings or their sex toys. They consider it their inalienable right supported by scripture. Most often, the females are used as concubines, cooks, sex slaves or human shields. They are kept bound or chained, gagged and starved. Often fed little more than ground dried maize once a day, many *sibya* die of disease within a few weeks of captivity. The prevailing logic, the male logic, is survival of the fittest. If a *sibya* is too weak to survive her captivity, what good could she have been in the first place? As with many *ISIS* bases, Aliyu's *Boko Haram* camp has a lye pit where dead women are heaped daily. It is an earthen dumpster for dead *sibya*, and it is always full.

Nigeria, Afghanistan, Iraq, Syria—everywhere people have been weakened and made into cogs by religious fanatics—it's always the same. The older women are used primarily as cooks until their captors grow weary of their monotonous cuisine. Then they are used as human shields. Theirs is a horrid demise. To be a human shield when the enemies of *ISIS* launch an offensive means a grueling death that is almost certain. This is a fate they must accept in a world devoid of humanity and personal freedom. Both are luxuries in scarce supply.

Human shields don't die cleanly. These women suffer. Inevitably, these unfortunate women will be cut down by waves of gunfire as they shield their captors, the brave men of *ISIS*. Maybe devastating .50 caliber rounds will be fired into these women from the back of a beat-up, rusted out Toyota Hilux or some similar crappy white pick-up like they always show in the news. The massive bullets will shear the woman's legs off at the knee caps, even cut her in half at the waist. Shrapnel bursts from mortars lobbed from some unseen position in the distance will tear the women's guts wide open so their intestines pool around their quivering bodies. Bombs dropped from U.S. drones operated by some anonymous, twenty-five-year-old gamer turned soldier sitting in a command trailer somewhere in Willow Grove, Pennsylvania, will reduce these women to a bloody soup of guts and bones.

The women used as human shields pray for death to take them quickly, but that is rarely the case. Only the lucky ones are killed instantly. A swift death . . . it is an odd way of conceptualizing God's mercy. When the skirmish ends, *ISIS* fighters won't waste bullets putting these women out of their misery. Instead, they will be left to suffer and pass as they may. Only those on the wrong end of a weapon understand how the universe shifts. With it shifts the rationale the rest of us carry through life.

Life becomes suffering and death brings relief. It is fundamentally counter-intuitive, but it's the way these women live. When death is working overtime for the Islamic State, the "one legitimate State," there is little time for mercy. This is not an act of cruelty but rather an act of supreme logic. For these women are *sibya*. Their value is less than that of a single bullet. So how can one waste a greater resource on a lesser? It is fundamentally counter-intuitive.

The fate of the young girls is much different from that of the older women. Aliyu's home country of Nigeria is rich in natural resources, especially oil. Nigeria is a member of OPEC. For Aliyu, however, Nigeria's boasts another natural resource . . . girls. They are his primary source of income. Girls thirteen through fifteen are prized most highly. When they are first taken, these young *sibya* are used as concubines for the *Boko Haram* men. The men rationalize it simply. If these girls are not virgins, they are not virtuous. If they are not virtuous, they do not deserve respect. Thus, impure girls may be treated as sub-human. They are *ashawo*, young whores in Nigerian, in Arabic a *junub*, one made impure through sex. Raping an *ashawo* is not morally wrong because for the men of *Boko Haram*, morality does not apply to sub-humans.

But their relative youth also translates well in both the "work slave" and "sex slave" markets. They command high prices because they can be used for many more years before wasting away, or so the theory holds. So many of these girls are sold off at some point in their captivity. Of course, no virgin is touched. They are for trade only. No rape or concubinage is permitted. "Pure" girls, virgins, *houri*, are the most valuable because they have not been soiled by sin. A girl's virginity maintains a man's reputation. And his wife (or wives) can't really resent him for adding a fine, young, pure girl to the stable.

It's like cruising a drive-through for a burger and fries versus dining on rack of lamb in a fine restaurant. Most of the men are happy enough to have a burger and fries with that shake. Tainted, non-virgins are purchased for a few hundred dollars. That's enough to buy several AK-47s or a crate of frags. Those with power and affluence prefer to hold out for only the very best and so are willing to pay an extraordinary price, as much as one thousand dollars on the open market, for a *houri*, a young virgin. This is the kind of action a group like *Boko Haram* can't afford to pass up. Aliyu and his men are always on the lookout to take *houri* for resale.

Muslim girls are used as concubines but never as human shields. If a Muslim girl has become boring and unappetizing, she is sold into slavery. Having had her virginity ripped from her by her captors, she is used goods. But technically, she is not impure because her virginity was taken by a devout *Boko Haram* terrorist. She gave herself honorably to serve the one true Islamic State. She will fetch a few hundred bucks. Her body is worth six RPG rockets. Aliyu calls her a "good lay," not an *ashawo*. He likes girls like this.

No matter how terrible the treatment of Muslim girls, the non-Muslims have it worse. Any non-Muslim girls may be killed immediately or taken as concubines until their captors use them up. As non-Muslims, they may be treated savagely without repercussion. When the men have their fill, the girls will be used as human shields. It will be the last time they are exploited in their miserable lives, so the girls are often thankful for their impending doom. No matter how violent and painful their death, it is preferable to the beatings and the rapes meted out around the clock when they are non-Muslim concubines.

Many of the girls taken from the village in Aliyu's raid were non-Muslim. They are divvied up first. Because any of the girls sixteen and older are most likely married, they are not virgins. Aliyu's men are permitted to have these girls only. Aliyu is a businessman first and foremost. Muslim or not, he wants the girls sold as sex slaves. They will be listed for sale on the Internet, but not the Internet most people know. This is not the world of Google, Amazon and iTunes. The girls are sold on what can be called the "darknet," a sinister underworld where one can find anything . . . drugs, prostitutes, real child pornography, weapons, sex slaves.

These things are sold all over the darknet via websites like Silk Road and Agora, sites that look like any we may see on eBay or Amazon. But the wares are very, very different. Aliyu purchases weapons from arms dealers via the darknet. It happens every day, everywhere around the world. The exchange is conducted in bitcoin, not conventional currency. Completely untraceable, bitcoin is the currency of a new generation of "online shoppers" who buy and sell anything illicit, including people. They operate completely outside the system and specialize in the taboo. Hate groups, child pornographers, drug dealers, arms dealers and sex traffickers proliferate on the darknet because of bitcoin. They flourish because millions and millions of people want hate, want drugs, want pictures of children having sex and want a real-life sex slave of their own.

Aliyu and countless other anonymous terrorists make the darknet their virtual home. Kofi Achebe knows this. Knee-high in human depravity, he has spent several years probing these murky depths. It all flows through the darknet, right beneath the surface of everyday life. Kofi knows he must shed light on the darknet because that's where the girls are sold, that's where the weapons used to annihilate whole villages are coming from, that's where terrorist groups like *Boko Haram* sell drugs and natural resources to fund their operations.

The United Nations is Kofi's chosen forum, but that is not working. Nobody listens to the cries of "bring back our girls." The girls keep disappearing. Nobody listens to the deafening silence that was once a village where several hundred people lived. Kofi Achebe knows cogs are replaceable and that's how the world wants it. Otherwise, good people prefer not to know, because when they know, they have to do something about it. Most people prefer to do nothing about it, so they prefer not to know. The logic is simple.

Every time a person surfs the net looking to purchase a nice blue ottoman or a lovely floral gift basket, there is beneath the surface a very different array of transactions taking place. The darknet is always active, always thriving. All one needs is an onion browser, so called because it layers identity, making users untraceable, completely anonymous, out of reach from the system, unencumbered by constraint and truly free from the controls of law and morality. With the right connections to the administrator of any of these darknet sites, one can buy just about anything imaginable, no matter how perverse, decadent or degenerate. It's like a Mafia movie. When someone vouches for you, there's no turning back. You're in all the way.

Aliyu purchased the AK-47 rifles used to gun down Yabani's village from an arms dealer in Chad. The dealer has an online store where all his wares are laid out on display as if he were selling hammers for Home Depot. Aliyu operates the same sort of darknet online store for his girls. He has built a solid reputation as a sex trafficker and has many loyal customers across the globe. Smuggling the girls is a task Aliyu leaves to another man whom he met on the darknet, a man who specializes in bringing human chattel to its destination. The systems are all already in place. All men like Aliyu have to do is acquire goods to sell and then leverage the system. In his case, the goods are girls.

It's easy to imagine this as a "third world" problem or an African problem. But Europe and the United States are by no means exempt from the flesh trade. Sex trafficking has flourished for years in these first-world countries as well. Wherever there are men, there will be an incessant, insatiable demand for the flesh of girls and boys alike. The world is full of buyers, and the darknet has sprung up as the marketplace. It's completely modern, completely modernized, and it's here to stay. It's a machine that swallows up children as easily as cows graze.

Some of Aliyu's girls will eventually end up in a sex stable for some mega-wealthy Arab or ex-KGB Russian turned oil tycoon when the wall came down. They will be beaten at whim and forced to perform all sorts of sexual acts. There is no part of their young bodies that will not be violated in some way. But, generally, they are fed and kept disease free. Others will end up as inventory for a large-scale pimp in countries like Germany, France or the United States, where their dark skin commands the price of an exotic oddity. Political connections, forged with large payouts, keep these pimps in business. These girls will be circulated and screwed until they are deemed used up or too old.

Heroin keeps them docile. Once their addiction takes over, there's nothing these girls won't do to get their next fix. They cease to be the beautiful souls someone once loved. When it is deemed they have become skanky or too old, a "sand man" is called in. It is the sand man's job to kill the useless girls like one might put down a horse. He administers a heroin overdose that takes her out of inventory for good. The position is quickly filled by another young girl purchased on the darknet. Thanks to men like Aliyu, there is an endless supply.

It's primarily in Russia where they like to film it all. That's where the most unfortunate girls end up. The demand for genuine porn snuff films is booming on the darknet. Videos and live streams of girls being raped and murdered, from simple strangulation to actual dismemberment, command the highest price. This is the real deal, and there are men willing to pay millions for good snuff. It's all there for them on the darknet, the new Hollywood of debauchery, where the most despicable acts command the highest price.

Once his girls are sold off, Aliyu does not care. They exist for him, if they ever "existed" at all, as a commodity and nothing more. He considers himself an entrepreneur first and a *jihadist* second. He has to be both to run a gang for *Boko Haram*. Kofi knows his work will take him beyond the battlefields and burned-out villages. He may be able to intercept a convoy and free some girls. More often than not, though, he has to plunge into the ocean of filth that is the darknet if he is to save even one girl after she is abducted. Unfortunately, neither his colleagues at the United Nations nor the good people of the Council on Women and Children have the stomach for such a thing despite their wellspring of good and genuine intentions.

Like a pernicious weed, darknet traffic grows at over 1000 percent per year. Terrorists groups like *Boko Haram* continually fill the pipeline with girls, drugs and weapons to meet the burgeoning demand of men and their phallic egos. Sometimes conventional warfare helps Kofi's cause. Other times, he must fight this war differently, using unconventional tactics. That is why he carries in his pocket a picture of Camille O'Keefe Rosemore he clipped from the *London Times* the day before. She may yet have the answers he's been looking for. As for now, he must make his rounds through the decimated village.

Chapter 7

Beads of sweat reappear on Kofi's brow. The sun is intensely hot. The dead bodies have been bloating and rotting in the heat for several days. They are barely recognizable as human. Some of the corpses have burst from the pressure of the body gas buildup and look like gruesome dolls torn at the seams. Kofi surveys the scene. Left to right he turns his head. Yes, this is all too familiar to him . . . the stench, the bodies—some clearly mangled from wild animals. He exhales deeply and inspects the nearest corpse. It was once a middle-aged man, proud father of three boys. His body was hacked up with a machete courtesy of *Boko Haram*. His belly has been picked at, clearly a meal for a vulture, wild dog or some other such creature scavenging off war.

This is what it's like to be an African, Kofi thinks to himself. There is a food chain. He knows billions and billions of oil dollars flood into his country. The oil flows out, and the money flows in. But there is no money, no riches, no wealth for the 150 million Nigerian people. For them, there is only a cycle of death and destruction that ends with one's mangled corpse being gnawed on by a wild dog.

Kofi scratches his head. The girls are part of this food chain. So, too, are the men who traffic them, the men abroad who buy the girls and the darknet that provides the marketplace. Kofi knows groups like *Boko Haram* thrive in places like this because the people are weak and have been made into cogs in a global machine fine-tuned for looting and killing. He knows what happened in this village— what happens in villages all over Africa—could never happen in a country like the United States. Countries like the United States don't produce cogs for the machine. Countries like the United States operate the machine. It makes him sick that even girls can be pillaged like a natural resource.

Kofi takes another look around. It's impossible to tell from his demeanor what he is feeling. He could be numb, or he could be incensed. He doesn't give it away. He reaches into one of the cargo pockets of his camo pants and pulls out a tin of Skoal. Dipping tobacco was a habit he picked up from the U.S. Special Ops guys who trained him back in the day. He kicked the habit twenty years ago. Since he started making these trips into the post-attack villages, he's picked it up again. He figures there are worse vices.

After "popping a lipper" as the Americans called it, he slides the tin back into his pocket. He turns to speak. He speaks sharply over his shoulder before launching a stream of dark-brown spit into the dirt at his feet.

"You coming out, or are you gonna sit in the truck all day as if that camera can operate itself?"

Olawale Cisse snaps to attention in the passenger seat. "Sorry, Kofi." He hurriedly grabs the camera from the bag by his feet and opens the door. He hops out with the trepidation of a child diving into a pool for the first time. He's been working with Kofi for only a month or so. His uncle made his fortune working with a large, multinational bank providing liquidity for corporations looking to do business in Nigeria, the Congo, South Africa and so on. Through his uncle, he has all the connections necessary to amass wealth and power. Olawale can have any job in finance he wants anywhere in the world. He chose to work with Kofi and the Council on Women and Families. His uncle has not spoken to him since.

Olawale grimaces. "I don't like it here. The smell is terrible." He chases after Kofi, who is already walking among the mass of dead bodies.

"You'll get used to the smell," Kofi says. He bends down next to the body of two little children. They are still wrapped in each other's arms.

Olawale snaps pictures. "I can't even tell their gender."

"It's a boy and a girl." The annoyance is apparent in Kofi's voice. "Better you not talk."

"They must have been hugging each other when they were shot."

Kofi corrects the young man. "Executed. These people were executed. Poachers shoot elephants. Terrorist thugs and murderers like *Boko Haram* execute innocent people. There's a difference."

Kofi spits again. Some inadvertently lands on the dead children. He wipes the tobacco juice from where it hit one of the children's arms. He stands up and continues toward the center of the village. He silently apologizes to the child.

Olawale chases after him again, snapping pictures hastily along the way. "Why are some of these bodies scattered all over the place and others lined up neatly in a row?"

Kofi stops and contemplates something. He bends down and picks up a few spent shells from the thousands scattered around the area. He smells one. The sharp scent of gunpowder mixed with CLP (gun oil) sends him back to his days when he was a man of war. He still considers himself a warrior, only now he fights his battles against men he knows are evil. This time around, there is a clear right and wrong.

"Do you not know?" says Olawale, jarring Kofi from his memories. "About the bodies?"

Kofi spits. "The Muslim bodies are lined up. Apparently, our friend Aliyu Adelabu feels he owes them respect after murdering them." He inspects some of the corpses more closely. "It is not uncommon for *Boko Haram* to kill Muslim men . . . sometimes women. Their twisted logic allows for this somehow. Notice that these people weren't mutilated like the other non-Muslims, but their hands and feet were bound. Make sure you get pictures of the bruising. And make sure you photograph them lined up this way because any Muslim seeing these pictures will know that *Boko Haram* is killing Muslims, too." He points out where he wants Olawale to photograph.

Olawale snaps pictures of the long line of corpses. He shoots Kofi a disturbed look. It's not just the mass of dead bodies that's giving him trouble. Kofi has seen that look enough times before to know exactly what's on the young man's mind.

"I know what you're thinking," says Kofi, removing his shades and wiping his brow with his cuff.

Olawale's voice cracks. "I thought *Sharia Law* prohibited Muslims from killing each other? How can these people claim to be pious Muslims when they slaughter other Muslims?"

Kofi spits and puts his sunglasses back on. "This is not the work of people, Olawale. This is the work of monsters. Aliyu Adelabu can call himself whatever he wants. He is anything but pious. He is a scourge, like a virus, only worse because we allow him to spread like the plague right in front of us while we stand by and watch. In the end, *Boko Haram* is nothing more than a gang of thugs, slavers and murderers. If you forget that, you will be forsaking what these poor people sacrificed."

His ambivalent demeanor gone, Kofi is clearly angry now. "You ask too many questions. I could have brought one of the other fellows, someone saltier. But I brought you here for a reason, Olawale. Take a good look around." He gestures to the destruction. "This is happening all over the world. It is happening right here in Nigeria, *our* Nigeria." He thumps his chest. "You have connections. You know what I say is true. People like your uncle, the power brokers in finance, know perfectly well what's happening. They try not to know. They hide their eyes. But they see all the same."

Olawale lowers his eyes in shame. He knows his uncle could do much more. That's why he opted to work with Kofi to begin with. "You want to take it out on me, but they decide for themselves to ignore it," he says.

Kofi rubs his face and nods. "Then you are learning, boy." He gestures for more photos to be taken. "You do not work in finance or the Department of Oil and Mineral Resources, Olawale, although you may now wish you had followed after your uncle."

"Don't count me out too soon."

Kofi looks at him without expression. "We need to burn these bodies. I have enough gasoline in the back of the truck."

Olawale lowers the camera. "You knew what to expect, didn't you?"

Kofi says nothing.

Something occurs to Olawale. "Doesn't *Sharia Law* say they should be buried as quickly as possible, within one day even?"

"I guess the pious Mr. Adelabu forgot that. Maybe you should send some of these photos to your uncle, too."

Olawale feels this is unfair. "I am here for a reason. I made my decisions in conflict with my family. My uncle has not spoken to me since."

"Tell it to them," says Kofi, pointing over his shoulder.

"I will make a difference, Kofi. It's not just about you. This is my country, too."

Kofi cracks the first smile of the day, a day that started for him at four in the morning. "Perhaps this job will put hair on your balls after all, Olawale. For a minute there, you sounded as if you had what the Afghans call *nang*. Having *nang* is having a sense of dignity and shame, honor and duty. I almost thought I was speaking to a man."

Olawale scoffs. "I know this term. You are not the only one who has travelled the world. I will be *nangialáy* and bring honor to my family name. You wait and see."

Kofi laughs just a bit. "Better you grow hair first, boy. Now get the gasoline cans from the truck. Then put on the hazmat suit in the back and pile up the non-Muslim bodies. Burn them and release their poor souls."

Olawale looks horrified. "You want me to stack *those* things?"

"They are people, Olawale, not things." He spits. "At least they were." He kneels down next to a dead woman whose empty eyes stare straight into the sun. He gently touches her forehead.

Olawale is repulsed. "You have seen too many dead bodies I think."

Kofi shakes his head. "Death like this reminds us how low we can sink as a people." He kneels next to a dead woman and touches her hand. "When I touch the dead body of someone whose life has been tragically ripped from them, I can feel their story. It becomes part of my life, part of the story that I must and will tell anyone who will listen. I am not afraid of these dead bodies, Olawale. To the contrary, I am in dialogue with them. Talking with the dead . . . that is my purpose for coming here today. They have much to tell me."

Olawale doesn't know what to say. He is disgusted and fascinated at the same time. The smell is beginning to get to him as well. The sun is baking everything. A large, black bird with an enormous wingspan glides in silently and lands in the middle of some bodies. Several other birds follow like paratroopers.

The birds began pecking and pulling at the rotting, festering flesh. One of the birds plucks an eyeball from the head of a young child. Olawale's head is spinning. He looks at Kofi. Why isn't he chasing the birds away? He is suddenly aware of a pounding headache. It feels like the birds are plucking at his head as well. He raises his camera and tries to photograph the gruesome sight. He faints before he can click a single picture.

When he awakens, he is lying back in the reclined passenger seat of Kofi's truck. The air conditioner is running full blast. He sits up quickly and tries to get his bearings. His head is still pounding. He rubs his eyes, recalling what Kofi said to him. He is not happy with himself. "I fainted because I have no hair on my balls," he thinks to himself. The moment quickly vanishes when he sees a large pyre burning.

Kofi took care of burning the bodies himself. He expected as much. He knew Olawale was not ready to process what he would see. He brought the kid half out of anger toward his uncle. He supposes he was punishing the young man for the sins of his uncle. But Kofi has no time for remorse. In a matter of days, Aliyu and his thugs will attack and pillage another village. He has to finish up here and move on in workmanlike fashion.

Olawale gets out of the truck and walks slowly over to the fire. Kofi hands him his camera. "All the pictures are taken," he tells Olawale. "I pretty much did your job for you."

"Thank you. I am sorry."

Kofi reaches into his pocket and puts in a fresh lip full of dip. Staring into the mesmerizing flames, he thinks for a moment before spitting. He feels he must pull the young man back in. "Why are you sorry? You have feelings. That is good. It is nothing to be ashamed of. If more people had feelings as deep as yours, things like this would not happen as often."

"But how do you manage it? You are much stronger than I."

"I do not feel much of anything anymore. Maybe anger, some sorrow . . . mostly anger. But I know I feel much less now than I did a few years ago. And I know I will feel even less a few years from now than I do today."

"As I said, you are very strong."

Kofi spits into the flames. It hisses. "No. That is not strength. It is feeling less. That's all. It's neither weak nor strong. My strength comes from talking with the dead. My mind is like a giant story that keeps growing. Here we are standing in front of a heap of burning bodies, chatting as if we were sitting around a campfire. This is a strange tale I have to tell."

"You are related to a great writer. That is why you have that power."

Kofi turns and heads for the Land Rover with the same assured stride he had when he first arrived. "Yes, my great-uncle was a gifted writer with a sharp eye for the dark truth that lurks beneath the surface of Africa. He speaks to me . . . in my head. Who knows . . . maybe speaking with the dead is like writing."

"Who knows?" agrees Olawale. "I would very much like to go home now. I have to attend to all the paperwork for this attack."

Both men climb back into their truck. Kofi starts it up and turns it around so that the passenger side is toward the pyre. He rolls down Olawale's window.

"Listen one last time before we leave."

"What am I listening for?"

"What are they saying to you?"

Olawale concentrates. He smiles and nods. "They are saying 'thank you.'"

Kofi turns to the young man. There is the faint glistening of a tear in the old warrior's eye. "That is why we do this job. We bear witness."

Kofi redirects the truck and speeds away, as if the reality of the village will diminish with every mile. But it is already stored away in his head indelibly where it will never fade away.

Olawale glances at the compass built into the dash. "Why are we heading north still?"

Kofi does not answer. He freshens his dip, reaches for an empty Gatorade bottle, pushes some napkins into it, and uses it as a spittoon.

"I thought we were going home? I have paperwork."

Kofi spits. "Change in plans. Paperwork doesn't matter shit to these people. Call someone in the office and have them do it."

"How do I do that?"

"Use my sat phone. It's in the black case in the back." He hands Olawale a business card with both Arabic and English writing. "Also call this man. He is an Imam. He will know what to do regarding the dead Muslims. Unfortunately, we've been working together quite a bit lately."

"It must be tough to be a religious leader and see this sort of thing happen."

Kofi nods. "I don't think he bargained for this. I think he's surprised by the number of Muslims murdered by *Boko Haram.* Anyway, you can call him when we arrive."

"Where are we going?"

"Lake Chad."

"Lake Chad?" exclaims Olawale.

"Is there an echo in here? We are going to Lake Chad. Specifically, Koulfoua Island."

Olawale rubs his temples. His headache is beginning to throb again. "Why?"

"More than five thousand refugees have fled to Koulfoua Island. We need to speak with them." He spits. "It is only a matter of time before *Boko Haram* attacks the island and slaughters those people by the thousands, so we may be speaking with the dead for quite a long time."

He reaches into his breast pocket and hands Olawale the article about Camille he's been carrying around.

"Her name is Camille O'Keefe Rosemore. She is an American, very famous. I want you to call her, too, and make arrangements for us to meet. Anywhere in the world she wants. I must speak with her."

Olawale takes the article and begins reading it.

Kofi pats him on the leg. "Get some sleep now. We have a long drive ahead of us. And I don't want you fainting on me when we hit a pothole."

Olawale sighs and reclines his seat. "No wonder the last guy who had my job quit."

Kofi plows the truck forward down the bumpy road. "He didn't quit."

"He just got tired of you, huh?"

"No, he was blown up by a land mine."

Chapter 8

Camille grabbed her cell phone and dialed Johnny Long. Johnny was a money manager. For the last forty-five years of his life, he'd dedicated himself to building investment strategies that could be applied to any number of situations. He sought to benefit all sorts of people regardless of their personal wealth. As he liked to explain, the stock market doesn't know how rich you are. The thing about Johnny Long was his humility and belief in human equality . . . not common traits among rich businessmen. People gravitated to him because he rarely put on airs. He could be a bit cheeky at times, it was true. Generally, though, Johnny Long had a deep respect for people as people, as a value unto themselves.

Johnny stood out among his peers because he didn't let his success go to his head in an industry where other money managers often turned to grandiosity as a measure of their self-worth. His tremendous financial success stemming from his three investment strategies enabled Johnny to undertake projects that had worldwide significance beyond rate of returns. He actively sought out opportunities to "turn things around for people," as he liked to say. His work with endowment trusts at hospitals, schools and countless foundations gave positive meaning to his life in a world where so many of his colleagues counted the value of their lives in terms of their own net worth.

Camille and Johnny were all about change. They got along well. When Johnny first met Becket Rosemore, he had recognized a singular opportunity to bring prosperity to a wider array of Americans. He pitched his dividend plan, a program whereby companies with a market cap of five billion dollars would be required to pay out 25 percent of their net profits in the form of a dividend. "This is the true meaning of participation," he told Beck. "Dividends are the true means of participation, whereas a stock is merely a certificate that is traded on an exchange." Needing a solid domestic platform for his presidential bid, Beck reeled Johnny Long in by promising to champion the dividend plan.

What Beck liked most about Johnny's plan was the notion that capitalism was the best system in the world for generating prosperity and democracy alike but had grown stagnant in a world where multibillionaire CEOs like Mark Zuckerberg amassed more money than they would ever need. Johnny's dividend plan would reinject that capital into the system in the form of dividends to shareholders, who would, in turn, either spend it (the "little guy") or reinvest it into new start-ups (activist investors like Carl Icahn). Either way, American capitalism would move forward toward a greater good.

As soon as Beck became president, he dropped Johnny and his dividend plan as fast as he could. Beck never intended to make the program a reality. Instead, he used Johnny Long to attract a broader segment of the voting public. In reality, Beck wanted as little change as possible. He left Johnny in the lurch and Camille at home while he spent what little free time he had sleeping with as many women as possible. That was just his way. He figured it worked for so many powerful men in the past, so why change things now?

Writing *This Soul's Journey through the Eye of the Storm* was a periodic moment of triumph for Camille. Once she finished it, her anger dissipated, and she slipped into a funk. She no longer loved herself. She no longer saw a purpose to her life. It would have been easy to say Beck took all that from her. But "easy" was not Camille's way.

This Soul's Journey was her attempt to shine a light on a great problem—why do we let our most powerful and successful men behave so badly even to the point of admiring them? When she put the final period in the book, she submitted it to her agent and went dormant.

Things were about to change dramatically. Once *This Soul's Journey* hits the market, Camille would no longer be able to hide from her destiny. She would have to face the fact that the road to her Self runs through herself and not through someone else, least of all Beck. She would start a firestorm of controversy. She had yet to decide where to go with it, where to go with her Self.

"I feel like I'm spinning my wheels," complained Camille, tossing a wet towel on a large, pink, Queen Anne style chair. She quickly slid into a thick, white bathrobe and shifted her cell phone to her other ear.

"This accident has been a real setback for me. I feel out of sync with the rest of the world. Things are happening so fast, and yet I'm moving so slow."

She plopped down onto her large bed. The billowy white comforter lovingly absorbed her. "I'm serious, Johnny. You wouldn't believe how many symposia on this subject are taking place across the globe right now. People are beginning to recognize that we are entering a time of huge awakening. It's the age of the crystalline solar self."

Johnny Long laughed. He was sitting in his office about to wrap up for the day. The financial markets had closed about an hour earlier, and he was more than ready for a good dinner. "I don't understand most of what you just said. It sounds as if you're saying I've been asleep all this time."

"Sure," chirped Camille. "We've all been asleep. In the process, we've lost connection with our higher selves. But that's all about to change. The Mayans knew this. That's why their calendar came to a sudden end. It's the end of the old times. We are entering a new era of spiritual connectivity."

"Ah . . . I thought the Mayan calendar ended because there were no more Mayans to keep it going. My bad."

Camille got up and walked over to the full-length mirror, opened her robe and pulled it aside, admiring her toned body and the large tattoo that adorned a good portion of her flat stomach. When she saw the scars on her leg, she cringed and closed her robe abruptly. She sighed.

"My leg looks horrible. It's gross," she said. "I have so many pins in it, I could set off a metal detector from a hundred yards away."

Johnny found her amusing. "Does it still work, your leg?"

"Mostly," she replied with a chuckle. "It gets me where I need to go. Still hurts, but Nicole is doing a great job with my physical therapy."

"So what's the problem? Some people find scars sexy."

"Are you one of them?"

Johnny laughed, mostly at himself. "Camille, at my age, a stiff breeze is about as much as I can handle. Never mind scars."

"Okay, I guess that qualifies as too much information."

"Hey, you asked," said Johnny.

Camille opened her robe again and gave it another shot. The scars looked just as bad as they did a minute ago. She admired the large tattoo on her stomach. What a *coup* that was. Beck nearly strangled her when he found out. It was a Japanese dragon koi that came alive against her pale skin. The bright yellows, reds and oranges appeared to glow with a sort of radiance and multidimensionality that was rare to achieve in tattoo art. The symbolism was equally important. Thought to possess the power to transform itself into a powerful dragon, the dragon koi had a special meaning in Japanese mythology. It symbolized overcoming challenges and power through a spiritual awakening. She got the tattoo on a trip to Japan with Beck before he became president. It meant a great deal to her, so much so that she made it a permanent part of herself despite the disgust it caused Beck. In a way, she knew even then that the tattoo would remain with her long after the man had come and gone.

It wasn't her first tattoo, and Beck wasn't always disgusted by her eccentricities. When they first met, he was enthralled by her edginess and loved the sunflower tattoo that spiraled around her foot. That sort of stuff about Camille used to turn him on. He would buy her ridiculously expensive shoes to show off her tattoo and would massage her high arches for hours while they chatted. There was a time when Beck found Camille's work as a past-life regressionist intriguing. It made her unique and, having written numerous books on the subject, something of a fringe celebrity around D.C. In fact, her client base included some very powerful politicos.

Becket Rosemore was single-minded. His thoughts were always directed toward accumulating power for himself. What worked with Camille in the past lost its luster as her value diminished. He was never too interested in what Camille had to say, but he faked it well enough because, back then at least, he found her body irresistible. For a man like Beck, a man who collected panties as souvenirs from each sexual conquest, this was all the motivation he needed. He also needed a foot locker to hold all those panties because he'd accumulated so many.

During that time, she'd come to trust Johnny Long. She and Beck first met Johnny at one of Beck's town hall–style talks just before he announced his run for the presidency. A brilliant money manager who'd dedicated his life to helping good people and good institutions find the road to financial independence, Johnny provided Beck with a radical idea to use as his economic platform during the election.

Thinking about all the unfulfilled potential irritated Camille almost as much as her scars. She turned sideways and took a good look at her leg again. "I guess every time I look at the scarring, it makes me feel weak." She closed her robe abruptly once again. "I hate feeling like that."

"It makes you feel weak or it makes you feel vulnerable?" asked Johnny. "They are different concepts."

"Ah," she scoffed. "You men and your concepts. Always parsing things into small morsels your huge egos can easily digest."

"Can't you perform a past-life regression on yourself? Seriously. . . ."

"No need. I already know I have been a man's plaything for thousands of years. I always end up getting killed in the most heinous ways. I'm usually a slave of some sort. That's why I have big feet and hands. I'm a worker. Only this time around, my job is to work with people's spirits. I'm meant to sow the seeds for spiritual connection . . . at least that's what I thought before I met Beck. He put an end to all that "freaky crap," as he called it. Lovely. So much potential . . . wasted."

"Well, if you'll pardon my huge ego, I would like to note that 'weak' connotes a feeling about one's self in the present, in the here and now. 'Vulnerable' suggests one is afraid of danger lurking in the future, so one is afraid to move forward. I think they're different concepts."

"Oh good God," said Camille. "How does your wife make it through dinner with you? But I get your point. I am definitely stuck because I'm afraid to move past all this. I know what you're saying. I feel like there's one of those cartoon safes waiting to drop on my head. And, of course, my darling husband is the Road Runner who always gets off scot-free."

She picked up the TV remote. The flat screen mounted on her bedroom wall popped to life. Beck's face was front and center on some cable news channel. He was deflecting questions about Camille's forthcoming book. She listened to him sling barbs at the show's host in an attempt to distract.

"Lovely, he's calling me shameless and self-serving," she said.

"Who is?" asked Johnny.

"The guy in the White House who can't keep his wang in his pants."

"Bill Clinton?" quipped Johnny.

Camille laughed out loud. "No, the other guy, my soon-to-be ex-husband. He's dodging questions about my book by attacking me."

Something more occurred to her, and she shuddered. It hit her viscerally and made her a bit queasy. "I wonder how many women he's been with while we were together? I mean . . . it's pathetic. Like . . . when we were having sex, back when he actually found me attractive, how many other women was he sleeping with? It's like he was rubbing them on me. It makes me sick now. But when we were together I tolerated it. It's like I was numb or something."

Johnny turned more serious. "Hmm . . . you wrote a book about it, didn't you? Beck's not getting off scot-free this time, my dear. And it's all thanks to you. Think about how many women are in your position. Think about how many rich men we put in power even though they do despicable things not just to women, but to all people. Open the newspaper and read any article on Africa. It's unbelievable how low people can sink."

"I don't do the news . . . TV or papers. I try to find positive stuff to focus on."

"That's why your book is going to be absolutely huge. It's a different format. People will take to it. Not to mention the fact that you are a worldwide celebrity. The car accident you lament so much also made you a sympathetic heroine. Women all over the world know your name. They love you, Camille."

She changed the channel to a program about Africa. It was a segment on *Boko Haram*. She tossed the remote on the bed. "Well that's ironic, don't you think? What's next, I die and become a martyr?"

"No, just the opposite. You begin to *live* again like you did before you met Mr. Happy Pants. At least that's what you tell me. You say you want your life back. You say you want to begin living again. Well, I've got news for you. When your book comes out next week, you're going to take the world by storm. The Red Dragon Lady will tell the truth for all the world to hear."

"Ech, who came up with that Dragon thing anyway?"

Johnny laughed. "I think it was a Marjorie Williams from the *Post*, right?"

"I guess. My agent keeps telling me the magazines are dying for a full body layout of me and my stomach tattoo. She says everybody wants to have the Red Dragon Lady with her dragon koi tattoo splashed on their cover. I feel like a piece of meat."

"Naw, there's a great story behind that tattoo and it links right into what I was saying about living your life again. And besides, look what happened when Bruce Jenner—"

"It's Caitlin now, thank you very much."

"Ah, yes," said Johnny, chuckling. "Sorry. Remember what happened when, ah . . . Caitlin Jenner posed for the cover of *Vanity Fair.*"

Camille sprawled out on a comfy chaise lounge. She propped her bad leg up on a few pillows. "Let's see . . . do I remember what happened? Well, I'm sure Beck thought to himself, *hey, I'd do that chick if nobody would find out.*"

"I bet he wasn't alone."

"Yeah, that's why everyone wants to see me naked on the cover of some magazine. There'll be a copy of it in the bathroom of every sperm bank. It's that need you all have to put manhood into anything that moves. It's disgusting."

She could dance around it all she wanted, but Camille was stuck. On the one hand, she longed to return to the life she once enjoyed before she met Beck, when she was motivated and felt her life had meaning. Now she felt empty, devoid of anything that would really count when she was on her deathbed.

She turned her attention to the TV. "Have you seen the news lately?" she asked. "Disgusting."

"I thought you didn't watch the news . . . too negative?"

"Call it a momentary lapse of reason. One of the cable news networks is running a piece on these *Boko Haram* nut jobs."

"Your husband never mentioned them?"

Camille grunted. "Please. If it didn't have to do with his China deal or with getting a piece of ass, it never crossed his mind. Apparently, these lunatics executed several thousand people so far this year for blasphemy and being gay. They're showing pictures of two children who were crucified for not fasting properly during Ramadan. Really?"

She sat down as the reality of what she was seeing sunk in. Camille was highly empathic, so things like this affected her viscerally. She was deeply connected to the world at large through the great collective unconscious she'd believed in since she first read Jung on the subject.

"Are you okay?" asked Johnny, sensing her unease.

"These are not just pictures on TV for me, Johnny. You know that."

"I guess it comes with being a medium. You sense things other people don't. That's your gift. That's why women all over the world love you."

She ran her hand through her thick, red mane. "That's why I need to be doing more. They're crucifying children, for God's sake. I mean, who does that? And they've got the nerve to say it's God's will. Are they insane?"

"Did you know *Boko Haram* is connected to *ISIS*, too?"

"No, I didn't. Like I said, it wasn't on Beck's radar."

"Yeah," said Johnny. "But it seems like these *Boko Haram* guys in Nigeria are the guys who kidnap women and girls to be wives or sold as sex slaves. Of course, there's the whole other problem of children being used as soldiers in places like Sudan. They sell for, like, six bucks a kid. I read somewhere recently that the United Nations estimates there are over 300,000 children being used as soldiers throughout the world. It's amazing."

Camille sighed. "It makes me sick. Beck could call attention to that sort of thing with all his power. But he can't line his pockets saving African children, so why would he bother? I'm sure that's how he figures it."

Johnny just exhaled loudly.

"Exactly," agreed Camille. "That's what I'm saying. I need to bring some sort of higher meaning to my life. I lost all that when I took up with our esteemed president. Once the divorce goes through—"

"How's that coming?"

"Believe me," she snorted with a hint of acerbity. "He can't get it processed fast enough. We should be done with it in a couple of weeks or so. I'm not fighting anything. I'll never have to worry about money again, that's for sure. I think Beck believes he can buy me off for trashing him on the publicity circuit once my book hits. At the same time, I will be totally excommunicated. It's gonna be new. You'll manage all the money for me. The book money, too.

I'll be free of a lying, cheating husband. I will be rid of the Secret Service robots who tail me night and day. But. . . ."

"Yeah?" prompted Johnny.

"But then what? I can't help feeling like we're entering a time of great spiritual opportunity, like a window of opportunity for people to connect with their higher selves. At the same time, take a look at the news. It's like the world is on fire. We're murdering each other in the streets, in villages, in cities . . . everywhere. Pop culture is stultifying our young people. Video games are numbing kids' minds. There's a disconnect somewhere, Johnny. I'm sure of it. We've fallen very far from our source."

"Look, I've been saying it for years. We're in a downward spiral. What did Jim Morrison say? 'I want to get my kicks before the whole shithouse goes up in flames?' I just try to positively impact my little piece of the world through my work as a money manager for good causes."

Camille jumped up. "No, no, no. . . ."

"Whoa," said Johnny. "Someone just woke up from her spiritual slumber."

"You've got it all wrong. There's always great discomfort during periods of great change. Right now, we are experiencing a period of huge spiritual growth as the universe allows us to expand in this dimension in ways we've never been able to do before. Naturally, people are going to act out because they are uncomfortable. All the garbage is being pushed to the surface. That's to be expected. But when the cleanup is finished, it's off to the races. You know the babies being born now are the first generation in over five hundred years to come to this world completely free of karmic burden? "

"Wow, I have no idea what you're taking about, but it sure sounds exciting."

Camille snapped back. "Don't patronize me. Beck used to do that all the time. There are a lot of people who feel like I do."

Johnny thought for a second. "Well . . . maybe it's time for you to assume a leadership role of your own. If you feel there's something you need to champion, then you have to do something about it.

Right now, Camille, you have the world's attention. When your book hits, you'll have a universal stage from which to speak. Who knows how long that will last? Beck will certainly try his best to shut you down, and he's the most powerful man in the world."

Camille's energy lowered. "Yeah . . . there's that."

"But," stressed Johnny Long, "you can be the most powerful *woman* in the world. What do you think about that? You are the Red Dragon Lady. You and your fabulous dragon koi tattoo that nobody but Beck and some Japanese tattoo artist have ever seen."

Camille pursed her lips. "That's interesting. I never thought of it quite that way."

"That's because you're too busy blaming Beck for ruining your life, as if that's even possible. Think about those girls in Africa who are sold into slavery. *Their* lives have been ruined. Your life is filled with freedom and opportunity. So take advantage of it."

"You know I could be offended by what you just said."

Johnny laughed. "You could be, but you won't be."

"What makes you so sure, Johnny Long?"

"It's been my job for the last forty years to tell people what to buy, when to sell and what to do with the proceeds. My rules for investing apply to life as well. You've sold off your shares in Becket Rosemore."

Camille had an epiphany. "Wow, so something just hit me. Now that I have cashed out of Beck's life, it's time for me to reinvest my emotional proceeds in myself. Instead of spending my life trying to help someone else—some man—find greatness, I need to find the greatness within myself and follow that path."

"That's the only way it can happen, Camille. You know that."

"It's funny. I spend so much time as a medium helping people look within themselves to find their path to the purpose and greatness that I guess I forgot to apply my advice to myself as well."

"Change can only happen through discomfort."

"Okay, okay. . . . I wrote that in the preface to my new book. If you don't stop throwing my own words at me, I will never send you an advance copy again."

"Do you think you have something great to share with the world, Camille?"

She dismissed him with a grunt. "Of course. My slave days are over. This lifetime is going to be different for me. I know it."

Johnny started laughing out loud.

"What's so funny?" Camille wondered with a beautiful smile on her face.

"The Red Dragon Lady is back."

"I hate that name."

"It's better than Koi Fish Lady."

"How about Camille O'Keefe? I think that's a good name."

"Then you'd better hurry up with the divorce."

"I don't need a piece of paper to tell me what I already know. I've been gone for some time now."

They wrapped up the call with promises to do lunch. Camille was due to start her book tour soon, and Philly was one of the first cities she'd be visiting. She would definitely get together with Johnny and his wife. She always got along well with Johnny's wife.

Camille tossed her phone on the bed and took one last look at herself in the mirror. She forced herself to hold her robe open, exposing her feelings of vulnerability as much as anything else. She nodded to herself. Yes, that scar would heal. Some aloe, some vitamin E, plenty of sun and lots of positive energy. Soon enough, it would be just a memory in time.

She laughed to herself. Maybe she should take a cue from Caitlin Jenner. Maybe she should pose alluringly on the cover of some popular magazine. Let the world get a good look at Camille O'Keefe and her fabulous koi tattoo. She smiled. That would wake some people up.

But then what? What was she to do after the buzz wore off? How was she going to ignite a wave of spiritual growth for women worldwide? Yeah . . . that was the question. She vowed to build something out of the ashes. Like a phoenix. She wondered if perhaps Johnny was right. Maybe this was her time. Maybe the women of the world were finally ready.

She was about to go into the shower when her phone rang. She knew the ring tone. It was her agent, Claudia Brenner.

"Hey," said Camille, slightly out of breath. "I was just about to jump into the shower. Well, actually, I was about to limp into the shower, but you get my point."

"I won't keep you, hon."

"Five days and counting," sang Camille. "I can't wait for the book to hit. Beck is gonna have a conniption. Are we all set for next week?"

Camille was referring to her upcoming appearance on *The Interview*, a wildly popular program featuring interviews with the hottest celebs.

"We sure are, hon. You're going to knock them dead, Red."

Claudia was a selling machine. Always upbeat, always "on." She was known to be firm but eminently fair. Camille's book was going to be a blockbuster. She had landed a deal for Camille that would eclipse anything even Bill Clinton got.

Today, however, her tone was unusually cautious. "So," she continued. "Something really weird happened this morning."

Camille was concerned. "Oh?"

"Yeah. I got a call from some guy at the United Nations."

"Really?"

"Yeah. Weird, right? He's some bigwig named Kofi Achebe. Anyway, he gives me this whole spiel about women and children being killed in Africa by some terrorist group."

Camille was equally perplexed. "Hmmm, never heard of him."

"Well, he says he's totally legit, with the UN, and must meet you. He says you have to hear what he has to say. He says you can change the world."

Camille was curious. "Oh my God, what did you tell him?"

"I told him he was damned right. You're the Red Dragon Lady. Of course, you can change the world."

Camille shook her head. "You, too, with that name? You didn't give him my contact info, did you?"

"Of course not, darling. I gave him my office address. I told him he had to meet with me first. Maybe he'll get to meet you someday, maybe he won't. Anyway, he'll be here the day after *The Interview*."

"Are you crazy, Claudia?"

"Camille, darling, of course I'm crazy. That's why I'm the best damned agent you'll ever have. Let Claudia Brenner do her job."

Camille sighed. Too much controversy and conflict always got her down. She wondered how on earth she was going to handle the firestorm that would ignite when her book hit. "I guess that's what I pay you for, Claud."

"And pay me you will, my dear. Gotta go. *Ciao!*"

Chapter 9

"It's a damned outrage!" Beck launched Camille's book across the Oval Office. It hit Sammy the staffer square in the nose. Sammy's real name was Samantha Browner. Beck kept her around because she could suck a golf ball through a garden hose, and he felt entitled to carnal privileges—sexual *quid pro quo*. This included "getting a Lewinsky" on demand in the Oval Office. It that sense, Samantha Browner took brownnosing to a whole new level. As far as Beck was concerned, it was all acceptable within the terms of the presidential code of conduct that sounded more like divine fiat.

Beck knew he'd made a mistake as soon as he sent the book flying. All Beck saw was Camille's smiling face on the back cover as the book sailed along its trajectory, pages fluttering. When it struck Sammy, there was a collective gasp. Her fashionable Donna Karan frames did little to protect her as they cracked and flew off her face. Blood flowed instantly from her nose. Sammy let out something like a yelp, flew backward, papers fluttering into the air, and hit the ground like a 115-pound bag of sand.

At first, nobody moved. Everyone stood silently staring at the blood seeping into the carpet.

"Don't just stand there," yelled Harry Pierson. "That's the damned rug in the Oval Office. Move your asses."

The other staffers scrambled to action. One man, whom Camille took to calling Pansy in response to his constantly talking down to her, pulled out his handkerchief, pushed Sammy's head aside, and began patting up the blood. It was unlike Camille to resort to name-calling, but he had it coming. Another staffer, an older woman of little interest to Beck, collected the papers that Sammy had sent flying into the air on impact.

Pierson gestured silently to a Secret Service agent, who proceeded to escort Sammy out of the Oval Office (once and for all, as she would later find out). There was nothing quite like getting the bum's rush from Harry Pierson. He was so smooth, by the time Sammy's nose stopped bleeding and her head stopped spinning, her termination papers and non-disclosure agreement were already being sent to her apartment via certified mail.

"Would it have killed her to duck?" said Beck with mock innocence. "I mean really . . . she bends over for everything else. And what moron decided to put a beige rug in here anyway?"

Pierson cleared his throat.

Beck got the hint. "It was Camille, wasn't it?"

Pierson gave him a sympathetic smile. One of the staffers picked up Camille's book and placed it on the desk in front of Beck with the back cover facing up so that Beck was staring right at Camille.

The president plopped down in his chair. "Look at that smirk on her face, Harry. The bitch is enjoying all this. Spiritualist my ass. What kind of so-called spiritualist writes crap like this?"

"Yeah, well . . . her new book is sitting on the most famous desk in the world. It's hard to believe."

Beck picked it up. Fearing themselves the next target, several of the staffers scattered like insects. "Everybody relax," said Beck. "You're acting as if I meant to hit Sammy for Christ's sake." He let out a disgusted grunt before summarily dismissing them all.

"Admit it, you have been known to express yourself freely. I mean, LBJ would blush," said Pierson with a sardonic, menacing laugh.

"Yeah, yeah. You're a funny guy, Harry. Whatever, everybody get out. I want to talk privately with my vice president if you don't mind."

The staffers didn't need to be told twice. On her way out, Margaret Manfred turned to Beck. Manfred was a top dog among Beck's handlers. She focused primarily on popularity polls dealing with social issues.

"You know, Mr. President, you need to do something about that woman and her book." Manfred often referred to Camille as "that woman." She shook her head in disbelief. "She's already at the top of the *Times Best Sellers* list, and it's only been out three days." She pointed to the large window behind the iconic desk that is so familiar the world over. "She's killing you out there."

Beck held the book up next to his face so that Camille's picture was facing Manfred. "She's killing me?" he said in a saccharine tone. "This redhead right here? *She's* killing *me?*"

Manfred was in no mood. She hated Camille. "You need to do something drastic."

"Maybe I should play God and shoot her myself!" He pulled the book back like he was going to fire it at Margaret Manfred. It was enough to send her through the door and down the hall with the rest of the crew.

"You see what I have to deal with, Harry? All these women?"

Harry grabbed a seat on one of the two couches running perpendicular to the president's desk. He gestured for Beck to help himself to the other couch so they could sit face-to-face.

"Maybe you should stop screwing them . . . all these women . . . you know?"

"Oh boy." Beck rubbed his face. "Is this going to be one of your famous 'Come to Jesus' meetings? Because if it is, we'd better order lunch . . . and dinner. We're gonna be here a while."

Pierson laughed. "You exaggerate, my friend. And I know you hit Sammy on purpose."

Beck smiled. "Was it that obvious?"

Pierson shrugged.

"Can I tell you something, Harry? I've wanted to do that to her for a while. She's like . . . one of those chicks you just wanna crack in the jaw just to see what it feels like. You know she's gonna go down like a sack of potatoes, but there's nothing quite like seeing it. "

"I wonder what Camille has to say about your past lives? You must have been one mean, slave-owning ballbuster. She writes about it."

Beck pointed at his vice president. "Forget about it. How do you think I got where I am today? If there is any truth to the craziness that woman spouts off, it's that great people coming to power isn't an accident. It's all meant to be." He thumbed his chest. "I'm meant to be."

Harry Pierson found this all very funny. He couldn't help laughing. "You certainly don't lack in self-confidence what she says you lack in the bedroom."

Beck's ego deflated instantly. His anger filled the void. "She wrote that?"

Pierson confirmed this. "Let's see . . . how did she put it? Ah yes . . . *The president has a disappointingly small capacity for truly pleasuring a woman despite his huge imagination to the contrary.* I think that's what she wrote. It was something like that. I laughed out loud when I read it."

Beck sat down on the couch across from Pierson. He was stunned and looked completely flattened. He simply wasn't used to being treated this way by women or subordinates. In this case, he considered Camille both. He preferred instead simple, black-and-white roles, as he termed it. In other words, Becket Rosemore liked everything in its place as he defined "everything" and "place." He felt ordered and focused when everything in his life was neatly squared away. To his dismay, the more success he gained the less orderly his life became. The more power he garnered, the more loose ends there were to trim. Recently, he felt his life was more a process of pruning away what he couldn't control than anything enjoyable. This whole ordeal with Camille's book only reinforced his deep-seated loathing of anything or anyone outside of himself.

Beck only trusted himself. And recently, he was beginning to question even that. When Camille had announced to the world in an unscheduled press conference from the Rose Garden that she was throwing him out of the White House because of his cheating ways, Beck's world began closing in around him. It was becoming stifling, restrictive to the point of debilitating. He knew that's why Pierson was there . . . to remind him that this was not acceptable from the president of the United States.

To clarify, Harry Pierson would undoubtedly refrain from any criticism of Beck's womanizing. Pierson couldn't care less. What bothered the vice president was Beck's demeanor, his appearance of weakness over this whole thing with Camille. Recognizing that his own political career was inextricably tied to Beck, Harry Pierson could not tolerate weakness from Becket Rosemore, the man to whom he'd hitched his cart.

Seeing Beck, the most powerful man in the world, slouching in the couch before him made Pierson angry. As far as he was concerned, Beck could do whatever the hell he wanted so long as he didn't blow their gig. He didn't consider it his lot to blow up from Beck's arrogance. Just thinking about it made him resentful.

For Beck, it was more a matter of emotional need than want. Beck preferred to stroll down Easy Street. But there was a time when he had sought a difficult path. The hardships of life in the armed forces were something he chose, knowing it would distinguish him for the rest of his life. He never thought twice about undertaking the most rigorous challenges. The intensity of the training, the isolation from the rest of the world, and the sheer brutality of war and the classified engagements entrusted to him as a special operator came as a package deal for which he enthusiastically signed up. He believed it would make him a better man. His definition of "better man" had since changed as his wealth and power grew.

The structured life in the military even helped Beck manage his deep-seated need for emotional distance. Beck could name only a few women other than his mother who had played a significant role in his life. Before meeting Camille, he remained adamantly single.

Any sort of serious relationship would have been too much baggage. Just like he found the very thought of a serious relationship cumbersome to the point of distraction, Becket Rosemore found life much easier painted in black and white. Gray was a shade of ambiguity he preferred to avoid at all costs. He enjoyed his colorful array of short-term affairs, knowing that life would take him elsewhere.

He really hadn't changed much over the years, and he was disgusted with himself for getting involved with Camille in the first place. What was he thinking? Why on earth would he bring a wife into the White House? He knew the reason. He knew he took her on more as a marketing ploy than anything else. He was learning the hard way . . . his way of thinking, his code of conduct, would always be a catch-22.

God, he hated that book. He was dying a slow death by his own hand. He didn't know how to handle his own failure. At least in a foxhole, he knew where he stood. The guy next to him would give his life to save him, and Beck would do the same. In a foxhole, the universe was only as large as what he could shoot. Nothing outside of the current situation had meaning greater than what was immediately at hand, namely, life and death. Intimacy in battle meant having another man's intestines blown in your face after the next mortar round hit. Intimacy in battle was Beck feeling the blade of his knife slide right between two ribs, instantly deflating the lung so that his victim could not cry out in warning.

Camille O'Keefe had learned something the hard way as well. The kind of intimacy that couples share did not exist for Becket Rosemore. He could kill a man without a second thought. It came easy for him. But women . . . they were a different opponent altogether, one whom Beck had no training to handle. His emotions always got the best of him in relationships, so he stopped having emotions about them.

It was easier for him to imagine himself free and invincible. Men like him could pull that off with ease. Before meeting Camille, his life was progressing exactly as planned, and he remained stolid in his conviction to avoid the sort of contrivances and emotional manipulations he felt defined relationships with women. To his chagrin, being a politician meant compromise, it meant affinity with people and ideas he might find objectionable but necessary for his own political survival.

He tried to keep things as basic as possible. The single life, no matter how solitary, afforded him a comfortable distance from his own emotions. His formula was simple—if he wasn't overly involved with a woman, he would never have to be too intimate. This rule of thumb was one of the principles underpinning his emotional life. Camille O'Keefe was the polar opposite of Occam's razor. She made things very difficult indeed. Perhaps more correctly surmised, since meeting Camille, Beck had twisted his own life into a convoluted mess.

This whole thing with Camille was proving to be his undoing. He felt he should have followed his gut and run as the "Bachelor President" or something like that which the media could make sexy. Instead, he was foolish enough to believe he could treat a woman as nothing more than an old sock or T-shirt he used to wipe up after pleasuring himself. Now he was screwed, and Harry Pierson was there to let him know just how bad it was about to get. It was time to pay the piper.

"I don't know," said Pierson with a sneer. His resentment was evident, and he really didn't mind revealing it, even to the president of the United States. "I look at you slouched there like a sulking teenager, and I wonder to myself what happened to the badass who took the world by storm? What happened to the cut-throat negotiator who redrew the map in the entire Middle East while flipping the bird to anyone who protested? Where'd that guy go?"

Beck cleared his sinuses and sat upright. "She's killing me out there, Harry. What am I supposed to do?"

Pierson waved him off in disgust. He was on a roll now. "Stop with your whining, will ya? You know why this kind of shit doesn't happen to Putin? I'll tell ya why. Because people are afraid of him. All the nasty crap that guy pulls on a daily basis, and what does the world hear about it? Nothing. And believe me, that son of a bitch is always up to something. It's just that people are afraid to cross him. Do you think one of his mistresses would publish a book like Camille's?"

Beck smiled. "She wouldn't be alive to give her first interview."

Pierson slapped the table in front of him. "Exactly, Beck." He pointed to the iconic view of the huge presidential desk poised against the large window, the famous view of the Oval Office and all it stood for.

"Look at that view, Beck. That's a power seat. That's your seat. Man, after your China deal, there wasn't a journalist out there who would write something bad about you. Now, it's like a feeding frenzy since that damned book came out. The vultures are gnawing on your ass."

Beck ran his fingers through his hair. He was still imaging Camille's obituary, how he would tear up at her funeral while appealing to the world to spread love and respect in her name. He needed something like that to turn his fortunes.

"We need something big to turn this thing around, Harry. Either that or I need to become an African dictator and simply take control of everything . . . leaving a pile of bodies in my wake."

"That's the problem with America, Beck. Sometimes we need a good dictator to kick a little ass, but everyone's all soft from too much comfort and freedom. We're a country of pansies now."

"Yeah," agreed Beck. "Sometimes I think we have too much freedom, you know? It doesn't sound right to say it that way, but you know what I mean."

"Sure," replied Pierson. "Sometimes you just want to clean up a mess the way it needs to be cleaned up. But you can't. That's the problem. Too many damned personal rights."

"Watch this," said Beck, picking up the remote that was lying on the table. He hit a button and a panel in the wall slid open, revealing a large flat-screen television. "I'm just going to pick any cable news channel." He flipped through several channels. Camille's face was everywhere. "She is ubiquitous, Harry. The bitch is like water."

He tossed the remote onto the table between them. At the same time, Pierson got an incoming text and checked his phone. He groaned as he picked up the remote and flipped over to the popular daytime talk show *The Interview*. Both men sat watching the host, Regan

O'Neill, interviewing Camille O'Keefe. It was the media event of the year. Camille O'Keefe had the world's attention, and her agent was going to maximize the opportunity.

Regan O'Neill was tossing out softballs that Camille hit out of the park. She was scoring points left and right, especially where women's issues were concerned. Camille spoke without reservation, revealing the most intimate details about her life with the president. She recounted the many nights when she could smell another woman on Beck's hands or clothes. The audience of mostly women booed loudly. Camille even discussed the time she found Beck's secret stash of panties he had accumulated from each of his sexual conquests. Beck thought they were well-hidden. Seems he was mistaken.

"What the hell is she doing?" cried Beck.

Pierson had already moved to the wet bar in the adjoining room. He returned with two glasses of Scotch. He put one on the table in front of Beck and kept the other for himself.

"That's in case you decide to start drinking again," he said to Beck, who had been dry since leaving the service years earlier. "Should I get you a revolver with one bullet as well?"

"She could drive me to drink, Harry. Listen to those women in the audience cackle like hens. You'd think I was a pedophile. Did all those women suddenly forget what Bill Clinton liked to do with his cigars? Like I'm the greatest villain of our era? Please . . . spare me."

Pierson downed his Scotch, put the glass on the table and took the other. "Did you really have hundreds of girls' panties stuffed in a footlocker or something, you sick bastard?"

Beck shrugged it off. "So I'm eccentric. I'll tell you one thing, Harry, I had the best-smelling steamer trunk of any damned president."

"Yeah, I'm sure the Smithsonian will want them for your installation . . . provided Bob Guccione doesn't get them first."

Their conversation stopped abruptly. Camille was answering a question about faking her orgasms. Harry Pierson immediately downed his second Scotch of the morning. And yet . . . he was glued to Camille's every word.

"So much for the nobility of the presidency," said Pierson as he headed solemnly back to the bar.

Chapter 10

The live audience on the set of *The Interview* burst into laughter when Camille admitted to "faking it."

Beck's jaw hung. "She was faking it?"

Regan O'Neill addressed her audience directly. "I think we all know what she's talking about, don't we, ladies?"

The women in the audience let fly with a volley of applause.

"Oh, I'm sure I wasn't the only one of his women left . . . wanting," added Camille almost as an afterthought. "No matter how many women the president has been with."

The women in the audience went wild, much to the chagrin of the men in attendance. Camille O'Keefe was a star thanks to her blunt honesty and Regan's unique rapport with her audience. She had a way of making them feel like her friends. The set was comfortable—large, plush couches for herself and her guests. A smooth jazz band off to one side filled the interludes. The lighting met filming requirements without seeming too sterile. And nobody in the audience left a show empty-handed. This morning, they each received a free copy of Camille's book.

"Sorry, guys," said Regan O'Neill. "But hey . . . ignorance is bliss, right? Right?"

"Unfortunately, I'm a medium, so I know things I wish I didn't," said Camille. "That's how I ended up here in the first place."

Regan turned serious now. "I think I speak for every woman in the world when I say we know your pain. It hurts deeply when we discover our men have been unfaithful." She sipped her coffee and sat back awaiting Camille's response.

Camille did not speak immediately. The camera zoomed in. It was clear she was tearing up. "Very deeply. It made me feel dirty, scummy, you know? I felt that I wasn't good enough. But then I started to get angry. I started feeling like I deserved more than being treated like just another sex toy belonging to a rich and powerful man." She wiped her tears away.

Regan handed her a box of tissues. "And so we have your book, *This Soul's Journey through the Eye of the Storm*. Those of you out there in TV land who haven't read it, you need to get it today. Every woman in the world needs to read this book. And so do all you men, know what I'm saying?"

Camille smiled sheepishly. "It's already been translated into ten languages."

"And I'm sure you will be blasted in all ten different languages by men who are threatened by what you have to say."

Camille shrugged. "Maybe. I can't control any of that, you know? It's funny. . . ." She paused as tears began welling up again.

Regan reached over and squeezed her leg. "We all know how difficult this is for you. You're a remarkably strong woman."

Camille cleared her throat and composed herself. "It's just that I am not confrontational. I'm an empath. People like me avoid conflict at all costs. I'm not looking to hurt anyone. I don't do revenge, you know? But I felt I had to write this book. I felt it was my obligation to the universe to speak my truth so women everywhere can see they are not alone and that we can do something about it. I also hope that the men who are daring enough to read it take a good look at themselves."

"*This Soul's Journey through the Eye of the Storm* is very controversial, Camille. There's no way around that. Your book threatens the power structure, undermines men's control of things."

Camille shook her head. "That wasn't my goal."

Regan was a bit surprised. "But you took on the president of the United States. Becket Rosemore is the most powerful man in the world." She held up her hand. "Wait . . . I misspoke. Becket Rosemore *was* the most powerful man in the world."

A thunderous applause echoed through the studio.

Camille shook her head again. "It was never my intention to attack Beck in that way . . . to get even or anything like that. I have tremendous respect for the presidency. That's why I wrote the book . . . to remind people that we are allowing our most precious institutions to be diminished by poor values. Remember, there was a time when I dedicated my life to helping Beck become president. I really believed in him. That's another reason I wrote this book. There was a time I truly loved him. I honestly felt like I had a duty to show him what he'd become. I loved him."

A stunned silence descended over the audience. Regan O'Neill couldn't believe what she was hearing. As Camille's comments seeped in, the beauty and light of her disposition began to shine through.

Regan searched hard for the right words. "So . . . you're trying to, like, hold a mirror up to the world?"

Camille exhaled loudly. "Yes! That's a great way of describing it. Every person who reads *This Soul's Journey* will see a bit of themselves coming to life in the pages. It was my intention for the book to be a mirror, as you put it. I like that. A mirror. . . . That's how I feel about it. I am not here on earth to hate. None of us are. This world, this third dimension, is like boot camp, you know? We all come here with a purpose. It's hard work."

"You call that our 'soul purpose' in the book," noted Regan.

"Exactly. So, each of us has a soul purpose when we come here. It all ties into our karmic burden, the spiritual debts we have to square away for our behavior in past lives. We either move toward that goal or away from it. Free will is critical."

"That all relates to the president's philandering?"

The audience liked that term, but Camille did not. "Let's say his 'behavior' instead. Holding up a mirror like my book creates a great opportunity for each of us who reads it to take accountability for what we've done in our own lives . . . men and women. After all, karma is the ultimate ledger in that it carries over our behaviors from our past lives. We can't escape the ledger of our lives."

"That probably strikes most Americans as a bit weird," said Regan.

Camille had heard this a thousand times before. "It might. But a third of the world already knows what I'm talking about. The Hindus, the Buddhists . . . they get it. We are experiencing a time of great change, Regan. My book is a part of that. It's not about attacking; it's about moving forward. We can only advance as a people when we act as if each individual person is part of a collective spiritual Self. For all the despicable things he's done to me, Beck will be held accountable by the universe and its universal laws. But spiritually, I have to forgive him. I have to move on, move forward. Beck the person did me wrong. But his spirit will always be pure." She pointed to the heavens. "We're all pure up there."

Camille wiped her tears away again. Only this time, they were tears of happiness. "I'm sorry," she said. "I am very happy to be feeling this way again. I was not myself when I was with Beck."

Camille received a lengthy, heart-felt standing ovation. Many women in the audience were crying, while the men sitting next to them were worried this new way of thinking did not bode well for their plans to spend the upcoming NFL season parked in front of the television sixteen hours per week.

"So you think men should read your book as well?" asked Regan.

"Of course I do. We all need to take a good look in the mirror from time to time, right?"

"What do you think is happening in the White House right now?"

Camille scratched her head. "Most of it I cannot mention on TV."

Regan O'Neill threw her head back and let out an exaggerated laugh.

"Seriously, though," Camille continued, "if I know Beck, he's yelling at Harry Pierson, and Harry keeps poking him back. Beck probably threw all his staffers out of the room. I'll tell you, Regan, when he gets angry, his staffers tremble."

"Even the ones he's sleeping with?" asked Regan sarcastically.

Camille smiled demurely. Her pain was clearly evident for the entire world to see. "Especially those women."

"You wrote that the president even slept with a staffer's wife? That's incredible."

Camille nodded. "Yeah . . . I kept the guy's name private, of course. In this case, instant karma got him. He was always very nasty to me. He liked to talk down to me because that's how Beck spoke to me. His staffers are like his children. They behave as if he is their father. That's why it's so important that people everywhere read my book . . . men and women. It's the same all over the world. When we admire powerful men who treat people badly, it is inevitable that we will, in turn, emulate that behavior. It's no good. The cycle must be broken once and for all."

"And yet you said you loved Beck?" Regan clucked her tongue in dismay.

Camille crossed one leg over the other revealing the sunflower tattoo on her foot. Her red dress was cut just right, revealing only enough of her leg to suggest elegant beauty tempered with humility.

"I said I loved him once, yes. I also said I must forgive him to move forward. Moving forward is a big point of my book. I want women—all people, but women most of all—I want them to recognize how readily we promote men to power even though their behavior is reprehensible."

Regan latched on to the implication. "It sounds as if you're saying women have to be accountable, too."

"Of course. As women, we have to be accountable for the things we accept from our men. Actually, this is true of all people, not just women. But it's the women of the world who seem to get the brunt of things most often. I mean, my book uses the American president as a touchstone, but take a look at how women are treated in Africa and the Middle East."

"Be careful," joked Regan. "You don't want too many world leaders coming after you."

Camille rubbed her hands together and then brushed her hair from her face. "You know, Regan, men are going to try and marginalize me and make *This Soul's Journey* into some sort of rant from a crazy, scorned redhead. I just hope women like you, women with a voice and an audience, keep pushing my message out to the entire world for all people to hear."

Regan liked the sound of that. She fancied herself a celebrity, but valued the responsibility that came with it. Like Camille O'Keefe, Regan O'Neill felt she had an obligation to speak the truth from her position of privilege.

"And what would you like to tell the world, Camille?"

Camille bit her lip and thought for a moment. "That it's imperative for men and women to recognize the universe of the soul, the one great force that binds us all together outside of time and history. This is boot camp, remember? But it's equally important for each of us women to move forward, to find ourselves."

Regan took another sip of coffee and returned the network mug to the table in front of them. "But Camille, come on. . . ."

Camille cocked her head. "What?"

"You know as well as I do—and I'm not saying this is what I think, but you know. . . ."

"What?" repeated Camille.

"People are gonna wanna know why the hell you stayed with him? I mean . . . people are gonna say that you saw an opportunity for fame and fortune, and, well . . . what makes you any different from, say, Hillary Clinton?"

Camille took a deep breath. "It's funny, my agent said the same thing. And I told her, I wish Hillary did what I did after that whole sordid thing with Monica Lewinsky. She could have taken the world by storm, and I wouldn't have needed to write this book. Instead, I kinda feel like she let the women of the world down."

Regan liked that answer. It would make a great sound bite. "So you think writing your book differentiates you?"

"Well, sure. I wrote the book to urge action. That's what I want. People to take action and change the way we behave toward each other. Look, when I first met Beck, I believed it was my cosmic duty to promote him, to help him realize his potential. I felt myself through him, defined myself through him, related to myself through him. That's why I was so prone to accept his terrible behavior. I think that's why we all tolerate things we shouldn't.'"

"Because we over-identify with a person we would otherwise find questionable?"

Camille agreed wholeheartedly. "I once believed my purpose was helping Becket Rosemore find his path and fulfill his karmic destiny. What I didn't understand—what is really critical for women to understand—is that the path to fulfillment runs through oneself. A person can't find themselves or define themselves through another. Lord knows we try. But it will always end up at a dead end. The universe intends for each of us, man or woman, to discover our way within ourselves. Each and every one of us has a unique path. The beautiful thing is they all wind their way to the same final point, an entirely different dimension where none of this world's pettiness exists. It's a place where we are all free and equal."

Regan didn't quite know how to respond. "Well, I would sure like to be the one holding the copyright to that map, but I'm sure Apple will beat us to it."

Regan turned to the camera and began wrapping things up. "Well, it's been my great honor to speak with Camille O'Keefe this morning. She has been, for a short time, the First Lady of the United States. She is now our very own flamboyant clairvoyant, the Red Dragon Lady, a best-selling author armed with the truth about the president, ourselves and a good bit of karma as well. And you know what they say about karma. Everyone in my studio audience received a free copy . . . yes, even the men. So listen, ladies, it's our responsibility to ensure that *This Soul's Journey through the Eye of the Storm* hits the world hard. There's going to be a lot of fallout from this book. We know that. More important is that we struggle to grow, as Camille has said. That's the point."

The audience rose to their feet and gave Camille her second standing ovation.

Blushing, Camille waved. "It's all about intentions. Just be true to yourselves. The rest will follow."

"Oh, before we go," added Regan over the din. "I have to ask you one last question. There's a rumor going around that you are going to pose nude on the cover of a very famous magazine and that you have a gorgeous tattoo covering, like, your entire torso. So, will we be seeing *all* of the Red Dragon Lady?"

Camille rolled her eyes. "Oh my God, you sound like a man. And I hate that Red Dragon Lady thing."

Chapter 11

Back at the Oval Office, Pierson was on his fourth Scotch. Beck was growing paler by the minute. He looked at his vice president. "Well, it was a nice run, wasn't it, Harry? Short, but nice."

The sauce was starting to kick in. "She just kicked you in the balls, Beck, like a dozen times. I agree now. We've gotta do something about this bitch."

Beck stood up and stretched his arms. "You sound like me now."

"I'm serious. Not only can you forget about a second term, you're going to be the laughingstock of the world."

It suddenly hit Beck. Pierson was right. Camille was about to ruin him and torch everything he had spent his life amassing. He played it out in his head. He would spend the next few months backpedaling. The press would have to try to humiliate him at every press conference. His entire legacy was destroyed by the Red Dragon Lady.

Beck's resolve returned. "So we agree. We need to do something. We need to hit her hard. Call your people in the Bahamas."

Pierson was a bit surprised at the depth of Beck's vehemence. "You want to bring the Agency into this?"

"Absolutely. They're the only nasty sons of bitches still in business these days."

Chapter 12

Somewhere in America, a dad sits down in front of his computer. He is well employed, a senior executive at a mid-level marketing firm. He, his wife and their two daughters are not wealthy, but they enjoy most of the middle-class luxuries a household income of $170,000 can accommodate. It is around midnight. His wife dozed off in bed an hour ago while watching a special about the liberating gender politics of transsexuals wandering the margins of social norms. The wife doesn't really understand all that. She is not steeped in post-modern gender theory, has never heard of Luce Irigaray or read Foucault's *Herculine Barbin*. It's okay, though. She still tears up when Caitlin Jenner speaks of her newfound liberty.

As she lies sleeping in her comfy king, little infiltrates her slumber. Bringing the girls to school and gutting it out through Pilates is on top of her morning agenda. From there, she will fire up her computer and get cracking on her next project. She is a graphic designer and enjoys working from home, the freedom of creating when inspiration strikes. She works half as much as her husband but makes almost as much. She drew a cute cartoon about it. It hangs magnetized to the refrigerator to troll him.

She's free to buy whatever she wants whenever she wants. Her husband does not control the purse strings. She holds an MFA that counterbalances his MBA . . . lots of Latin acronyms. Her mother never went to college. She was a legal secretary who handed her paycheck over every second Friday. It's all good. When she fires up her laptop and starts creating art, it's progress.

The girls—one five and one ten years old—have long since been tucked away in their matching pink and green beds. They enjoy their lives, what little they've lived of them. They never fear the night, never lie in bed, eyes wide open, wondering if they will be murdered or taken and made into sex slaves. Unlike their African sisters in spirit, they don't know anybody who has been murdered in their sleep, they've never been beaten or gang-raped by so-called "police" demanding sex in exchange for "protection." They have never heard gunfire, and that's a good thing.

A hand-painted mural of a fairy kingdom adorns their wall and welcomes them each night into fantasyland. Their mother painted it in her second trimester. It was a gift of love, and that love still radiates from the eyes of the fairies. There is a Fairy King and Queen who look down from a hill. But from the way they are drawn, it is clear they are not looking down disparagingly on their subjects. The woman drew them to embody familial love. Even the big, red dragon in the corner seems like a symbol of valiant dignity rather than some foreboding harbinger of death. In this way, the red dragon in the mural is a lot like Camille, the Red Dragon Lady.

But tonight, dad has a very different fantasyland in mind as he powers on his laptop in the den. He's logging into the darknet looking for really hard-core porn. He's in the right place. He knows what he's doing. Sitting there in his pajamas, this average, middle-class father of two girls connects to his crypto VPN, opens his Tor browser, checks his virtual dark wallet for bitcoins and begins his clandestine search. He is totally anonymous, untraceable, unaccountable thanks to modern technology that ensures his freedom to do whatever he wants online.

The world's brightest coders and hackers have dedicated their lives to moving people outside the system. The man welcomes all this progress and innovation as he deftly navigates to a Tor Hidden Services list to find what he wants. The list amounts to a smorgasbord of dark delights, including everything his imagination can conjure about sex, drugs and porn. He can't imagine life without the freedom to do whatever he wants in the privacy of his own home. He is American through and through.

He pauses . . . lowers the volume on his computer . . . listens. He thinks he hears his wife stirring upstairs. When he is sure she is asleep, he continues. He does not know why he does this in secret. His wife is game. They have great sex. She even keeps a stash of adult videos in her sock drawer. But something else drives him now, something outside all that. Something only the darknet can deliver directly into the dens of Middle America . . . child pornography.

He doesn't know how it happened. It just did. One night, he was browsing the surface net like millions of other men across the globe. His wife watches her share of streaming porn. But somewhere along the line, the man got diverted, lost in the darknet. It started the night he was looking for "barely legal." What could it matter? Everyone had to be at least 18, so he took it with a grain of salt. It was all just fantasy. It was all just a show. One night he clicked through a few times, and there it was . . . a site with real kiddie porn.

At first he panicked. How could it be? How could there be real children having sex right out on the web like that? He was shocked. But he kept clicking through, clicking through. Amazingly, videos of children were everywhere. That first night, he stopped himself. He closed his everyman Firefox browser and deleted the history. He went straight to bed and wondered what sort of man would enjoy watching children getting molested and raped.

A few months later, the darkness called him back. He was at work. He didn't know why, but he had to see more. His firm had been discussing the potential of marketing within the darknet. His colleagues were raving on about "crypto browsers," and bitcoin, and secret drug markets that "regulars" didn't know about. There was money in it, big money, especially the porn and drug markets, and his company discussed the best ways to tap the opportunity. That's when the man began venturing into the darkness for real.

And so there he sits alone in his den, his wife and girls asleep upstairs. He thinks nobody will ever find out. Somehow, he thinks that makes it okay. He clicks through anonymously to his favorite kiddie sites to watch live streams of children being raped. He pays with bitcoin that he washes through an online exchange. It's a billion-dollar industry. He is as horrified by what he sees as he is aroused. Maybe that's why he watches it? He doesn't take the time to reflect on it. He doesn't take the time to imagine his own daughters exploited in such a way. He just takes in everything he sees on the screen as if it's only another movie on Netflix.

When he is finished, he changes his pajama pants and heads up to bed, back to the world of fairies. He has everything to lose. He just doesn't care. He needs the darknet like a fiend needs a fix.

Chapter 13

The rickety motorboat eases up against the shore. It struggles to make way under the weight of six men. The water laps gently against the aluminum sides, making a soothing noise. The men onboard, however, have not come on a mission of peace. The men are *Boko Haram* recon, five soldiers and their leader, Aliyu Adelabu. They have ventured across Lake Chad to get the lay of the land, to see if the giant refugee camp on the island is well protected or wide open for a massacre.

The small beach is hidden by a cove, but nobody is keeping watch anyway. Aliyu now knows his assault on Koulfoua Island, when it comes, will progress relatively unchallenged. He is not surprised. He knows Chad officials want nothing to do with the Nigerian refugees. If not for the United Nations, Chad police forces would likely have killed the refugees themselves. And he knows the United Nations doesn't want a fight. They prefer instead to dispatch politicians dressed as soldiers, "peacekeepers" who are reluctant to intervene. At any rate, thinks Aliyu, any United Nations troops will likely be bound by crippling rules of engagement preventing them from posing any real opposition.

The refugees are people of flight. The United Nations are people of empty rhetoric. The men of *Boko Haram* are men of deadly action. Aliyu Adelabu tells this to his men time and time again. This test run is just a precaution. When the time comes, his men will creep like a spreading disease up the beach into the camp about a mile away. Once they penetrate the perimeter, the only thing slowing them down will be taking the time to reload. They will need thousands and thousands of rounds because they will kill thousands and thousands of refugees, along with anyone else who dares stand in their way.

Aliyu remains on the boat as the other men tie off and take inventory of their surroundings. He breathes deeply, taking it all in. He enjoys the calm before the storm. As the fresh air fills his lungs, he feels his strength course through him. It makes him feel powerful to know he will soon bring death and destruction to disrupt the complacency that he sees hanging over the island. In his mind, the Muslim women need proper discipline. The non-Muslim women are as good as dead. As for the girls, Muslim and non-Muslim alike, they mean just one thing . . . money.

Aliyu reached out to some sympathetic "friends" in Chad. At first, they seemed eager to assist. But now, they seem less inclined to help him round up the girls. He loathes bureaucrats and politicians for their ambivalence and even cowardice. If the government of Chad will not assist him, then Aliyu must act for himself in the name of Allah. For weeks, he has promised his men great rewards, assuring them that these refugees will not escape divine justice simply because they have found their way to Koulfoua Island. He has told them over and over that there will be a thousand *sibya* for them to take as their own before selling them off. He has formed a sacred bond with his men and means to keep his word.

All seems clear. The men give Aliyu the thumbs up. He steps off the creaking motorboat like he is Idi Amin walking into a party in his honor. His ego reaches the shore before his boots hit the sand. He carries with him a large machete. His favorite toy, it is well worn. The ivory handle bears the scars of many encounters with other people's skulls.

It is no coincidence that the handle is ivory. When he was younger, before *Boko Haram*, Aliyu smuggled ivory into Sudan. They traded the ivory tusks for weapons. Aliyu and his group would sling entire elephant tusks on their shoulders and hump hundreds of miles through thick jungle to avoid detection. It required superhuman strength and determination. Their degree of resourcefulness was incredible. Once there, he would meet with Sudanese Army officials, sent by President Oscar Al-Baluri himself. Capitalizing on his position of power, President Al-Baluri was one of the largest ivory traders in the world.

When Aliyu decided it was too much work for too little return, he stepped up his game and established himself as a middleman for war diamonds used to fund the savage civil wars in Sierra Leone, Liberia, Angola and everywhere else horrendous atrocities were perpetrated by men using tens of thousands of child soldiers to do their murdering for them. Like so many of the men roaming the African continent, Aliyu Adelabu was a ruthless gangster trading blood-soaked commodities like ivory and diamonds for cash and weapons he and his men could use in their holy war upon innocent men, women and children. In this sense, Aliyu Adelabu has always been a merchant of death, selling valuable African resources on one end in order to sell African sex slaves to the open world market on the other.

Resources, money and innocent lives were fed into the machine in order to grind girls out the other side. Men like Aliyu take what they want by force and push it through the darknet on the other side. This makes Aliyu something of an entrepreneur, wending his way through life deal by deal, raid by raid and girl by girl. It is this paradox of riches that plagues Africa at its core. A continent rich with natural resources, it is also one of the poorest on the planet. Wealthy interests, largely from China but also from the West, cut deals with dictators who consider themselves "President for Life" and crank out billions for themselves and their cronies by selling mining and drilling rights to the highest bidders.

The amount of money that passes hands is staggering. It is also largely undisclosed, for there is little democracy here. It is not necessary. In this world of entitlement for the few and devastation for the masses, governments levy few taxes and ask nothing from their people. In return, their people get exactly what they pay for . . . nothing. There is neither taxation nor representation. There is only exploitation in a land where people are a thing to be harvested or eradicated, bought, traded and sold. Billions of dollars are controlled by the few who have become corrupt enough to elevate their heads above the pervasive stench of human decay.

In a world where enough is never enough, Aliyu Adelabu finds his own space in which to operate. His entrepreneurial spirit, his drive to survive, takes the form of radical Islam now. He calls himself a Muslim, but he is not a pious man. He represents radicalism, not Islam. Like the handful of oligarchs who rule the African continent, Nigeria included, Aliyu Adelabu takes what he needs and sells it to the highest bidder. And on Koulfoua Island, there is a vast untapped resource of females to be taken and sold on the open market.

It is more than he can resist. He can almost smell thousands of women as he and his men make their way on their recon. Aliyu spits. His flagrant disregard about being observed impresses the other men.

"When we take this island," says one of the men admiringly, "I want to get an ivory-handled machete like yours, Aliyu. That is something a real man can carry around. It says to the world, 'I am somebody.' It says, 'I am dangerous.'"

The other men agree. They would each love to have something like that, a symbol of their prowess.

"Especially," jokes another of the men, "when I slice open some smelly refugee whore from her throat all the way to her dirty parts. She will look at me, see the fine ivory handle in my hand, and her last thoughts on this earth will be of her own shame and my power to erase her from existence."

The men all laugh. "You have no ivory-handled machete yet," quips one of the others. Again, they appear to care little should they be observed.

"That is what I enjoy most about what we do," notes Aliyu. He is pointing his storied machete into the darkness toward the refugee camp. "I like having the power to kill an entire family . . . gun them all down where they stand and bring an immediate end to their family line. It's like killing stray dogs on the street . . . rounding them all up and killing them. Only this is far better because I can end a bloodline . . . just like that . . . gone from existence."

One of the men agrees wholeheartedly. "Yes, rounding up people is more satisfying."

Aliyu replies without hesitating. "To be honest, it's all the same to me. That's what gives me my power. I can see women for what they really are . . . things to be taken, bought and sold. That is the way of our world. It is not my place to change it. Most women are shameful. All women are poison. The problem with the West is that men have grown soft and allow their women to influence their minds."

Apparently satisfied with the recon, he stops in his tracks and breathes in deeply again. "Yes, this is going to be easy," he tells his men. "No *wahala*," he tells them, no worries.

They like the sound of that. They are not looking for warfare. They are looking to take as many *sibya*, as many female hostages, as possible without encountering resistance. They are looking to execute the rest gangland style. They don't want any trouble. Easy murder is by far their favorite.

"When will we attack, Aliyu?" asks one of the men.

"Soon, God willing," Aliyu replies. "Very soon. The world is beginning to hear about us. They are beginning to watch what happens to these people. We must strike before people care too much about these people."

He spits and thinks it over. "Let me correct myself. I am wrong to call these women people. They are refugees. More accurately, they are things." His words drip with contempt.

"No big deal," agree the men. "It will be easy."

One of the men grabs his crotch. His name is Kashim. Like many of the men in *Boko Haram*, he is Kanuri. "I will find myself dey trippin some hole," he says, feeling himself. He means he will find himself an Igbo girl to rape, maybe thirteen years old, if that. Aliyu's men hate the Igbo people who live in or near Northern Nigeria and take every chance they can to slaughter them en masse. The mere sight of an Igbo man makes Kashim want to kill him as slowly and painfully as possible. If he sees an Igbo woman, he can barely restrain himself from beating her, raping her and then leaving her to die a slow, painful death so she has time to contemplate his power over her. As for Igbo girls, well . . . they command as high a price as any other if they are virgins, so respect that.

"Yes," Kashim continues. "A nice *chu ezi* for me." He uses the Igbo term *chu ezi,* because that is what this girl will be to him, a pig vagina suited for raping and not much else.

The other men laugh at Kashim. They call him a faggot in Igbo, which is twice the insult to his manhood. "*Your fada, sagba.*"

Kashim is livid. He raises his AK-47 and, clack-clack, locks and loads it. The round that he forgot was already in the chamber ejects harmlessly into the air and lands in the sand near his feet. The man obviously intended to make a show of his power, but the ejected round makes him seem rather impotent.

The other men laugh even harder at Kashim's lackluster show of bravado. "Did you not like the bullet that was already in your chamber, *sagba?*"

Another one of the men chimes in. "He shot his load early like a boy."

Deeply insulted, Kashim lunges for the man. Aliyu throws his machete into the sand. The weapon that has severed countless limbs stands at attention in the sand while Aliyu intercepts Kashim and grabs him by the throat. Kashim immediately drops his weapon and stands limply as Aliyu begins crushing his esophagus with his bare hand.

"We are here to work," Aliyu reminds his men. "We are here to do Allah's work, not here to embarrass ourselves and . . . *and* His good name." With his other hand, he grabs Kashim's balls and squeezes. "Do I make myself absolutely clear, *sagba?*"

The other men apologize and stand looking down at the sand. "I think we can all agree that we do not want our balls squeezed," offers one of the men, a true tactician.

That much they can all agree on. Aliyu releases his grip, and Kashim, who seconds ago was ready to stick it to some pig whore, falls to the ground choking and spitting up into the sand.

"No *wahala*," says Aliyu, again. "No problems. Understand?"

Kashim nods. "No *wahala*, boss."

Returning to the matter at hand, Aliyu takes his machete from its sticking point and points up the beach. The darkness is pierced only by the luminescent glow of fires burning in the nearby refugee camp. The United Nations and the Red Crescent helped set it up. They are there to help, but there is little the politicians will allow them to do. The aid workers are limited to providing basic services, some food and water, digging pits in the sand for latrines, administering basic first aid. There is little money at their disposal. They are for the most part babysitters for thousands of displaced people who have nothing.

"They are right there for the taking," he tells his men. "We will bring all of our men, and we will decimate them. Those we do not kill outright will drown in their own blood. I promise you this."

The others turn and look at the fires burning away. They cannot wait for the bloodbath. It will be like a holiday for them. The backlighting of the moon reflecting off the water behind them casts a beautiful albeit foreboding glow. The men stand pondering the bounty before them, their evil intent juxtaposed against the cool glow of the moonlight.

"There are so many to kill," says one man. "How will we kill them all?"

"Yes," agrees one of the others. "It will be very busy work to cut them all down. This is why the Americans drop big bombs from planes. It is better for killing many at once."

One of the other men disagrees. He spits on the ground at the mention of America. "*Your fada*, screw you with your Americans. They drop bombs from high in the sky because they are cowards. They let bombs do the work their men cannot do themselves. It is different with us. We are *Boko Haram*. We are real men. We kill with our hands, not our technology."

"The Americans do not like to see blood on their hands," said one of the other men. "But we like it very much. I cannot wait to have blood on my hands, blood of infidels. We are doing them a favor by killing them. Do not forget that. They live their lives in sin. We are freeing them from that, *inshallah*."

Yes, agree the others. *Inshallah . . . inshallah.*

Aliyu likes what he is hearing. The men are coming together nicely. "Allah willing, we will attack in several days."

The others are concerned. They will need boats to hold the thousand or so girls they will take. And they will need much ammunition for the thousands of infidels they will kill. Almost a thousand girls are waiting to be taken. But first they have to kill so many. How will they manage with only fifty men?

The others nod. They are legitimate questions. It is a matter of logistics.

"We will need many boats," adds one of the men.

"The boats are not a problem," replies Aliyu, somewhat annoyed at the implication that he is not prepared. "I am in the process of securing enough boats from a man in the Nigerian police. In return, he will get two girls per boat. That is fair, is it not?"

The other men agree. It seems fair enough.

"We can carry a lot of ammunition as well," comments one of the men.

Aliyu nods and draws a circle in the sand with the point of his machete. "This is the camp." He places an X outside the circle. "This is where we are now. He draws a second X about a foot above the top of the circle. "This is the Chad police station for the region." He draws a line from that X through to top of the circle. "I am working on getting some police to attack from here . . . help us herd them in."

The men are astonished. "How did you arrange that, Aliyu?" asks one.

"In return for their assistance, each of them will get to take three girls younger than twenty-one but not younger than fifteen."

"That is why you are the boss, Aliyu," compliments one of the men. "You have power. You make things happen that we cannot."

One of the men seems uneasy. His name is Ahmad. "But I thought the Chad police were rounding up *Boko Haram* in Chad? Just last week, I heard it is forbidden for Muslim women to cover their faces? It is said they want to kill us."

Aliyu nods. "Yes, but that is a game. You understand? It shows they are doing something to protect their people. But they do nothing unless they are getting paid to do so. If they round up a certain type of people, it is because someone is paying them to do so. If they attack and kill thousands of refugees, it is because we are paying them to do so. In the end, they will report that the refugee camp was really a terrorist hideout, and they will look like heroes. Then they will move on to the next party who wishes to pay them for something."

"So it is business for them?" notes Ahmad.

The others agree. It is just business.

"Yes," answers Aliyu. "These refugees are scum. It takes very little to convince people to help remove scum. Still, there seems to be some resistance, and I am not sure they will help in the end. You just never know."

"Are they turning against us?" asks Kashim.

"I don't know that they will help, but I do know they are not our enemies. They are businessmen. The police in Chad are like anyone else . . . Greece, Turkey, Austria, Britain . . . everyone hates refugees because they are diseased scum. Who wants these animals living in their country? We will stand up tall like men. And we will keep shooting until they all lie dead in puddles of their own blood that has yet to sink into the earth. Then we will exercise our claim on the girls. I don't care if we kill the women. After twenty-five, they are worth almost nothing. Just keep shooting. The rest will fall into place. You will see. Have faith. *Inshallah*."

Before the others can speak, Aliyu is already heading back to the boat. He whistles, and the others run back to the boat and began pushing it out into the water. As they depart, Aliyu runs his assault plan in his head yet another time. He feels the Chad police might turn their backs on him, but he doesn't fear any resistance from them earlier. That is the most important thing. He knows there might be a few United Nations soldiers at the camp, but what good will they do when taken by surprise? More importantly, the beach will be unguarded. That's what they came to find out. He smiles to himself as he thinks things through. Yes, he thinks, they will walk right up to the camp and begin killing. The ensuing panic will be all they need to ensure their own protection. No *wahala*, no worries.

Twenty minutes into the journey back across Lake Chad, Aliyu stands and walks up behind Kashim, the man who was grabbing his crotch and boasting back on the beach. He grabs Kashim's AK-47 in one hand. With his other, he raises his machete and drives the ivory handle into Kashim's skull, sending him flying into the pitch-black water. Aliyu still has Kashim's gun in his hand.

He sheaths his machete and points the automatic weapon at Kashim, who is flailing half-conscious in the water. Aliyu opens fire. Without so much as a thought, the other men follow their leader and join in the frenzy. Kashim is ripped to shreds as men empty their magazines into him. Parts of what was once Kashim splay across the water. Seconds later, Kashim is no longer visible and the boat moves on across Lake Chad toward home.

"That is what you will do when we attack," instructs Aliyu. "Just keep firing. Reload, and keep firing. What happened to Kashim is what happens when you lose sense of our purpose. I hope you understand that."

The other men are silent. They are men of *Boko Haram*. Better they clean their weapons, say their prayers and prepare for the task ahead.

"We need to get a replacement for Kashim," says one of the men. "I think my cousin would be interested."

Aliyu smiles. "Now that's the sort of initiative I like."

Chapter 14

The fires are beginning to die down on Koulfoua Island. It is nearly midnight. Not a single person among the five thousand knows Aliyu was there that very evening scouting the island and plotting their murder. There is still some activity around the tents. There are three or more families in each. There are no sides. They are really just large blue poly tarps on poles. A large UN shipment is due any day. Until then, about half the people have cots. There are some blankets, but not enough to go around. There are some diapers, but the babies far outnumber the nappies on hand.

A little girl, Nmaku, sits in the sand, her little feet buried. She finishes the last bit of a peanut butter packet provided by the Red Crescent a few weeks earlier. The only other thing she's eaten all day is a packet of high-calorie cookies. There are fifteen people under her tarp. Abani, a four-month-old boy from one of the other families sharing the tent, will not survive another twenty-four hours. Like so many children in Africa, he will die of dysentery, something unheard of in the West. But it is a fact of life—and death—in this part of the world.

Nmaku is pondering something. "Mother?"

Her mother, Ezewani, looks listlessly at her daughter. "Yes, Nmaku?"

"Why are we here?"

Ezewani musters a brief smile. This is quite a question. "I don't know how to answer that, Nmaku."

"I don't like it here. I want to go home," says Nmaku, unburying her feet.

A tear runs down Ezewani's cheek. She gives Nmaku a small amount of water. It is more water than she can spare. She finished her last packet of potable water the day before. The other families cannot be expected to give her some of theirs. She knows they will likely die there on the beach if the United Nations does not do something soon.

"We don't have our old home any more, Nmaku. This is our home now."

Nmaku doesn't understand. "Why?"

"This is who we are," she explains to the child. "This is what our life is meant to be. You remember what Father Mason said in church when we were there."

Nmaku nods. She remembers the man with the funny white collar sweating in his black shirt and pants.

"It is God's will," Ezewani clarifies. "It is up to us to discover the blessing in it."

Nmaku bites her cracked lips. She contemplates standing up until she realizes she doesn't have the strength to do it. "So then why did we run away?"

Ezewani knows she will not be seeing her daughter much longer if this keeps up. "You are a smart girl. I don't know why we run. We are all doing what we can to survive. It will all end the same way no matter what we do. That is what I meant when I said this is who we are. So it must be God's will."

Nmaku thinks again. The effort is exhausting. "Will I go to heaven like the priest said?"

"If anyone goes to heaven, my darling, it will be you." Ezewani tries to move and grimaces. She has a deep wound in her leg where she was cut by a machete while fleeing a raid. It is severely infected. There are no antibiotics yet, and she will likely die before any arrive. Her jagged, festering wound, barely concealed under a crusty, threadbare bandage, stinks of her impending death.

"Will the men chasing us go to heaven? Will they chase us there, too?"

Ezewani does not answer.

A few minutes later, Nmaku speaks again. "I am ready to go, mommy."

"Go where, *obim*? Go where, sweetheart?"

"To heaven. If you say it's okay. I will be pretty there all the time. Not ugly like I am now."

Ezewani chokes back tears. "You are more beautiful than you will ever know, Nmaku."

The two fall silent. Soon, everyone in the tent is asleep. Abani, the baby boy with dysentery, does not awaken the next morning. He is dead. His parents lack the strength or the fluids to cry. Even their grief was stolen by *Boko Haram*.

The UN shipment of supplies containing the antibiotic for Ezewani's leg is delayed by Chad military authorities who seized the trucks until a suitable bribe was paid. Ezewani is dead two days later. Her body is laid into the lye pit, a mass grave, next to the baby boy whose empty eyes are permanently open. A layer of lye is shoveled on top of them. That much the few aid workers can do.

Nmaku opens a packet of peanut butter. It will be her only food until dinner time when she gets some boiled white rice. Soon, she thinks, she will see her mommy in heaven where they will both be pretty all the time.

It is true, she thinks . . . this is what her life was meant to be.

Chapter 15

It was an odd feeling, travelling abroad without her husband, the president of the United States. Even odder for Camille was the mandate that she travel under the protection of her First Family security detail, handled, per usual, by the Secret Service. When she decided to leave Beck, Camille hoped also to leave behind all the pomp and circumstance that filled her days as First Lady. She found it ego driven and largely counterproductive to her spiritual growth. She came to this conclusion when she realized how connected she'd become to her extravagant wardrobe. Occupying a separate part of the White House with all its amenities until the divorce was finalized was one thing. But when she found herself having difficulty contemplating leaving behind several hundred-thousand-dollars' worth of shoes, clothing and accessories, she realized how much she had changed over the last few years . . . and not for the better.

She resolved to give it all away. Being First Lady was never about acquiring material wealth for Camille. To the contrary, she originally embarked upon the journey at Beck's side because she felt it was her obligation to help him fulfill his potential. She saw it as part of her karmic burden. Lost in the process was her own sense of self. Likewise, her own tremendous potential was completely consumed by Beck's personal needs and ambition.

This would have to change. She began the process with a thunderous declaration of self when she announced to the world at a press conference in the Rose Garden that she was throwing the adulterous president out. She knew she didn't have the power to actually evict him. But she also knew she had the power to touch the world—especially the women of the world—with words that resounded with faith in herself, in her own autonomy, and, most importantly, in her own potential. She knew her speech would fly out to the women of the world who were once deaf to the possibilities of their own selves, just as she once was. As she said in that speech, if only some of the other women who had previously occupied the White House had taken a similar stand, hers would not have been necessary.

But it was. It was very necessary. Camille knew that. What she did not realize at the time was how attached she'd become to all the material things that filled her life. And now, flying on a secured jet accompanied by a Secret Service detail made her feel as if she was right back where she started before declaring her independence. She asked Johnny Long to accompany her on the trip because she wanted someone around for advice who was not part of Beck's establishment. Having just embarked upon a spiritual journey in a totally new direction, Camille felt she needed a friend like Johnny to help take the rudder until her divorce was completed and she could leave it all behind. She had to completely walk away from all the materialism as well. She hoped Johnny and his wife would simply pull her along if necessary when it came time for her to leave behind all the trappings of her former position like the clothes and other amenities. This she had to do if her journey was going to lead her back to herself. That's why she decided to shed that skin, give it all away and begin anew.

Camille could sense her security detail didn't like having Johnny around. She figured it was because outsiders made their job harder. She peered out the window of the Gulfstream C-37B out of Andrews Air Force Base. This was the standard transportation she flew.

The specially outfitted plane was equipped with military-grade encrypted communications capabilities, enhanced radar and weather tracking and a classified list of ultra-high-tech defense enhancements meant to protect Camille and other high-ranking government officials such as members of Congress and military commanders as she headed for her meeting with Kofi Achebe in the Bahamas.

The twin Rolls-Royce engines whined as their descent began, and Camille could see the scintillating teal water that called to her. The meeting with Kofi Achebe was arranged by Camille's agent, Claudia, after she screened Kofi. Claudia set it up in the Bahamas in order to give Camille a little breathing room and maybe even a bit of fun . . . who knew?

Camille looked at Johnny and breathed what sounded more like a sigh of relief than anything else. "It's so beautiful. I feel like a different woman already. Look at the color of the water, Johnny," she continued. "You never see anything like that back home. We're suddenly in a different world."

Three Secret Service agents were sitting in the cabin with them. Pete Gunning was Team Leader. He was relatively new to the detail. One of the agents rolled his eyes just a bit. It was ever so slight, and usually this sort of disrespect would never be tolerated. But there was little, if anything, usual about Camille O'Keefe. Once she announced to the world that she was leaving Beck, she became even more of an outcast than she was when faking her way through being First Lady and pretending to be fulfilled.

Camille caught the agent making that gesture. It didn't bother her, though. She knew the security detail accompanied her to the Bahamas only as a formality. She knew Beck wished she were dead. Beck, the White House, the exclusive events, the Secret Service . . . it was all in her rearview mirror now.

"I don't think they like it that I brought you along," she said to Johnny, but looking right at the agent while she spoke. She'd grown accustomed to making little stands like that with Beck's staffers, who tended to treat her like either a new age freak or a gold digger.

Johnny smirked. He didn't notice the agent roll his eyes, but he had no doubt the men on the detail resented him being there. "Gee, you think? The last thing these guys need is an outsider like me tagging along." He looked at Pete Gunning who just smiled back at him.

Camille raised her seat up and slipped on her Prada shoes. "God, I'm going to miss these shoes. I'm just going to donate all my clothes, you know. Let a charity auction them off or something. You might have to knock me out first. Would you do that for me? Donate it all while I'm unconscious." She laughed at herself.

Johnny imagined the event unfolding. "Can't lose what you never had, right?"

Returning to the matter of the agents, Camille spoke her mind even though they were sitting right there. "Believe me, we're both outsiders. I can feel their resentment. It's like a thick sort of film that lands on your skin." She made a sourpuss.

"Kind of like pollen?"

"Well, I'm allergic to both. I don't like it. I'll be very happy when we land. The first thing I'm going to do is take off my shoes and walk barefoot in the sand. I need to do a little grounding."

"Yeah," agreed Johnny. "My wife doesn't get here until tonight, so I may just join you."

This time, Johnny noticed the glance from one of the other agents. He had to admit, it made him feel uncomfortable being scrutinized like that. Almost as a controlled response to the surveillance, he added, "It's too bad my wife couldn't fly with us this morning."

There was no hint of sarcasm in Johnny's comments. Camille looked contrite nonetheless. "I'm really sorry about that. If you ask me, it's all too much. Why would she want to spend time with me while all this mess is going on?"

She was referring to the security measures put in place ahead of her visit. Following First Family protocol, the airspace around Lynden Pindling International Airport, formerly Nassau International, would be completely closed down before, during and immediately after

Camille's arrival. All planes were grounded from the moment her flight left D.C. and would remain so until Camille was off airport grounds. Likewise, no one got in or out of the Bahamas by plane until Camille was clear to land in and depart her plane. All the while, thousands of unsuspecting passengers thought their flights were delayed due to some unseen storm front somewhere out there.

"They're much stricter after 9/11," she said. "You know . . . commercial planes are weapons of mass destruction now, so they put a TFR in place wherever I go."

"TFR?" asked Johnny, seeking clarification.

"Temporary Flight Restriction," Gunning answered in a monotone.

Camille shrugged. "Apparently, since I announced to the world that I'm leaving my husband, millions of people love me. At the same time, millions of people hate me, or so I'm told. Either way, I still need all this protection everywhere I go. Isn't that right, Pete? Of course, as soon as we're divorced, these three guys here will drop me like I have herpes . . . thank God."

Johnny sighed. "Tell that to my wife. When we got married, having to travel separately was not part of the arrangement. She's a bit miffed about that."

"Too bad nobody was there to protect me from myself before I married Beck. Anyway, I'm sure a day at the spa will clear it all up with your wife. It's on me, of course."

Johnny nodded. "Of course . . . that ought to do it."

Camille grimaced as if something suddenly occurred to her.

"Uh-oh," commented Johnny. "Are you rescinding the offer already?"

She groaned and turned to Pete Gunning. "Are we following full protocol, Pete?"

"Yes, full protocol. You still get the top shelf."

Johnny decided to say something. "It seems advisable considering the First Lady's popularity."

Gunning exhaled and closed his magazine. He slid it into the black bag at his feet. "True, but we're more concerned with the people out there who may want to harm her. Believe me when I tell you, sir, there is always someone out there lurking. It's my job to make sure that doesn't happen. Not on my watch, not so long as she's still the First Lady."

He cleared his throat and adjusted the cuffs of his crisp, white shirt. He was antsy, though, unsatisfied with his answer. "Look," he said to Johnny, "who the First Lady chooses to accompany her on this trip is her decision. But I'm not putting a man on you. You can come and go as you see fit. As for the First Lady, we have full protocol in place. We don't know much about this Kofi Achebe guy except that he works for some NGO affiliated with the United Nations. What we do know about his past is not pretty. Plus, there have been issues with the First Lady in the past."

Camille grew uneasy. Gunning was alluding to an incident that hurt her very deeply. Back in the day, a man named Frank Lonza headed up Camille's security. He and Camille were as close as the boundaries of professionalism allowed. At one point, he even contemplated a transfer lest his emotions interfere with his ability to do his job. Frank was one of the few men around her who was actually repulsed by Beck's constant philandering and womanizing.

Frank Lonza was killed in the line of duty tracking down a skeleton who emerged from Beck's closet. Camille was devastated. It was Beck's dark past catching up with him and, of course, Camille found herself the target of someone looking to hurt Beck. Nobody revealed what had really happened, but Camille knew it was shady. She never trusted them after that.

"What do you mean?" asked Johnny. "Is there a chance something might go wrong?"

"There's always a chance something might go wrong," said Gunning, matter-of-factly. "That's why we're here. Suffice it to say, Kofi Achebe had a pretty nasty reputation back in the day when he was moving weapons for the Kotimbo administration. He ran a shell corporation called Motubabe Exchange Limited that functioned as a conduit for billions of dollars paid to Kotimbo and his cronies in exchange for drilling and mining rights. The guy may have good intentions now . . . or he may not. I find it best to assume the worst, especially with guys like this."

"Business as usual," opined Camille without turning from the window. She seemed resolved to these facts of life. "The things I could tell you about the world of shell corporations." She laughed to herself. "It used to really bother me when I first met Beck. Now I'm numb to it. It's just another part of myself I've lost."

She turned away from the window and looked at Johnny. He could see the weight of her current life in wrinkle lines that had recently begun appearing on her forehead. "That's one of the reasons I need a change," she said. "I'm numb to all the things I used to feel passionately about."

Johnny speculated. "Maybe that's why you're here for this meeting?"

She smiled. "Yeah . . . maybe."

Gunning seemed determined to finish his point about Kofi. "As you may know, the shell corporations that used to manage African mineral rights often venture into . . . shall we say more dubious endeavors."

"What do you mean?" asked Johnny. Again, he was concerned that Camille was not.

Gunning pursed his lips while he tried to word it suitably in layman's terms. "Well, in Africa, a handful of men run everything. It doesn't really matter which country you're talking about. It's almost always the same. Unbelievable resources are there for the taking. It's wide open. These guys come in, set up shop—calling it a 'government' or whatever—and systematically sell off the mineral rights to the bidders of their choosing. It usually goes to the highest bidder, although not always. Some funny deals find their way into the portfolio, you know the story."

Johnny instantly got the drift. "Wow, that's a lot . . . I mean, a lot of money . . . billions into their pockets?"

"More like their secret Swiss bank accounts," said Camille. "The Swiss have the most ample pockets in the world."

Johnny nodded. "Now that's something I know about. Swiss bankers drive me crazy. They're like hyenas. As soon as the animal dies, they feed off the carcass. They hide away trillions of dollars for history's worst people, and then ingest it all into their own coffers when these despots and such die off."

"The problem," noted Camille, "is that while all these oligarchies prosper beyond our wildest imaginations, they give little back in return."

"That's because there is no democracy," explained Johnny. "When a government asks nothing from its people in the way of taxes, it gives nothing in return, including the right to vote."

"I don't know," said Camille. "I haven't had much experience with Africa and all that. I just know I heard about some pretty amazing shenanigans with shell corporations. That's all I'm saying. It really is a shell game, pun intended."

Johnny thought for a moment. "I thought you spoke with one of Mandela's daughters before agreeing to all this? You vetted this out, right?"

"Yeah, I spoke at length with Zindzi Mandela. She knows Kofi personally and vouched for him. Zindzi Mandela's word is good enough for me."

Gunning wasn't buying it. He was no fan of the Mandela family, either. "All I know is that Achebe has a past," said Gunning.

"I know," replied Camille. "She told me about all that. It is what it is. His current role with the United Nations Council on Women and Families seems to be all people care about now. Anyway, I've known Zindzi for a few years now. In fact, she's speaking at the conference on human trafficking where I am heading after here. If she says Achebe is okay, then as far as I know, he's okay. The rest I leave to the universe."

The pilot announced their final descent into Lynden Pindling International. Gunning motioned to the other two agents to prepare to go to work.

"This is true," agreed Gunning. "Achebe's NGO is cleared with the State Department, so you can meet with him. But we're taking full precautions. We have to assume the worst, as always, and prepare accordingly. That's my job."

Johnny leaned toward Camille. "Full precautions?"

She grimaced. "Yeah, that means our route from the airport to the hotel will be secured. When we get there, the hotel will also be on lockdown until we are settled in. I assume we will occupy an entire floor. I think they're shutting down the marina, too."

Johnny sat back flabbergasted. He never thought of Camille in this capacity before. They were closing airspace, roads, marinas, entire floors of luxury hotels . . . yet she seemed completely nonplussed by the whole thing.

Johnny tightened his seatbelt. "You really meant it when you said you have become a different person. I mean . . . you're talking about shutting down airports, roads, five-star hotels in which you take up an entire floor as if you do this sort of thing every day."

Camille looked at him. "I do. It's become no different than choosing my entrée. This is what it's like to be the First Lady. I'm rarely free to do anything. But all that should change soon."

Gunning turned to Camille one last time before landing. "Whatever is going on between you and the president is no concern of mine, ma'am. As far as I'm concerned, you are the most popular, influential woman in the world, and it's my job to make sure nothing happens to you. There's no way we're cutting corners on this. If something were to happen to you, it would impact every woman in the world." He sat back and rubbed his temples. "So I apologize about any inconvenience to your wife, Mr. Long. As crass as it sounds, the woman sitting next to you is far more important."

Not knowing what to say, Johnny looked at Camille for a cue. On the one hand, he felt like Gunning had just insulted his wife. On the other hand, he realized Pete Gunning was right . . . the larger-than-life, tattooed redhead sitting next to him was, by far, the most important woman in the world.

A few minutes later, the flamboyant clairvoyant, the Red Dragon Lady herself, touched down in Nassau.

Chapter 16

As predicted, the airport was totally secure. Secret Service agents had arrived on site a few days earlier to ensure the proper precautions were in place. This was customary. Less usual were the tight confines. When she travelled, Camille was either received on a private runway with Beck or else she scurried through large airports in large cities across the globe. This was very different. The runway was long enough to accommodate any plane in service, yet the rest of the airport was relatively tiny and looked more like some rich guy's beach house.

As she entered the airport accompanied by her entourage, Camille looked around and took note. The boarding area was completely cleared out. In such a small airport, the effect was distinct. "I feel like I'm in a zombie movie."

"You left the zombie back home," joked Johnny, in a whisper.

Gunning stayed close to Camille while the second agent took point and the third the rear. Every shop and stall in the immediate area was closed.

"I wonder where all the people are?" said Johnny.

Camille sighed. "I hate this. I really do."

"They're probably all waiting outside in an angry mob with their pitchforks and torches."

"Thanks for reminding me, Johnny."

Gunning mumbled something into his cuff and directed Camille and Johnny toward an exit to their immediate left. It led back down to the tarmac. They followed Gunning down the steps, out the door and into a white limo with blacked-out windows that was waiting for them. The vehicle was reinforced, bulletproof and pre-loaded with weapons and medical supplies, including Camille's own blood should a transfusion be necessary. The two other agents emerged behind them and hopped into a black Suburban, also sporting blacked-out windows. A third car, another black Suburban with four more agents, idled at the ready. All this was the "secure package," a motorcade consisting of two agents in Camille's limo, three in the first Suburban and four in the second Suburban.

Camille slid into her seat with ease. It was all so old hat for her. Johnny, on the other hand, was blown away.

"Who pays for all this?" he asked.

Camille smiled. "You do. Anyway, I like the white car. Black limos make me feel like I'm at a funeral."

Gunning spoke into his cuff again, and the secure package made off toward a rear airport exit. The small security hut at the restricted exit was manned by yet another Secret Service agent who opened the electric gate. And just like that, the secure package was gone. Not a single refrigerator magnet, bag of mangoes or puka-bead necklace was purchased along the way.

Camille snapped her fingers. "Poof! The Temporary Flight Restriction is lifted. Just like that, planes are allowed to take off and land again. Amazing, isn't it? All this for me? All those people standing around outside or, like your wife, wondering why their flights are delayed two hours . . . they have no idea it's all because the Secret Service is moving my ass around behind the scenes. It's all very cold and aloof. I feel like a chess piece when they take over."

"Ah," said Johnny, whimsically wagging his finger. "Let us not forget that at one time yours was the president's favorite ass. I guess that counts for something." He was citing a ribald if not tasteless editorial that had appeared a few weeks earlier in one of D.C.'s tabloid papers.

"Yeah, yeah . . . can you believe they printed that? Only a man would consider that journalism. What else did he write?"

This time, Johnny wasn't joking. "He wrote something like . . . now you're just one of the masses of women throughout the world with nothing better to do than complain about their ex."

"Lovely." She sat back and closed her eyes. "Hey, thanks so much for tagging along. I know it's a hassle for you. I really needed a friendly face, you know?"

"Are you kidding? Don't mention it. My wife and I are looking forward to a little fun in the sun . . . if she ever gets here." He held up his hand before she could protest. "Just kidding, just kidding. You're buying dinner, I know. Give her some kind of fruity drink with an umbrella . . . she'll love you a long time."

Camille pressed one of the buttons next to her seat. A lighted makeup mirror emerged from the roof of the limo. She began primping. "I can't wait for it to end. I can't wait to move on. There's something out there for me, Johnny. I just have to find it."

They turned onto John F. Kennedy Drive to begin the twenty-minute ride to the Breakwater Coastal Hotel, the ultra-exclusive resort where they were staying. In their wake, the agent manning the security hut confirmed into his cuff that the secure package had successfully departed. Like clockwork, the dozen agents of Advance Team A working the airport emerged from the woodwork and dispersed as quickly as they had descended several days earlier. They made their way to a Gulfstream C-37B of their own that was already fired up and waiting. Within minutes, Advance Team A was en route to secure the site of Camille's next stop, a visit to Austin, Texas, where she was the keynote speaker at a conference on human trafficking. This was the event Camille had mentioned earlier at which Zindzi Mandela was also speaking. Ever since that fateful day when Camille had addressed the world with her own declaration of independence, people had followed her everyplace she went.

When it was announced that Camille would deliver the keynote address, 20,000 tickets sold out within six minutes. All proceeds went to Camille's foundation.

The Red Dragon Lady became a lightning rod for women's issues ranging from income equality, to abuse, to child rearing and even to the sex-slave trade that continued to flourish right in front of people's eyes. It all struck her as odd. She never sought fame but only tried to do what her karma demanded her to do. Then again, as her agent noted many times over, nobody told her to go out and write a tell-all about the man who used to be the most popular president in U.S. history. That choice Camille made on her own.

In an attempt to maintain equilibrium with the universe, Camille opened a foundation called the Society for Balance and Justice, through which she funded various causes and initiatives benefitting women, children and families worldwide. As surprised as she was about her explosive popularity, Camille O'Keefe was even more shocked when millions of dollars began flowing into her foundation. Camille O'Keefe suddenly had the means to make her life significant and touch those less fortunate in a truly meaningful way. She had at her fingertips more power than she'd ever had standing at Beck's side, helping to promote his agenda.

She regained her powerful vision and her insatiable drive for spiritual growth. All that she lacked was that one window of opportunity to put it all together. She agreed to meet Kofi Achebe because his emphasis on women and families intrigued her and because a voice inside her—her intuition—told her this was the opportunity she was looking for. Outside of that, she had no idea what to expect.

Chapter 17

It all came down to intentions and intuition for Camille. That was her measure of things. She knew intuitively that this meeting with Kofi was a gateway through which she would move forward along her life path. She may not have known exactly what to expect. But her intentions were pure. She was not looking to exploit Kofi's organization or, more importantly, the people he was trying to help.

So when her motorcade pulled up in front of the Breakwater Coastal Hotel, she was feeling excited as she peered out at the towering coral-colored hotel building. She tousled her hair a bit. "I am learning to trust myself again, that's all. It's amazing what happens when you trust yourself, Johnny. Everything seems natural, like I am in the flow with a greater order of things, like I'm connected to a source. Think about it. We have everything we need inside us from the moment we are conceived. Then we're born, and our egos take over. From there, it's a lifetime of departure from our true selves."

Johnny thought about it for a moment. "Well, that makes me feel a bit unfulfilled." He laughed. "I mean . . . is it really all downhill from birth?"

Camille turned to Johnny, stretched her arms and answered him. "Yes, for most people. Sorry, Johnny. Welcome to life in this low-vibrating third dimension. But it doesn't have to be that way. Take Taoist masters for example. They spend their life learning to die while they are alive. They spend their lives shedding their egos and return to the source from which they came. Times are changing. There is a great awakening coming to pull us up from the pit we've fallen into. Pretty cool, huh?"

Johnny shrugged. "Um . . . I guess. I'm really just hoping to retire in time to get in three or four years of golf before I die."

They both laughed as the white limo pulled onto the resort grounds and came to a standstill in front of three bellhops standing at attention about forty feet away. They looked like they fell from the annals of Old Britannia in their crisp white linen shirts and khaki shorts. Their knee-high white socks and pith helmets completed the look.

"This is it," said Gunning. He mumbled something into his cuff. "Roger that." He turned to Camille. "Okay, ma'am. We're secure. Off you go."

Advance Team B was in charge of securing the hotel and grounds. As with the airport, the lobby was empty except for basic staff. The dozen agents on Team B were positioned around the lobby and grounds, while the group travelling in Camille's motorcade fanned out in preparation for her entrance into the hotel.

One of the agents opened the limo door. Camille and Johnny stepped out. They both looked the part of affluent vacationers arriving at one of the most prestigious resorts in the world with one exception . . . the immediate area had been completely vacated. None of the other guests were allowed in the lobby until Camille checked in and was safely on the entire floor that was blocked out for her. There were no explanations given to the other guests. They had no idea that Camille O'Keefe was on site to meet with Kofi Achebe, a salty, war-torn Nigerian looking to stop the impending massacre of almost five thousand people and the enslavement of a thousand girls.

Johnny looked around. Even the front of the hotel was beautiful, transformative. It took him to another place entirely. And still, it felt weird. "So . . . where are all the other guests right now?" he asked Pete Gunning.

"We've established a perimeter of 100 yards," he replied. "They can go anywhere they like, just not here."

"Do you think anyone will recognize me?" asked Camille.

"You're joking, right? They would have to have a telescope."

Camille nudged him on the arm. "I was being facetious. Like I said, I hate all this. They isolate me all the time."

"It's for your own good, Camille. If anything happened to you, the world would be far worse off than it is today."

"I'm just one woman," she said, as she affixed a cream-colored, large-brim hat on her head. "There are billions more to take my place." She put on a pair of big, round white Gucci sunglasses. Half her face was instantly eclipsed. She looked like a star from the Hollywood Studio Era, comfortable yet classic in a pale yellow beachy Chanel dress with spaghetti straps that left her shoulders bare, something that would have thrown Beck into a rage had he been there. As Camille liked to say, the president preferred his mistresses half naked but his wife one step from the Madonna.

Johnny looked equally timeless, like Cary Grant to Camille's Ingrid Bergman. Johnny was as sharp as always in his seersucker suit and suede loafers. Not everyone could pull off seersucker, but Johnny knew his limits. He looked perfectly at home in the British Empire environs of the hotel.

"You need to be totally average looking like me," he joked.

"Stop . . . you know what I mean. This isn't exactly the time for me to wind up on the front pages of the tabloids in the company of some strange man."

"You look ravishing, but no different than most every other rich woman here. It is, after all, one of the most expensive resorts in the world. I imagine all these beautiful, affluent people are pretty pissed off right now after getting the bum's rush from the lobby while you check in."

"I know," said Camille. "It's a good thing they can't tell who I am from 100 yards away. It would be bad for my street cred."

Johnny smoothed out his jacket. "With that red mane of yours? Never underestimate the power of a zoom lens, my dear." He looked around. "Anyway," he reasoned, "You can just lay low until your meeting with Kofi. Just don't go promenading around the pool."

"Like my blue-suited friends would allow that. They're always speaking into their cuffs. And they call me weird for talking to the spirit world? And they never, ever sweat. They're like robots. Pete Gunning is a cyborg, I'm sure of it. Honestly, I think all men are wind-up screwing machines. And that's another thing. . . . It's okay when Beck wants to make an unannounced stop at a burger joint or, as we know, slip away for a private rendezvous with one of his chippies. But no such luck for me, especially now that we've separated. They keep me on a short leash."

"They know you can't complain to the president anymore."

Camille grunted. "Exactly. But even when I was still the respectable First Lady, they never really showed me the type of deference they would have shown Nancy Reagan or Michelle Obama. I'm so ready to be gone from all this."

Gunning's men took their positions and checked in with Team B covering the lobby and adjacent grounds. They were just about ready to proceed to check-in. They were delayed unexpectedly when a sleek silver Bentley limousine circa 1956 attempted to breach the circular driveway in front of the hotel lobby. An agent at the gate stopped the car and informed the driver that the access was closed for the next twenty minutes as a security precaution. Gunning pressed his earpiece and listened.

"Hold the First Lady," he said, into his cuff.

"Shit," said Camille, wearily.

"What?" asked Johnny Long nervously. "What's wrong? What shit? No shit. Shit not good."

Camille looked at him apologetically. "This is the kind of stuff that happens when men talk into their cuff. It never happens when I talk to spirits."

In an instant, one of the agents standing next to the lobby door took Camille by her arm and stood between her and the Bentley that was still parked idling about fifty yards away. He opened the door to Camille's white limo and slid her inside. His movements were instinctive almost second nature. The way he gently slid the First Lady back into her seat was gentlemanly even as the other half of his body was poised to kill somebody.

Johnny Long was left standing alone for a few seconds, not knowing what the hell was going on, least of all what to do. Camille held the limo door open as the agent tried to close it.

"Get in," she said. She patted the seat next to hers.

For the first time in a long time, Johnny Long noticed he was sweating. He climbed into the back of the limo with Camille, although his was not nearly as graceful a maneuver. They both turned to look out the back window.

"I guess I'm not on the same protection plan you are," he joked.

Camille patted him on the back. "Eh . . . they sell insurance for that sort of thing. You may want to look into that if you plan on hanging with me. Anyway, this should be interesting."

"Yeah, that's some car. I bet the guy sitting in the backseat isn't used to being told no."

"Funny that you assume it's a man and not a woman sitting in the backseat. Tsk, tsk, Johnny Long."

Johnny watched in awe as the protection plan for Camille unfolded in front of him. Gunning gave instructions into his cuff. Camille's agents formed an umbrella around her vehicle. Two more agents from Team B headed toward the Bentley to assist the gate agent who stopped the car in the first place. Camille's limo driver cleared his throat and waited calmly for instructions. Johnny realized that the driver never actually opened the door for them when they arrived like a civilian chauffeur would do. Instead, he remained at the ready behind the wheel. It was all part of the safety plan that was drawn up "just in case." And every so often, "just in case" goes down.

Johnny and Camille looked on as the rear door of the Bentley opened. Apparently, the man sitting in the backseat of the priceless vintage limo did not like taking orders. He came out of the vehicle mad as hell. Unfortunately for the man, his attire could not have been more ill-chosen. He looked every part the angry Arab. He wore a white *keffiyeh* with a black *agal* on his head . . . typical for an affluent

Saudi. His long, tan *thawb* robe seemed comfortable enough but didn't quite go with the supple Bruno Magli loafers he was sporting. A perfectly trimmed goatee and a dark pair of aviator sunglasses topped it off. He was the kind of guy they print up for moving targets at the Secret Service training range.

The man was yelling in Arabic before he even stepped one foot from the vehicle. When he realized the gate agent was American, he switched seamlessly to English. "Let me pass. I am a guest at this hotel."

"You can go anywhere," said the gate agent. "But you can't go there. Not for another twenty minutes like I told your driver."

"You have no idea who you are talking to," yelled the man. "You'd better be a very powerful man, because when I find out who you are, you will be begging to clean the soles of my shoes."

"I work for a woman," replied the agent in a monotone. He ought not to have said it, but he did. Mentioning a woman in power would only troll the irate Arab. He also stepped toward the Arab, getting far closer than was the cultural norm in the Middle East.

When the man heard that his needs were being subordinated to those of some woman, he turned red. "Are you crazy, man? This is an outrage. You have no idea who I am. There is no woman on this planet who comes before me. What kind of a country is this? We are not in America, my friend."

The man's driver stepped out of the car. He was obviously the man's bodyguard as well. That was a mistake. The two back-up agents stepped in front of the driver and each grabbed one of the driver's wrists. The man was gigantic. His wrists were bigger than either of the agents could grasp with one hand.

The Arab quickly surveyed the situation. Men in blue suits, ear pieces, perfectly positioned to back each other up . . . this would not end well for him. He looked at his bodyguard. "*Khalass . . . khalass.*"

Everybody relaxed a bit except for the Arab man and the agent with whom he was standing face to face. They were so close, the agent could see himself reflected in the Arab's sunglasses.

"This is not the last you've heard from me, little man in a blue suit." The Arab man slid his foot enough to land a bit of dirt and gravel on the agent's shoes.

"Heads up, Zeus," said Pete Gunning, into his transmitter. He was speaking to his sniper perched above, covering everyone's ass. Call sign Zeus.

The agent motioned for the Arab man to look up and to his right . . . two o'clock . . . on top of a five-story parking garage. Perched up there was the Team B sniper, a man who did not wear a blue suit or sit with the other men on his team, a man who slept with his MK11, his lightning bolt, and delivered instant death from above. That's why they called him Zeus.

The Arab man got back in the Bentley, as did his driver. He sent gravel flying as he gunned it out of the gate area.

"Americans. Women," said the Arab, as they sped off. "Take me to the marina. We will take the *Odyssey* out. Yes . . . bring me to my ship. Take me away from all this nonsense."

Camille and Johnny watched the whole thing like they were watching television.

"It's all so smooth, right?" asked Camille.

"It's amazing to watch," Johnny observed. He sat back and looked at Camille. It was an epiphany moment. "I mean . . . all the planning and training that the guys go through, not to mention the expense. You're a really, really important person, Camille. These guys would take a bullet for you, and they probably don't even like you. They just do it because you occupy a position of power."

Camille sat back. She was pensive, contemplative. "I know . . . I know. I think about that all the time. That's exactly the problem with men like Beck. People are so quick to respect rich men and give them all this power. But we expect them to behave on a higher plane, you know? They do whatever they want, and people just keep buying into it. The responsibility is on me now to set a different standard. I feel responsible to the people who send money to my foundation . . . millions and millions of dollars. They do it because they have expectations for me to do something better. If I start acting like Beck, I will attract all that negativity back, and I will fail miserably. I am here for a purpose. I cannot fail this mission."

Chapter 18

Having re-secured the area, Pete Gunning opened the door to the limo and let Camille and Johnny out.

"I apologize for the delay, ma'am. We just had to finish locking things down. You are now free to enter."

They stepped out of the limo just as they had done a few minutes earlier.

"I can still feel the negative energy from that Arab guy," said Camille. "He's not a good guy."

"You can tell that?"

Camille nodded. "Of course, intuitively."

Johnny laughed. "Wow, could you imagine if all women had your superpower. Men would never get a date."

Camille snorted. "Ha! Especially the married ones. And by the way, we do all have superpower intuition. We just haven't learned to use it, so we remain obedient to all you penile cyborgs."

"Thanks," said Johnny, straining to catch a glimpse of the Bentley he feared could reappear at any moment. He was not up for being stuffed back into Camille's limo. "I wonder what that angry Arab is thinking right now."

"He's cursing me. He doesn't approve of a woman being put before him . . . unless she's on her knees of course." She snorted. "Ha! I guess it doesn't help that I was badly beaten and tortured by an Arab informant looking to get at Beck. That was before he was president. But I still relive it in my mind. That's what Gunning was alluding to back on the plane."

Johnny had no idea what to say. Camille was so matter-of-fact with that tremendously personal detail, he didn't realize she was being serious. When he saw that Camille was not joking, he was horrified.

Desperate to change the subject, he took one last look at the magnificent façade of the Breakwater and gave Camille the once over. "I also wonder what Kofi will think. I mean, that dress you're wearing probably cost more than a destitute African family earns in ten years."

Camille sighed. "I know. How ironic, right? And look where we're staying. I guess I haven't completely shed my head-of-state lifestyle yet."

"Do you think he will be offended?" asked Johnny, showing his naïveté.

Camille was entertained. "Who, Kofi? Offended? That's a laugh. Believe me, these United Nations special envoy guys live pretty high off the hog."

When everything was a green light, Gunning motioned to the three bellhops who had been standing at attention this entire time, even during the episode with the angry Arab. Excited to finally receive their cue, they went straight to it.

"Welcome to the Breakwater Coastal Hotel," said one of the bellhops, as he waited for the driver to pop the trunk. "We have everything you could possibly desire at your fingertips twenty-four hours a day."

"Ah, nothing like the Bahamas," noted Johnny, as he slung his seersucker jacket over his shoulder. A second bellhop assisted with the luggage under Gunning's watchful eye while the third held the door open wide for the First Lady and her guest. Camille and Johnny headed into the lobby. Theirs was one of the more discreet, albeit one of the most lavish, buildings on the Breakwater property.

"Wait until you see this place," said Johnny. "You will love it. I've stayed here once before."

"I have too," she said, with a wink. "I've been here several times."

Johnny corrected himself. "Sorry," he said. "I forget sometimes that you're the First Lady. As impressive as this place is, it's probably nothing compared with what you've seen."

"I know," she said. "I just don't seem like First Lady material, right? I'm used to it."

Johnny was uncomfortable. "I'm not quite sure how to answer that."

"Stuff like that doesn't offend me. I answer to a higher authority."

"Yeah . . . my wife is much better at delicate phrasing than I am. I've spent too much time in finance. Having too many New Yorkers in my life is like drinking wormwood. It rots the insides."

"Oh, stop with yourself," Camille quipped. "When is your wife coming? Because you're in one of those weird, rhapsodic moods that takes people before auspicious events."

Johnny smiled. "Later tonight. I just hope I stop shaking by then. All that Secret Service stuff really freaked me out. I'm used to brokers screaming out in anguish whenever the market's down big, but none of them have been perched on a rooftop with a sniper rifle. Jumping off a roof . . . well, that's another story."

Camille rolled her eyes. "She's coming tonight? Thank God. She can take you off my hands."

"We're looking forward to a nice little vacation actually. This place is very romantic."

They went through the magnificent lobby. Camille walked over to one of the huge tropical plants growing in the lobby. It was more like an indoor tree. She touched the leaves and started talking to it. Her grandmother used to do that. Needless to say, the woman had a greenhouse full of plants that would make any botanist envious.

"Well," she said, turning back to Johnny. "I get to enjoy the company of my security detail and, if I'm lucky, a call with my divorce attorney that will cost me, like, a thousand dollars."

She sighed before continuing. A wave of melancholy overcame her seemingly out of nowhere. "That's my romantic getaway. Sound like fun? Anyway, all these guys running around in their blue suits talking into their cuff and armed to the teeth . . . they're just men like all the rest. Sure, they did a great job today. Our guys are the best in the world. Still, as soon as I filed for divorce, they began treating me like I was some sort of weirdo. In that regard, they're like everyone else surrounding Beck."

"Like I said before, they bust your chops because you're on the way out. You won't be running to Beck complaining. Or maybe they're envious?" He grinned.

Johnny handed her a glass of champagne he took from a waiter who was offering free refreshments in the lobby. "Free champagne. I didn't get that when I stayed here. Is that why you chose this place?"

"Exactly," she said, winking again. "Cheers."

They clinked glasses.

"Good stuff for lobby freebies," remarked Johnny.

Camille couldn't resist laughing at him. "Really?"

Johnny didn't get the joke. "What?"

"This champagne is from the White House cellar. Anything I eat or drink on the road is controlled by the Advance Teams or whatever they call themselves this month. You probably didn't notice the earpiece in the waiter's ear either, did you?"

Johnny grimaced and took a look. Damn if she wasn't right. How the hell did he miss that?

"So drink up good citizen," said Camille, jovially. "You're paying for it."

She clinked Johnny's glass again.

"Oh my God," said Johnny. "Who are you?"

"I'm the Red Dragon Lady, remember?" She stopped kidding and said in all seriousness, "All that media hype aside, I know who I am, Johnny. Well . . . I am working on rediscovering that great woman. More importantly, I know beyond a shadow of a doubt that I am here for something far bigger than being Beck's squeeze . . . not even his main squeeze, just his First Lady. Still, I would love to have a dollar for every time one of Beck's cronies told me I don't exactly fit the mold."

"Oh, you'll have a lot more than that once your divorce settlement is finalized."

Camille smiled. "It's all good. Things unfold a certain way for a reason. It's just as much about the time as the place. I'm nervous as hell, but something tells me this is going to be a very important meeting in terms of my life's work. My internal meters are off the dial. Something big is about to happen for me. I feel like I am about to take a monumental step forward in my life plan. Again, I have to thank you for coming down here with me. I know it was a weird request. Your wife must think I am after her man or something."

"Oh, please. She's happy to have a day to herself without smelling me reeking of Bengay. To be honest, I couldn't pass it up. I have no idea what to expect. I'm just going with the flow. So I assume we don't actually have to check in or anything like that, right?"

Camille almost spit her champagne. "Well, *you* might have to. But I don't. The guys take care of that . . . they charge it all to the full faith and credit of the United States of America and all that. I don't mind loitering here for a while longer though. I'm actually beginning to relax. It's beautiful here. Where else will you get a place like this all to yourself for twenty minutes?"

"Heaven?"

Camille snorted as if Johnny was being absurd. "Silly, places like this don't matter in heaven. Physical manifestations of beauty don't exist on that dimension."

The majesty of the hotel suddenly demanded their attention again with the same sort of pull that drove the waves up and down against the beach on which the magnificent hotel sat. They both stopped and looked up at the large brown tubular lights descending from what seemed like a hundred feet up in the air. The far end of the lobby was completely open to the beach and water just beyond. Giant sheer drapes billowed in the ocean breeze, making the two agents positioned there seem very small in comparison. The azure sea spread out lazily across the horizon like a giant negative-edge pool. The sides of the lobby were open as well, making the place a unique intermingling of nature and construction. Camille connected to it intuitively.

"I guess this is a pretty good place to go with the flow," said Johnny.

"Everyplace is a good place to go with the flow, Johnny." She downed her champagne. "Now where's that secret agent waiter guy? I'm ready for another."

Pete Gunning informed Camille that her floor was secure and ready.

"Great, Pete. Give me a minute while Johnny checks in."

Gunning hated the idea of keeping everything on hold while they waited for a civilian to check into his standard King with an ocean view.

Camille pointed toward Gunning's sleeve. "Go ahead . . . talk into it. It'll only be a few minutes more."

That was exactly what Gunning did. Camille was delighted. "God, I crack myself up sometimes. Hey, if I don't, who will, right?"

As she and Johnny headed toward check-in, Camille stopped short in her tracks. She let out an exhilarated, "Oh my God!"

"What?" asked Johnny, unaccustomed to such outbursts.

"Look," she replied, pointing to a yellow and green hummingbird hovering above a brightly colored sign advertising dolphin swims for guests.

Johnny read the sign. "Swimming with the dolphins?" He was perplexed over Camille's zeal.

"Yes," she said. "But look at the hummingbird."

"Jeez, I can't believe I missed that," said Johnny. "It's so damn fast and small."

The hummingbird flew toward them, hovered over Camille, and then sped off through the open end of the lobby toward the ocean. Camille stood smiling and somewhat transfixed as if her body was here but her spirit was somewhere else.

Johnny pursed his lips. "You seem . . . ah . . . to be someplace else."

She held up her hand to shush Johnny for a second. "I'm communing."

Johnny stood there feeling rather awkward, wondering how this sort of thing must have played in the White House. It was a wonder Beck didn't kill her. Then again, rumor had it that he certainly tried.

Camille casually returned to the present moment. "Wow. . . ." She ran her hands through her hair. "That was really interesting." Her tone was matter-of-fact.

"I'm afraid to ask," said Johnny, shifting his seersucker jacket from one arm to the other.

"That wonderful creature was more than just a bird."

Johnny chuckled. "I must have missed it."

"Don't be silly. It's unbecoming for a man like you. Of course it was a sign. Come on . . . a hummingbird landing on a sign about dolphins. And then flying up and hovering over me? Don't they teach you anything in money school?"

Johnny laughed. "Believe me, they don't even teach about money in money school."

Camille turned to Johnny and looked him square in the eye. She spoke with absolute certainty as if she was Moses having conversed with the burning bush. "I'm telling you that was no mere hummingbird."

"What was it?"

"It was Wayne Dyer."

Johnny was stunned and amused at one and the same time. He knew Camille was a renowned medium, but he hadn't really experienced her in action like this before.

"His spirit left his body, yes. And that same spirit just came to me in the form of that hummingbird."

Johnny tried to sound as nonjudgmental as possible. "Okay . . . this is the part where I don't know what to say."

Camille smiled at him. "That's fine. Silence is perfectly acceptable. I knew Wayne . . . not really well, but enough to say hello whenever we bumped into one another at a conference or something. He changed my life. He used to tell a story about a hummingbird. He found them deeply spiritual. And now he's telling me everything is going to be alright with this Kofi."

Again, Johnny tried not to judge. "The hummingbird told you that?"

"No, silly. The spirit of Wayne Dyer in the form of that hummingbird told me that. Spirits can incarnate as animals, too, you know."

Johnny chuckled. "So that's a spirit having a bird experience." He said it tongue-in-cheek, but Camille took it literally.

"Maybe it's not too late for you after all. He said I am about to undertake a very important challenge, but it will be very difficult. He said that although I should welcome difficult challenges, I should not experience difficulty. I should keep the two separate. Always face challenges, never feel difficulty. It's tough advice but very true."

Johnny couldn't refrain from posing a bit of a challenge. "You're sure about this? To be quite honest, I am worried about this meeting. It's none of my business, and I know it doesn't involve me, but I feel out of my comfort zone."

Camille smiled and exhaled loudly. "Me, too. I mean look at me." She held her arms about and spun around. "But I don't shy away from difficulty. That's when the learning happens. Challenge equals learning. Everything is going to be alright."

Johnny found it difficult to let it go. "I had a similar experience during a big investing contest I entered a few years ago. It was called *The Battle of the Quants*. I had to make some serious changes in the way I went about my business. It was pretty uncomfortable for me, though."

"And what happened?"

"I won."

"I know," said Camille, with a wink. "I Googled you. It was a rhetorical question."

Johnny shook his head. "It's amazing how differently we see the world. I can't even imagine how Beck reacted to all this stuff."

"Oh, rest assured he would have killed me with his own hands if it was legal. He's killed me in many previous lifetimes. I know it. He knows it. Unfortunately, we're not finished. We have too much karmic baggage to be done with each other just yet. More importantly, I'm done playing his victim. That much is different this time around. That's what really matters . . . progressing."

Camille walked up to the dolphin sign and touched it as if it had an energy all its own. This irked Pete Gunning and the rest of the guys, who were anxious to see Camille safely to her floor. Her insistence on staying with Johnny while he checked in annoyed them enough as it was without her meandering.

Although she could sense their annoyance, Camille paid them no mind. "You know, everyone's talking about dolphins these days. They vibrate at such an incredibly high level. Their energy is off the chart compared with us low-vibrating earthlings plopping around in our meaty bodies worrying about our fragile egos."

Johnny tried to mimic a dolphin sound but sounded more like a gagging Muppet.

"Really?" laughed Camille. "Don't try to be a dolphin, Johnny. You might hurt yourself. I'm telling you, a lot of people are starting to believe dolphins are spirit guides that have come here to help us. As amazing as it sounds, I've never swum with them."

She turned to Pete Gunning. "Don't let me leave here without doing it."

Gunning arched a brow. "I wouldn't dream of it, ma'am."

"I'm a perpetual thorn in his side," she said.

"Maybe he doesn't believe in spirit guides?" said Johnny. "Hummingbirds, dolphins? I keep thinking of Beck. I'm sorry to keep bringing him up, but I find it funny to imagine his response when you say things like this."

"Beck has trouble letting go of the material things he loves most. As a result, he's never been able to realign with his higher self. He clings to his notions of entitlement and eschews humility."

Johnny held up his hand. "Wait, did you just use the word 'eschew?'"

Camille nodded. "Indeed, I did. I have yet to unlearn all those fancy First Lady words. It's a simple concept really. With Beck, as with so many men like him, ego replaces source. So he would tell me to stop being a moron or tell me to get real. He would make some snide remark about my weight or my tattoos to try to make me self-conscious in public. He would do something like interrupt me and tell me that nobody cares what I have to say. Or he would tell me that people just want to look at my ass, which is getting big, so why aren't I in the gym? Then he would go out and find himself a new piece of ass that, apparently, looked better. You know, that sort of stuff. It's all a means of his ego protecting itself by belittling me."

This made Johnny sad. For a moment, he felt Camille's pain. She sensed it and let out a near-perfect dolphin sound, and they both laughed. "Don't worry about me, Johnny. I have the dolphins on my side. I can't lose."

Johnny snapped his fingers. "What was it Douglas Adams wrote about dolphins in *The Hitchhiker's Guide to the Galaxy*? Dolphins are really here to study us? We're like their experiment. One of his other books was called *So Long and Thanks for All the Fish*."

"Funny, that's probably what the dolphins said just before they split this low-energy dimension of ours."

Johnny laughed. "Exactly."

"Well, that Douglas Adams guy is right. We are all one big dolphin experiment. But they don't really need to eat fish. They just do that to make us feel special when we see them gobble them down."

Camille made another dolphin call and smiled at the woman, behind the check-in counter. The woman returned a huge tropical-island smile, the sort that melted away any semblance of mainland worry that may have stowed away in a visitor's luggage.

"I see you speak French," noted the woman referring to Camille's dolphin call.

The hummingbird reappeared near the counter.

"There he is again," said Johnny.

"We have a lovely hummingbird garden just outside to your left," explained the woman behind the counter. "This little guy must have decided to stretch his wings a bit."

"No," said Johnny Long. "This one is different. This little guy is a guru."

The woman smiled. "Ah, I see you speak Hindi."

As Camille stepped into the glass elevator that whisked her up to the top floor, she looked down onto the lobby below and thought this must be what it looked like to leave the planet. On her way up, she was afforded a marvelous view of the grounds. To the rear of the main building where Camille was staying was the resort marina where the world's wealthiest nautical adventurers docked while staying at the property. It was the same marina where the angry Arab's 200-foot *Odyssey* was docked. As Camille arrived at the top floor, her floor, she could see the marina through the large window that constituted the entire ocean-side wall. There she noticed that same classic Bentley limousine pull around to the main entrance of the marina. Once again, the limo was met by a Secret Service agent who, once again, informed the driver that the facility was still on lockdown.

Camille watched as the car swung around to depart, stopped and then reversed to where the agent was standing. The angry Arab jumped out of the car and began flailing his arms at the agent in what Camille assumed to be an irate tirade. She was right.

"What do you mean I cannot access the *Odyssey* for ten minutes? Do know who I am? Do you see the size of that ship? You could not even be a galley hand on that ship."

The agent simply stared at the Arab and shook his head. "You can go anywhere. You just can't go there for another ten minutes."

The Arab threw his sunglass down and stomped on them. "You idiot Americans. Your women will be the end of us all." He turned to his driver. "Don't just stand there. *Ahbal!* Hand me another pair of sunglasses."

Chapter 19

Kofi Achebe arrived about an hour later. He rode in a town car, not a limousine, and his driver was Olawale Cisse, not a hired chauffeur. After the scene in the village, Olawale contemplated hanging up his camera and going to work with his uncle after all. Kofi didn't blame him. But the morning he went in to say goodbye to Kofi, something strange happened to him, and his resolve was tempered once more. He came across a very old church about three blocks from Kofi's office in Lagos. The façade was riddled with bullets. Graffiti was spray painted across the front. It was in Arabic. Had Olawale been able to read it, this is what he would have seen: *Tell your false God to make room. You will soon be joining Him.*

Olawale might not have been able to read Arabic, but like everyone else in the area, he knew who was responsible . . . *Boko Haram.* It wasn't about religion for him. He hadn't stepped inside a church in years. Nor was it about politics, even though his uncle had such political sway. For Olawale, this was merely one more example of a systematic assault on the most valuable antiquities of the world by *Boko Haram,* something they learned from *ISIS* and *Al Qaeda* before them. It was a strike at what made people human, and this bothered him. For years, these two terrorist organizations full of murderers and thugs destroyed as much great art and architecture as they could in order to announce to the world that idolatry, creativity, beauty and diversity would not be tolerated. Hundreds of precious works and great buildings were thus summarily destroyed as if they had never existed at all. That was the whole point for groups like *Al Qaeda* and *Boko Haram* . . . wipe out the people, places and things that fortify difference. Fortify rigidity with ruthlessness, make people believe that they are fleeting in the face of violence.

For Olawale Cisse, the issue was freedom. It seemed like *Boko Haram* was everywhere, now even in Lagos. And everywhere they went, death cleared the way for freedom to settle over the land. When Olawale saw the bullet holes and graffiti, he felt sick to his stomach. It was different this time, though. It was not like the nausea he felt when he saw all those dead bodies rotting. No, this feeling of nausea was completely different. It was existential, as if some essence at his core was trying to scratch its way out. It was as if he carried the angst of the world in his belly and its weight on his shoulders. If you destroy a people's antiquities, you eradicate their historical significance. Destroy a people's past, and you destroy their future along with it. This is the goal of groups like *Boko Haram*.

Kofi Achebe drew his motivations from elsewhere. For him, Africans devastating Africans had to stop. The rest of the world was all too willing to throw fuel on the fire, so he figured it was incumbent upon him, an African man with access to United Nations resources, to step into the line of fire. Like Olawale, Kofi did not go to church. But he believed he would be held accountable one day for the sins of his past, a part of himself he ran from every day. He believed he would be condemned on high when it was his time. At the same time, he felt he had these years left to mitigate the death and destruction he had once participated in. And so he dedicated himself. He placed himself in harm's way in an attempt to make recompense for the deeds of his youth. The young man, Olawale Cisse, sought a return to humanity that connected us all while the older man, Kofi Achebe, sought humanity in order to return to the people.

When the valet drove off, Kofi and Olawale were left standing in the awesome shadow of the main building where Johnny and Camille had stood admiringly just a short time earlier. Kofi had travelled the world, but tried to be respectful of his cause with the Council on Women and Families and make relatively modest accommodations while on the road. When he flew, he flew economy, not first class. When he rented a car, he either drove himself or had Olawale drive rather than hiring a driver, unless he required specialized knowledge of the local surroundings.

When Camille O'Keefe had suggested they meet at the Breakwater, she didn't have to ask twice. The business at hand was grim enough. Kofi welcomed the sunny, copious environs of the Breakwater if for no other reason than to lighten the atmosphere a bit. He had been following Camille in the papers ever since she made her famous "I'm throwing the president out" speech in the Rose Garden. The more he saw of Camille, the more he was convinced of her unique power to connect to the mass of the world's people who were struggling to survive or, at best, yearning for something more in their lives then finding their next meal.

He had Olawale reach out to Camille's agent after *This Soul's Journey through the Eye of the Storm* came out. That didn't go so well. After leaving several messages, Olawale passed it back to his boss, frustrated that he couldn't get a return call from the agent. Kofi then reached out to Zindzi Mandela, who had participated in several conferences with him on Women and Families. He received a call back from Camille within an hour. From there, some arrangements were made over the course of the next week, and there they all were . . . in the Bahamas in all its grandeur.

They were greeted by the same attentive bellhops that helped Camille. "Welcome to the Breakwater Coastal Hotel. We have everything you could possibly desire at your fingertips twenty-four hours a day."

The bellhop took their luggage and pointed the way to the reception desk.

Kofi instructed Olawale to "tip the gentleman."

Olawale fumbled through his wallet and gave the bellhop a few bucks. "You are good at spending other people's money, Kofi."

Kofi laughed. "Indeed. That is the best kind to spend."

Accustomed to the intense African heat, neither man removed their jacket. Kofi wore his usual business attire. When he was "in the field," when he was out investigating the scene of some atrocity, he wore fatigues, and carried an M4 assault rifle and a Sig M11 pistol. When engaging "an erudite audience," as he put it, he appeared quite differently—a dark blue Armani suit (one of only two suits he owned) and one of three crisp white shirts he had made for him by a Baker Street tailor in London. His black wingtip shoes were Bally, the only pair he bought in the last five years. They were well worn but always polished and re-heeled when necessary. He accented his outfit with a black and gold tie clipped with a United Nations pin.

It was important to Kofi that he look dignified when meeting with people who were not shooting at him. He felt it was too easy for people to pigeonhole him as "unintelligent" or "unsophisticated" because he represented the cause of destitute and dying Africans. It didn't help matters that he was a huge man. When he shook hands, his consumed the other person's hand like some sort of eclipse. His head needed every muscle of his bulky neck for support. He knew he frightened people, especially white people who were too inclined to see him as a "big, angry African."

At the same time, people expected to see a certain conflict-hardened grittiness underpinning his comments in order to take him seriously. Still, he was sure to speak impeccable English and good French. He went out of his way to display etiquette and protocol as only a member of the United Nations could. He knew this was who he had to be—an African man somewhere between rebel leader and Oxford intellectual—in order to be heard, and so that was the role he crafted for himself.

Olawale Cisse was entirely different. Before coming on with Kofi, the most conflict he'd seen was a tough soccer match between rival halls at the university. Olawale could barely shoot photos of dead bodies, let alone fire a gun resulting in a dead body. Where Kofi Achebe was a straight bourbon guy who drank to forget the things he'd seen and done, Olawale Cisse was more of a fellow prone to bouts of insomnia if he ate too much rich food. Still, Olawale was kindhearted, and his intentions were usually pure. Camille would like him.

He wore a smart blue blazer, pinstripe button-down shirt and khaki pants. He looked the part of a well-mannered young man who had studied at a British university as, indeed, he had. Cambridge was where his uncle sent him to study. He had travelled Europe and, of course, seen much of sub-Saharan Africa. But he'd never seen anything like the Breakwater Coastal Hotel with its gigantic draperies flapping like sails as the ocean breeze wended its way through the open lobby. The modern furniture decorating the lobby reminded Olawale of Zurich for some reason. He assumed it was the clean lines and neutral tones. This was how he saw the Swiss, as well.

"This is rather extravagant, isn't it?" he asked.

Kofi clucked his tongue. "You have a lot to learn about Americans, my boy. This is how they operate. Remember that Camille O'Keefe is the First Lady of the United States, even though she is getting divorced from their president. Remember, too, that Ms. O'Keefe is one of the most famous women in the world right now for her outspoken position on women's rights."

Olawale was skeptical, perhaps because he got the cold shoulder from Camille's agent. "I don't know, Kofi. Is this really the best woman to go to for help? I mean . . . look at this place. How does being here in the lap of luxury connect us to our mission to promote the welfare of women and families? Our problem is an African problem. I don't see how an American celebrity can advance our cause."

Kofi smiled and took a glass of champagne from the waiter who, as Camille noted, was part of her security team. Unlike Johnny, Kofi noticed the waiter's earpiece immediately. He cordially thanked the waiter. His eyes darted around the lobby . . . the waiter, the man reading in the corner wearing jeans and a polo shirt . . . the man standing next to one of the billowing draperies. . . . Kofi made them immediately and reminded himself just how important Camille O'Keefe was to the world.

Kofi returned to their conversation. "As I was saying, exactly what is Africa? What is 'an African problem' as you say? The world comes and takes $350 billion in natural resources a year from sub-Saharan Africa. So why is this just an African problem? It is the world's problem because the plight of African women and families is directly tied to the looting of resources by Africans and non-Africans alike."

The waiter offered Olawale a glass of champagne as well. "You drive me to drink, Kofi. I hope you are happy." He reached for a glass and drained half in a single sip. He never noticed the waiter's earpiece. He was content enough with the free drinks.

"Careful, Olawale. You don't want to be guilty of overindulgence. What would the African people say?" Kofi smirked.

"You may check in right over there, gentlemen," said the waiter, who played his role expertly. He gestured toward the large reception area that was now staffed by three stunning women and two of the fittest men Olawale had ever seen.

"Does everybody in the Bahamas look like that?" Olawale asked the waiter.

"Only here, sir," replied the waiter in complete seriousness.

Chapter 20

The meeting was set for later that day. They had agreed to meet in a conference room in the hotel that Camille's security team arranged. Calling it a conference room was like calling a Bugatti a car. The room was astounding. Again, Olawale felt the setup was too extravagant for the matter at hand. He reminded Kofi that their enemies in *Boko Haram* lived in tents and ramshackle huts. *Boko Haram* was hardened from having nothing and not softened by luxury.

"That is why they seek to take everything," Kofi responded. "People who have nothing to lose will lose nothing, so they resort to committing atrocities. The same holds true for the Palestinians, I suppose."

As he was accustomed to do, Olawale reasserted his protest. "But, Kofi, think of the Congo. Think of Angola and Rwanda. There are powerful men in charge who own everything. Has that stopped them? They always want more."

Kofi patted his mentee on the shoulder and then picked a piece of lint from his pinstripe shirt. "I think you have it wrong. Katoma, Kabinias, Salatus, Kagitoma . . . any of those guys . . . they are just names. They are façades like the shell corporations they hide behind. Sure, there is a small group of men who own everything, sell everything and surround themselves with countless cronies. These rich men had everything to lose, so they did not commit atrocities. Instead, they let them occur regularly. It is different. You must understand the nuances and complexities."

Olawale grimaced. "It's the same thing to me, Kofi."

"If there's one thing I wish you to learn from your time with me, it's that no two things are ever the same in politics. Being African, you should know by now that each situation is unique and must be dealt with individually according to its own set of rules. Perhaps I should write a book some day? I envision something between fact and fiction . . . like *factory*. That would be a shocker, would it not?"

Olawale was about to protest vehemently with a comment about morality superseding everything. Before he could speak, Kofi held up his hand. "Eh . . . eh . . . I know what you are about to say. Just remember. Compromise is everything if it resolves a problem and saves lives. We are surrounded by palm trees here. When a hurricane hits, the palm trees bend deeply, but they do not break. I dare say the palm tree is better for it. Living things are malleable and bendable; dead things are rigid and unyielding."

And with that, the two men stepped off the elevator and found themselves on the conference-room floor of the resort building. The entire floor was on lockdown. Gunning's men, the group that had accompanied the secure package from the airport, were in charge of security during the conference.

There was a single concierge permitted. He greeted Kofi and Olawale as they emerged from the elevator. Before he could do anything else, the security team subjected the two men to a methodical frisking. They then waved both metal and explosive detectors around the men. Before they passed the detectors over Kofi's attaché case, he stopped them.

"Gentlemen, that is my attaché case. Let me save you the trouble by telling you that there is a Sig M11 handgun inside."

Gunning tensed up. It was uncomfortable to say the least. One of the agents passed a detector over the case. Sure enough, it screamed its warning. Gunning opened the attaché and removed the gun. He ejected the magazine and cleared the chamber. A round popped out.

"Now why would you be taking a loaded handgun into a meeting with the First Lady? And with a round in the chamber? What am I supposed to think?"

Kofi nodded. "That was my mistake. I forgot I had it. I take it with me whenever I travel abroad."

Gunning handed the gun and clip to one of the other agents. "You took this on the plane? Is that what you want me to believe?"

"No, no," replied Kofi. "I always check the gun with my luggage, but it's at my side at all times after arrival no matter where I am travelling. I survived one assassination attempt quite by luck. I was unarmed. After that, I vowed never to be caught unable to protect myself even in a place like this. A man like you will understand."

Gunning stared him down. He understood completely. But it wasn't his job to empathize with the men he was surveilling. It was his job to anticipate problems before they occurred.

"Come on," implored Kofi. "You know who I am."

"Exactly," replied Gunning. "That's the problem."

"They're clean otherwise," said one of the agents.

Gunning thought it over for a minute. "Put two men in the room. You can bring the First Lady up." He nodded to the concierge to proceed.

"May I take your jackets, gentlemen?" asked the concierge.

Kofi answered for the both of them. "You may take the young man's. I will keep mine, thank you."

Olawale shot him a glance.

Kofi nodded at him. "It makes me look better. You, not so much. What can I say?"

The concierge hung up Olawale's blazer and provided a quick overview of the facility as he took them and the two agents to the conference room.

"Gentlemen, you have at your disposal every amenity of a high-tech office suite. You have phone, fax and Internet, of course. I must advise you that they are unsecured lines. If you require secured phone lines and encrypted Internet capabilities, we can provide an IT consultant to establish your secure connections. We provide such services regularly for our more discreet guests. Of course, this will be an added expense item."

"Of course it will," said Olawale, in a tone laced with sarcasm. He imagined the list of "discreet guests" included some of the very men Kofi was trying to bring down.

The concierge smiled back politely. "You have a full bar and assortment of snacks available to you at the service station along the window." He gestured toward the room-length window that looked out over the crystal aquamarine ocean some thirty stories below. The service station was stocked with a wide assortment of beverages, fresh fruit and snacks. "Should you require more privacy, I can close the automatic blinds."

"Everything looks fine," said Kofi. "Your hospitality is very much appreciated."

"Very good, sir," said the concierge. "Let me get back to my station to receive the First Lady properly. Should you require food service or anything else, simply dial 11 on any of the phones in the room." He smiled again and stood almost at attention.

Kofi motioned to Olawale a few times with his head. "Come on, then."

Olawale rolled his eyes and huffed. He then reached into his pocket, removed ten dollars, and gave it to the concierge.

Kofi cleared his throat.

Olawale removed another ten and forked it over as well, pushed the concierge toward the door and gave him the bum's rush albeit with a wonderful air of *bon homme*. "Thank you ever so much, kind sir. Your work is wonderful . . . top of the range . . . quite a bit of alright."

He returned to Kofi. "Did you forget your wallet again?"

Kofi placed his worn attaché case on the long, solid boardroom table and took a seat facing the ocean. It was much to his liking. As if the expansive, wall-sized window wasn't enough, the furniture was equally impressive. The dark wood table perfectly matched the other pieces. The couches and chairs adorning the room were classic British Empire style with fabrics and worn leather that evoked a bygone time when colonialism was the rule. The irony was not lost on Kofi, a man who'd seen both the light and dark side of colonization.

The two agents accompanying them took up positions standing at either end of the room. They had already swept the area. It was secure. Now their concerns turned to these two Africans, one of whom had tried to walk into the meeting strapped. Kofi noticed they were speaking quietly into their microphones. He knew what they were saying. Olawale had no clue, but Kofi had seen too much not to recognize the machinations at work. Kofi was certain Gunning was instructing his men to keep his big, African ass on a very short leash. Were Kofi to make the slightest aggressive move toward Camille, the agents were to take him out . . . and Olawale, too, for good measure. The First Lady was everything; Kofi and Olawale were nothing.

No need to let that interfere with the matter at hand. Kofi knew Olawale was different, less likely to acquiesce to power. It was his youth but also his nature. He looked at Olawale. Yes, the young man who still maintained his youthful enthusiasm and sardonic vigor. Olawale still believed in people, still believed the world was populated by far more good people than bad. Kofi recognized himself in Olawale, although that would have been a long, long time ago, back when Kofi still dreamed of a world where people treated each other as vibrant individuals and not simply crammed into cramped, confining boxes of "ism," causes and ulterior motives.

That youthful part of himself had departed a long time ago. Now that Kofi was looking for a new road to journey down, he recognized how seriously flawed he was. His view of mankind was more pragmatic. He wasn't looking to change the world, nor did he believe there were many truly good people in it. Unlike Olawale, Kofi Achebe felt most people were selfish, self-serving creatures of habit living life in fear of change. Who really owned what? Where did the money come from? The mega yachts, the mansions, the skyscrapers, all those billions . . . follow the money, follow the money. It's all being funneled. When he looked around a big city,

Kofi Achebe saw a universe built with bones and cemented with blood. It was as simple as that. Where most people saw diamond rings, gold necklaces, cell phones, gas stations, knockoff handbags and the myriad of other things that filled daily life, Kofi saw the empty eyes of the dead staring off into nothingness that lay piled up behind the façade. Everything he saw left a trail of blood. No wonder he could be a stone-cold fighter sometimes.

These are the things Kofi learned when speaking with the dead, with all those empty shells of former people piling up at his feet more and more. He yearned for silence while at the same time craving a redemption that was only possible through engagement with the brute reality of life. All he was looking to do now was help change his little part of the world in hope of clearing some space for the few good people left.

He looked at one of the agents. Despite Kofi's huge physical stature, the agent was unintimidated and staring right back at him. Kofi decided to avert his eyes. He couldn't afford trouble just now. Instead, he considered the large, hand-carved humidor sitting on the conference table near him. He had no doubt it was full of Cuban cigars. He leaned in and opened the top. Sure enough, there were some real beauties lounging around in that cedar-lined box. And they were, indeed, *Cubanos*. He thumbed through them gently, with respect for the craftsmanship that went into making each one by hand. . . .Romeo and Julietta, Cohiba, Partagás. Out in the field, Kofi preferred to pack a fat lipper of Skoal like he'd done that day in the village when he was examining the massacre that took place. He dropped a bit of cognac into each new tin, letting it soak in. The cut tobacco gave him the jolt he needed to handle such things. But in his private time, the time when he lowered his walls and allowed the ghosts that hovered around him to speak their piece more fully, the moments when he spoke to the dead most concertedly, he turned to straight bourbon and the mellow, nutty plume of a fine *Cubano*.

A man close to Castro once told him that Cuban soil had a very high lithium content, the same element prescribed to treat bipolar disorder, and that smoking a Cuban cigar was tantamount to self-medicating. Often, he would slip into moments of deep reflection when he recalled the many victims whose mangled corpses he'd come across. Each one of them had a story to tell. They spoke to him about their reality, not literally like Camille could do, but contextually, circumstantially. Each dead body provided Kofi with clues about the truth and reality of things happening that nobody wanted to discuss. He worked for those ghosts, but he had to keep them in abeyance all the same, for they were angry and pushed him to avenge their brutal demise in ways that he had sworn off years ago. Whatever it was, Kofi Achebe needed those moments of solace, reflection and conversation with the dead lest bitterness take over his life entirely.

Kofi leaned back in his leather chair, one of a dozen surrounding the rectangular boardroom table, and looked up at the ceiling fan that was rotating slowly overhead. Olawale sat down next to him. He knew Kofi well enough now to know when he should give the man some space. He stood up and ventured over to the bar, all the while under the watchful gaze of the two agents. The close surveillance made Olawale nervous. He felt like a criminal, and he resented being made to feel that way. His hand shook as he poured a drink for Kofi. He thought to himself that this must be how a black man in America feels.

The young man returned to the table and carefully placed a neat bourbon in front of his salty mentor. Kofi rejoined the present moment. His keen eye caught Olawale's hand shaking a bit as he placed the glass down on the table.

"I didn't notice you go over to the bar," said Kofi. He rubbed his eyes.

"You were talking to the dead, weren't you?" asked Olawale. That was the term Kofi had given to those moments when he slipped away into deep thought.

Kofi did not answer. He took the beveled crystal rock glass, held it up against the backdrop of the ocean stretched out across the room before him, and admired the caramel color of the bourbon.

Olawale looked at the two agents as he settled back into his seat. "I wonder about the people who meet in rooms like this. What deals did they broker that nobody knows about? What entitlements did they grant for themselves that cost people their lives? I don't know, Kofi . . . it makes me angry sometimes when I think about it . . . like the world is spiraling out of control and nobody cares because they are too caught up in their own little lives to worry about other people. That's why I decided to stay on with you. To be honest, I almost quit after you took me to that village. But then I realized that would make me like everyone else. I am not here to be like everyone else, Kofi. I am determined to make a difference."

Kofi nodded as he listened. "Yes, I used to feel the same way. A word of advice, though. Don't presume to call other people's lives 'little.' That's not for you to judge. But I completely understand how you are feeling. I was there myself. That's when I committed myself to stop killing other people in a war that really amounted to a gang fight for turf and money. I swore people would know my name and read about my great deeds as I travelled the road toward redemption."

"That's what motivates you now?"

Kofi wagged his finger. "No . . . no . . . I no longer need a gold star to validate what I do. Leave the gold stars for people who need that sort of thing. What I care about now is learning how to be humble. That's the only way to make real change."

"But you've told me you have killed men since then."

Kofi scratched his head. "True. I had to defend myself from people who were trying to kill me."

Olawale clucked his tongue. "Then they should be dead. You were doing the world a service."

Kofi smiled at the boy's naiveté. "I will suffer for it all the same one day, boy. Call it final judgment, call it karma. Whatever you call it, I will pay recompense for the lives I have taken. That's how it works. The value system of this world is not the same as that in heaven."

Olawale was uncomfortable speaking of such things with Secret Service agents in the room and changed the subject. "It's funny that the décor is British Empire. I feel like I am in some story about men in pith helmets and Africans with spears charging at one another. You know, God save the Queen and all that."

Kofi laughed. "Those days are long gone, my boy. Now the Colonialists who occupy our continent speak Chinese and carry bags full of money instead of weapons. Do you know that there are over one million Chinese workers in Africa now? And you know how they multiply."

"I knew there were a lot of Chinese shipped in, but I had no idea it was that many. I bet most people don't know that. Someone needs to write a new story then."

"Yes, someone definitely needs to write a new story, one about a handful of African rulers who have somehow managed to take for their own all the riches God put there for the African people to enjoy. Those few men have stolen God's gifts, and the people take the lives of each other."

Olawale sighed. "You've seen much more than I have. Nothing ever changes, does it? The children repeat the sins of the father. In both cases, they are usurping what God has given to His people."

Kofi looked up at his protégé. "That was very well put. But I also blame God for allowing it to happen. What sort of God is that? With a God like that, who needs the devil, eh? But don't fret, Olawale. Something tells me the story of Camille O'Keefe may very well be the new story you are looking for. Yes . . . and what a story it will be."

They could hear Camille arriving at the concierge desk. Olawale smoothed out his shirt and pulled on his cuffs in preparation for Camille's arrival. Kofi downed the quaff in a single gulp and handed the glass back to Olawale, who quickly deposited it in the sink and returned to Kofi's side. The boy was learning.

Kofi stood up, and both men prepared to meet the Red Dragon Lady whose voice they already heard through the door.

"So begins the first chapter in the new story, Olawale."

"What will it be called?"

Kofi smirked. "Judging from the state of things, I'd say *Angle of Attack* would be perfect."

Chapter 21

Camille glided into the room accompanied by Pete Gunning. Kofi and Olawale stood before her, taking it all in. As Kofi expected, Camille was as elegant in person as she appeared in the press. He was immediately aware of another quality as well, one that radiated from the Red Dragon Lady . . . repose. This struck him, for he expected Camille to be brimming over with vivacity. Instead, she was calm, even a bit demure.

"It's an honor to meet you, Madame First Lady," said Kofi, accepting the hand that he waited respectfully for Camille to extend. Her hand was warm and steady, her shake was more humble than firm. Kofi left his grip loose, taking care not to envelop her hand in his.

"Yes," said Camille. "It's nice to meet you finally in person. Zindzi Mandela speaks very highly of you. She says she has yet to bump into you when you don't have something startling to say."

Kofi withdrew his hand respectfully and stood tall. He knew the effect his large frame had on the much smaller woman. "I am afraid Ms. Mandela is correct. It is unfortunate that I have seen so much sadness. It seems every time I return to the field, I am witness to some new atrocity. I wonder sometimes if it will ever end or if this is the fate to which I have been condemned."

Camille smiled. "There is no such thing as seeing too much, Mr. Achebe. Your work in the field is invaluable. Every time you return there, you cast light on darkness. Returning is the way of the Tao, it is the way of growth. Welcome it. Remember, sometimes we have to journey back as a way of moving forward at the same time. We will inevitably arrive where we started anyway."

Kofi was blown away. He'd met the First Lady of the United States for a mere minute or two, and already she was engaging him on a level well above what most others could grasp.

He was hard-pressed to come up with a suitable response. "Ah . . . you really are a woman of paradox as all the papers claim. I have now witnessed it firsthand, Madame First Lady."

"Call me Camille."

"Call me Kofi."

And so there it was, the niceties of two diplomats complimenting each other in lofty terms as a way of breaking the ice. Olawale didn't care for it, however. What he'd seen in the field sickened him. Looking through the lens of his camera as he tried to photograph the carnage was, for him, like looking through a special scope that laid bare the stark depravity of man.

Camille's comments rubbed him the wrong way. He felt anger rising in his stomach. This was not good, not good at all considering there were now three Secret Service Agents in the room with them, each one armed well enough to cut down fifty men. As for Pete Gunning, he didn't like the look of Olawale one bit. He viewed the young African as a radical and most certainly a threat. Gunning was just looking for an excuse to hurt Olawale because he felt the entire trip was a waste of his time.

Camille graciously took the glass of iced cucumber water one of the agents handed her. She sat at the head of the table. It never occurred to her to sit anywhere else. This might be Kofi's meeting, but it was her show. And yet, as Kofi noticed immediately, Camille had a calming way about her as if she was completely comfortable with who and where she was.

"I trust in my own nature," continued Camille. "I believe we all come to this world with a blueprint for our lives. So when terrible things happen to people, I tend to think it is part of their life lesson. Then, of course, there's karma, always ready to impose a penalty or impart a reward."

An uncomfortable silence descended over the group sitting around the table. Camille sensed it immediately, but before she could elaborate, Olawale jumped in. He could restrain himself no more. He obviously didn't see in Camille what Kofi saw. Olawale resisted the lure of the most powerful woman in the world, the one they call the Red Dragon Lady. At the very least, he was unwilling to give her the benefit of the doubt.

"That is very easy for you to say when you are not the person suffering. Do you really believe the words that just came out of your mouth? Are we really to give up control of our lives like that? Should we excuse the atrocities because it was part of the victims' pre-life plan or whatever you called it?"

Kofi rubbed his temples. "Please excuse Olawale. He is young and still a bit brash. He is curious more than anything else, but he has not yet learned the value of respect for what he does not understand."

Olawale's response was just as harsh. "What I understand is that African people are struggling to survive but have no problem dying. It is an outrage how so few are taking notice. I suppose the West cannot see from behind the stack of gold that obscures their vision."

He regretted his tone as soon as the words left his mouth. Camille was unoffended but nonetheless taken aback at the young man's vehemence. "They may gain the world, but they lose their soul, Olawale. The universe has a way of sorting things out. Trust is more important than control. Trust is the way of the Tao; control is the way of the ego."

Olawale was seething inside. He didn't know what came over him. Ordinarily, he wouldn't dream of speaking to a woman that way, let alone Camille O'Keefe, the most influential woman in the world. Yet the words flowed from his mouth like venom from a viper. He was shocked at his own behavior and yet, at the very same time, exhilarated to have a voice at all. If Camille O'Keefe was, in fact, the most influential woman in the world, shouldn't he speak the truth?

This was what Olawale wondered as he continued to insult the Red Dragon Lady.

"Exotic metals for sophisticated electronic gadgets, oil and petrol to fuel their polluting machines, fake designer bags to tote around as if they were the genuine thing . . . women, children and slave labor . . . that's what it all comes back to."

Camille looked dumbfounded. A million things ran through her head. She could have been offended, could have been irate or mortified. She could have reacted in any number of ways. Were Camille O'Keefe like most Americans, she would have dismissed Olawale as a raving liberal or even a kook. Were she like Beck, she would have mocked the young man to his face before having security detain him just for the fun of it.

Instead, what occurred to her most was what it would mean if Olawale was right. What if the developed world ran on the blood of Africa? What did that mean for humanity? What did that mean for her? The young man ranting before her was feeling the overwhelming power of his convictions. She respected that. More importantly, she listened to him because she heard her karma calling. What Olawale just described was a place on earth, Africa, rich in every imaginable resource but one . . . love.

For Camille, love was the most precious resource, a gift to be shared among all people. She didn't care how hokey or flakey men like Beck thought she was. Cynicism didn't change the immutable laws of the universe . . . love was much stronger than hate could ever be. And yet, it was so much easier to turn toward hate. Likewise, she didn't begrudge Olawale for his passion and conviction as Beck would have done. Instead, she recognized in the young man a hole in his center that was devoid of love.

This was the new story Camille was looking for. Something in what Olawale said called to her. It resounded with her premonition that a new opportunity was about to present itself, one that would help her to move forward with her life plan. She'd been looking. But she knew that's not how the Law of Attraction worked. People don't manifest what they want; they manifest what they are. That was

Olawale's problem. She began to recognize her calling intertwined in this fateful meeting.

Her interest in him aside, Camille was now concerned for Olawale's safety. She sensed tension rising in Pete Gunning. Having been around the block a few times, Kofi also noticed Pete Gunning moving closer to Olawale. He couldn't afford a mishap here, even if it meant offending Olawale. There was too much at stake for Kofi to worry about hurting the kid's feelings.

Camille took charge. "You have nothing to apologize for, Olawale. You are speaking from your soul. That is the voice of truth. Sometimes, that voice can sound a bit harsh to new ears. People who get offended easily are people who are unwilling to listen. I can only imagine how my comments sound to people. Isn't that right, Pete?"

Gunning did not respond. Olawale was still visibly upset. "That is the point. Nobody's listening to anything other than the sound of money."

Camille understood entirely. "I think what I am trying to say is that we are spirits having a human experience, not the other way around. Accordingly, we need to trust in our own nature, trust that we will inevitably return to where we started, return to our source. What happens to us here, what happens to this mass of flesh. . . ." She squeezed her arm for emphasis. "That is momentary, a twitch in eternity which is where we will return."

Gunning moved closer to Olawale. The two other agents did the same. It became clear things were about to get very sticky. Camille had no doubt the agents needed very little provocation to get forceful with Olawale, a young African man whose presence the agents already resented. Olawale seemed to be the only person in the room not getting the message. Such was the myopia of youth. Like so many well-educated African young men, he had much to say, much that was ugly but nonetheless true. Unfortunately, the vigor in his words was received more as vinegar.

Pete Gunning was not about to let things get kooky. He would take Olawale out at the drop of a hat. Who would really care? Gunning didn't like Olawale or people like him, people who thought they were better and believed they had the answers to everything when, in reality, they had no clue about what went on behind closed doors. Gunning didn't believe in answers; he believed in control. When he had control, there were no problems. When there were no problems, no answers were needed. Africa was a massive shit hole to Pete Gunning. The respective governments lacked true control, and so they had nothing but problems. As a result, people like Olawale began thinking they had the right to lash out and cause trouble.

Olawale felt Africa's anguish on a genetic level that could very well cost him his life, if not today then sometime in the future. That's why Pete Gunning hated Olawale. He hated people like Olawale because they started trouble. And people who start trouble make life difficult for Pete Gunning. In his ideal world, Gunning would be free to clean things up. "Clean things up" meant getting rid of troublemakers like Olawale however he saw fit. He would also love to start with these two shady African bastards. What kind of world was it where he couldn't gun down scumbags like this? Answer . . . not a world in which Pete Gunning liked living. He was a sanitation engineer waist high in a world of shit.

So when Camille saw Gunning reach under his blazer, she worried big time. She imagined his palm sliding onto the grip of his Sig P229. This would be very bad. It was something Beck would love . . . his soon-to-be ex-wife and turncoat getting herself in heaps of trouble as soon as she set out on her own. He would be thrilled should one of Camille's "crazy ideas" get a young African man killed.

She intervened and addressed Gunning just as he placed his hand on Olawale's arm. "Great idea, Pete. Why don't you take this young man outside where he can enjoy the amenities while Kofi and I conduct our meeting?"

Olawale pulled his arm from Gunning's grip a bit too forcefully for his own good.

"That is a wonderful idea," said Kofi, also trying to bring the emotional level way down. "Olawale, please take the next two hours to yourself and enjoy the facilities. Who knows when you will get another chance to visit such a lovely place as this?"

Camille nodded to Gunning who stood down. "Pete, please see to it that the concierge sets this young man up in the spa. I am quite sure he can arrange things. Tell him it's a personal favor for me. Put it on our account. The American people owe this young man a debt of gratitude."

Kofi glared at Olawale. His gaze spoke volumes and silenced the young man immediately. "Excellent idea," he said, emphatically accentuating each syllable.

Gunning escorted Olawale out. When they were in the hall, safely out of earshot, Gunning whispered in Olawale's ear. "There's only one thing worse than an African son of a bitch . . . it's an *educated* African son of a bitch like you who thinks he has it all figured out. You're one of the guys I would line up against the wall first . . . before I moved on to shooting any of your backwater dictators. That's what I think of you."

Olawale was scared, but he had a pair of balls on him (even if Kofi considered them hairless). "I don't remember asking."

Gunning shoved Olawale in the general direction of the concierge. "Set him up in the spa for a few hours." He stared at Olawale. "Better yet, find him some island whore who won't mind touching him. Maybe she'll teach you a thing or two in the process, smart guy. You never know."

The concierge, a black man himself, was startled. "This is the Bahamas, sir. We have many people of Afro-Caribbean descent."

Gunning made no effort to mask his disgust. "Yeah . . . we can only hope the next hurricane is big enough. You people aren't very buoyant, are ya?"

Chapter 22

Kofi breathed a sigh of relief. "Thank you. That was going to get ugly. You handled the situation like a true head of state. I am humbled, and I will apologize to you in seven different languages if that helps."

"It's not necessary. There's already too much ugliness. That's why we're here in the first place. What we just witnessed is a microcosm of the way we handle problems throughout the world. Force confronting force. No love."

Kofi stroked his chin and contemplated how to get the meeting back on track. "What you say is very true. It is too easy for the world to think African people are somehow less than human because that's how we are always portrayed . . . starving, indigent, tribal, savage, ignorant. Unfortunately, in too many instances, this is exactly how we behave. That's why it's so important for us to clean up our own backyard, as you say in America. But I need your help, Camille."

"I'm listening."

"What bothers people like Olawale is that the vast majority of African people have never been allowed to evolve with a strong sense of self and spirit. Even asking for your assistance bothers him. But I am different. I accept that even in this post-colonial age, we are controlled by outside interests wielding vast amounts of money. Africa remains the world's colony. Everybody wants a piece and the highest bidders get all they can eat. Even China is involved as one of the leading players now. As such, help must come from the outside as well. It is an odd paradox, but nonetheless true."

Camille stood up and walked over to the window, where she poured herself a fresh lemonade from the pitcher that her personal chef had prepared in the kitchen prior to the meeting. She took a sip while soaking in the view.

"Since you mention it, Kofi, why have you asked to meet with me? I mean . . . I certainly welcome a trip to paradise like the next person. But as you know, I've gone out of my way to accommodate you with a meeting without really knowing what you have in mind. Ordinarily, I wouldn't do this."

Kofi nodded. "Yes, I thank you for that. I owe Zindzi Mandela much thanks for her endorsement. I know that's why you came."

Camille looked at Kofi as she returned to her seat. She noticed again how big his hands were. When they shook earlier, she felt like Kofi could crush hers with only the slightest effort. Kofi's 6'3" frame was intimidating and didn't make her feel quite safe. Kofi got this reaction all the time and understood there was no use in being offended. He was savvy enough to understand that his looming African appearance scared the white folks. As he did so often at times like this, he spoke French to convey the grandeur of his mind in addition to the quality of his physique.

"*De mauvais grain jamai bon pan.* A golden bit does not make the horse any better." He held up his hands. "I am unadorned. What you see is what you get with me. I have received many awards and recognition for my work in the field, but I am only one man. I have seen many things but can only speak so loudly. I have reached out to you because I desperately need your help. There are about five thousand refugees who have fled to an island between Nigeria and Chad. They are about to be slaughtered by *Boko Haram*. To help stop this, I need what only you can do."

Camille sat back in her chair. "Wow, I wasn't expecting that."

"How could you?"

"All of them?" she asked.

"Many will be taken as sex slaves . . . the girls mostly. The rest . . . yes . . . those who are not taken as sex slaves will be slaughtered down to the last. Their bodies will be left rotting in the sun until I burn them in a giant pit. The collective memory will not miss them because these people are alone in the world to begin with. Except for me . . . and, I hope, you, Camille O'Keefe."

Camille breathed deeply, taking in the moment. As connected as she was to the forces of the universe, she could feel the pain and suffering Kofi was foretelling. She was feeling things, measuring them, assessing them. "I felt something like this all day. I knew this was going to be a very significant meeting in terms of my life's work and the lives of others."

Kofi smiled. He had the perfect response. "Everything starts with a thought, an idea. Ideas manifest into things."

Camille laughed. "Oh, stop quoting me, will ya?"

"People around the world are quoting you. Your book is a smash. You also wrote that when we have a new awareness of something that touches us deeper than anything else in a given moment, we are obliged to act on it according to the Law of Attraction."

"Okay, do you have note cards tucked away over there?"

He kept pushing in hope that using Camille's own words would move her. "You mentioned love. Who loves these people?"

He struck a chord that resounded very deeply in Camille. She was silent for a moment. She drank her lemonade and listened to the ice cubes tinkle against the glass tumbler. "I never imagined we'd be talking about so many at once. Five thousand? Really?"

Kofi nodded.

Camille felt the emotion welling up in a single tear. She managed to hold it back. Still, her voice cracked just enough to be audible. "So much death."

Kofi wiped his brow and returned his handkerchief to his pocket. "It will be at the hands of *Boko Haram*. They calculate worth in cash and, of course, dead bodies."

"Yes . . . men tend to do this. When angry men feel they have something to prove, the meek had better start running."

"But the meek never do, do they?"

No," said Camille, sadly. "They stand and await their miserable fate, and carry their suffering with them into their next life."

Kofi got up and poured himself a lemonade, too. He held up the pitcher and motioned to Camille for a refill. She shook her head and pointed her thumb at one of the agents. "I can't. A Secret Service agent in the kitchen oversees everything I eat and drink while I am here. Now that you've handled it, it's considered compromised. You could slip me a Mickey, don't you know."

Kofi looked at the pitcher and made a funny gesture of being impressed. "These must be very special lemons."

"I think my security guys find you very threatening. You can imagine how they feel about the thought of you slipping me anything, if you know what I mean. It's downright un-American."

Kofi looked at two lemon halves floating nipple up in the pitcher. He grunted to himself and put the pitcher down gently. "I would not dream of touching her lemons," he said to the agents.

Camille laughed. "Maybe if you spoke more French, they would forget you are a giant African, but alas. . . ."

Kofi returned to his seat and put his glass down ceremoniously. "I will admire it from a distance but knowing full well it would be fabulous to taste it."

The moment was definitely uncomfortable, even for a free spirit like Camille. Beck would hate Kofi. She reminded herself that Beck probably hated her more.

"I have heard of *Boko Haram*," she said. "Groups like that remind us all that evil exists. It's right there in front of our eyes."

"And yet nobody wants to see it," said Kofi, quickly. "But you do."

"So much hate. That's what it is. A big, giant ball of hate that gets bigger and bigger with every person they murder."

"When I go out into the field, it is usually after the fact. I go where evil men have brought death and destruction. I step on African soil that is soaked with the blood of innocents. It is ironic considering the great riches that are buried beneath that same earth. Sometimes, I think that is the price we pay. Blood . . . we must soak African earth with the blood of innocents in exchange for what we pillage from it."

Camille was suddenly adamant. Kofi obviously pushed a button. "No, Kofi. Demanding human sacrifice is not how the universe works. It does not demand that we sacrifice the purest among us to reconcile the ledger of the heinous. You must stop thinking that way. You will manifest what you are, Kofi, so you'd better redirect your thoughts."

"But isn't this the story of Christ? It's the foundation of Western thought."

"Absolutely not. Jesus accepted his fate. These poor people you're talking about who get slaughtered . . . they are not willing participants. It's totally different."

Kofi was too jaded to lower his armor. He had seen too much to believe in anything but cosmic retribution. "I live in a world of universal retribution, Camille. You must understand, I survey the aftermath of massacres. I document. I try to be the eyes of the world. But I can't make them see. And now, I am faced with something completely different. I find myself *ahead* of the slaughter, and I don't know what to do to save these people. This is bigger than I am."

Camille remained decisive. "Remember something, Kofi. The circumstances of the moment may be bigger than you, as you say. I may even be bigger than those same circumstances and have the ability to help. But there is nothing . . . nothing greater than love. You deal with people—men—who let fly missiles and bullets, thinking that silencing people by killing them will change things. But it never does because you cannot change the immutable laws of the universe no matter how many people men kill. You cannot silence the dead."

Kofi liked what he was hearing. She was righteous. She was powerful. She was the real thing he was seeking. "You know . . . when I arrive at the site of a massacre and conduct my investigation, I call it 'speaking with the dead.'"

"Of course," she exclaimed. "I speak with them all the time. What do you think, everything about a person disappears when they die? That's funny. The laws of the material world disappear when we touch the universe, Kofi. The soul is infinite and loathes constraint. So instead, men should learn to send love instead of hate. The hate will dissipate."

Kofi laughed at the thought. "What you say is true, but it is very hard for men of war to become men of love."

Camille waved her hand at Kofi. "Nonsense. Men are people. People are love. Hatred is a choice, not an essence."

She sipped her drink and watched a droplet of condensation run down the length of the tumbler. Kofi was not entirely sure where this was going. Was Camille on board? He tried to pull her heartstrings again. "Five thousand is but a drop in the bucket compared with the millions who have perished already. But in this case, we can do something about it before the massacre occurs."

Camille cleared her throat. She was uncomfortable. This was completely new to her. Politics was never her forte and mass executions were certainly not something she'd ever dealt with. She began having second thoughts about coming in the first place. At the same time, she felt compelled to help. She felt drawn to those five thousand people, a sort of gravity that pulled her on a molecular level. These were strong souls in service on that island.

She decided to test Kofi a bit. "This is something that could become an international incident," she said. "Perhaps you'd better seek help from people who can advise you better than I can."

"You can't really believe you are ill-equipped to help. Your view of the world, coupled with your fame, makes you the perfect person to help save these people."

Camille looked at Kofi, who, in turn, was looking back at her expectantly. She thought this must be what it was like to be a powerful man like Beck . . . people always waiting for a thumbs up or down on matters that have great personal importance to them, even matters involving life and death, people who have no idea that a decision regarding their fate is being made.

She breathed deeply and kept testing him. "You know, I see in front of me a man with very personal concerns. Clearly, there is a greater good here. Just as important, there is a greater will here. What I mean is, there is a reason I am sitting here today. There's a reason I am here today, a reason greater than myself. In that sense, I am inclined to do everything I can to fulfill my own fate by helping these people. At the same time, I sense your expectations of me may be too high."

"But you are the Red Dragon Lady. You are one of the most popular and powerful women in the world right now."

There was that moniker again. It made Camille grimace. "I never liked that name. It raises expectations too high." She laughed. "There's a perfect example of what I'm talking about."

"Once you published your latest book, the world expected great things from you, Camille. Where once, perhaps, you were content with more personal projects, you are now on the world stage. Millions of people look to you, Camille O'Keefe, for advice, for help . . . to tell them what to do. When you took a stand against the president of the United States, the most powerful man in the world, and declared your right to respect, you inspired untold masses of women struggling daily to survive. You beat the most powerful man in the world, if I may say so. I'm afraid that makes you the most powerful woman in the world. That power, it seems, has found you."

Camille shook her head. "I don't want to tell people what to do."

Kofi sensed the negotiation was at a crucial juncture. "You cannot change that now. It is already done. Your power and renown have taken on a life of their own. It is bigger than you. The world wants the Red Dragon Lady. This is, as you say, your fate."

As Kofi went on detailing the atrocities he'd witnessed through his work with the United Nations, Camille lost herself in thought, ruminating about the situation before her if for no other reason than to protect herself from the savage in what Kofi was detailing. He was, she acknowledged, quite right about her fame. From the moment her book hit the street, she was a sensation. Her car accident, dubious as it was, only made her more of a hero in the eyes of the world. She also knew Kofi was correct about her stature in the eyes of women worldwide. For some time now, millions and millions of dollars had been flowing into her foundation, the Worldwide Fund for Human Equality. New money flowed in daily from small individual donations and magnanimous corporate grants. The amount of money in her foundation's coffers was more than Camille had ever imagined. What she lacked was a plan for putting it to work.

It was never her intention to be a fundraiser. She wanted to fund literacy projects, especially for girls in parts of the world where they were seen more as feral animals than human beings. Never in her wildest dreams did she think millions and millions of dollars would find their way to her cause. With Johnny Long at the helm managing the foundation's investments, Camille could start a global effort with all the necessary support mechanisms in place.

But what Kofi was talking about scared her tremendously. It was totally new, totally outside her realm of worldly experience. She could hardly believe what he was saying was true. Are masses of people really slaughtered like that? If so, how could the world turn a blind eye? It was hard, very hard, for Camille O'Keefe to envision a world where young girls are herded up and sold as sex slaves. How was this not a crisis issue?

The answers to Camille's questions were plain for her to see as she sat listening to Kofi documenting atrocity after atrocity. There was something greater at work here, some systematic evil running rampant across Africa and everywhere else love was lost. That was the great point for her. Where love was lost, hatred would spawn and grow like a weed, choking out everything else until there were no beautiful flowers left. That's what was happening in Africa with these *Boko Haram* people just like it was happening in the Middle East with *ISIS* and *Al Qaeda*. That much she was sure of, for she had often heard Harry Pierson railing against such groups.

Harry Pierson . . . funny he should pop into her mind just then. When she thought of Harry Pierson, new wheels began turning. Kofi had stopped speaking for almost a minute before Camille even noticed.

"You turned me off, didn't you?" he said. "I understand. I sometimes go too far when trying to win support for the cause."

Camille shrugged. "You tried to impress me with how much power I have. That doesn't interest me. How much good I do, how much love I send out to the world . . . now that's something completely different."

Kofi pursed his lips. He looked confused and didn't know what to say.

"You don't know what I am talking about, do you? Of course you don't. How could you? No matter how hard you search for peace, you are a man of war trying to bring peace through violence. Don't you see the problem in that?"

Kofi nodded politely. "It's what I know."

Camille really did feel for the man. "You are a giant in physical stature, Kofi. But I'm afraid your spiritual standing in the eyes of the universe is . . . let's say not quite as large."

"Where I come from, blunt power is the measure of the man. Point blank. I know it is different for you."

"Eh . . . power is power. Power is important. I just get mine from a different place and express it in different ways. This world runs according to the rules of the ego, Kofi. Our career, how much we make and have, what other people think about us . . . that's the ego world. That's not where real power lies. Real power is in *less*. What I mean by that is I get my power from returning to my source, not dressing it up with a bunch of worldly ornaments." She laughed at herself. "Although, as my official First Lady stylist will tell you, I have strayed quite a bit from the path of simplicity."

Kofi looked crestfallen. He was unaccustomed to being challenged in this sort of way. Ordinarily, he would always have a tin of Skoal in his pocket and his gun at hand. He was used to confrontation on these terms. So when Camille told him real power lies elsewhere, it put him outside his world, and he lacked the words necessary to describe what he was feeling. The statesman in him won out. He mustered a smile, faint as it was. He lacked conviction like a third grader posing for a school portrait.

"Your look of disappointment," said Camille, "underscores what I mean about your expectations. You shouldn't look to me for answers. Find them within yourself. Trust in your own nature. As I wrote in one of my books, *dharma* is the way."

Kofi saw Camille slipping away again. He wanted to lash out, to call her a hypocrite for remaining on the sidelines while thousands were murdered. He wanted to mock her in her ivory tower. He was angry and wanted to put his dark aviators on before she saw the vitriol seeping out of his eyes. This was the one thing he would always miss about being in the field—his right to settle things himself . . . definitively.

He suddenly understood what had happened to Olawale earlier. Damned if he wasn't going through the same thing himself. But unlike Olawale, he recognized the pitfall and was determined not to let it get the better of him. The experienced statesman stepped in again.

He made a desperate attempt to keep a sensitive woman like Camille engaged a bit longer. "So then you are not interested in helping save these people? Those who will be cut down are the lucky ones. Think of the hundreds of girls destined to a life as sex slaves . . . if you can call that a life. Is there really nothing you can do?"

Camille cocked her head and moved the hair from her face. She wasn't done testing him. "I didn't say that, Kofi. After all, I've come all this way. And like I said, I feel there is something important about to happen, but I just don't know if Africa is the path . . . *my* path. I know this is upsetting you. I can read it all over you. It's just that I am not sure. This is a big undertaking, and I want to work on my literacy campaign."

Kofi took a deep breath. He longed for his handgun, for the soothing feel of its grip. He brushed his right hand against his lip so he could smell the gun oil. It fortified him. He still wanted to yell at Camille. He wanted to demand answers to questions that never occurred to people of privilege in the West. She wanted to work on her literacy project? Literacy? Really? How can a dead woman read her own obituary? How does knowing how to read help a girl who is used as a sex toy at parties in Bangkok? The animals of *Boko Haram* decapitate the literate and illiterate all the same. That's what he wanted to say. A ten-year-old girl who is about to be gang-raped over and over for five hours straight only to be violated again one more time after she's dead...does reading the Bible help with that? Kofi had seen far too many young corpses lying in pools of blood, semen and shit. They always defecated themselves before they died. So what passage in Shakespeare should a young girl read to help her prepare for that day? Because that day will surely come for an African girl, but it will never come for women of privilege like Camille.

This, and more, he wanted to say. Instead, Kofi rubbed his eyes. He was so angry he could explode and kill everyone in that room. He realized now it was a damn good idea to take his gun away.

"You are upset, Kofi. I know."

He thought to himself... she had no idea. He thought to himself... I would kill you right now if I could, but that would only prove you right. Even a man such as him could grasp the bitter irony in that. He searched desperately for a new appeal.

"I know what you are thinking, Camille. You're not sure getting involved in Africa is the best idea right now. After all, you were recently in a terrible car accident. You have a best seller out and you are also embarking upon a new life apart from President Rosemore, and that has to be finalized. Then there's the matter of expertise. You don't know very much about Africa other than what you see in the media and what you've heard about my professional involvement with some very ugly events. You know how dangerous things can get. I mean . . . we're talking about thousands of refugees being slaughtered. We're talking about places like Rwanda or Nigeria or Chad . . . places like that, right? It's very, very dangerous, especially for a woman."

Kofi saw Camille bristle at his last comment. He saw another way in. He would attempt to goad her. He cleared his throat. "Believe me, Camille. I understand. It is not a place for women. No, I shouldn't put it that way. What I mean to say is that most women would shy away from such places. After all, the women in those parts of the world are being tortured, raped and murdered, so why would a successful woman like you want to get involved in places like that?"

Camille stared at Kofi, trying to discern if he was trolling her or if he really believed only men should undertake acts of heroism. She couldn't decide . . . most likely both. "You make me sound like some sort of bourgeois prig who only feels safe in a drawing room lest she be whisked away to an asylum for hysterical females. I don't even know what a drawing room is much less a prig. But those are the words that come to mind."

Kofi smiled. "I apologize. That was not my intent."

But of course, it was. Camille knew this. It bothered her. She crossed her legs and flicked the hair from her face. "Your comments bother me, Kofi. Yeah . . . I am bothered. Surely you know firsthand what difference one person can make? That's why you called this meeting in the first place."

"Point taken," replied Kofi.

Camille held up her forefinger. "Let me finish. I dare say, there is just as much difference one *woman* can make, especially when that woman is me, Camille O'Keefe, the Red Dragon Lady, one of the most popular women in the world."

"I appreciate that," said Kofi.

She held up her forefinger again. "Let me finish, please, because I am not sure you do appreciate what I am talking about. Gender is not the issue here. The issue is control versus trust. I trust in my own sensibilities, in my own intuition. Sure, this whole thing worries me. I won't lie to you . . . all this talk of mass murder, rape and slavery scares the hell out of me. I can feel their pain, you know. It's part of my gift. So part of me wants to run away. That's the logical part. But my spiritual self, my intuitive self, knows I am needed. I am connected to those poor people in a way that transcends the confines of ego that usually define money, war, politics and all that man stuff. I am needed as a woman, and I am needed as the specific woman *I am*."

It seemed that Kofi's last-ditch effort had worked when he suggested Camille wasn't "man enough" for the job. He sat back and breathed a sigh of relief but dared not speak for fear of undoing what he seemed to have achieved.

Still annoyed, Camille pressed him for a comment. "So what do you have to say?"

Kofi sat up straight. "It seems to me these are precisely the sort of people who need help and spiritual guidance the most."

"Yes," she said. She thought before continuing. "The fortunate must seek out the unfortunate. It is universal law, and I can't ignore it. What else do you have to say before we wrap up?"

"I want to show you something." Kofi reached into his attaché case. The two agents tensed, so Kofi moved very deliberately. He took out a manila envelope and walked it over to Camille. He laid it down in front of her and returned to his seat.

Camille was hesitant to even touch it. "My God, the energy emanating from this thing is terrible. My ears are ringing like bells. I can only imagine what's inside."

Kofi wanted the power of that unopened envelope to weigh heavily on Camille. He'd seen the photos. There was a terrible darkness inside trying to get out. It was the darkness of the dead. It was unmistakable to a medium like Camille. That's why she felt it so viscerally. The ringing in her ears was the collective voice of the dead trying to tell their stories all at once.

Camille placed her hand on the envelope and pushed it back immediately. "Wow . . . wow." A tear welled up in her eye. "Take it back. I don't need to see what's inside to know how terrible life is for those people."

She nodded to one of the Agents, who took the envelope and returned to his post.

Kofi was undaunted. "So I know that you have seen both sides of the world . . . the richest and the poorest among them."

Camille said nothing. It struck her as ironic that this man was pleading for her help when only two years ago, she was nobody of note. Like Beck, Kofi's ego dominated him. But she saw his willingness to make positive change where he could. Failing to do so was Beck's greatest failure.

She had just about made up her mind to walk away from the whole thing. "One last question, Kofi. Why can't you assemble a delegation from the African nations to help? Why is Africa not handling this?"

Kofi had heard this many times before. It annoyed him now no less than the first time it was thrown back at him. He knew that the more people were able to shove human savagery into some remote corner of the world, the more they could distance themselves from the truth of their own complicity and collusion.

"Why do you think this is an African problem?" he replied. "Why is *Al Qaeda* or *ISIS* just a Muslim problem? It is the world's problem."

"That's what the United Nations is for," said Camille. "You know that. Why come to me? Why go outside your own organization?"

Kofi's frustration showed. His voice grew louder. "Because my organization is part of the problem."

He collected himself and went to the service area for some fruit. It was a welcome respite for creating some space for cooler heads to prevail. Kofi thought for a moment as he returned to his seat and enjoyed some fresh pineapple chunks.

"Tell me," he said. "You have voiced your concern about the perils of Africa. But again, what makes you think this is solely an African problem?"

"I suppose that's a fair question."

Kofi wiped his fingers on a napkin and pushed his plate away. He reached into his attaché case again, pulled out a piece of paper, and read from it. "As with the rules of nature that are so applicable to the essence of our spiritual selves, sometimes faraway people and distant places can reveal a great deal about ourselves right here where we stand today." He put the paper back into his case.

Camille laughed out loud. "Oh, boy. Here we go."

Kofi folded his hands and smiled. "You, Camille O'Keefe . . . you wrote that in your book *The World Is a Looking Glass* twenty years ago. Have you changed that much?"

"It was twenty-three years ago," chirped Camille. "And there's no need to remind me."

"You are able to walk in so many different worlds," continued Kofi. "That's what makes you so great. You are the woman who attended so many political events and White House functions. You are also the sparkle in the world's eye for being brave enough to expose not just the truth about the president and other unscrupulous men we hold in high esteem, but also to reveal your own vulnerability and deep hurt at the same time. You have an amazing ability to connect with everyone because you practice humility and wield it against your own inclinations toward egotism. That is why you are the woman I came halfway across the globe to recruit."

"More Red Dragon Lady stuff?"

"Only moments ago, you referred to yourself by that name. You are becoming that idea."

Camille rolled her eyes.

Kofi didn't know what else to do. He slapped his giant hand down on the table for effect. The glassware vibrated. It startled Camille. "I know you look at me and think . . . this large African man is here today wanting something for himself. And that it is an African problem. But it is not. Africa is the world's problem because the world is Africa's problem. We can fill this room with tales of African woe perpetrated by the world at large. That is what you see on television. We all know that tale already."

He reached his long arm over to the humidor from which he earlier took a few cigars. He opened the lid. "Perhaps President Rosemore liked to enjoy a fine cigar from time to time?"

"Oh, yes. God knows what else he did with it in the Oval Office."

Kofi motioned toward the humidor. "Pick one randomly . . . indulge me, please."

Camille reached in. Her arms were not nearly as long as Kofi's, so she stood up to do so. She held up the stick as if it was a bingo ball.

"Ah!" said Kofi. "A Cohiba Black. Cuban, of course. Would it surprise you to know that the one cigar you are holding sells for $25?"

To Camille, it was an absurdity. "$25 to smell like an old ashtray? Maybe I should sell my old socks?"

Kofi laughed at the thought of the Red Dragon Lady selling her dirty socks on the Internet because he knew there would be many men out there willing to pay top dollar for Camille O'Keefe's foot stink. He would be one of them, but he kept that to himself. "As your new friend, I would advise against that."

Camille gasped. "You don't think. . . ."

"Oh, I'm quite sure there would be a bidding war," said Kofi. He would be right there in the midst of it. Again, he kept that to himself.

Kofi took another Cohiba and held it up like a second bingo ball. "What we hold in our hands, Camille, is almost three week's wages for the average man in Angola, to name but one country. $1.75 a day. That's about average. In the Congo, the world's poorest country, the average is $1 a day. This little bit of rolled tobacco that we light up so casually and at our whim is far more than a luxury to the average African. It's unthinkable."

There was silence. Camille was a bit embarrassed, especially considering the grandiosity of their surroundings, not to mention the cost of her *haute couture* clothing and accessories.

Kofi slid the cigar into his attaché case. If nothing else, that was coming with him. "This is the story you are accustomed to hearing about Africa, yes?"

Camille sighed. "Point taken."

"And yet not all Africans are poor or dying or getting slaughtered. There are many wealthy Africans in Angola, to use the same example. In fact, there are residential communities in Luanda where houses cost half a million dollars and up. It's ironic, but Olawale's uncle owns several for investment purposes."

"I get that there is tremendous income inequality," replied Camille. "But there needs to be significant movement toward spiritual freedom in those countries if change is going to happen. Then again, I feel that way about all people everywhere."

Kofi nodded. "Point taken, as well. So, there is the Africa the world sees on television. What the cameras don't show you is that the Chinese built those homes in Luanda and helped clean up the slums of Chicala as part of a side deal with Vice President Vincent

Mobande in exchange for oil-drilling rights. And by 'clean up' you know what I mean, don't you Camille?"

"Unfortunately, I do."

Kofi continued. "Needless to say, a handful of people in Vincent Mobande's circle have made themselves rich beyond every imagination, selling off Angola's oil rights to the Chinese and, frankly, any other nation quick enough to cut a deal."

Camille began to see where Kofi was going with all this. It dawned on her that maybe Kofi was right, maybe there was a global story here.

"Men like Olawale's uncle represent European banking interests that finance everything. It's a global web encompassing Africa's largest front and shell companies like Sissegal. Of course, the Swiss happily provide the coffers and shell corporations through which corrupt African leaders, hand-in-hand with world banks, siphon, funnel and stash their billions. And when one of these corrupt leaders dies suddenly, as they often seem to do, the Swiss system simply absorbs the cash that nobody else knows is there. It's a booming resource industry for China and the West, and a nice little side gig for the Swiss.

"And your point?"

"My point is simply this . . . it all ends up in the West. It all becomes the cars, and petrol, and jewelry, and clothing, and widgets that fill the days of Americans and Europeans. Point blank, there it is."

"Is that why Olawale seems to take this so personally?"

Kofi clucked his tongue. "His uncle has facilitated many deals with Sissegal. Olawale is ashamed. It comes out as anger and defensiveness in a young man."

"I understand. One day he will learn that the process of letting go of the things we are most attached to is a process that yields the most fruit."

"The problem is that men like Olawale's uncle are respected throughout the world. You wrote about that in your latest book, Camille. I remember it . . . you ask 'why do we tolerate and even admire such terrible behavior from the people we put in power?'

So few control so much and so many, Camille. You said it yourself. This is perhaps more true of Africa than anywhere else in the world. That is why we need your help."

"Yeah . . . I guess I did say that. Ego is a powerful thing. It runs the mindless, man-driven drilling machine you're talking about."

"God has blessed the African people with a vast array of natural resources," continued Kofi. "The most in the world, I'd venture to say. And yet, our people have the least. It is the greatest embarrassment to humanity of our time. Sissegal is just one in a vast network of large shell corporations set up to funnel billions of international investment dollars for oil rights into the pockets of a few guys. The Chinese are there . . . the Dutch are there. . . . What's unique about Africa, though, is that politics is enforced with the gun and calculated in body counts."

Camille leaned back in her chair. "That's one way of putting it. I'm beginning to see what you mean when you say the world is Africa's problem."

Kofi grew more serious. "Make no mistake about it, Camille. I am asking you to help prevent the slaughter of thousands of innocent people. But sooner or later, everything is connected to the big business of pillaging Africa's resources."

Camille was honest about her inexperience. "It's so different from America."

"It is, and it isn't. The story does not stop with Angola, I'm afraid. The same things hold true for oil in Nigeria, tantalum in the Congo and Rwanda, diamonds in Zimbabwe. The list goes on. If you look closely enough on a map of Africa, you will see a long line of multinational corporations lining up to transact deals with small groups of powerful men who control the continent.

"As for the people, they are systematically chewed up in civil wars, wars funded by the sale of these very same raw materials. When the people get in the way, they are systematically murdered. Even terrorist groups like *Boko Haram* have ties to the diamond trade and smuggling knockoffs made in China through Africa and out to the Western world, where materialistic consumers wait to snatch them up."

"Really?"

He shakes his head. "They're not even real."

"What is real?" asked Camille. "The only thing that's true is a thing that doesn't change. So nothing in this dimension is true."

He looked straight at Camille. "And *that* is why I say this is not an African problem but rather the world's problem. Because the world is Africa's problem. Make no mistake about it, Camille O'Keefe. Your involvement may bring peril your way. If we get too close to the bloodline of money, your life may be in danger. I cannot guarantee your safety."

"There are never any guarantees, Kofi. Not long ago, I was lying upside down in a car wreck nearly dead. Who's to say where things will lead? I need to do what's right. Then, at least, I know my path will lead me in a virtuous direction. That's really all I can believe."

Kofi just nodded. He knew all too well that a delicate woman like Camille didn't comprehend what it felt like to visit the site of a devastated village after a "cleanup," after the systematic roundup and execution of hundreds, even thousands, of people . . . gone without a trace as if they never existed. How could she contemplate such a thing?

Camille's was a world of spiritual transcendence. She believed with all her heart that what happens to people in this physical world is merely a fleeting manifestation of a life plan one's spirit agrees to before entering a body. But as Olawale pointed out, it's easy to say when you're not the Rwandan boy whose arm is lopped off with a machete because he refuses to execute his parents. It was all very difficult for Camille to imagine because she was not the girl praying for death while being gang-raped in all orifices simultaneously.

Divine contract? Who would agree to this? And yet, for Camille O'Keefe, life was an exploration, even if it meant witnessing great horror. She was aware that she was on the precipice, on the verge of experiencing something new. But never for a moment was she to assume that it would be comfortable. Quite the contrary, as their conversation developed, she began to recognize for the first time in her life that she had come to this world with a mission as yet unfilled—to bear witness to crimes against humanity that nobody else was willing to see even though they were happening all around us all the time.

Yes, there was a new story to be written, an intricate yet brutal pastiche of hope set against incredible savagery. Camille had the power to bring light to darkness and send "love to hate," as she was fond of saying. At the same time, the story might be so much bigger than she. It could be so big, in fact, that it could consume her completely and whisk her away viciously.

Sitting there in the Bahamas, Camille O'Keefe decided that Kofi passed the test. It was a risk she had to take. This was the moment she accepted it all . . . including calling on Harry Pierson, of all people, for help.

"I hope I have not scared you off," said Kofi cautiously. "I just want to be honest about the risks."

"No, no. It's okay. I feel I need to warn you, too."

Kofi was amused. "You warn me?"

Camille shrugged. "I can do my best to get this issue in front of the right people. In fact, I have the very man in mind. He is different from me, though. I believe in love; he is a man of war like you. I can try to enlist his help, but I cannot guarantee what he'll do. It can be anything from a flat-out refusal to a clandestine operation that kills a whole bunch of people. I really don't know."

Kofi made nothing of it. "Like you said, there are no guarantees. More importantly, I interpret your comments to mean you have agreed to help?"

"Of course, I will help. How could I do anything else? After all, I am the Red Dragon Lady."

Kofi stood up and stretched his enormous wingspan. "Perhaps this is a good time to order some lunch? I would like a big salad . . . with lobster."

And so it was done.

Chapter 23

Maiduguri is the heart of the Borno State and the nerve center for *Boko Haram* in Nigeria. The city represents the struggle for control and self-determination that characterizes Nigeria and many other African nations. It is a microcosm of the global struggle between freedom and intolerance, between life and death, that takes the weakest and most defenseless first. These people are the low-lying fruit for *ISIS, Al Qaeda,* and *Boko Haram* factions everywhere.

To Aliyu and his men, as well as all his supporters in the region, Maiduguri would always be Yerwa, the original Kanuri name. The Kanuri are Muslim and have rooted themselves in Northern Nigeria for centuries. They hate the non-Muslim Igbo people and exterminate them whenever possible. Aliyu's faction is but the most recent manifestation of a war over ethnic cleansing that has been raging on for as long as people have been killing each other. Maiduguri bears the scars of the conflict. Local police are no match for *Boko Haram*. Fires burn and gunshots fracture the otherwise serene night. Bombs explode randomly often enough to keep non-Muslims in constant fear but not so often as to expose Aliyu and his men.

The fight expands consistently, diligently. Maiduguri is about 100 miles from Lake Chad where thousands of refugees go about their lives like bugs completely ignorant of when they will be squashed underfoot. Aliyu and his men will drive up past Zundur and then on to Monguno, where they will meet the arms dealer who has the extra weapons and ammunition they will need for the slaughter. Then it's on to Doro Gowon, where their contact will equip them with the boats they need to transport their *sibya* back to Maiduguri. The girls will be divided up, some taken as brides and concubines by the *Boko Haram* men, and the rest transported down the A4 to Bama where they will be sold off to slave traders. From then on, the *sibya* will cease being human beings. From then on, they will be nothing more than brides and orifice holes for filling before they're finally snuffed out. Nobody will remember these girls, for most of their families will have been cut down on the island. Like bugs underfoot, they will have come and gone without notice in the cycle of life that characterizes modern-day Africa.

Maiduguri sits between the A3 and A4 highways. It is most definitely a crossroads. There is a definite hustle and bustle to the city. The streets are choked with rusted, wheezing cars and trucks that are held together with spit, mud and duct tape. The gunfire and bomb blasts have become so familiar that nobody flinches when the vehicles cough and backfire. Ubiquitous mopeds dart in and out of traffic. Those fortunate enough to have cars—those who can afford the petrol—feel entitled to yell at the myriad of pedestrians roaming about. Goats meander everywhere as well. The scene has an air of the carnivalesque. Even the ramshackle structures passing for houses seem a bit ludicrous, with their bleached stucco walls and brightly colored corrugated roofs that look almost Mediterranean.

The evening draws near, casting a golden hue over the dry dirt and scrub brush that stretches for miles outside Maiduguri. As the sun prepares to set, it casts a shadow across the city, a visible reminder that life in Maiduguri is thus divided in two. On one side is the general population, the thousands of people going about their business in all those rusted-out cars and buzzing mopeds, or hoofing it around amid the goats and cinderblock houses with cracking plaster. Life for these people can be as depleted as the river Ngadda Maiduguri in the dry season . . . caked, cracked, stunted, and shunted.

Simultaneously, the steady flow of wealth has found its way into a few hands, as it always does in a resource state like Nigeria. Another world exists in Maiduguri as if tucked away in another dimension. It is replete, energetic, effusive and enthusiastic. This is the world of gated communities and luxury high-rises, private schools, the university and teaching hospital. The lavish villas in the gated communities boast fancy landscaping, the luxury high-rises tower above the desiccated earth, scorched asphalt and human refuge below.

This other landscape is not congested with dilapidated vehicles but rather accented with fine Mercedes sedans. The lawns are piped for sprinklers and always green. There are no goats grazing out on the manicured lawns in these gated communities. The resource state erects gates and fences to keep them safely separated. These lofty high-rise condos stand too high above the dusty, quasi-urban landscape below to allow reality to infect the air of success. Where most Maidugurians never have enough of anything and must root around for slop sustenance, the fortunate few feed off the marvelous cornucopia that is the African resource state as it doles out billions to those connected to shell corporations like Sissegal and a host of others. Fancy restaurants characterize this part of town, restaurants where a single entrée costs about as much as most people earn in a month.

But life has changed in Maiduguri now. There is something new growing in the interstitial spaces of the city, something viral and festering that, like HIV, will soon overwhelm the continent. And just as disease spreads from person to person, so, too, grows the scourge of *Boko Haram* and radical Islam. The undercurrent of violent change has become too loud to ignore. In places like Maiduguri, it has already happened. The undercurrent has become the predominant tenor with a frenzied pitch. The simple divisions between the Haves and Have-Nots are eroding quickly according to plan as mosques and other Islamic buildings are built or renovated at a swift pace and stand as a testament to the power of Allah, not just in Maiduguri but on the entire continent as well.

Sporadic gunfire pierces the otherwise serene evenings in Maiduguri. The cityscape is littered with burned-out shells of cars and non-Muslim buildings that have been destroyed by *Boko Haram*.

The more buildings that are destroyed, the more mosques and related facilities are built in their ashes—zoning plans brought to you by *Boko Haram*. The Maiduguri police are overwhelmed. Aliyu and his men are better weaponized, better financed and better connected. If the police arrest or kill one of his men, the repercussions are swift and severe. Aliyu has already taken out entire families as retribution. The Nigerian government could step in, and sometimes it does as a token gesture for the world media. But too much violence might disrupt the resource state and the flow of oil money. In the end, the resource state is about the resource state, so municipalities like Maiduguri are left to fend for themselves on a level that will not attract anyone's attention because, really . . . who cares about these people? It's about the money, not the people.

A resource state like Nigeria has an underworld in Maiduguri that operates in much the same way as the surface world. As it is above, so it is below. Graft is the path of least resistance, and Aliyu usually opts to buy off his opposition. Once the local authorities are bought, Aliyu and his men pretty much have their way. Occasionally, he must orchestrate a bombing just to remind everyone who's really in charge of the streets. Bombings also serve notice to non-Muslim Nigerians . . . *Boko Haram* is coming to systematically eradicate all non-believers whose very existence insults the good name of Allah. What *ISIS* did in Paris, Istanbul and Brussels, *Boko Haram* does in Maiduguri regularly. The only difference is that Maiduguri is not Paris or Brussels. When Aliyu tortures, murders, kidnaps and rapes anonymous African women, few people know or care about it so long as the cash flow of the resource state is not disrupted.

The myopia of greed prevents everyone in power from seeing the inevitable—*Boko Haram* will come for them, too. It's entropy, violent energy leading to complete human demise. The safe distance created by the resource state through fear and corruption will not last. Modernity, no matter how advanced the appearance, cannot hold out against a never-ending onslaught of cave dwellers seeking to return us to the Stone Age by any means necessary. The great aspirations of the resource state—the gated indulgence and the high-rise aloofness—cannot withstand the force of radical terrorism forever, for radical terrorism dishes out an ancient vehemence powerful enough to erode our modern institutions.

Aliyu Adelabu and men like him are hungry for change, and they will stop at nothing short of complete annihilation. *Boko Haram* is a modern-day anarchist group the likes of which the world has never seen because the world has never seen a movement seeking to roll back the clock so far. Aliyu Adelabu is *Boko Haram*; *Boko Haram* is radical Islam. The transitive theory is at work. Eventually, Aliyu will knock down every door in Maiduguri. He will riddle every statue with bullets and destroy every architectural remnant of cultural antiquity because it is the work of infidels. He will murder writers, journalists, cartoonists . . . anyone forsaking his perverse definition of Allah. He will erase infidel history as if it never existed. He could teach Hitler and Stalin a thing or two about making people vanish.

In Maiduguri, Aliyu hunts these people down, just as he prepares to hunt down thousands of refugees hiding out in the middle of Lake Chad. Exposure is one of his goals. It's only a matter of time before he tears down those gated walls with a degree of savagery and vehemence the world cannot ignore. He loathes those people and knows there are no gates or high-rises tall enough to withstand the mighty force of Allah, *inshallah*. He will bring that force.

For the time being, though, the power of wealth, the power of the resource state and shell companies like Sissegal, still hold sway over him, for he needs the resources to buy and sell on the black market to fund his private war. He pays for some of his weapons and ammunition using bitcoin he receives from selling coltan. Coltan is a key component in just about every cell phone. His coltan was smuggled out of the Democratic Republic of Congo, where Aliyu has a source. Aliyu uses diamonds, too. That's how he purchased the boats necessary for transporting the sex slaves off the island. The diamonds were smuggled by one his men from nearby Central African Republic near the border with Cameroon. It's all transacted on the darknet.

Diamonds are not a slave girl's best friend. Neither are coltan, ivory and oil. Without these resources there could be no raid on the island. Without these resources there could be no *Boko Haram*. Without the resource state, *Boko Haram, ISIS and Al Qaeda* could not exist, for they are financially dependent upon the very system they wish to bring down in flames. Men like Aliyu live with the irony. Theirs is a relatively two-dimensional world in which lesser evils are tolerated for the greater will of Allah as they choose to define Him. Recognition of hypocrisy is not a strong suit among these guys. It does not matter to Aliyu that his parents live in one of those gated villas and that their banking money sent him to private school in Johannesburg and then on to the London School of Economics. This only makes him angrier and more self-righteous. He will show his parents that he is truly a free man, a man of Allah.

Chapter 24

Aliyu's house does not convey the degree of power he holds in the city. It sits near three mosques on an unnamed road near a large park off Kashim Ibrahim Road. The cinderblock structure is plastered, but the sun has taken its toll. What was once a bright white façade is now faded and cracked. The cinderblock shows through in places, and a rust-colored band runs around the perimeter of the upper and lower portions of the exterior walls. The terracotta-looking roof is not actually made of terracotta tile but rather corrugated metal painted to look like tile.

Aliyu is well-educated; his parents are rich. He believes his faux terracotta roof is a bourgeois fake. He lives with it. So do his four lieutenants sitting around him. They are all well-educated . . . England and Belgium. They became radicalized in different ways, but their stories are largely the same. They came from money but lacked purpose. They were depressed and angry at nothing in particular. They were just angry. They all fell into dissatisfaction that happened within various malcontents in the Muslim student population. Although none of them knew each other when they returned to Nigeria, Aliyu and his four lieutenants became an extended family that helped them to refocus their depression and resentment. Allah became the way for them.

From there, it was only a matter of time before they came into contact with a much darker element. That's how radical terrorist organizations recruit. They find alienated young people, bring them into an extended family and then drive a wedge between the new recruit and their real family. That wedge is radical Islam, and there is no going back. The massive outreach is a systematic program wending its way across the globe via social media sites powered by various *jihadi* groups like *ISIS* and *Boko Haram*.

They use the same encryption technology that powers the darknet. This gives them instant access to millions of young people searching for ways to channel their rage. They communicate out in the open, flagrantly, via Twitter and other mobile platforms using apps that offer the same encryption capabilities. Thanks to darknet-style encryption, people like Aliyu are everywhere and yet nowhere to be seen.

Several months after returning to Maiduguri from studying abroad, Aliyu was on the verge of suicide. This, also, made him much like his future comrades in arms. Unlike his four lieutenants, who are Nigerian Muslims by birth, Aliyu is not. He turned to Islam for salvation, as a means of transcending what he saw as the meaninglessness of his life. He learned discipline and commitment. He learned of Allah's greatness. He changed his name to Aliyu and no longer muttered the infidel Christian name his parents gave him when he was born. The man who was raised in a gated community, attending the best private schools, found Allah in order to be reborn as something glorious . . . Aliyu Adelabu.

He met his four fellow *jihadists* in a Maiduguri *madrasa* for adults where radical Islam was able to pull them in like a cult does with alienated American college students. The malicious *madrasas* produce terrorists who detonate themselves in the name of Allah like cults produce bald vegans selling pansies. In the *madrasa*, Aliyu learned that suicide is vehemently forbidden and would bring great shame to his memory. But as a *fedayeen*, as a *shahid*, as a holy martyr, his name would live on forever. Sacrificing oneself in the name of Allah is not the same as suicide. It is the exact opposite. Aliyu learned to sever the relationship with his infidel Christian family. He learned the depression and anger he felt could not result in suicide but could properly lead to his becoming a holy martyr worthy of reverence.

It was akin to *ISIS* overthrowing *Al Qaeda* for prominence in the Middle East, just as *Al Qaeda* overthrew *Hezbollah*, and so on. The son eventually comes to kill the father. *Al Qaeda* lived in caves and operated in secret. *ISIS* openly recruits young people via social media, boasts affluent members among its ranks and makes no qualms about thumping their chests in public. *Al Qaeda* sent the world fuzzy, outdated videotapes shot in front of shabby façades clandestinely smuggled by faceless couriers; *ISIS* delivers its message through the masses, through the *umma*. They say it a thousand different ways . . . *we are coming for you.*

That's how Aliyu came to understand that "suicide bomber" was a derogatory term invented by the West to disparage and shame righteous *jihadists*, which is what he came to consider himself. He learned that the media was propaganda and a tool of Zionism. One day, the five of them were discussing the Jewish threat to the Al-Asqa Mosque and how they wished they could wipe the Jews from the map. Israel was so far away, though. What could they possibly do to make a difference? That's when they met some men from *Boko Haram*, thugs, wannabe gangsters, looking to recruit more thugs and wannabes. Unlike the average terrorist who is reduced to violence through abject poverty, displacement and hopelessness, Aliyu and his four friends—charismatic, well-educated, committed to the cause—fit the bill to become the future leaders.

They immediately recognized the opportunity to amass power for themselves. It took only six months for Aliyu to rise to the top within the organization. That's what Aliyu and his cohorts loved. They longed for that kind of power, that kind of respect. Their fathers bought respect from people through corrupt resource deals. Their mothers married into it. In contrast, Aliyu and his lieutenants sought to grab it for themselves. When they first joined up with *Boko*

Haram, they considered the men in charge to be imbeciles. That was the old regime . . . outdated, weak, running around disorganized in crappy white pick-ups, firing their rifles in the air and robbing smugglers. That was not the life for Aliyu and his men. They sought to bring respect to Allah and, in the process, command respect for themselves, respect they could never have living in the shadow of their corrupt fathers. This was what they learned when they became radicalized. The wedge was driven deep.

In a matter of months, Aliyu and his lieutenants overthrew the *Boko Haram* leadership. It was easy. They acted like they were in an American Mafia movie. They even put plastic down on the floor before assassinating the old leader. They were waiting for the fool in his own house, the very same house Aliyu now occupies. Each fired a single round into the man's head. A headless body was all that remained of the former *Boko Haram* leader. They then paid a visit to the remaining chain of command. Each man met the same fate . . . five bullets exploding his head. That night, they dumped the bodies and the larger pieces of skull and brain in the middle of Maiduguri and served notice . . . we are coming for you. Twenty bullets, exploding four heads, and the deed was done.

Aliyu was now in charge. He took up residence in the dead leader's house and the very next day set about instituting the new agenda for *Boko Haram* Maiduguri. They had the city's attention . . . and its respect. Next, it would be Nigeria, then all of Africa . . . and then the entire world. He vowed to continue his war until he took up residence in the Aso Villa, the Presidential Palace in Abuja. From there, he would not rest until he stood atop the mount overlooking the Al-Asqa Mosque, proclaiming himself the man who finally drove out the Jews.

As for his family . . . he had a special plan in store for them.

Aliyu Adelabu was the man with a large ego. He wanted to be Camille O'Keefe's greatest nightmare. She does not yet know who he is. But she knows the darkness he brings forth wherever he goes. She felt it when she touched the envelope Kofi handed her. She refused to touch it again because she knew it contained images of pure evil. That's why she agreed to help Kofi.

Chapter 25

When night falls, the interstitial places come to life in Maiduguri. Gunfire and explosions may shatter the quiet. Nobody knows for sure except Aliyu and his men. Four of his closest confidants sit in a semicircle in front of him as they discuss the pending attack on the island. A king without a proper throne, Aliyu sits on a couch facing the others. From within these walls, Aliyu has built an impressive network for selling black-market resources either traded or hijacked from smugglers. Most of all, he has an amazing knack for the coltan market, and moves a great deal of the sought-after metal in order to fund his operation. He studied economics at the university.

There is still an hour or so before the sun turns into a burning orange ball and plunges into the horizon. *Salat al-Asr,* afternoon prayer, is over for Aliyu and his men. *Salat al-Maghrib,* the evening prayer, will not begin until sunset and will last until the sun's luminescent red light is gone from the sky. That gives the men time . . . time to plan the murder of thousands of refugees. Later, the mosques sound out their *adhan,* their call to prayer. Arabic will echo through every street and household in Maiduguri. Then they will pray the *Maghrib.* For Aliyu, it is far more than a call to worship God. It is a declaration to the city that Allah is here and that

Islam will envelop everything. Aliyu is devout. Five times a day he prays, just as Muslims do all over the world. Each time he hears the *adhan* boom through the city, Aliyu is pleased. It feels to him as if the city is momentarily returned to its former glory, when it was known as Yerwa.

The couch Aliyu sits on is a faded gold and green. It looks like crushed velvet, but it's really velour. The cloud that poofs up when the cushions are beaten is genuine Maiduguri road dust. This ubiquitous, gritty silt has infiltrated every nook and cranny of the house. Aliyu likes this. It reminds him of the way he plans to infiltrate every corner of the non-Muslim world as he works to make his caliphate and pan-Islam a reality. On each side of the couch is a lamp atop unadorned, circular end tables. Neither lamp has a shade. The generator chugs along out back, but both lamps are turned off. The coffee table in front of the couch is battered but serves its purpose. Five steaming cups of tea sit around the teapot in the center of the table in much the same way that Aliyu's four lieutenants sit facing him.

His lieutenants are as dark-skinned as he. It is difficult to see their faces with the lights off and the shades drawn. They all wear *kaftans* of various colors. The robes distinguish them from non-Muslims. So do the head scarves they wear. Underneath their *kaftans* they wear army fatigues. The juxtaposition is exactly what they want, for it embodies the duality of their lives as *jihadists* . . . they fight, but they fight for Allah.

The living room is as drab as the seating. The white sheetrock walls are dirty and cracked. The remainder of his three-room house reflects a sort of pragmatic negligence. All the windows are shaded, of course. Aliyu demands that the meals his men eat be equally ascetic. He does not exclude himself from this mandate. The kitchen eating area is sparse . . . an old fridge, a few plates, a table with five austere wooden chairs. One pan and one pot constitute the cookware. It's all he needs. He eats mostly white rice accompanied by some morsel that meets his fancy at the time. A few plates and glasses sit on the counter next to an old bread basket. A single, dirty light bulb attached to a white cord hangs down from the center of the room.

His bedroom is equally Spartan. A thin mattress covered by a faded blue sheet and worn blanket sit in the corner. The window is boarded up as he cannot sleep without the added sense of security. There is a *musallah*, a prayer rug, on the floor, a dresser with basic clothing and a lamp on top of it. There is no central air, no walk-in closet or Jacuzzi tub. There is no television, no Blu-ray player, no Xbox. There are just the basic necessities, a cell phone and his plans . . . always plenty of plans.

No family pictures hang on the stark walls, even though his family lives a short distance away in one of Maiduguri's finest gated communities. He disavowed his family long ago as part of his commitment to *Boko Haram*. When he converted, they could not comprehend what he became. In return, he found them disgusting for their bourgeois vices and lack of proper divinity. They weren't Muslim, so they could never understand how offensive they were to him. In the *madrasa*, his values were completely erased as he was reprogrammed with a new code, *Sharia Law*, and a new way of thinking.

Now, several years later, Aliyu sees it all so clearly. His family is part of the problem, part of the infidel virus that has to be eradicated. He is no longer the weak, depressed, misguided bourgeois youth he once was when he went by the name he dares not speak. In his new position as leader of *Boko Haram* Maiduguri, Aliyu Adelabu is a powerful man, a man worthy of respect. His men are willing to kill for him. His men are willing to die for him. Every morning before he prays the *Farj*, Aliyu reminds himself that he decides life and death. He reminds himself that this is real power.

He acknowledges the simple logic of the *jihad*—one day, he will storm the gates that surround his parent's villa, kick down the door of the home he grew up in, and throw his worthless parents against the wall along with his whore of a sister who screws any soccer player she can get her hands on. Taken as a whole, Aliyu's family—the family whose name he will no longer utter—is an embarrassment to him.

He is thinking just that as he sits there on the couch. He strokes his beard as he praises himself for the hundredth time this day.

His four lieutenants are watching a YouTube video on one of their cell phones. They are laughing and yucking it up.

"Listen to that," says one of the men.

One of the others punches his arm. "How are we supposed to hear if you keep bleating like a goat?"

The two men begin arguing while the others chide them.

"Okay, okay. . . . I will restart the video."

He swipes the screen and the video restarts. The men lean in and watch with pride. They are watching a video clip of a soccer game played in Turkey two days after the *ISIS* attacks in Paris that rocked Europe from its somnambular complacency. During a moment of silence before the game, tens of thousands of Muslims began whistling wildly, their way of booing the moment of silence. Then comes the bit the men love the most . . . the crowd starts chanting *Allahu Akbar, Allahu Akbar.* The chant morphs into *Martyrs will never be forgotten . . . Martyrs will never be forgotten. . . .*

"Listen to that," cries one of the men. "*ISIS* is everywhere."

"The West does not understand," says Aliyu without looking up. It is difficult to see his face with the lights off. "They are still trying to fight *Al Qaeda* in some cave somewhere."

"Or *Hamas*," jokes one of the men. "Maybe they don't even know Arafat is dead?"

The men enjoy a good laugh over this one.

Aliyu continues with a great fact he knows to be true. "They haven't figured out that *ISIS* is a movement of the people. *ISIS* is every Muslim man and woman. And we are having many Muslim children to carry the movement forward, *inshallah.*"

"Europeans are more stupid than the Americans," says one of the men, as their laughter dies down. "They are all easy to kill off. I wish I could kill them all myself."

"We need a nuclear bomb," exclaims one of the others. "That will be the end of them all, *inshallah.*"

Aliyu looks up. "Yes, there is no doubt we will see that day come. It will be a day when the infidels are destroyed by their own technology. We can only hope that we are the holy men who make that happen."

One of the lieutenants rewinds the video. "Listen to them chanting!"

"The power of the Muslim people is glorious," boasts another.

Aliyu plants his feet firmly on the floor and sits up straight. "*ISIS* is giving strength to average Muslims because average Muslims want power and respect. *ISIS* delivers that which has been denied to the Muslim people for centuries." He makes a fist. "That time is over. It is our time now."

"Look," says the man with the phone. "I am reading on Twitter that *Al Qaeda* has taken over a hotel in Mali. They are executing people one by one."

"It is truly a glorious day," adds another.

Aliyu holds out his hand. "See . . . it is spreading. Person, by person, by person . . . bullet, by bullet, by bullet . . . it is spreading. And we are multiplying our numbers every day. The more children we have, the closer we come to taking over. Germany, France, Belgium, England . . . they will be predominantly Muslim soon. And then we can make change with the vote as well as with our guns."

The men look at Aliyu. "Do you believe we can capture the world like that?" one asks him.

Aliyu smiles and offers his men a reassuring gesture. "We are making waves throughout Africa. But it is true. Europe and the Middle East have dominated the world picture. That will change as we take over more of this continent. Once we have taken control of the resources with which Allah has blessed us, then the rest of the world will have no choice but to acknowledge us as the greatest power on earth."

His lieutenants love this. They need their leader to speak like this. They sop up the power and respect that overflows from him. It is a trickle-down effect, but the tap is wide open and they thirst for more.

And when we annihilate those five thousand scum, we will make sure the world media see it all on video."

The men nod. They understand their role in the movement entails more than leading guerillas in an assault. They are college-educated. They can speak to the public. This is vital to Aliyu's plan.

"You nod," says Aliyu. "But I am not sure you fully understand the challenge. The world sees us as starving, illiterate Africans.

They actually think *we* are the savages and feel garbage like those we are about to wipe out are in need of assistance."

"Yet they do so little to help them," says one of the men.

Aliyu nods. "In the end, we are all just black savages to them. They would like to call us by a different word, but they are no longer allowed to use that word. Instead, they pretend to help and love the African people. But really . . . we are all animals in their eyes, and the amount of help seldom surpasses the verbiage."

The men sit in silent contemplation for a moment.

"One day, we will get the bomb," says one of them suddenly. He is enthusiastic.

"We will," replies Aliyu. The shadows in the room cut across, making him look ominous and foreboding. The effect is almost *noir*. "But until then. . . ." He makes a fist and holds it in front of his face like a boxer at a press conference before a fight. "Until then, this animal will strike."

"Will we take many *sibya* for our own?" asks one of the men. The others also want to know.

Aliyu strokes his beard. He has told them at least fifty times already. "As I have told you many times, I must give some of the girls to our friends for the assistance with the attack . . . police, army, weapons dealers. This is customary. It seems 12-year-old girls are becoming more valuable than diamonds." He grins.

One of the men grabs his crotch. "I cannot make sons with a diamond."

"But you can get a blonde American whore to marry you if the diamond is big enough," jokes one of the men.

The others burst out laughing. The man insulted spits on the floor. "Screw the Americans."

Aliyu throws up his hands. "Hey, *ode buruku*," he yells. "What are you doing by spitting on my floor, you idiot?"

The man is embarrassed and apologizes. Smelling blood in the water, the others poke fun at him some more.

"You forget your place," says Aliyu. "Anyway, we need to finish planning the attack on the island. Then we need to talk about a bombing attack on the Gomboru marketplace. I want to hit it from both sides off Waziri Kayari Drive," he explains, making a pincers motion with his fingers. He thinks a moment before continuing. "And I want to do it just before Christmas. The place will be full of Christians. Let them go to their false Messiah. It's time we focused on cleaning up our own city. A few bombs here and there won't do the trick. We need something bigger, a campaign. Bombing the marketplace will mark the beginning of a glorious period in our history, my brothers."

There is an abrupt knock at the door. The men jump up and grab their rifles. Aliyu raises the .45 that is always at his side. There is a series of small clicks as each lieutenant flips off the safety on his weapon. Then everything is quiet except for the sound of car horns in the background.

"Who the hell is that?" asks Aliyu.

His men shrug.

On the other side of the door is a white man. He is wearing baggy green camouflage pants. His shirt, untucked, is an off-white Cuban-style *guayabera* smoking shirt complete with pleat work. His hiking boots and the rucksack he carries on his shoulder are worn and covered with a layer of the same omnipresent dirt that has worked its way into every ramshackle house in the city. There is dust in his scruffy black beard and shoulder-length mop of hair as well.

He takes off his sweat-stained baseball hat and uses it to wipe his forehead. He's rocking back and forth whistling *Lucy in the Sky with Diamonds*. He looks over his shoulder suspiciously and knocks again.

The lieutenants look to Aliyu for their cue. He stands up and moves off to the side, out of the line of direct fire.

He nods.

The demeanor of the men changes instantly as they fan out without hesitation. This group of young African men who, seconds earlier, looked like a bunch of grad students hanging out now show another side of themselves. Their movements are fluid, coordinated. They look like hardened killers, well-trained and organized, each man tested and tempered with countless kills under his belt . . . infants, women, the young, the elderly . . . it's all the same to them. The day before, they were watching a soccer game. There was no moment of silence, but they are still.

The first man glides to the side of the door and prepares to open it. Two of the other men instantly take a knee, one aiming at the front window, one training his weapon on the front door, ready to empty his clip into the street. The fourth stands tall in front of Aliyu with his AK-47 pointed at the front door as well.

There is a palpable tension as the essence of death looms. The darkness is right there at head level. Aliyu nods again. The man positioned next to the door opens it and stands to the side ready to fire. The others prepare to fire as well.

"What the hell?" yells the man standing at the door when it flies open. "It's me, for God's sake."

The men lower their weapons and stare at the man standing in the doorway.

The scraggly white man looks ticked off, odd considering he is staring down five barrels. "What the hell? Put those damned guns away, will ya?"

The men look at Aliyu, who bursts out laughing, perhaps for effect. "Ah, it's the American man! What are you doing here, Dr. Harvey Gut-man?" He pronounces the last name as if it's hyphenated. It comes off as patronizing . . . exactly as Aliyu intends.

Dr. Harvey Guttman looks over his shoulder again to make sure nobody is following him before stepping inside. "Would it kill you to turn some lights on in this joint? What'd you forget to pay the electric bill? Oh, I forgot . . . you don't have Con Ed in this shit hole of a neighborhood."

Aliyu nods, and the men turn on the lamps on either side of the couch. The lieutenant who lets the doctor in pokes his head outside, takes a quick look around, and then slams the steel door shut, sliding the three dead bolts into place in the process.

"That's better," says Guttman. "You crazy bastards almost shot me."

Aliyu laughs boisterously once more. "Perhaps someday we will, but not today. You are the one American I want to keep alive, Gut-man. Please . . . sit. I will make believe I did not hear you call my neighborhood a shit hole." He motions for the doctor to sit down on one of the chairs facing the couch.

Guttman sits down and tosses his worn olive rucksack on the table.

"What are you doing here?" asks one of Aliyu's men. It is clear he despises the American. "You are not due until the first of the month."

Harvey Guttman shrugs as if it's no big deal that the man asking him questions is holding an AK-47 and would like nothing more than to blow away an American doctor. "I have other business in the area."

The men eye him suspiciously. What other business could he have here? They did not like the sound of it, but it was not their place to call out Aliyu's contact. Guttman continues on as carefree as ever. He leans forward and helps himself to a cup of tea. He knows he ought to wait for Aliyu to offer, but he also knows hospitality is more of a right than a nicety in a Muslim household, and Aliyu would never refuse the basic comforts to a guest . . . even an American doctor whom he'd rather kill.

As he pours the tea, he can feel their stares burning right through him. If it were a comic book, they would surely have laser beams shooting out of their eyes. It makes his visit all the sweeter that they loathe him . . . except if they kill him, who will they buy their drugs from?

"I'll tell you what, Aliyu . . . I can't say much for your interior designer, but you got yourself some damned good tea."

Aliyu thanks him out of custom. All the largest tea suppliers in the world have operations in Nigeria. But he gets his straight from China via smugglers. The handbags they move might be knockoffs, but his tea is the real deal.

"It should be," hisses one of Aliyu's men. "It is *Da Hong Pao*, the finest tea in the world."

"That tea you are drinking costs more than gold," says another.

"Well then I guess I'll help myself to another." He empties his cup and refills it.

The men are livid at his arrogance, but what can they do? The rules of hospitality forbid them from acting brashly.

Aliyu strokes his beard. "I am pleased you like it. I get it from some people who work in the . . . transportation business. Of course, they give me special rates. Not like you, Gut-man. I think you enjoy overcharging me."

Guttman slurps his tea in protest. "Hey, my sources aren't cheap."

"You have your sources, I have mine," replies Aliyu. "So where are the goods?"

Harvey Guttman holds up a finger. "Yes, of course. Down to business. I have everything right here." He finishes his tea, places the empty cup on the table and pulls the rucksack closer. He unbuckles the leather straps and reaches in like a bad Santa. He tosses a large baggie on the table. "Five hundred Valium to keep you relaxed and happily amnesic."

He tosses a second bag on the table. "Five hundred Oxycontin for your wounded men . . . or anyone the Valium didn't work on." He stops to grin. "Tell you what, pop one of those Hillbilly Heroin with a couple shots of tequila and you'll be seeing Allah for sure, my friend."

One of Aliyu's men grabs his rifle and puts the muzzle against the doctor's temple. "If you blaspheme again, I will kill you myself. I don't care what you bring us. We will find another criminal to take your place."

Guttman holds his hands up. "Okay, okay . . . Jeez, who knew you were so touchy?"

Aliyu reaches over and inspects the two bags. He speaks without looking at Guttman. "First, we do not drink alcohol. You insult us to suggest otherwise. Second, the great name of Allah should never pass the lips of an infidel like you, especially a man like you. You understand. We enjoy your service, but take care not to go too far. You are in our world here, Gut-man. Show us respect or one day when you visit us, that will be the last anyone hears from you."

The doctor gently moves the rifle barrel away from his head and hangs his hat on it. "Okay, okay." He takes his hat back and wipes his brow with it again before putting it back on his head. "But . . . buying drugs from an American doctor . . . that's okay? I'm just sayin' . . . you know . . . it strikes me as a bit ironic, that's all."

Aliyu clarifies his position. "We are holy warriors. We need these things to continue waging *jihad* against the world full of infidels. It is our obligation. There is no shame in it. There is only glory. America is a country plagued with drug addicts. You understand, Gut-man. You came to this continent, stole our people and turned them into crack addicts so you could put them all in prisons."

One of Aliyu's men jumps in acerbically. "That is why so many of your black Americans are turning to Islam. They will find the righteousness inside themselves that could not be stolen from them. In Islam, they will find dignity. And then they will take your country for their own. Just wait. You will see."

Another of the men piles on. "The first thing they will do is exterminate the enemies of Allah."

Harvey Guttman shrugs. He knows full well they're full of shit. He has no doubt that some of the drugs are for the personal use of the men sitting in this room. "Well, I'd better find time to fit in that trip to Disney World before Mustafa Jones lines me up against the wall, huh? Anyway, I have the rest of this month's order here as well."

"Hurry up. It is almost time to pray the *Maghrib*."

Guttman emerges with a third large baggie and tosses it on top of the others. "Eight hundred Prozac . . . enough happy pills to go around. I feel better just looking at them."

Aliyu just nods.

"And for my final act. . . ." With both hands, Guttman lifts out several large baggies duct-taped together. He lays the package on the table with far more respect than he displayed when tossing the others around. "Five thousand Captagon for resale. You must be making a killing selling this stuff. The market price keeps going up. It's all you terrorists gobbling them up."

Aliyu is curious. "From our usual sources in Syria?"

"But of course. And this is the real deal, not like some of the fake shit that they're putting out in Syria now."

"I expect no less from you," says Aliyu.

"It's amazing," opines Guttman. "If you told me a few years ago that manufacturing and selling amphetamines was going to be big business in the Middle East and used to fund world-wide terrorism, I would have laughed in your face."

Aliyu holds his hands up in understanding. "How do you say it in America . . . the worm turns?"

Guttman smirks. "I guess so. The only worms I like are at the bottom of a mezcal bottle. But what you say is true. You terrorist folks have a way of taking Western practices and turning them against us. Kudos to you, my friend. Jeez, you can even buy big quantities of this stuff on the Internet nowadays . . . delivered straight to your door. All that freaky-deaky darknet stuff. Guns, drugs, girls . . . but you wouldn't know anything about that. It's not pious."

The men laugh at the thought.

"I don't think that would work out," says Aliyu.

"Right, right. I forgot. You live here, but you don't really live here. Having me as your personal courier is far better."

Aliyu is pleased. He smiles broadly. He motions to one of his men who instantly takes the bags and brings them to the boss's bedroom. He lifts the mattress that sits in the corner covered with a worn blanket and props it up on its side, revealing a steel trapdoor that looks like a large safe. Kneeling down, the man spins the dial back and forth three times. He slides a latch open and raises the door. The first few steps of a wooden staircase are just visible in the dark. He grabs the multiple bags of pills and carefully descends into the darkness.

A moment later, a light snaps on. The lieutenant carefully places the pills on a shelf between some cases of Gatorade and three crates of RPGs. The secret basement is a storeroom excavated when the house was first built. It's about half the size of the one-story house above. This is where Aliyu keeps his cache of weapons, drugs and money. Crates of guns and ammunition are piled up against three of the walls . . . mostly AK assault rifles and some .45 handguns. The two M60 machine guns and several crates of 7.62 millimeter rounds were newly acquired when Aliyu and his men took down a NATO supply truck attempting to bring food and medical supplies north via highway A3. They also confiscated food and medicine in the process. Stores of plastic explosives are kept in lockboxes until the terrorists need them for bombing public places like the marketplace just before Christmas.

Capable of unleashing 600 rounds per minute into a throng of people, the two M60s will be invaluable to Aliyu during the island raid. Having that kind of firepower means his men can fire twenty rounds per second, and will enable *Boko Haram* to execute en masse line after line of undesirables as fast as the terrorists can line them up. It will be a furious slaughter. The ammunition is standard NATO issue. Aliyu likes the irony in it. Let the world media suck on that.

The man makes his way over to a safe to which he has the combination. This safe contains the group's working capital. "Working capital" is what Aliyu and his lieutenants call it in their collegiate way. As for the other men of *Boko Haram*, they are the barely organized dirtbags of Africa. Aliyu's men are desperate hired thugs, the African equivalent to gangbangers. The men know Aliyu has a way with money. That's why they follow him. He takes good care of them so long as they remain obedient. The boss is sure to dole out girls, drugs and enough cash—cheddar or pepper bar, as the men call it—to help them with their meager expectations.

Aliyu keeps a private safe down there as well. In it he keeps vital documents like fake passports and statements for *Boko Haram*'s Swiss bank accounts as well as his own personal accounts. He also uses the safe to store gold, diamonds and stock certificates, all of which are as liquid as cash in his world of smugglers, racketeers, corrupt government officials and corporate side deals. His knack for keeping the money flowing to and from the right people has enabled Aliyu to amass an empire for himself in a very short period of time. He expects no less of himself.

Aliyu has maintained secret accounts in Switzerland since he seized power. He uses the organization's Swiss accounts to shelter the vast sums of money he receives from selling female slaves, trading resources like diamonds and coltan, and selling Captagon. He also uses these accounts to facilitate huge inflows of untraceable money from wealthy supporters in northern Nigeria who are worth billions from their own dealings with the resource state. Other billionaire benefactors hail from the Middle East and pump millions of dollars into *Boko Haram*'s Swiss coffers in an attempt to see the Middle East, North Africa and sub-Saharan Africa unite in their quest for pan-Islam. These are men with upstanding reputations and high-profile positions. Much like the darknet, the Swiss system enables them to maintain secret sinister identities operating in the seedy underside of civil society. Aliyu knows this and uses the system to great advantage.

His operation would be impossible if not for the Swiss. His secret personal accounts will provide for him well into the future . . . should he live that long. He siphons off millions from his *Boko Haram* business dealings . . . the slavery, the trading, the drugs. He also takes his "scoop"—his 10 percent commission, as his Saudi friends call it—from the millions of dollars coming in from faceless benefactors the world over. He learned from the Saudis that "scooping" was one of the most lucrative careers possible. He considers it his privilege, his entitlement, as leader of *Boko Haram*.

The Swiss system embodies the classic Swiss neutrality. Money is always welcome, no matter the source. Aliyu rose to power by murdering his predecessor. He will likely meet his demise in much the same way. The Swiss banking system will simply swallow the millions and millions of his hidden money when he is gone just like it has done with every other villain, despot and scoundrel who has met a violent end. For nobody outside the system knows what happens to money that never publicly existed in the first place. It's as beautiful a symmetry as any Swiss watch. As for his lieutenants, they have the foresight to stash their money away in much the same way. They are largely satisfied. They are very different from the rank and file of *Boko Haram*, the desperate losers and thugs who do not fear dying because they have nothing to lose. They do not respect life because there is no respect for their own.

The man in the secret storeroom is a millionaire many times over. His fingers are comfortable fanning through stacks of hundreds.

He deftly spins the dial and opens the safe. Inside there is about $300,000 in cash. The terror group uses this money for daily expenses. Cash flow remains steady thanks to Aliyu's talent for trading girls and natural resources. The man takes four $10,000 wraps of hundred-dollar bills, closes the safe, spins the dial and clicks off the light. He returns to the living room after re-securing the trap door beneath Aliyu's mattress.

When he enters, Aliyu and Guttman are talking about next month's meeting.

"Excellent," says the *Boko Haram* boss. "Next month, I will need you to pick up a package from Lagos before you come here."

The man holding Guttman's forty grand stands by quietly. The others are silent as well. There is an air of anxiety. They are waiting for something.

Guttman takes off his hat and scratches his head. He brushes his messy hair out of his face. "I have a feeling this is gonna be somewhat out of my job description."

The man tosses the forty thousand on the table in front of Guttman. "Your job description is to do what we hire you to do."

Guttman picks up the four tight-wrapped packs of cash, thumbs through them quickly, and slides them into his rucksack. Another clean deal, thank God.

"Yes," says Aliyu, in a thunderous voice that startles even the doctor. "See how you scooped up that money, Gut-man. You are all in, just like we are. There's no turning back for you. Our fate is your fate."

The doctor sits back in his chair, scratches his chin and exhales loudly. The Oxycontin he washed down with a couple of Star lagers forty minutes prior is kicking in and starting to give him the itchies.

Guttman laughs. "Yeah, let me tell ya, it's a good thing I went to Harvard. I mean . . . picking up packages . . . that's high-level stuff."

"As I recall, Gut-man," responds Aliyu Adelabu, "you were arrested for writing prescriptions for money. You wrote a lot of prescriptions and you made a lot of money. The American media called you Dr. Feelgood." He turns to his men. "I like that name. Dr. Feelgood. It has a good ring to it."

The men laugh.

"Hey," says Guttman, scratching his arms. The itches have ahold of him now. "What can I say? Harvard Medical School was expensive."

Aliyu wags his finger. "We obviously have needs that overlap, doctor. You have fled to Nigeria to hide from your government, and we operate outside of ours. So let's stop pretending, shall we? You will pick up a package in Lagos and bring it to me with our next shipment. You are not to open the package. You are not to be distracted in any way en route here."

"That means no drinking and no whores," adds one of the men with disdain.

Guttman smiles. "So you know about that, huh?"

"You cannot fool us. We know everything about you, Gut-man. You think you can travel about in my country without my eyes on you? I'm the reason you are allowed to travel about freely in the first place. The police or the army would have pinched you a long time ago. They know you are with me . . . unless they hear otherwise."

"This might be a good time to pop one of the Valium, buddy," says the doctor.

Aliyu ignores him. "If you deviate from the plan in any way, you will not live to see the next sunrise. In return, I will pay you an additional hundred thousand dollars."

Guttman drops his head as he mulls things over. Whatever it is he's being roped into, it must be very, very important. Very, very important means a lot of innocent people are going to die as a result. He figures it has to be red mercury or maybe actual nuclear material for a dirty bomb of some sort. More likely red mercury which he knows is a hoax, but try telling that to a terrorist. They are all convinced red mercury actually exists and is the missing link to creating nuclear weapons for themselves.

Guttman looks up. If only they knew. "Okay," he says. "You're the boss, Ali-yu."

"We will get you the location of the exchange when the time draws near. Until then, you will discuss this with no one. I assume we understand each other?"

Guttman nods. Inside he is laughing. It has to be red mercury . . . it is too easy. "Like I said, you're the boss."

Aliyu stands up to signal the meeting is over. "Please excuse us. It is time to pray the *Maghrib*."

Guttman stands up unceremoniously. "So glad to hear it. Now if you'll excuse me, I have to find myself a clean bar and a seedy hooker. Wait . . . reverse that."

He picks up his rucksack and heads for the bolted steel door leading back out to the street. One of the lieutenants slides the bolt and unceremoniously ushers the doctor out and locks the door behind him.

The men prepare to offer their prayers. "What is all this about a package?" asks one of the lieutenants excitedly.

Aliyu clasps his hands together. "It is from our friends in Iran. It's coming through one of our people in Pakistan. I promised you untold glory, and you shall have it. It is only a matter of time before the entire world knows *Boko Haram*. We will detonate a bomb that will change the world. People will shudder when they speak our name."

"You have finally acquired the red mercury? You are truly masterful."

Aliyu smiles and bows slightly, basking in the moment.

One of the men rounds up the tea cups to bring them into the kitchen.

Aliyu stops him. "Our lips should not touch that man's cup. Make sure you destroy it. Consider it a glimpse of things to come."

Before beginning his evening prayers, Aliyu runs through his head what needs to be done to arrange the money for the red mercury exchange. He will have to contact André Lamon, his banker in Switzerland, and arrange to transfer $85 million to the seller, a series of nameless, faceless entities, one inside the other and so on, like a set of nesting dolls. From there, the $85 million will disappear as it wends its way through the Swiss system in a series of undisclosed transfers, a meandering river sprouting small tributaries along the way.

André Lamon will arrange it all at Aliyu's command. He will also arrange to get the money into the *Boko Haram* accounts. Only Lamon knows the exact accounts into which the $85 million will flow. Lamon also knows there are several associated accounts at the bank into which the money will go from there. He knows more than any one of the individual account holders or their operatives. He is the gatekeeper. That's how the Swiss system is set up to work. But once the money leaves his bank, once it's on the outside, it will be virtually untraceable. Money moves at lightning speed, making the world a very small place indeed.

That will satisfy Aliyu's obligation to the seller. He also has to arrange for the cash to pay Guttman. He could tap his working capital, but he needs that for the island raid. He could use the proceeds from the girls he will sell off after the island raid. But that's a bit too cumbersome. Instead, he intends to sell all the Captagon in one fell swoop to a certain General in the army. That will cover Guttman's expenses. No price is too great for Aliyu where red mercury is concerned. He'll do anything to get his hands on it.

Chapter 26

After leaving Aliyu's place, Guttman walks several blocks without looking back. Slung on his shoulder is his rucksack containing forty large, a tidy sum for his services by any measure. His timing is according to plan as Maiduguri begins its evening prayer. There are far fewer people about than usual. When he reaches the park, he stops, drops the rucksack to the ground and looks around carefully. Nobody seems to be following him. Never one to be too sure, he flips the bag over. Obscured in a corner seam is a zipper which he opens, revealing his Sig 226 and some extra clips. He takes the pistol and checks the safety. As always, there is a round ready in the chamber. He zips up the secret compartment, slings the bag on his left shoulder, leaving his trigger hand unencumbered, and slides the gun into his belt.

After walking a bit along the park, he makes a right onto Maiduguri-Lake-Kukawa Road and heads toward the American University of Nigeria which, of course, specializes in petroleum science. As he approaches Kashim Ibrahim Road, he stops and looks around again. He senses he's being followed, but can't make out anyone behind him. He just feels off. Maybe someone is on to him? Maybe Aliyu had second thoughts about keeping him around? In Africa, it doesn't take much of a reason.

He slides the safety off. As the university comes into sight, he picks up his pace. That's when he hears a single twig snap. It comes from behind the dense, eight-foot hedgerow that lines the park along the path. His first thought is to cross the street and keep making for his destination. His second thought is to start shooting into the shrubs. He finds neither option particularly advantageous. He quickens his pace again, knowing the hedgerow will end within fifty yards. He can hear the footsteps pick up on the other side of the hedges. Somebody is definitely coming for him. A few more steps and the hedgerow ends. He'll be face-to-face with an unknown.

Five steps before he reaches the end of the block, Guttman makes out a thin spot in the hedges. Without a second thought, he turns from the hunted into the hunter by thrusting himself through. The bushes snap as he drops the rucksack with his left hand and draws his Sig with his right. He couldn't have been any smoother. In a split second, Guttman is through the hedgerow and standing two steps behind the Nigerian man who has been following him for the last hundred yards.

But Guttman has the drop on him. The man is completely taken by surprise. Guttman cracks the handle of his pistol against the back of the man's head, dropping him to his knees immediately. Before the man can gather his senses, Guttman delivers a second pistol whip to the man's face, pummeling his jaw. Two teeth fly from his mouth. The man falls flat on his back moaning and barely conscious, the knife he is carrying still gripped in his hand.

Guttman sees the knife and steps down hard on the man's wrist. Regaining consciousness, the man shrieks and opens his hand. Guttman quickly bends down and takes the blade. Having rendered him completely defenseless, Guttman is about to slit the man's throat when he notices he wears no beard. He is not a Muslim. He is not one of Aliyu's assassins from *Boko Haram*.

Guttman withdraws the blade from the man's bare throat. "Who the hell are you?" he says in a sharp staccato voice. Guttman sounds nothing like the laid back, play-it-cool cat he was with Aliyu. A different man has emerged.

With his jaw possibly broken, the man can hardly speak. He slurs something repeatedly that sounds like, "I'm sorry, mister. I have a family."

Guttman leans in closer. He's getting frustrated. "What? I don't understand what the hell you are saying?"

The man repeats himself as best as possible.

Guttman closes his eyes and shakes his head in disbelief. "You've got to be kidding me," he says to himself. "Dude, you picked the wrong tourist to mug. I would have killed your African ass without a second thought. Jesus. . . ."

The man can only moan.

Guttman sighs loudly. "I really don't need any hassles right now." He unloads a vicious kick to the man's exposed ribs, sending him over on his side. "I really don't have time for this shit," he continues, kicking the would-be mugger again. "I really hate distractions," he adds, just before launching another kick.

The man is clearly messed up. Blood is pouring from his mouth. The butt of the pistol must have caught the man's nose as well because it's clearly broken. His mangy green soccer jersey is already soaked through with his own blood. One of his worn sandals is lying a few feet away. The impact of Guttman's attack was fierce enough to send the sandal flying. There is just enough light left for Guttman to see how dry and cracked the man's foot is. His toenails are yellow and misshapen.

For a moment, Harvey Guttman wonders if it's even a human foot at all. One thing is clear, though. This man has walked many miles on those feet. They embody the ugliness of his world. Karma has not been kind to this one. He seems destined to live many lifetimes of misery. Singling out Guttman as an easy mark was just another miscalculation by a man who was buried by the weight of repeated attempts to better his situation as if completely unaware that the chips were stacked against him from the day he was born.

As the man begins to regain his senses, the pain from his broken face overwhelms him. He begins crying and begging for his life as best he can. He extends his shaking, open hand. Guttman immediately realizes he really messed this guy up and there's no way he will get adequate medical care. The man is no different than a wounded animal out on the savannah. Guttman knows he will not survive.

It's a meager, pay-to-play existence with desperate, destitute people like this man. The irony hits Guttman, and he takes a deep breath. Surveying the area, he bends down hastily and feels through the man's dirty red Bermuda shorts for some sort of identification. He pulls out a creased driver's license and shoves it into his own pocket. He then pulls out a small wad of 40,000 Nigerian Naira, about two hundred bucks back in the States. He puts the money back in the man's pocket.

"Damn it," says Guttman in disgust.

He collects himself, slides his gun into his rucksack and jogs the rest of the way to the university. When he hits the campus, he heads straight for the maintenance shed behind the main administration building. He opens the lock without hesitation and quickly slides inside undetected. The shed smells like gasoline and grass trimmings. He throws his rucksack on top of a workbench over which several hand tools hang . . . assorted hammers, screwdrivers, clippers and the like. He pulls several tools by their handle. They are actually levers, and the workbench clicks as it unlocks from the shed wall.

Guttman pulls the workbench forward. It swings away from the wall like a door. The top of the bench is hollow and lined with lead. Inside are several handguns and an Uzi. There is also ammo, cash, more pills, fake passports from an array of countries and a satellite phone. He grabs a Brazilian passport and the satellite phone, and two more clips for his Sig. The rest he will leave stashed in case he's deployed there again. He powers up the satellite phone and dials a number he knows by heart . . . it is André Lamon, Aliyu's money man in Switzerland. But there is no André Lamon just like there is no Harvey Guttman. These are their cover names. They are both CIA operators.

Neither man has any idea about *Boko Haram*'s plan to raid the island. The scope of their work is limited to posing as a drug dealer and a Swiss banker in order to set up Aliyu and whoever else is helping him. For almost three years, they have been setting a trap for Aliyu Adelabu and his band of bearded scum. It's now time for the big payoff.

After several rings, Lamon answers. "Yes?"

"Hey, it's Dr. Feelgood."

The two men go through their security verification protocol.

"Candy came out on the island," says Lamon. His accent is authentic. Guttman smiles. "In the backroom, she was everybody's darling."

The protocol was met. Using a Lou Reed line about a transsexual, drug-using hooker was Guttman's idea.

"*Gava?*" asks Lamon in French.

Guttman tosses his baseball hat on the bench top and scratches his head. "Oh, just peachy. I just had to lay the wood to some poor bastard planning to mug me."

Born to play a Swiss banker, Lamon rarely showed emotion. His voice was flat and steady. "I guess he picked the wrong man."

"Yeah, I messed him up pretty bad."

"Did you call to tell me about your evening exploits?"

Guttman opened his Brazilian passport and double checked the expiration. "I'd love to chat, but it's time to move. Wire some money into my Canary Islands account."

"I assume, then, I will be receiving a call from our friend Aliyu?"

"Oh, yes," confirms Guttman with a bit of delight evident in his voice. "It's been a long time coming, but he's finally taken the bait. He will be calling you to transfer $85 million to buy red mercury."

Lamon finally shows some emotion and laughs. "Really?"

"Hey," Guttman replies, with a shrug. "Who am I to convince him there's no such thing. Sometimes, there's just no convincing people, you know?"

"Excellent. Once we have the information, we can follow the money."

"Exactly, my friend. I have been looking forward to this day for many years. I can't wait to nail those bastards." He pushes the workbench back against the wall until he hears it click. He gives it a tug to make sure. "But first, I need to get out of this shit hole. Time for me to lay low for a while."

"Heading home?" asks Lamon. They've been working together long enough to share some details they would otherwise keep to themselves.

"Nah," says Guttman, stuffing his things into his rucksack. "I'm heading to the Caribbean for some R&R while you do your dirty work. Dr. Feelgood needs his fun, too. I can't remember the last time I saw a blonde. I'll be seeing you soon enough, though. We have to finish this *Boko Haram* thing. We really don't know where this money leads. It will eventually get laundered out in the open and morph into dividends, and bonuses, yachts, real estate, and all that rich people sewage that flows out of all this corrupt bullshit."

"Okay, safe travels. Watch your back."

"Yeah," says Guttman. "Hey, don't forget to transfer some cash into the Cayman Islands for me so I can pay my bar tab. It's gonna be a biggie."

"Don't worry about a thing," says Lamon. "It's my turn now."

They were about to cut the connection when Guttman remembered one last thing. "Oh, hey, I need you to do me another favor."

"That depends. I remember the last time you asked me to do something for you. As a matter of fact, I had that damned Brazilian monkey of yours for two months before I could find someone to take it off my hands. The bastard tore up all my curtains."

"It was a capuchin monkey. And I'll have you know that 'monkey,' as you call him, actually stole the prototype for an Iranian nuclear detonator. Anyway, that guy I tuned up." Guttman takes the mugger's license from his pocket. "He lives somewhere in the Gomboru district near the marketplace. I want you to see that he gets a good chunk of money."

Lamon grunts. "If he's anything like the last guy you greeted with your fists, I'm sure he will need it."

"Yeah, pretty much."

Lamon chuckles. "No worries. I will send it via courier. Send me his name and address."

Before he departs, Guttman takes one last look around. Everything appears neat and tidy. His work here is done for the time being. The next time "Dr. Feelgood" makes his rounds things might be very different. The next time he's in Maiduguri, there might not be any more *Boko Haram*. *Inshallah.*

Chapter 27

From the moment *This Soul's Journey through the Eye of the Storm* hit the market, Becket Rosemore was inundated with intense scrutiny from all sides. Up to that point, Beck was Teflon, his professional reputation as impregnable as he liked his women. His meteoric rise to fame made him a formidable adversary. At one point, he had enjoyed the highest popularity rating of any U.S. president ever.

Beck's opposition could do little more than lie in the weeds, waiting for a magic weapon to appear from the Gods. Camille's book was the Trojan Horse they were waiting for, playing right into the hands of his political opponents, who were desperate to find something they could hang on the president. Beck's personal conduct astounded the world. Camille revealed his Achilles heel. She handed Beck's opponents the secret to her man's fatal weakness. As with all tragic heroes, Beck's own hubris would finally prove his undoing. It was a watershed moment in American politics. Once Camille revealed the other side of the great American president—once she exposed the arrogance, conceit and base depravity of the man whom the world held in the highest esteem—the arrows flew at him from every direction. Both sides of the aisle were scandalized.

Beck wielded his power ruthlessly. But once word of his womanizing became public, he could no longer keep his critics locked under his thumb. There were always people who had resented Beck's rise to power. They felt he'd usurped the presidency with some sort of backdoor information that helped to forge a deal with the Chinese and redefine the Middle East. Those whom Beck had stomped on en route to the White House felt vindicated, for they knew firsthand how low he could go to get what he wanted. These people began coming forward to spew their vitriol in public and get their revenge. This contingent felt Beck had yet to pay his dues, and so they were all too happy to sit back with their popcorn and enjoy the show while he was pilloried. To make matters worse, Beck received little defense from colleagues and "friends" in his own party. Those who sat on his side of the aisle began assailing him if for no other reason than to distance themselves from the dumpster fire. They were in sore need of a peace offering after allowing Beck to demagogue his way to the top as if issuing royal fiat.

In what seemed like an instant, Beck became fallible and mortal. He knew he'd made a lot of enemies on his way up. In the end, they were all the same . . . men of ego and deceit. That's why he was so determined to keep them down. What surprised him was the extent to which his "friends" abandoned him. He thought for sure his people would rally the troops and circle the wagons around him to protect the good name of their president. He was shocked by many within his own party when they crawled underneath a rock when the shit hit the fan. He stood alone to face the hailstorm of criticism, and he wasn't weathering it very well at all.

His numbers plummeted to historical lows after the book. He was losing badly in the court of public opinion, and everyone knew how to hurt him on the political battlefield now that his vulnerability was exposed. Any thought of a second term was inconceivable to anyone but Beck, who still clung arrogantly to the belief that he was too invaluable to the world to be cast off so easily. What the president didn't know was that his own party was conspiring to ensure he would not be the nominee in the next election. The man who would be king was about to find out that he was really an emperor with no clothes . . . ironic given the sexual exploits that had landed him in his predicament to begin with.

Beck was mostly a ball of rage. He reared up and bared his teeth every time Camille O'Keefe was said to have gotten the better of him in the war of words. He hated her, loathed her, despised her, reviled her . . . he used every synonym he could think of to describe what he felt most toward Camille—disgust. Her very existence disgusted him. He found everything about her an affront to his sensibilities. When he thought of her in the aftermath, he really did feel she was less than human. As he said to Harry Pierson, "If I could rip her vagina off and light it on fire . . . yeah . . . that might satisfy me. No one knows more about her putrid red twat than I do."

The mention of her name sent him into fits of rage that resulted in the resignation of two female staffers, one of whom was the woman he had hit in the face with Camille's book. She got a nice settlement offer and was happy to be gone. Another resigned after commenting that Beck could not hope to win a PR war with the Red Dragon Lady. Beck threatened to "staple her lips to Camille's ass" so she could kiss it better.

The few loyal staffers who remained by Beck's side begged him to lie low and ride it out. He vowed to do just the opposite. He pledged to be as public as possible in his day-to-day life and show the world that it would take more than some flighty, redheaded bitch to bring down the world's most popular man. For the most part, there was nobody left but Harry Pierson.

As it turned out, however, even he was ready to strike a blow.

Chapter 28

Many U.S. presidents have kept one special place from their past where they can visit to escape the madness, if only for a while. Beck's house up near Cooperstown, New York, was his refuge. Even in the White House, he felt like the walls had ears, and he was dismayed by how many of his own inside people were turning on him. He left D.C. for Canadarago Lake shortly after his last two female staffers resigned. He had lost what little respect he had for women and the Beltway, both of which now left a putrid taste in his mouth.

He had spent a lot of time at Canadarago Lake when he was fresh out of the service. The early-morning sunlight bouncing off the lake soothed him. He needed the clean air and expansive mountain vista to help realign him with the world he had left behind when he opted for the Special Forces. Things had seemed much simpler then, despite the complexity of his feelings. He was toying with the idea of going into politics, but he hadn't yet committed himself. There was too much he had to bury deep inside first, too many memories of his life as a special operator floating around in his consciousness. He had to lock them away deep inside before he could enter the civilian world again.

What he liked most about the large, white and green Victorian was the porch that ran around most of the house. He figured he could sit there for hours putting everything away in his head. He hoped that the small towns dotting the landscape around Cooperstown would act as a sort of time machine through which he could reconnect with himself. Back then, Becket Rosemore sounded a lot more like Camille O'Keefe, and he wasn't afraid to look at himself as part of humanity instead of above it. That was precisely the part of him that connected with Camille years later. It was the intersection of their past lives together.

Living in Cooperstown meant living in the shadow of the Baseball Hall of Fame. That storied building with its magnanimous, larger-than-life memories of bygone times gave Beck something he was sorely missing. It was like returning to a time when America was united, solidified and moral. Baseball was a game built on those values. Cooperstown itself was a town frozen in time like a Norman Rockwell painting. That's exactly what Beck was looking for when he left the service.

Folks up there liked to name their houses. Beck named his "Rockwell House." He hoped that every time he stepped into that house he would be stepping through a portal into a Norman Rockwell painting. He did his best to make it a reality. He fished in the morning. After he'd stop at one of the local diners, hit the batting cage or the gun range, and then spend the afternoon watching Little League games at the Field of Dreams, a fantasy world where young boys and girls from all over the country came to culminate their childhood and play one glorious final tournament with their buddies before moving on to high school and life thereafter. Everything in Cooperstown was, similarly, a rite of passage, and Beck needed to feel a part of something greater like that.

When the winter came, Beck would hunt and read for hours at a time. He also quit drinking because it brought back all the memories he had stuffed away. After two years, he was ready to return to the civilian world and make his way. He reintroduced himself to society and the rest was history. He became a household name, reunited with Camille and amassed massive power for himself.

He never foresaw the landslide that would take him under.

Chapter 29

Feeling abandoned and under siege, Beck wanted nothing more than to return to Canadarago Lake and reconnect with a piece of himself. Nothing the "toxic, redheaded bitch" could touch. This was how he referred to her now. He could barely pronounce her name without launching into a tirade. He desperately needed to get away. Why not? Everybody was saying he was a *de facto* lame duck anyway. So he made off for Rockwell House without much ado.

His solace lasted about thirty seconds, as the president of the United States goes nowhere without much ado. Before heading to his retreat, Beck had to notify the Secret Service who, in turn, mobilized a presidential away team. What Beck intended to be a spontaneous escape quickly turned into the usual rigmarole of logistics and other tedium which had really begun weighing on him now that his popularity had plummeted. What had once seemed like pomp and circumstance weighed like a burden on him, now that his own party considered him a useless, deadweight liability.

Beck imagined a convoy of black Suburbans descending upon Cooperstown. It was like poisoning his personal slice of idyllic Americana just when he needed to taste it the most. It didn't sit right with him anymore now that the world had turned against him. The truth of the matter was quite different. From the moment he took office, the requirements of his position mandated that Rockwell House be ripped from its place in Beck's imagination and modernized to allow for secure presidential visits. On that solemn day when he took the oath of office, Rockwell House became a presidential compound, a matter of national security under the purview of the Secret Service.

Two days after Beck won the election, work began on Rockwell House to bring it up to speed. State-of-the-art security systems were installed, including motion sensors that could detect two mice screwing. The original eighteenth-century window frames were replaced to support bulletproof glass with special tinting that rendered completely blurry any photograph taken from outside. The fire-suppression system looked like it was pulled from a skyscraper. His prized solarium, where he had once spent the better part of a year learning to identify the myriad birds of upstate New York, was similarly refitted with the same glass. In addition to flummoxing would-be paparazzi, the coated glass had the strange effect of frightening off the very wildlife Beck had come to recognize within seconds. But something about the glass confused the birds who repeatedly flew into it, killing themselves instantly.

One of the five bedrooms was converted into an impenetrable safe room, stripping the space of its original architectural charm. Another bedroom was converted into a bunk room for Secret Service agents, and the kitchen was modified to accommodate a small staff while the president was in residence. A third bedroom was outfitted to become an operating room should the need arise. And while Beck appreciated the kitchen upgrade and the Viking appliances even if he didn't know how to operate them himself, he considered the conversion of his mahogany-and-marble trimmed smoking room into a tactical communications room almost more than he could emotionally digest. He was appeased only by the addition of a sniper perch in the cupola up on the roof. Having a crack shot up there gave him a sense of well-being that helped assuage the redesign of his happy place.

In the event of a national crisis, Beck could essentially run the world from Rockwell House. When he first took office, this made him feel important. He wasn't happy with the changes, but his sense of self-importance overshadowed his nostalgia as only a swollen ego could. Now that he was essentially a disgraced lame duck, his ego was not nearly as swollen and large. He suffered ego dysfunction. Now that he was despised by millions of women who had once adored him, the alterations to Rockwell House seemed like an intrusion. He was glad to be rid of D.C. for a while, and D.C. was thrilled to be rid of him as well.

Everyone except Harry Pierson.

The vice president wasn't going to let Beck slip off that easily, not after Beck had destroyed his political career by banging his way across the country. Perhaps worse to a man like Pierson, Beck was subsequently unable to control his wife. If Beck was going to bring him down, Harry Pierson pledged to make sure Beck suffered every minute of their mutual fall from grace. Beck suspected as much. But what choice did he have when Pierson arrived unannounced at the front door of Rockwell House?

When Pierson arrived, the president was sitting in the study reading *Huckleberry Finn*. He was wearing a pair of jeans and a T-shirt just like in the old days, and sitting in his favorite worn leather reading chair. He was also wearing a red smoking jacket, something he picked up in Thailand along with the herpes he later gave Camille.

Pierson strode in without knocking and didn't bother to wait for an invitation to sit. Instead, he showed himself to a chair directly across from Beck's. Beck could feel Pierson's angry energy and put the book down on the carved wood coffee table that separated them.

Pierson leaned over and took the volume in his hands. He smelled the book. "I love the smell of old books," he said. "It reminds me of the one woman I actually loved. She worked in a rare book shop in Annapolis. That's the woman I should have married. Not the screwup cannonball I'm chained to. Imagine if it were legal to kill one person in a lifetime. Funny . . . we would both whack our wives. The only difference is that you would screw yours one last time after she was dead, you sick shit."

Beck pursed his lips and reminisced. "Yeah . . . right. Remember when everything smelled like gun oil back in the day? Life was simpler then."

Pierson tossed the book back on the table. "Yeah, well . . . that's all fiction, boy-o. Huckleberry Finn, war stories, glory days, your dumb gun oil . . . it's all shit in the shitter now."

"That's why I keep this house. It's a place where I can bring it all back to life."

Pierson shifted in his chair. He was agitated. "It seems to me you're more like Dr. Frankenstein now."

Beck pointed to the built-in mahogany bookcases that lined the wall across from the large stone fireplace. He was proud to have read every book and not, like so many people he knew, simply to have hired an interior designer to fill the shelves with impressive titles.

"There's life in those pages, Harry."

"It's fiction, Beck. Maybe that's your problem? Maybe you can't tell the difference between fiction and reality anymore? Maybe the lines have blurred so much you can't even tell when your life is fiction? Maybe fantasy is a better word?"

Beck shrugged. "It worked for Clinton. And let me tell you something, Harry. The greatest men in history—the men who made this world run—were all dreamers. More importantly, they believed in their own stories. Men like me are our own heroes."

"Unfortunately for you, Camille is not Hillary Clinton. She didn't sit by and cover for you because she doesn't give a crap about your world. Like you always say, her story is entirely different. She doesn't read books, she reads tea leaves for Christ's sake. You let a woman like that into the White House?"

"It's all just different narratives, Harry. Nobody cares about the truth. People just want to be entertained. So why worry about the truth if nobody wants it? That's what Carter could never understand. You should take some time to get away. You will see things differently."

Pierson prickled at Beck's nonchalance. It pissed him off something fierce. "Is that right? Who the hell are you all of a sudden? What, have you traded in your *Penthouse* for the *Atlantic Monthly*? You've single-handedly killed my political life. You realize that, right? I mean . . . there's no coming back in *this story*, my friend. That's not fiction, it's a damned fact. Like I said, you've created a monster in that woman. You're Dr. Frankenstein."

Beck inhaled deeply. "Don't worry about that toxic, redheaded bitch. It'll blow over soon enough. Americans have memories as small as their brains."

He looked at the Secret Service agent standing in the double-wide doorway that led into the great room. "Could you leave us, please?"

"Wait," ordered Pierson. "Bring me a drink first." He looked at Beck. "Whataya got to drink in this joint?"

Beck gestured to the wood-topped bar that matched the book cases. "It's eleven a.m., Harry."

"I agree. It's too early for a martini. Scotch," he declared, decisively. "Three rocks. And none of that crap the president leaves sitting out for these local yokels. Give me the stuff the British Prime Minister gave him. He stashes it in the right-hand cabinet."

The agent sprung to life.

Beck smiled and obsessively centered the Twain book on the table. "Is there anything you don't know, Harry?"

"I know my career is over, but it doesn't take a genius to figure that out."

One of the agents addressed Beck. "Excuse me, Mr. President. Will you be having a drink as well?"

Pierson answered for him. "No. The president doesn't drink. He only drives everyone else to."

After handing Pierson his glass, the agent stepped out of the study and closed the French doors behind him.

Beck broke the ice. "So . . . what brings you here?"

"Oh, you know . . . books . . . same as you. Only I'm not talking about Mark Twain and two bumpkins on a rafting adventure. I'm talking about Camille O'Keefe and the damned president of the United States and his marathon hump fest. Jesus, Beck, she's killing you. And you sit there in your sissy bathrobe telling me not to pay her any mind."

Beck looked down at his crimson attire. "It's actually a smoking jacket. Hugh Heffner gave it to me. When I bumped into him in Phuket years ago."

"Bumping into Heff can be interpreted in many ways, you know."

"It's all good, Harry. It's all good."

Harry Pierson downed his Scotch in a single gulp. "Are you high? What happened to President Furioso? See, that's exactly the kind of crap I'm talking about. You can be all cavalier about things, but you're taking me down with you."

Pierson stood up in disgust and went over to the bar to fix himself another drink. Beck stared into the yellow Arabesque wallpaper, hoping to find some suitable answer.

"Do you even know what I'm talking about?" asked Pierson, in dismay. It was almost a plea.

"I understand you're angry, but things will blow over. I've done too much to simply disappear from the world stage."

"Oh, you've done enough, Beck. You've certainly done enough." He returned to his chair and sat down. "My God, man, you're deluded. You're, like . . . worse than Reagan in his last year. In case you haven't noticed, nobody is on your side. Camille has thrown you right off that world stage you so grandly refer to and has taken it for herself. If it didn't mean the end of my career, I might actually admire the bitch."

"Please don't do that," said Beck. "You'd be surprised how things can work out."

Pierson rubbed his temples. "I don't think you get it. Your opponents have been making hay from this thing. Christ, even the pathetic bastards in our camp have begun throwing you under the bus to distance themselves, and those are even the guys who were your friends. Those poor bastards are so afraid Camille might rat them out next, they wouldn't dare speak up on your behalf. Wake up, my friend. You're marooned on a damned island, and there's no rescue ship coming."

Despite his best attempts to play it cool with Pierson and deny him any sort of satisfaction, Beck gritted his teeth. "That toxic, redheaded bitch."

"Yeah, well . . . that toxic, redheaded bitch as you call her is running rampant out there." He jumped up and grabbed the remote off the table before Beck could snatch it first.

He switched on the TV. "Just look at her."

He flipped through the channels. Camille seemed to be everywhere. And everywhere they seemed to be trashing Beck.

"She's killing you. She's killing *us*." Pierson tossed the remote on Beck's lap. "Not so sexy anymore, is she?"

Beck turned off the set and stood up. At first he was very calm, even deliberate. But he couldn't keep it together. He exploded and hurled the remote into the fireplace where it shattered into pieces against the stone.

One of the agents opened the French doors and popped his head in. "Is everything okay, Mr. President?"

Beck turned on him. "Get out! If I want you, I'll call you."

"Wait," yelled Beck.

"Yes, sir?"

"Cancel the damned cable."

"Yes, sir."

"Wait," yelled Beck again.

"Yes, sir?"

"Just have them send a new remote. Tell them I lost it."

"Cable . . . no cable . . . you can come up here and stick your head in the sand all you want," said Pierson. "It's not going to change a thing out there." He walked toward one of the windows. "And out there, we're done. That glass might be bulletproof, but you're certainly not. Not anymore. One term . . . that's it. One and done."

Beck turned to him. "What do you want from me, Harry? Huh? You make it sound like I never did anything for you. Remember, it was thanks to me that you're vice president in the first place. You're bitching about serving only one term? Nobody would even know who you are if it wasn't for me."

Pierson laughed. "Exactly right, Beck. Nobody would be associating me with you and your sexual escapades. Nobody would be associating me with the biggest political fall from grace in U.S. history. And for sure, my damned wife—that freaking crow of a woman—wouldn't have moved me into one of the guest rooms because she assumes I was dipping my wick along with you. Do you understand what I am saying?"

The vice president took his drink from the coffee table and paced around the room, mindlessly staring at the assortment of luminescent Jim Schanz landscapes. They captured the duality Beck once sought when he first bought the place . . . ethereal yet rooted, transcendent yet earthy.

Looking at the expensive art set Pierson off again. "See . . . no matter what happens, you will always be able to buy expensive art and bed the hottest women. Of course, now you'll have to either slip them a roofie or go to some remote part of the world where they don't have television. You blew it sky high, man. I don't have the world at my fingertips like you did. Sure, there's plenty of deals out there for you so long as nobody knows you're involved. Take those Chinese connections of yours. What do they care if your reputation is ruined here so long as you can 'consult' and provide valuable information? You'll always have millions of dollars. But not me. I'm stuck at home with a cannonball living in a world of complete shit because of you. This is all I have. And thanks to you and your libido, I'm about to lose it all."

"You underestimate yourself, Harry. The world is still your oyster, as it is mine. There's nothing Camille can do that can hurt us in the long term. She's just another whacko with a book deal. Americans barely read. And soon enough, some new scandal, or celebrity divorce, or war someplace nobody cares about will replace Camille O'Keefe."

Pierson turned away from the painting in which he was trying to lose himself. It wasn't working. Neither was this conversation with Beck. "Man, you really don't get it, do you? You think this is all fleeting and that Americans are morons."

Beck stood up and went over to the wall of bookcases. "Some of the greatest works of literature sit on these shelves, Harry. And I'll bet 90 percent of voting Americans haven't read more than ten of them. Americans want men like me in charge. They want a strong man in the driver's seat. That's me. Why do you think guys like me get all the women? Why do you think guys like me rise to the top so fast?"

Pierson shook his head in dismay.

Beck continued on undaunted. "Because I get things done. What . . . do you think I'm the first president to mess around on the side? They all did it. Big deal. Nobody really cares anymore."

Pierson finished off his second scotch and put the glass on the mantle. "You're all alone on this, Beck. I need to distance myself from you."

Beck waved him off. "You're crazy, Harry. That toxic, redheaded bitch is a flash in the pan. Trust me."

Pierson rubbed his chin. He was deeply disturbed by what he was hearing, if for no other reason than he finally recognized how capable the president was of immersing himself in complete denial. It unsettled him.

"Sit down for a second, Beck."

Both men retook their seats.

"Okay, I'm sitting down. What now?"

Pierson thought over his words carefully. It was going to be hard to get away from the fallout. He knew there was no coming back for him. But he still felt a sense of loyalty to his president. "Have you read Camille's book?"

"Read it?" said Beck, incredulously. "I lived it. Why the hell would I want to read it?"

"I have," confessed the vice president. "It's more than just some sensationalist rant. This book is a well-written, well-thought-out commentary on the state of affairs between men and women."

Beck repeated the words mockingly. "State of affairs . . . are you making some sort of pun? Are you trying to be funny?"

Pierson managed to laugh a little. "Actually, that's the first line of the book."

"Really, Harry? You're citing the bitch now?"

Pierson held up his hands. "You've gotta admit, she has a way with words."

"It's her editor, for God's sake, Harry. Did you ever read one of her other books? It's like they were written for children. The soul is eternal Oneness . . . what does that even mean?"

"Be that as it may, Beck, *This Soul's Journey through the Eye of the Storm* is the new manifesto for women's rights everywhere. It's a call to action against men who believe they are entitled to do whatever they want, whenever they want, simply because they have power . . . power that women grant them."

Beck was getting pissed. He'd heard about enough and was ready to send Pierson as far away as possible. "Is that another line from this fabulous book?"

"No, I made that up myself, thank you. Anyway, she's sold millions of copies in something like twenty different languages already."

Beck stood up abruptly. "Oh, spare me this crap. Are you saying Camille O'Keefe is the new Becket Rosemore?"

The question hung in the air like a ball thrown in slow motion. As the two men stared at each other in silence, it became very clear that Beck's sardonic question was actually the truth. Camille had supplanted Beck on the world stage.

"You know what?" asked Beck. "I think it's time for you to leave. I'm going hunting."

"Okay," said Pierson. "But there's something you should know. They're planning on preventing you from running for reelection."

Beck didn't believe a word of it. "You mean those dingbats in the other party want me to step down because they're tired of me kicking their ass?"

Pierson shook his head. "No, Beck. Although the other party pillories you in the media, they would like nothing more than for you to run for reelection. They'll wipe the floor with you. I'm talking about the members of our own party, Mr. President. You're done."

Beck was enraged. "That's the most ridiculous thing I've ever heard. Why?"

"Because you're poison," yelled Pierson. "Face the facts, Beck. Nobody wants you around anymore."

"Is that why you came up here, to stick the dagger in, you ungrateful Judas son of a bitch?"

"You mean Brutus. He stabbed Caesar. Judas betrayed Jesus . . . and you're no Jesus."

"You know what I mean, you pompous prick."

"Actually, Beck, I promised them I wouldn't say anything to you."

"Wow, you'll just betray everybody, won't you?"

"No, I came here out of loyalty to you. Like you said, I owe you a lot. But this is the end of the line for us."

"So you've said."

"I mean you and me . . . our partnership. It ends here."

"Okay, Al Gore."

"I mean it, Beck. Your own party is going to do you in. They're not going to risk losing the White House to that buffoon who'll be running against you."

Beck was prepared for something like this. He had played it out in his mind time and time again. But now that it was actually happening, now that there were secret meetings about him and all that, he was floored. His anger started to turn to despair as the reality of what Pierson was saying began to sink in. He had to massage his temples.

"It's really not a big deal, Beck. One term was more than enough for you to make some serious connections. Like you said, you'll be fine."

The president looked up at his vice president. His voice was forlorn. "I suppose they have you tagged to take my place?"

Pierson tried his best to keep a stiff upper lip. "Actually . . . no. I'm going down with the ship. I'm done, too."

Beck rubbed his forehead. Pierson tried to ease the blow, but Beck interrupted him. "Just get out of my house."

Pierson tried to speak again, but Beck just raised his hand. Pierson knew better than to press it.

Chapter 30

Beck stood at the window watching Pierson and his security detail pile into the limo and head down the road toward Route 28. An incredible loneliness overtook him. He knew he had so many options, and yet he felt completely disempowered. He could see his reflection in the window as Pierson's motorcade drove out of sight. Disgusted with what he saw, he turned away and walked over to the bar. He poured himself his first drink in almost two decades.

He knocked it back and poured himself another. He downed the second just as fast. The alcohol hit him quickly now that he'd been sober for so long. Trying to muster what energy he could, he decided it was the ideal time to kill something. He called for one of his security detail.

The man was there in seconds. "Yes, Mr. President?"

"Let's get ready to shoot. I want to get some good hunting in while I can."

"Your rifle bag is already packed, sir."

"Good. We'll head over to Senator Brogan's property. It's crawling with pheasant."

Beck could see the agent was hesitant.

"What?" asked the president.

"We contacted the senator as you instructed . . . to let him know you were going to hunt on his land."

"Okay, so what?"

"Actually, Mr. President . . . the senator's people said that he would prefer you to hunt someplace else."

Beck's hands dropped to his sides. "What?"

The agent was praying for any excuse to leave the room.

Beck was so angry he stuttered. "This is the same Byard Brogan . . . the same . . . the man who magically became Majority Leader after I picked up the phone for him?"

"I'm sorry, sir. People can be fickle."

"Whatever, just get the car ready."

"Where are you hunting then, sir?"

"I have no idea. But I am damned well gonna shoot something before this day is done. I don't give a crap if it's a cow out to pasture."

The agent left, leaving the president mumbling to himself and pouring out another drink. "I'm the damned president of the United States."

He walked over to the bookshelf and removed a beautiful edition of *Julius Caesar* bound in dark, faded leather, smelling faintly of antiquity, of bygone values. He sighed. He felt alone. He was still mumbling to himself. Beck thought about Pierson correcting him about that whole Brutus and Judas thing. What did the details matter? The point was the same. Betrayal was betrayal.

"You too, Harry? You too?" His words lacked conviction. The daggers were already sunken in too deep.

Chapter 31

It started with an op-ed in a major D.C. paper. From there, it spread like wildfire over the AP wire. Within hours, every major paper carried it, in turn spawning dozens of other articles speculating on the rift between Beck and his vice president. Nothing could have pleased Harry Pierson more. Indeed, that's why he planted the piece in the D.C. paper to begin with.

Harry Pierson did not rise up through the ranks of the intelligence world by being passive and fair-minded. A man like Harry Pierson could go a long way in Washington. His ability to cauterize his emotions when it came to human life gave him an iron stomach when things got nasty, and his knack for self-preservation made him both an ally and an enemy to everyone at all times. He was one of the most calculating, connected, conniving men in D.C. That's why people turned to him when dirty work needed to be done. Even Beck had turned to Pierson on several occasions when he needed certain matters handled, matters that simply couldn't become public.

Always willing to make a deal, Pierson was a modern-day Rasputin, collecting secrets as precious as a first-born baby. Pierson was a facilitator to some, a deal maker to others, walking a tightrope, amassing his power by turning everything he could into political gold.

More than anything else, people feared him as one of Washington's greatest extortionists. Many high-placed people crossed paths with Harry Pierson, and more than a few needed his help managing situations that could crush their careers, marriages, hopes and aspirations if they became public.

With the pressure mounting to get Beck off the ballot for the next election, members of the president's own party were busily plotting his fall from grace. Pierson was the obvious go-to. Unbeknownst to Beck, senior members of his party, led by Harry Pierson himself, devised a PR campaign that was set to roll out in a few days. The goal was to sacrifice Beck, but in such a way as to restore the party's reputation in the capricious court of public opinion. It could be done, but it wouldn't be easy.

They decided not to go negative by attacking Camille. They may have loathed her, but they were smart enough not to cross her. They would only appear callous and misogynistic if they did. Instead, it was Beck they planned to offer up as a sacrifice to burn at the stake. But first, they needed their Rumpelstiltskin, Harry Pierson, to weave his magic, turning Beck's bullshit into gold so they could later spin out a new candidate. It was a perfect assignment for the vice president.

The entire plan was Pierson's idea in the first place. He put the machine in motion two weeks before he headed up to Lake Canadarago. He made the trip with a very specific agenda in mind. Sidelining Beck would be easy. The president was a ticking time bomb. He was also predictable, easy pickings for a man like Pierson, who was confident he could manipulate Beck as if the president was a marionette.

At the same time, Pierson had to distance himself from Beck if he had any hope at all of remaining in politics. This was a matter of personal survival. To pull the thing off, Harry Pierson had to set up two people—Becket Rosemore and Wagner Van Dorthman. At one time, both of these men were very close to him. But a man like Harry Pierson will always use that against you. Close as they once were, he had no qualms knocking them down like bowling pins if it meant saving his own ass. He had to jettison both in order to stay afloat. It was never really a tough decision. Instead, it was a matter of pragmatic common sense.

Like so many times in his past, Harry Pierson turned off his emotions so he could take care of business without hesitation. His first task was to push Beck's buttons and precipitate a falling out of sorts. That was his primary reason for surprising Beck at Rockwell House. Getting Beck to flip out would be easy. And so it was. Several references to Camille, a few lines from her book, a comment or two about Beck looking like a fool . . . that's all it took for D.C.'s Rasputin to weave his magic.

Setup number one was easy. Beck never saw it coming, not from his own vice president and closest friend. There was more work to be done, however. The rift between them had to be public. The hack job in the press would not come as easily as Beck's narcissistic rage. In order to distance the party—and, more importantly, himself—from Beck, Pierson's next job was to arrange an op-ed inflammatory enough to light the fire under the president's feet. For this, Pierson needed a hot topic with a lot of pop. He needed a public apostasy. He knew just the guy.

It was the obvious choice. And so Harry Pierson never thought twice about using another "good friend" as sacrificial lamb number two. He tapped his old friend Wagner Van Dorthman to script the op-ed. Van Dorthman was recognized by super PACs and other vital financial supporters. During Beck's term in office, Van Dorthman was as close as one could be with a sitting president. They were often photographed playing golf together, and Van Dorthman was a regular speaker at all the president's big fundraisers. His role was vital in Beck's ascent. Pierson would see to it that his role would be equally critical in Beck's downfall.

Harry Pierson knew if he could turn Van Dorthman, it would crush what little support Beck might still have. Such a betrayal would also hurt Beck very deeply on a personal level. Pierson desired both. Rasputin must have his recompense, too. He had nothing else to go on. For the time being, he was toast, a political dead man walking.

He had to do something. Desperate times required desperate actions. He was capable of anything. When things got nasty and the crap got thick, Pierson was the kind of man one sought out as an ally and prayed not to have as an enemy. Pierson knew he would probably go down with Beck. He also knew how fickle politicians were. If he could somehow orchestrate this maneuver against Beck, he might just ingratiate himself and curry enough favor to live another day.

It was time for Rasputin to sit behind his wheel and spin out the perfect plan to turn Wagner Van Dorthman. Because Van Dorthman was so close to Beck, Pierson had to go deep to find something damaging enough to Van Dorthman that he would rather throw Beck under the bus than risk his own ass. It had to be ironclad. It had to be something truly terrible. Fortunately for Harry Pierson, Wagner Van Dorthman laid it right in his hands around the same time the party decided to oust Beck. Once again, things just fell into place as if the universe had a guiding hand in the matter.

About two weeks before Pierson visited Beck at Rockwell House, Van Dorthman was in Ethiopia inspecting one of his new manufacturing plants. Cheap labor was Ethiopia's greatest resource, and the world's biggest designers quickly began sourcing their clothing to factories like Van Dorthman's that were popping up everywhere. As a result, a small, super-affluent class began to rise up along with the new skyscrapers. As a matter of course, certain dark elements also emerged in order to satisfy the more perverse tastes of the powerful, nouveau riche men in Addis Ababa.

Harry Pierson knew the rapid rise of a super-class in the Ethiopian capital meant new markets in the flesh and drug trades couldn't be far behind. Pierson always knew what he needed to know. He was sure an unbridled, carnal playground would flourish in Addis Ababa. He was equally certain that a man with Van Dorthman's taste for extreme pleasure would get himself in trouble sooner or later. Somewhere in there Pierson figured to set a trap for Van Dorthman, get him involved in something so nasty, burying Beck in the media would seem a very small price to pay for the billionaire to extricate himself.

And so, as he'd done so many times before, Harry Pierson mobilized his intelligence network. A day later, the sting was in motion. Van Dorthman was staying in an extravagant executive villa at the poshest hotel in Addis Ababa. Money flowed through those villas like the water flowing through the many fountains adorning the property. The three-story villa had everything the billionaire CEO of VD Manufacturing could want . . . luxurious bedding and fine décor, a private pool, private gym with sauna, even a chef and butler. For $25,000 a day, Van Dorthman's needs would be well met. Best of all, he could write it all off as a business expense.

Fine champagne and prescription drugs were only two of Van Dorthman's vices. Pierson knew the textile mogul had a penchant for exotic beauties, as young as possible. The two had joked about it many times over the years. Precisely because he knew Van Dorthman so well, it didn't take much for Harry Pierson to figure out the perfect plan to make him his stooge. All he needed to do was serve up delicacies of the flesh he knew the billionaire could not refuse.

The textile mogul was soaking in the Jacuzzi tub up on the third floor of the villa. He was more than halfway through an ice-cold bottle of champagne, a Krug *Privat Cuvée*. He knew it was a good buy at $2,000, especially at a hotel, so he sent the villa's butler for another. Still, he was a bit bored. The novelty of having everything at his disposal was giving him a sense of ennui lately. He wanted something more. He yearned for a greater thrill. He knew deep down inside that's why he came to Africa in the first place. He could have sent any of his operations people to check in on the progress of the new factory. Ethiopia was uncharted waters for him, a veritable frontier land where he felt he could get or do anything he wanted without fear of reprisals or repercussions. And he would have been right except for one minor detail . . . nowhere on the planet is outside Harry Pierson's reach.

When the butler knocked on the bathroom door, Van Dorthman welcomed the second bottle. Getting drunk on one of the finest champagnes in the world wasn't the worst use of his time. If nothing better turned up, he could always order up a couple of fine prostitutes.

"You may enter," he said, turning the Jacuzzi bubbles off.

The butler opened the door. Van Dorthman could barely restrain himself when he saw not just another bottle of champagne but two Ethiopian girls as well. They were dressed identically in matching outfits . . . wispy periwinkle blouses, beige miniskirts and sandals laced up the calf. He figured they couldn't be older than fifteen. Despite their relative youth, both girls embodied the exotic beauty of Ethiopian women . . . jet-black almond eyes, pronounced cheekbones and full lips, and a long, thin neckline and silhouette.

They were like two stunning bookends standing motionless on either side of the butler. They were exceptionally beautiful and exceptionally young. Van Dorthman felt like he was on top of the world. "Oh, my. What have we here?"

The butler smiled broadly. He knew a special gratuity would be in store for this. "I am sorry, sir. They did not have another bottle of that particular champagne."

Van Dorthman was not pleased. "That's ridiculous. I want what I want."

"If you will allow me, sir. The usual sommelier appears not to be here today. A British chap was working in his stead. I've never seen him before. A white man. He was definitely British, but very different looking. He was very tall. Yes, he was definitely British. More importantly, sir, he offered you this 1998 *Clos d'Ambonnay*. He said it was on the house, a special gift for Wagner Van Dorthman."

Van Dorthman was thrilled. "That's one hell of a rare bottle. Why the hell would he give it away like that? Did he know me? Are you sure you've never seen him before?"

"I have not, sir. I did not ask twice. As we like to say in Ethiopia, it's better to have an egg today than a chicken tomorrow. You are obviously a very important man. Perhaps he's heard of you? I hope you don't mind, sir."

Van Dorthman threw up his hands and laughed. "Mind? Just the opposite. I love you! And yes, I am a very important man." Turning his attention to more important matters, he looked the girls over. "I see you picked up something else along the way."

He put his empty glass down on the side of the Jacuzzi and stood up. He was buck naked. The sight of the two young girls made him visibly excited with anticipation.

The butler bowed ceremoniously as he held his hands out toward the girls. "I can provide many things for you, sir."

Van Dorthman smiled. "Where did you find these two lovelies?"

"They were waiting for me in the lobby. They say they were sent to you specifically . . . from a friend."

"Well, this must be my lucky day, my man. First, some substitute sommelier hands you a $2,000 bottle for free and then you throw in a couple of little girls, also for free? Let me tell you, my man, you've made this Bawana very happy indeed. I need to look into buying a house here."

"We'd be lucky to have you, sir."

Van Dorthman stepped out of the Jacuzzi and held his arms out to the side proudly. "Not bad, huh girls?"

The girls averted their eyes demurely. The butler neatly wrapped a towel around Van Dorthman's waist and began preparing three fresh glasses of champagne.

"Yes, yes," urged Van Dorthman. "Good idea. Give them some champagne. Both of these little birds will be flying high in no time."

The butler grinned. "I see you know how to handle girls like this. That is good." He handed each girl a flute of champagne. He told them that if they did not comply with every one of the white boss's requests, he would personally scar their faces with acid. They would be rendered undesirable and useless, destined to life as an outcast. A regional variation of the scarlet letter, this was a common way of punishing disobedient women around those parts.

"Do it," ordered the butler in English for emphasis this time.

What choice did they have? The frightened girls obediently drank the champagne. They were both clearly unused to drinking alcohol and had to choke it down.

Van Dorthman addressed the girls directly now. "The bottle of champagne you're drinking costs $2,000 a bottle. Do you understand what I am saying? That's a lot of money for you, isn't it? Yes, it is.

Remember who gave it to you. Remember to tell everyone how good the white boss is to you. Next time, we can have a big party with the rest of your little friends. There's plenty of champagne and plenty of me to go around."

"Don't worry, sir," said the butler. "They both speak English. And next time, I can bring as many girls as you desire. It is not a problem rounding them up. They are everywhere for the taking."

Van Dorthman looked at the butler. "They just showed up out of the blue asking for me?"

"That is correct, sir. They said they were a gift to you from a friend."

Van Dorthman thought for a moment, concluding some local official must have sent them as a "thank you" for the payoffs and other graft he had spread around Addis Ababa like jam on bread in order to get his factory approved and then built. It was no easy task. It cost him millions in bribes. But it was business as usual around those parts. So, too, he assumed, was this delectable, two-course gift of flesh.

"Thank you," he said. "That will be all for now. Please make sure that my dinner jacket is pressed for tonight. I'm dining with Mayor Dumior. And make sure both of these little beauties are gone from the premises when I am done with them. I'm sure I don't need to tell you that the utmost discretion is required, right?"

The butler nodded. He knew clientele like Van Dorthman depended on his secrecy.

Van Dorthman looked the girls over. Again, he figured they were no older than fourteen . . . fifteen at the most. For certain, they were younger than his own daughter. That was as far as he took the comparison. He removed his daughter from his consciousness, safely back home with his wife. These two African girls, though . . . he had plans for them. They had only just begun to mature. They were perfect, just as he liked them. As with fruit, he liked to pick his girls while they were not quite ripe.

Having two exotic girls under his complete control made him feel lightheaded. Maybe it was the champagne taking hold?

Whatever the cause, he swelled with desire that was woven tightly with feelings of power and rage. That was the emotional trinity that drove him to devour young slave girls just as it drove him to succeed in business. It was a glorious fusion of mind and purpose for him. Like Becket Rosemore, the man whom Van Dorthman promoted so fervently, power, control and anger were all orgiastic bedfellows in the act of sex.

The butler bowed and left Van Dorthman alone with the girls. They were both thin, maybe 110 pounds each. The champagne was hitting them already. They felt woozy, but their bodies were also buzzing with a sort of euphoric feeling beyond their control. Van Dorthman had done this enough times to know when a young girl was buzzing. He grew more aroused. He downed his glass, dropped the towel from around his waist, walked over and took a girl under each arm. He nestled their thin shoulders against his ribs. They were so small. It felt great.

He slid a hand under each of their skirts. "Who wants to play a game?" It sounded as if he was talking to children . . . because he was.

The action started after Van Dorthman and the girls knocked off the superlative bottle of champagne the mysterious new sommelier sent up with the butler. Bondage was one of Van Dorthman's favorite pastimes, especially with the young ones. He tied both girls to the bedposts. They were naked except for their lace-up sandals. He toyed with them lasciviously. They were his possessions.

It took him several minutes to realize that both girls had passed out. Shortly thereafter, Van Dorthman lost consciousness as well. The last thing Van Dorthman remembered was hearing a man's voice and seeing the fuzzy outline of a very tall man. It was definitely a British accent he heard. After that, he fell flat on his face in front of the giant canopy bed, his empty champagne flute shattered on the tumbled-stone tile.

An afternoon full of pleasant surprises had turned dark for Van Dorthman. When he finally came to, Wagner Van Dorthman tried to regain his senses. He had a splitting headache and couldn't really remember where he was. There was, indeed, a very tall man looming over him saying something. But all Van Dorthman could make out was a strong British accent. The words themselves weren't making any sense yet. He tried to sit up, but the tall man pushed him back down into a large fan chair. He tried to speak, but nothing came out. That's when Van Dorthman realized he was naked and gagged.

The tall man was dressed in hotel attire. He was, in fact, the very sommelier the butler had mentioned earlier. Of course, Van Dorthman had no way of knowing an elaborate setup was occurring. He had no way of knowing he would owe Harry Pierson forever or even that his friend was pulling the strings to begin with. All he knew was that something had gone terribly wrong, and he was in big, big trouble.

Van Dorthman strained to see as the tall man methodically removed his tuxedo jacket, folded it and laid it on another chair. He then pulled one end of his bow tie and let it hang down before opening his collar and cracking his neck from side to side. The man then snapped his fingers as if he'd forgotten something, went over to his jacket and fished out two black leather gloves from the side pocket. He then refolded the jacket. The neatness with which he conducted himself unsettled Wagner. This couldn't possibly end well for him.

The tall man pulled his gloves on, pushing each finger down one by one. They were quite snug and creaked ever so slightly each time the man clenched his enormous fists. He turned to Van Dorthman and smiled.

"I am very tall, and you are very small. Perhaps that's why you like having sex with little girls, eh matey? Well, I know one thing you'll never forget . . . when you see a gigantic white man in the middle of Africa wearing leather gloves on a ninety-degree day, you'd best turn and walk the other way. We've spared no expense for you, matey. Rest assured, I am top of the range at what I do. You're in for a real biscuit."

Van Dorthman tried to speak, but the gag just prompted more saliva. The man removed the ball gag.

"Do you have any idea who the hell I am?" hissed Van Dorthman, who had apparently regained enough of his senses to start leveling threats. It might not have been the best attempt at détente.

Without hesitation, the man let fly with a right hook that caught Van Dorthman squarely on the chin. The man's arm seemed to extend forever and gathered tremendous velocity that rippled through Van Dorthman's jaw, knocking him unconscious instantly. Clearly annoyed at the mogul's lack of fortitude, the man took some smelling salts from his pants pocket, cracked it nonchalantly between his thumb and index finger, and held it under Van Dorthman's nose. Van Dorthman shook his head as he began regaining clarity.

The man sniffed some, too. "Seems you're in a bit of a pickle as it is, mate; best you don't make it any worse by being daft."

Still put off by Van Dorthman's glass jaw, the man waved the smelling salts under the mogul's nose again. When Van Dorthman seemed alert enough for another round, he squeezed his nose, yanked his head back, and pried his mouth open with three of his massive gloved fingers.

"The thing is," he said, towering over Van Dorthman who looked immobilized in his chair like a butterfly pinned to a board, "I can pour a bottle of bleach down your throat right now. Or I could snap your neck like a twig. Hell, I could even have my way with you like you did with the girls there. A little respect on your part would go a long way toward making sure I don't tear your knob off so as you can't hurt any more girls."

He released Van Dorthman's head and pushed it back against the chair in disgust before continuing. "To answer your question, matey . . . yes, I know who you are. That's why I'm here. And by the way, I was expecting someone much tougher. But I guess a Yank who runs around drugging and raping little girls has no buttocks. You're a little arsemonger as far as I'm concerned. They're going to love you in Kaliti Prison, matey. Around here they call it the Gulag. I bet those inmates are gonna do a number on that pudding cup of yours, eh? Do you know they stuff hundreds of inmates in big cells? They're more like cages for that load of animals they've got locked up in there. I suspect you'll find out what it's like to be buggered yourself. It serves you right, you bleeding wanker. You just gotta love good irony, eh matey?"

Van Dorthman began to panic. He looked over to the bed. The two young girls were motionless. Their wrists were still tied to the bedposts and their heads were drooped. They looked dead. For a second, Wagner felt like he was going to faint as extreme anxiety overtook him.

The man looked over at the girls as well. "Ah, look at that, will ya? There's your handiwork." He walked over to the bed, stuck out a gloved finger, and poked the first girl in the cheek . . . nothing. He did the same with the second girl. . .nothing. He took each girl by the hair and pulled her head back. "Not much good going on here."

He let go of their hair. The girls' heads drooped again. "I can't understand your taste for little girls, matey. Not me, nope. I like my women to be women . . . nice titties, a nice arse. A woman knows how to operate, you know what I mean? I guess you like to feel like a big man though, don't ya? I mean . . . you're a bloody buggering nonce. You have a messed up brain and all. You're a maggot. But did you have to drug them and tie them up like you were Bill Cosby's protégé?" He noticed Van Dorthman was close to tears.

"It was all a misunderstanding. You have to believe me."

The tall man had a burning desire to knock him out cold again. He walked over to Van Dorthman and folded his arms. It was all he could do to restrain himself. "I've lived in this country for ten years now. These are good people just trying to survive like everyone else on this shit-hole continent. When big business comes knocking, though . . . well . . . everything becomes a resource to be bought and sold by men like you. Isn't that right, matey? I guess the people here don't mean much to you except as cheap labor or maybe something to satisfy your perverted fetishes."

The man was agitated and started pacing. "Now you've made me sound like a damned socialist or worse, a blithering feminist, and that really pisses me off." He unloaded another punch, this time into Van Dorthman's gut. "It's bad for business to sound like a revolutionary or an uppity bird. In my line of work, I must remain politically neutral. I wouldn't want to offend a potential client. It's unprofessional . . . you understand."

Wagner Van Dorthman was too busy gasping for air to attempt speaking. Instead he just nodded and gave the tall man a thumbs up.

"Excellent, then we have cleared the air about my political affiliations. It's still a bit dim of you." He gestured over his shoulder toward the two girls. "To leave them here like that? They look pretty young. They're not going to take kindly to this around here. You may see these people as bloody savages, man. But that's how they're going to see you as well. Or are you too daft to understand that?"

Van Dorthman tried desperately to comprehend what was happening. "Who are you?"

The tall man smiled. "You probably think I'm here to kill you. Actually, I'm here to help you get out of this mess. I'm your friend. My specialty is helping dodgy buggers like you, mate. That's why they call me The Angel . . . for Guardian Angel. I see to it that certain . . . shall we say, important businessmen like you don't get caught up to their arse in shit. And today, it looks like you're number one on my shit list."

Van Dorthman sat there staring at the girls in disbelief and trying to comprehend what the hell the guy was talking about. He considered the situation and how he was sitting there naked with those two girls tied to the bed like that. "So, you work for the U.S. government?"

The Brit laughed. "I am a subcontractor. I work for everyone . . . and no one. You know how that goes. I'm neutral . . . like the Swiss."

Van Dorthman was shocked. He didn't know what to think. As far as he could figure, he was either the luckiest or unluckiest man in the world at that moment. The last thing he remembered was stripping the girls and binding them. The rest was gone. "I didn't do anything to those girls. I don't know what happened. It was all in good fun, believe me."

The man peered over his shoulder. "They don't seem to be having a very good time of it, matey."

Van Dorthman still couldn't put it all together. "I don't know what happened. The butler showed up with the girls. He said someone sent them to me. I just assumed that's how it goes around here."

"Around here? In Africa, you mean? People just send little girls as sex toys? Is that how you see these people?"

Aside from his aching jaw, Van Dorthman's head felt like 10,000 volts were ricocheting between his ears. He'd never felt like this before and was sure somebody had tampered with the champagne. He was beginning to suspect there was more going on than he realized. The first thing that came to mind were the bribes. Had he left someone important off the list and now they were screwing with him? Or maybe it was a competitor trying to protect their turf? That jerkoff from Momamatu Textiles always hated his guts.

Wagner had to make a critical decision, and he had to make it immediately—could he trust the Brit? His splitting headache and throbbing jaw didn't make it any easier. The tall man may have hated his guts and wanted to kick his ass, but he might also prove to be the only one who could extricate him from what looked to be the end of everything. It was a precarious situation to say the least. But really, what choice did he have?

He sighed. "I remember the girls taking their clothes off, and then I tied them up. After that . . . nothing. The next thing I know I'm naked and a gigantic British psycho is punching me in the face."

The man laughed. "I keep thinking about the inmates in Kaliti Prison. Did I mention I love irony? I did, didn't I? Sorry if I'm boring you, mate."

Van Dorthman struggled to find the words to explain what happened because he genuinely didn't know. Obviously, the Brit wasn't buying it. "I didn't kill those girls, for Christ's sake. It . . . it must have been the champagne. My head's killing me. I feel weird, too. Someone spiked my champagne. I've been set up. I'm lucky to be alive myself. I'm telling you, I didn't kill those girls."

The Brit found this amusing. "Dead? For Christ's sake, man, they're not dead. They're unconscious, out cold. Do you think we'd be having this conversation if there were two dead little girls in your bedroom, you sodding lunatic?"

"I told you I have no idea what happened to them. I mean . . . I guess I gave them a lot of champagne." He pulled his arms in close to help cover his naked, vulnerable body.

"You gave two little girls a lot of alcohol? They can't weigh more than seven or eight stones. Think about that. And I'm supposed to help you?"

There was fear in Van Dorthman's voice. "I . . . I didn't think it would be a big deal."

The man walked over and examined the girls again. He pursed his lips and grimaced. "Even if you are a whiney prat, I don't think a couple bottles of champagne would lay them out like that. No spew or anything? Maybe you're right . . . somebody slipped you one."

Van Dorthman saw everything he'd worked for over the years evaporating into thin air. As he looked at the two girls lying limp across the bed, he saw his entire world crumbling before his eyes. What would he tell his wife? What would he tell his daughter?

"You've got to help me," pleaded Van Dorthman. "I will make it worth your while."

"Don't be a shit. I am very well taken care of," replied the Brit in annoyance. "Why else would I be here helping a dolt like you? Gone and gotten yourself into a real situation, you did. How did they get here? How did two young girls wind up in your villa for sex . . . which, by the way, is as illegal here as it is in the United States. When rich foreigners like you get involved with stuff like this, it starts a frenzy of greed and outrage. Trust me, mate . . . you're in deep right now. You're upset because I belted you twice. But believe me, it's a damned good thing I'm here. You must have some friends in very high places, matey. Today's your lucky day. Fate had a plan for you, and you managed to escape, you dodgy bastard, thanks to me. I hope you've learned your lesson. I doubt you're important enough to have another Get Out of Jail Free card."

"I swear to you . . . I swear on my children's lives—"

The man cut him off. "Don't say stuff like that. This is business. Leave children out of it. Didn't you just hear a bloody word I said?"

"Okay, okay . . . I get it. Your job is to bail out guys like me—"

"Maggots like you," clarified the man.

Van Dorthman was in no position to debate. "Fine, fine . . . I'm a maggot. But I promise you, something's not right here. It doesn't add up."

The man laughed. "You can say that again. It's a big world. Someone's out there trying to bring you down, while someone very powerful is willing to help you out. Like I said, you're the luckiest son of a bitch in the world today."

It was one man orchestrating both sides of the con—Harry Pierson, the vice president of the United States. And it was going according to plan. He fed Van Dorthman's depravity, cornered him and then handed him his escape. It was masterful, the kind of maneuver that made Harry Pierson infamous on the Beltway . . . and feared by all.

There was no way Wagner could have seen things for what they were. The reality of his situation was obscured by his own guilt and debauchery. The only thing he could see was his own culpability and the tremendous price he would pay. Nothing else mattered, not the girls, not his aching jaw, not even his new factory. Saving his white ass was his sole motivation. It was exactly as Pierson had predicted. After all, the vice president was busy saving his own life.

"What I mean is that I passed out also. So it couldn't have been just a pill and a bit of champagne. My head felt like someone hit me in the forehead with a sledgehammer even before you socked me. I'm telling you, it was the champagne."

The man went back to the girls and checked their pupils. "So you are trying to tell me that someone spiked your champagne?"

"The butler . . . where's the butler? Find that son of a bitch. He'll tell you everything. You'll see. He'll tell you everything."

The Brit scratched his head. "Ah, yes, the butler. That troglodyte who brought you the girls and the champagne in the first place."

Van Dorthman was beginning to show signs of life. "Yes, yes. He will tell you everything." Then he caught himself. As he recalled it, the butler mentioned a tall Brit was standing in for the regular sommelier. It had to be the same guy with him right now. If that was correct, then the Brit could have been the one who spiked the champagne to begin with.

"Wait, the butler mentioned to me that someone sounding a lot like you was standing in for the usual sommelier. Is that true? Were you watching this thing unfold the entire time?"

The Brit grinned. "I can neither confirm nor deny that."

Van Dorthman massaged his temples. "So you arranged the whole thing to catch me with these girls?"

The Brit looked him straight in the eye. "Maybe I did, maybe I didn't. What does it matter to you? Whether or not somebody wanted to put you in a pickle is irrelevant right now, don't you agree? I am your only way out. That's the only thing that matters to you right now. Of course, I can walk out and leave you to your own devices if you prefer."

"No . . . no. I see your point. I'm screwed either way."

The Brit gestured to the girls. "They got screwed. You got lucky. Big difference. Anyway, you have no choice. My job is to get you out of here unscathed. That's what I've been paid to do. Your cooperation is not required. You're coming with me one way or the other, so you might as well play nice."

"So then why did you set me up in the first place?"

The Brit stopped what he was doing and looked at Van Dorthman as if the question was completely insane. "Huh?"

"I said why did you set me up in the first place? Why go to all this trouble?"

"I didn't do anything to your champagne. But somebody obviously did. As for me, that was all part of the plan. It created the need for my services, right? If you're not in trouble, I can't save you from trouble. See how that works? If I stopped it from happening, there'd be no need to save your ass. In my line of work, you don't ask too many questions. Frankly, mate, I don't give a crap. I get a job, I do the job. I get paid."

Van Dorthman couldn't figure it out, but he knew one thing for sure. The Brit was right. He had no choice but to go along with the plan someone had painstakingly laid out for him. He was just along for the ride. He could figure out the details when he was back safely in the States. Someone had him drugged. Someone had him saved. That's all he might ever discover.

"So what about the butler?"

"Oh trust me, I had a little talk with the bloke. He's been pimping little girls like this for a couple of years now. Everybody knows about it. You're not the first rich white guy he's drugged. But the money keeps flowing. You know what I mean. The racket's big enough for some important people to take their share. The butler's not my problem right now, you are. These girls are going to wake up soon, and you need to be well on your way out of Ethiopia. And I don't expect to see you here again, so you better find some lackey to visit that factory of yours going forward. If I do see you around here again, it won't be business. It will be personal. Wankers like you make me sick. I'll snap your neck, prop open your mouth, and do to your face what you were planning to do to these girls. Then I'll go and have a few pints as if you never existed at all. That's how little I think of you. You're the lowest form of scum there is."

It sounded to Van Dorthman that the Brit was going to help him escape the scene and extricate himself from the whole sordid affair, but it was going to be a rough ride. Obviously, someone had arranged the whole thing. But why go to such lengths? He hadn't a clue, not yet. Whatever the truth of the matter, Wagner Van Dorthman knew one thing for certain. As things stood, his wife and kids would never find out. He had to play his hand right, though. He couldn't afford to fall from grace and land in ruin. As he had always said, he wasn't cut out for a life of poverty. The Brit was obviously some sort of mercenary. But he was no friend. Just because he was helping Van Dorthman today didn't mean he wouldn't kill him tomorrow. The whole thing was completely foreign to him.

"Thank you. Thank you so much for believing me," said Wagner.

The Brit held up his hand. "Don't make me hit you again. I never said I believed you. To tell you the truth, I'd just as soon let you rot in Kaliti Prison. But . . . I will say your dilemma was brought about by some outside interest. So I feel for you there . . . just a bit. It still doesn't excuse what you did. For that, I would prefer to cut off your balls and stuff them down your throat. Maybe some other time, eh?"

Van Dorthman stood up slowly. He didn't care that he was buck naked. He was overjoyed that the Brit was going to help him. "Thank you. Thank you so much."

"Don't thank me, matey. Like I said, you must have a very powerful friend in high places even if you have an enemy equally high up."

Van Dorthman tried to focus on moving things along. "How do you plan to get me out of here?"

"Leave that up to me. Pack just a small bag, your money, and we will get you out of here."

"But won't the police come looking?"

The man nodded. "Yes, because the butler will call them. He probably has already. That's part of his scam. Drug you and the girls, call the cops and catch you red-handed. The bribes roll from there. See how that works? You were an easy mark, mate. And if you don't pay them a small fortune, they will lock you away for a long, long time to serve notice to anyone else who may be considering playing without paying."

That was the last the Brit spoke of it. As promised, Wagner Van Dorthman was whisked away from the villa shortly thereafter. The Brit helped him climb over a whitewashed wall at a section where the barbed wire had already been cut away. A black Suburban was waiting for him on the other side. Van Dorthman's bag came flying over the wall after him, hitting him straight in the head.

A muscular white man jumped out of the passenger's seat. He was wearing a khaki shirt, jeans and combat boots. He also wore a floppy camo bush hat and dark aviators. He pulled Van Dorthman up, pushed him into the back seat of the truck and then threw the bag in, once again hitting Van Dorthman in the head.

The man looked at Van Dorthman before closing the door. He was American. "Boy, asshole, for a pedophile, you sure do have some powerful friends." He reached into his back pocket, popped out a tin of Skoal, inserted a fat lipper and spit. "Yeah, must be nice."

He slammed the rear door shut and jumped back into the passenger's seat. The driver, dressed in camo pants, a blue Hawaiian shirt and sweaty baseball cap, looked back at Van Dorthman. "So you're one of the world's largest clothing manufactures? We got us a real fat cat billionaire right here in the back seat."

Out of breath after running from the villa and taking two bags to the head, Van Dorthman just nodded.

The driver spoke up this time. "Well, it looks as if the emperor has no clothes . . . get it? Clothing manufacturer . . . no clothes . . . double entendre? " He put the truck in gear and started to drive off. "God I crack myself up sometimes."

Van Dorthman stuck to his story. "I have no idea what happened back there. It was all a setup."

The driver smiled. "I bet they were young, right? Yeah . . . guys like you can't resist a little exotic snack when you're shitting all over a poor country."

Van Dorthman looked completely lost. "Who are you? Where are you taking me?"

"You have no idea what's going on, do you?" asked the driver.

The man in the passenger's seat was smirking. He spit into an empty beer bottle. "Should we break it down for him? I hate to see these rich guys look so clueless. It shatters the image, you know? Hey, remind me to get beer later."

The driver nodded. He turned onto Gabon Road and sped north toward Airport Road. "I guess somebody has to." He looked back in the mirror.

"You can call me Dr. Feelgood. This other guy here is Bird."

"Yeah, I have a thing for cocktails," said Bird. "Like Robert Blake in *Baretta*, only I didn't kill my wife. She left me before I got the chance."

"*Don't do the crime, if you can't do the time*. . . . Wasn't that in the theme song?"

"Yeah," said Bird. "Sammy Davis, Jr. Damn, that's irony."

The two agents got a good laugh over that one. They didn't seem very concerned over Van Dorthman's fate. In fact, Bird whipped out a brown bag lunch and started eating a ham sandwich and some chips. "Saving your ass is making me hungry, dude."

Van Dorthman began to wonder if they were going to kill him. "Where are you taking me? Listen, you know I have a lot of money. I can pay you if you don't whack me."

Guttman and the Bird burst out laughing.

"Dude, what is this, the Sopranos? Whack? Really? You shouldn't talk so much. It doesn't suit you well."

"Yeah," said Guttman. "I thought you pedophiles were, like, the quiet lurking type. Here's what you need to know. The authorities will be arriving at your hotel shortly. You will not be there, you're welcome." He spit into an empty beer bottle.

Bird looked at his partner in disgust. "Dude, must you do that crap in the car?"

Guttman just smiled and spit again.

"Lovely," said Bird. "You're a real ladies' man."

Van Dorthman's head was spinning again. Trying to make sense of things only made it worse. "How did the police find out? Who notified them?"

Guttman looked incredulous. "The butler did, who else? He was setting you up. That scumbag has been setting rich businessmen up for years. He uses the same scam every time. Let me guess . . . he showed up with some fancy bottle of champagne to win you over. And look at that, he just happens to have two young girls in his company as well. He says he doesn't know how they got there, but they are a gift or some crap like that. Am I right? Am I right? That's all it takes. You rich pedos are all the same. You can't resist. Only that fancy bottle of champagne was laced with enough etorphine to knock you all on your asses just long enough for the cops to show up."

Bird laughed. "Nothing like a little animal tranquilizer to bag a pedo. It's kinda funny that he uses animal tranquilizer in Africa. It's like a safari gone bad." He laughed.

Guttman waved him off. "Please, dude. I see what you're trying to do. You can't outwit me. My 'emperor has no clothes line' was much funnier."

The more the guys joked, the more Wagner Van Dorthman began to palpitate and sweat. He ran the day's events back in his head.

It sounded like the Brit's story was more or less the same as Guttman's. If so, he had almost walked right into a scam that would have cost him millions. And who knew if it would end there? Once the police had the evidence, what would stop them from extorting him forever, especially with a factory set to open in Addis Ababa?

The Brit, Guttman and Bird really saved his ass. This one episode could haunt him forever. He was completely at the mercy of the butler and the police. "So the butler is a con man?"

"More like an extortionist," answered Guttman. "Those girls are in on it. They're his daughters."

"A real scumbag," added Bird. "Pimping out his own kids, drugging them . . . God knows what else he does with them. I'm sure there are videos. As a matter of fact, the British friend said he found cameras all over your villa. You were close to being a porn star, my friend."

"Yeah," said Guttman. "I can only imagine the look on your wife's face when she gets one of those hasty-ass pop-up ads for one of those darknet kiddie sites, and there's your little winkie staring her in the face."

The two men laughed, but Van Dorthman didn't see the humor. "We didn't actually have sex. I swear. I passed out first."

Guttman shrugged. "Maybe you did, maybe you didn't. I can tell you for sure that not everyone passes out beforehand. Those girls have been raped dozens of times. That's their job."

"Oh, my God," said Van Dorthman. "So then what you're saying is really true? The whole thing was a setup to blackmail me?"

"Of course it's true. If I could make up shit like this, I'd be a best-selling novelist. You know, you rich guys are funny. You can be as shrewd as hell sitting around the boardroom table. But out in the real world, you have no idea when you're being taken advantage of. What were you thinking, that you are such a big man around town, some kind of Bawana whose Mandingo brings him two young girls to have sex with? I mean . . . really? That was, like, 200 years ago, dude."

Van Dorthman sat back and closed his eyes. "He said they were a gift from an anonymous friend. Oh my God, how could I have been so dumb?"

Both men in front laughed.

"Men like you are all the same," explained Guttman. "As long as you have your ego stroked and you hear what you want to hear about how great you are, any dirtbag like that butler guy can play you like a cheap guitar."

"Hey, where does that saying come from?" asked Bird. "That cheap guitar thing?"

"How the hell should I know?"

"Just to be clear, I have a cheap guitar, and I sound great. Just saying."

Guttman looked back in the rearview. "Just ignore Jimi Hendrix here. Suffice it to say the local police would have had their way with you. I guess they think it's fair, considering you had your way with two local children, huh? It's funny how the universe works things out."

"Exactly," said Bird. "The butler was just the front man. Dirty cops are dirty cops everywhere in the world. They have a nice little racket running out of that hotel. We've known about it for years."

"Why don't you stop it from happening?" asked Van Dorthman.

"Why would we?" replied Bird. "Predictable corruption has its value. To be quite honest, we've extorted a kingpin or two ourselves, haven't we? You never know when you need to cash in that chip. Some pretty graphic video comes out of that place. I think every intel agency in the world monitors that joint."

"Besides," added Guttman. "If we put a stop to that sort of thing, how would degenerates like you get their rocks off?"

Van Dorthman was blown away. He never considered that he was being trapped, let alone watched by government agencies . . . including his own. He supposed there really was no end to the depth of surveillance defining the new world order, especially with everything going Internet and global. He considered it a gift from God that he got away with it this time.

"So the giant British guy works with you, too? He really helped me out."

"Yup," said Guttman. "Just like you, the butler never saw it coming. He switched bottles on you, but we switched sommeliers on him. By the time the authorities get there, our British friend will have the place completely clean. I'm afraid our Ethiopian friends won't have a rich American tittie to suckle off today. In case you're wondering, you're the rich American tittie of which I speak."

Bird chuckled. "Did I tell you to remind me to get more beer for tonight?"

"Wait, wait," said Van Dorthman. He was getting a bit testy over the agent's nonchalance. "Have the place cleaned? What does that mean? What about the two girls? What will happen to them? Those little bitches can identify me."

Bird held up his hand. "Whoa there, big fella. You're sounding a little too gangster, considering your position."

"The girls are none of your concern now," added Guttman. "Thanks to you, their fate is sealed. Like you said, we can't have any loose ends that can compromise you. That would render this entire operation futile. We don't operate carelessly like that."

Bird started singing. "Bye, bye black girls. Bye, bye black girls. You should be proud of yourself. A lot of trophy hunters would love to come to Africa and mount two native girls."

"I don't think he has the same definition of 'mount,'" said Guttman. "But it was a good joke. I'll give you that. Maybe there's hope for you yet?"

"So that British guy is going to kill them? I mean . . . I know I said they could identify me, but . . . well, I didn't mean I wanted them rubbed out. They're just girls," said Van Dorthman.

Bird turned around abruptly. "Really, bro? Rubbed out? Where do you get this stuff from? Rubbed out? Where'd you get that one from, *Dragnet*?"

Guttman honked the horn twice for emphasis. "*Dragnet* . . . good one. Anyway, douchebag, you should have considered their lives before you decided to molest them."

"And the butler? What about him?" asked Van Dorthman.

Guttman chuckled. "Oh . . . I'm quite sure our British mate has something special planned for that scumbag."

Van Dorthman sat back and exhaled loudly. He was completely overwhelmed. He knew the men were right. In the end, he couldn't afford any loose ends. It was unfortunate that the girls had to die. He wasn't happy about it, and he did feel bad. But he realized he had to stop himself from connecting with them. He had to cauterize his emotions. He should just let these guys do their jobs and thank his lucky stars.

"I guess I owe you guys big time."

"Not us," replied Guttman. "We're just the hired help. But you certainly owe someone very high up a very big favor."

Everybody kept saying that. He had to have a name? "Who? Who sent you to help me?"

Guttman shook his head. "Come on, dude. We can't disclose that. Trust me, though. He's the kind of guy who'll reach out to you when he needs a favor. Or maybe he'll send you a dozen roses with a card reminding you of what a complete moron you are running around Africa."

Bird was enjoying the whole circus. "Two girls just show up at your door? Can you be that stupid and make so much money, Doc?"

Guttman smiled. "How would I know? I just like to feel good."

Bird enjoyed that immensely. "Good ol' Dr. Feelgood's in the house." He turned back to Van Dorthman. "Listen up, bro. You don't utter a single word about this, or you'll end up like those two girls. Get my drift?"

Van Dorthman nodded.

"And like the doc said, sooner or later our guy will tap you for a favor. You can count on it."

Guttman made a sharp right onto Airport Road. He gunned it and turned on the radio. A popular song by Lady Gaga was playing. "I love this song." He started whistling. "It's like one of three songs they play in this shit hole."

Van Dorthman noticed several airport signs as they sped down the road. "Where are we going?" he asked Guttman.

"To the airport. Can't you read? There is a private jet waiting to take you to Gaborone, Botswana."

"Whose plane is it?"

Guttman shook his head again. "We can't disclose that either. Like I said, you'll find out soon enough."

As they approached the airport, Guttman veered the Suburban right onto a dirt road that looped around to the back of the airport. They pulled up to a guardhouse and were granted access to a private runway where a Gulfstream V was sitting in wait for departure. Guttman and Bird exited the car and escorted Van Dorthman on board.

"Someone will be there to meet you when you arrive in Botswana. By the way, you'll be needing this." Guttman tossed Van Dorthman his passport. "Courtesy of our British friend. You forgot about that, didn't you?"

Bird seemed genuinely disgusted. "You won't get far without that, douchebag."

"Thank you," said Wagner Van Dorthman. "Again, I really owe you guys."

"Oh, you really owe somebody. It's just not us," said Guttman.

Guttman and Bird turned and headed for the plane's exit. Before stepping off, Guttman turned back to Van Dorthman. "Hey, numb nuts. A word of advice . . . this is your only free pass. The next time you see us, you won't be this happy."

"Of course, of course," said Van Dorthman, ecstatic to get the hell out of there scot-free. "You have my word. I promise."

Guttman and Bird stepped out of the plane, and the flight attendant closed and sealed the door behind them. Guttman climbed into the passenger side of the truck this time. Bird took the wheel.

"I need you to drop me at the main terminal, Bird."

"Leaving our fair city so soon?"

"Yeah, I've got to be in Geneva to wrap something up . . . Nigeria."

"You're flying commercial? What the hell?"

Guttman shrugged. "Yeah . . . apparently Vice President Pierson wants to save Van Dorthman's ass bad enough to give him my ride."

"Wow, that blows."

"Tell me about it. They stuck my ass in economy."

"So is Switzerland part of Pierson's reclamation project for himself?"

Guttman shrugged again. "I don't know, dude. Who knows where the hot potato will land. All I know is that I've got to put some *Boko Haram* douchebag to bed. But I'll say this for the old bastard . . . when he wants something, you don't want to be the person standing in his way."

Bird wiped his forehead. "Yeah . . . just another day in the life of an operator."

Guttman made a disgusted grunt.

They turned back onto the dirt road and headed for the main terminal.

Chapter 32

In the meantime, the Brit was back in Van Dorthman's villa making one last sweep. The place was clean. Van Dorthman was successfully exited. Now he had to take care of the two girls who were just beginning to come to. He sighed. This was the tough part of the job. He would enjoy taking care of their pimp father, that bastard butler. But children . . . it always brought him down.

Two more operators, each dressed as if they worked for a cleaning service, arrived on the scene as well, each of them wheeling a large, five-foot silver canister behind them. The disguise was fitting. "Cleaners" were operators used to sanitize messy jobs in the field, especially the bodies left behind. Like the Brit, cleaners were experts at disposal and disintegration. There was no dirtier job on the planet.

The two men stepped out of the villa elevator onto the third floor, where the master bedroom was located. The Brit was waiting for them. He motioned toward the girls. "We need to move. The authorities will be here any minute. I still need to take care of their father."

One of the cleaners walked over to the bed and checked the girls' pulses. He looked at his partner. "About a hundred-and-ten pounds each, I'd say."

The other cleaner nodded in agreement. Without further comment, the first cleaner injected each girl with half a syringe of etorphine. "They'll be out for another six hours."

The Brit sighed. "I hate to do this."

"Why?" asked one of the cleaners. "It's better than living with their degenerate father. So really, they're better off."

The Brit sighed again and looked at his watch. "Okay, get it done quickly."

The cleaners wheeled their equipment over to the bed. Vital to the operation, the canisters were state-of-the art, high-tech units originally designed to smuggle defectors out of East Germany during the Cold War. They'd received some nice tweaks over the years, including a small unisex urinal, strap-in seats, a full five-hour oxygen supply, and pressurization capabilities enabling the precious cargo to be stowed in the baggage compartment of a plane if necessary.

The cleaners respectfully slid the unconscious girls into jumpsuits and each scooped them into their respective transport canister. They belted the girls in, turned on the oxygen supply and sealed the canisters.

"They'll be right as rain, my friend," said one of the men.

"No worries, Tony," said the other to the Brit. It was the first time that day he had heard his real name. "You did good. They'll be safely on their way to the U.S. embassy in Johannesburg within the hour. From there, some sort of United Nations Council for Women and Children or something like that will step in. Some Nigerian guy named Kofi Achebe is in charge. I hear he's a pretty straight shooter. I guess they help place girls like this with a proper family."

The Brit rubbed his face. "Are you sure?"

One of the cleaners chuckled. "This comes directly from the big man. The girls will be fine."

"Happily ever after and all that," added the other.

"This comes from the big man? He must be getting soft in his old age."

"Yeah," said one of the men. "President Rosemore must have broken him in. Our instructions are to deliver the girls safely. Look at it this way . . . whatever happened to them in the past has already happened. The important thing is that the rest of their lives will be better than anything they would have known had we not intervened. That's the whole point of what we do, right?"

All three men laughed at the absurdity. Then again, perhaps they laughed because for once, it was actually true.

"Now go take care of the father. Give him his one-way ticket."

The Brit nodded. "Right, then . . . thanks. Be safe."

He wasn't a big fan of politicians. He'd seen too much misery perpetrated by too many rich, powerful men who were elected to office on a platform of fantasy and lies by an electorate that didn't know any better because they didn't know the truth behind the scenes. But if it was true that Harry Pierson had intervened to save these girls, then maybe, just maybe, the vice president deserved to stand apart from Becket Rosemore, the president who disgraced his nation.

Now that the girls were safe and onto their new lives in the States, the Brit strode into the elevator with a newfound sense of purpose. That meant trouble for anyone he didn't like. He knew exactly where to find the butler. As predicted, he was waiting in the manager's office for the police to arrive and execute their scam. The Brit thought about the girls . . . about how their father drugged them and forced them to have sex with men, how he used them as tools or resources at his disposal. Yes . . . this was the part of his job he really enjoyed.

The Brit put on his black leather gloves, cracked his knuckles, strode into the manager's office and closed the door behind him. The butler checked his phone. The police chief and some men would be there momentarily. He checked to make sure he had enough memory in his camera to take enough incriminating pictures of his passed-out daughters.

The butler leaped from his seat when he saw the Brit. He tried to speak, but it was too late. In a split second, the Brit wrapped his massive hand around the butler's throat. His grip was so powerful, the butler went limp almost instantly. The Brit deftly reached into his pocket and drew out a syringe. He jabbed the needle into the butler's neck.

The butler stared straight into the Brit's eyes. Fear had overcome him. He knew this was the end.

"This is not going to end well for you, mate," whispered the Brit as he emptied the syringe into the butler's neck. "Before I'm done, you will beg me to kill you. By the way, you can call me Tony for the short remainder of your life."

The butler lost consciousness in the Brit's arms. He opened the office window and passed the butler out to the two cleaners who were waiting with their truck. The Brit slid out the window next, and they were off. The butler was never heard from again . . . and nobody noticed. The two girls were enrolled in a New Hampshire private school by month's end.

They would both go on to be . . . human again.

Chapter 33

Wagner Van Dorthman buckled his seatbelt as the jet began taxiing down the runway. He allowed himself to relax for the first time that day. It was crazy. Somehow, someway, he found himself on the brink of disaster and then plucked from the precipice by some unnamed benefactor as if a *deus ex machina* came down and saved him from certain disaster. He downed his second gin and tonic and closed his eyes.

As the plane moved into position, his cell phone rang. The number was restricted. His first inclination was not to answer. But after all that had happened to him that day, he figured he'd better answer it. He remembered Guttman saying the puppet master pulling the strings from on high might be reaching out to him in the near future.

"Hello?" His voice was tentative and wavering.

"You owe me one, you perverted son of a bitch."

Van Dorthman recognized the voice instantly. It was the vice president of the United States. "Harry?"

"Who the hell else would it be? Even in college, I was bailing your ass out. Still can't keep your prick in your pants, can you?"

Van Dorthman smiled like it was old times. "I forgot what a good memory you have."

"I know you are about to take off. I just wanted to check in on you to make sure you were okay."

"I'm good, Harry. Thank you. You really saved my ass. How did you know I was in trouble?"

"It's my job to know. I've been keeping an eye on you."

Wagner Van Dorthman was no match for Harry Pierson. He never saw it coming. "It's not like when we used to go girl hunting in college, huh? It's nice to know someone has my back. I owe you a big one . . . anything, anytime."

There was a moment of silence.

"Yes, Wagner . . . you owe me a big one. Since you mention it, I just happen to need a favor."

The jet engines began to whine. "Name it, Harry. Whatever you want."

"I need you to bury Beck in an op-ed."

Van Dorthman was shocked. "What? Really? I'm one of his biggest supporters."

"I know. That's why I need you. I have to distance myself from Beck. He's done. I can't go down with him. You can help save me with the party like I saved you today. I need you to do this for me."

Van Dorthman was silent. Betraying Beck was not something he welcomed. Neither was turning down his long-time friend and nascent savior. "Why are you doing this, Harry? We have a lot of history together."

Predictably, Pierson was unmoved. "History is written by the victors. That's the first thing you learn in politics, Wag. You're learning that lesson right now the hard way."

"Look, I can see your need to get some distance from Beck. But why do you have to make me look like a fool in public, doing a complete turnaround on my friend like I am some sort of pawn?"

"Because that's exactly what you are. Both you and Beck got yourselves into this predicament because you can't keep your genitals in their proper place. What do you want me to tell you, Wag? This is how it has to be."

"I don't know, Harry. This is really weird."

Wrong answer.

"Listen, you arrogant prick. I can turn that jet around right now. You'll be in police custody before you can say 'prison sex.'"

"Yes, Harry. I know that."

"Listen, Wag. Eggs have to be broken to make an omelet. Unfortunately, you're my egg, and I need an omelet in the worst way."

Van Dorthman breathed deeply. "Okay. But we're even after this."

"Sure," agreed Pierson. "Until the next time you get yourself neck deep in filth. Have a good flight. My people will be reaching out. Most of the piece is already written. We just have to sharpen the hatchet a bit more . . . hone it."

Van Dorthman turned off his phone and sat back for takeoff. He could hardly believe the course of events that had transpired over the last twelve hours. He was a businessman and not a politician. He never considered his old friend would exploit him like that. And setting him up with the butler in the first place? What did he know about how low Pierson could go to cover his own ass?

After all the years of friendship, Wagner Van Dorthman discovered for the first time that Harry Pierson was a Rasputin. He felt humiliated and ashamed now. What bothered him most about the whole incident was allowing himself to be hoodwinked by some half-wit African con man. He would have to be much more careful in the future. He couldn't afford to get himself stuck like this the next time he went out looking for a little "young" fun.

He had an upcoming trip to Bangkok to negotiate building another new factory, which really amounted to bribing the right people. He slipped off his shoes and reclined his chair. Yeah . . . he would have to play it safe when arranging more children to molest.

Chapter 34

Pierson never thought twice about it. He was determined to survive at any cost, and that's exactly what made him D.C.'s greatest ally and greatest adversary at one and the same time. He sacrificed Wagner Van Dorthman in order to save his own ass. There was no way he was going down with Beck. Pierson simply couldn't allow this to happen, not now, not after coming so far. He had worked a lifetime amassing power and influence. Like Cheney, he had the balls to take calculated risks in order to get what he wanted . . . or needed. He was strong-armed but also savvy when he had to be. Brilliant as the man behind the curtain, his seemingly endless labyrinth of covert meant his quiver was always full of arrows, some tipped with poison.

He wasn't about to give it all up now because Beck felt compelled to whip out his wang as casually as checking his watch. Instead, he would serve Beck's head on a platter to the party. To do this, he needed Van Dorthman to lop it off. As usual, Pierson's plan worked perfectly. What bothered him most was not Beck's womanizing. Frankly, he couldn't care less if Beck had an insatiable appetite for females. Pierson knew it was like a drug to powerful men who needed to prove their prowess time and time again. He depended on men's addiction to power over flesh in order to corner them. Wagner Van Dorthman was a perfect example.

No, what ticked Pierson off, what really set him at odds with Beck, was the way in which the president failed to cover his tracks. Pierson felt betrayed, abandoned, exposed. He would make Beck pay for the way in which he failed to control his behavior, the way in which he failed to "control his bitch," as Pierson was apt to say. The two of them were sinking his career right before Pierson's eyes. He had to deal with both of them. Beck's downfall was already well underway.

Wagner Van Dorthman was a bit sentimental about the whole thing, but that only annoyed Pierson. Once he condemned a man, he expected them to bear their punishment honorably. As for himself, Harry Pierson was willing to do whatever it took to escape judgment. If manipulating and humiliating Wagner Van Dorthman was what needed to happen, then he would make it happen. The only thing that mattered was his own survival, which he was willing to ensure by any means necessary.

As for Camille . . . Pierson hadn't decided what to do with her. He could easily crush her along with her ex-has-been. It wouldn't take much to set her up in a ruinous scandal. Wagner Van Dorthman, Becket Rosemore, Camille O'Keefe . . . they were all the same. They afforded their emotions too much freedom. It made them vulnerable. They left their humanity exposed for vultures like Pierson to peck on.

In some ways, though, Camille was different. Their politics certainly differed, and he would rather be waterboarded by Glenn Beck than be locked in a room with her for more than twenty minutes. Still . . . he didn't know why, but Harry Pierson felt a sort of affinity for the passionate redhead. Sure, he thought of her as a crazy-ass bitch. But it was with a stirring feeling of paternalistic affection. Only a true Rasputin can bifurcate like that.

Lately, Pierson began to understand Camille's predicament. After the whole shebang in Ethiopia, Pierson confided in his wife, something he hadn't done since he had admitted she was "sorta special" the night they got engaged. "It's like we've both been betrayed by that man. He screwed us both."

It scared the crap out of him when he suddenly realized what empathy felt like. It was the one emotion completely incompatible with his mode of existence. His wife was less moved by her husband's kitsch. She was never one to shy away from kicking him in the balls when the opportunity presented itself.

"Yeah, well . . . what did you expect, Harry? That guy will screw anything, even your wrinkly, old ass." She then handed him a copy of Camille's book. "Speaking of which, do you think you can get her to sign my copy?"

The message was clear. While millions of women now loathed Becket Rosemore, they loved Camille O'Keefe for having the power to stand up to the most powerful man in the world and say, "No! I'm not going to tolerate this anymore." This interested Pierson. She definitely had mass appeal, something Pierson could not garner for himself now that he was so closely identified with "President Hose-more," as one paper so eloquently put it. Pierson couldn't help wondering if Camille might yet become an ally. He spared her for the time being.

And so, one day, seemingly out of the blue, Wagner Van Dorthman wrote a scathing op-ed condemning the man he had so fervently endorsed for president just a few years earlier. It came out first in a D.C. paper but was picked up instantly by every major news outlet in the world. From there, Van Dorthman's poisonous comments made their way into the kitchens of America. To make matters worse, Pierson set up Beck by having him recorded off-mike making a derogatory comment about Camille to one of his aides. The sound bite instantly made its way around the globe, travelling the same path the op-ed already had cleared.

Despite his initial resistance, it took Van Dorthman all of thirty seconds to quell any misgivings he might have had. Of paramount importance was remaining in Pierson's good favor lest he suddenly find himself splashed across the front page. Self-preservation was his primary motivation, too, and it proved to be much stronger than any sense of loyalty he had for Beck. The rich and powerful often gnashed and gnarled at each other on their way up. It was a fundamental fact of life for Van Dorthman. Sometimes, in order to keep a powerful friend, another must be sacrificed. He had his money, he had his power and he had third-world little girls. He saw no need to fight it when it wasn't his place to try and change the world.

Once he gave himself over to his dark side, he found it surprisingly easy to let it fly. In a lightning flash that Washington insiders recognize as the crackle of back-room deals, Wagner Van Dorthman became a raging monster trying to kill his own creator. The anger in his words startled many readers. Needless to say, he captured the world's attention from the get go. #PresidickBlowsmore blew up on the Twittersphere instantly.

He called Beck a "slimy, two-faced womanizer" and "a pompous adulterer who effectively cheated on every woman who voted for him." "I was one of the president's most ardent supporters," Van Dorthman wrote. "He was also one of my closest friends. But now, after witnessing the way he degrades women, I can no longer, in good conscience, continue as either his supporter or friend. I cherish the women of this planet as our most vital natural resource."

The best part for Pierson was that he wrote the piece himself. He could really spin some shit into gold. That last bit about Van Dorthman cherishing women was his crowning moment, made tongue-in-cheek, considering Van Dorthman was a pervert with an insatiable appetite for little girls. Pierson's puerile knack for penis jokes reached new artistic heights . . . *Bang around town* . . . *pecker politics* . . . *Big Willie's protégé* . . . it was sheer genius. He could almost hear the world howling with laughter after reading that Beck was a "tuna fisherman who couldn't stay in his home port with the loveliest First Lady to ever grace the White House."

As if Camille's book wasn't enough of a sexposé, Van Dorthman drudged it up anew thanks to Harry Pierson and his poison pen. Displaying the kind of team-player attitude Pierson liked, Van Dorthman even added scandalous information of his own. For example, he revealed an episode in which Beck kept a young lady in a luxury hotel just one floor below where he and Camille were staying while on official business in Germany. While Camille slept like a rock after Beck slipped an Ambien in her Riesling, he made his way down to his fair-haired German lass, who let him run the gamut with her *glockenspiel* and the rest of her Teutonic body.

Ah, Germany, the home of Schiller and the aesthetic education of man . . . *long live my royal mistress!* And while many European men laughed at the article and how provincial and puritanical Americans could be, the overwhelming majority of women at home and abroad were whipped up again because men like Beck routinely found themselves rewarded with wealth, power and affluence. After Pierson and Van Dorthman were done with Beck, Camille's book seemed understated, if anything.

Out of Beck's ashes arose the fiery redheaded Phoenix stronger than ever. Her popularity and sphere of influence were never greater. She was a cause *célèbre* whose message meant different things to different people . . . a martyr, a feminist advocate, a role model, a hero, a troublemaker, a back-stabbing bitch. Camille O'Keefe now symbolized the power of possibility standing up to the forces of subjugation. Becket Rosemore was done. Camille's future looked replete. All that remained was for Harry Pierson to land on his feet.

Chapter 35

The call came from out of the blue. Pierson recognized the voice immediately. It was Camille O'Keefe. He laughed to himself. The girl was a weirdo, but she did have uncanny timing.

"Your ears must be burning. I was just thinking about you." He sat down at his desk and cleared his throat. He had no idea what was waiting for him on the other end of the line.

Camille made a low, throaty sound to underscore her incredulousness. "Are there actually women who fall for that, Harry?"

"Believe it or not, yes," he said grinning. "That's how I picked up my wife." He sat down and leaned back in his shoulder-high leather vice presidential chair. It might not have been the Oval Office, but he was sure happy to have it. It beat the hell out of his old digs in the Pentagon, where everything seemed to smell like an armpit, mold and salami.

"Lovely," said Camille. "I can only imagine the sort of women you've met since you became Beck's sidekick. Your wife must be thrilled it's all coming to an end."

Ordinarily, Harry Pierson would have bristled at such a barb. But something about today was not ordinary. Today, he was in a pretty good mood, all things considered. His plan with Van

Dorthman went off without a hitch, the party bigwigs were satisfied with his efforts, and, if they kept their word, he would land on his feet in some official capacity on some sort of committee should the party somehow manage to overcome the damage Beck had done and win the next election. He was still furious with Beck, but at least he had settled the score. Van Dorthman would get over it soon enough, too.

Suddenly full of energy, the vice president stood up, glided over to the bar in the far corner, and poured himself a very fine Scotch. "Ah yes, my darling wife. To tell you the truth, I think she's pissed because I'll be home more. Do you know she handed me a copy of your book for you to autograph? It's like asking O.J.'s family to sign the knife."

Camille relished the idea that she might have turned Pierson's wife. It made her feel like her message was more than just self-proclamation. She walked over to her bedroom closet and selected a couple of outfits. "Just think, now the two of you can take that world tour . . . just the two of you . . . travelling together for three months." She tossed the outfits on her bed next to her open suitcase, which was almost packed.

"I'm sorry to spoil your idyllic image, Camille. But let's not be too hasty. I may just survive this ordeal after all."

Camille laughed at the thought. She actually snorted. "It's funny you mention that, Harry. I was just thinking the same thing."

Pierson didn't catch Camille's intimation. He was too caught up in protecting his own ego. He returned to his chair, sipped his Scotch, and fired up a Cuban cigar from the humidor on his desk before reclining in repose once more. "Don't count Harry Pierson out yet, my dear." He tossed the torch lighter on the desk and blew a large cloud of smoke into the air as if to give his point weight.

Camille neatly folded her outfits into the suitcase and zipped it up. "I assume you saw Wagner's piece in the paper?"

Pierson relished the moment by letting another thick puff waft up above his graying head. "Hmm . . . Wagner . . . Wagner. . . . Do you mean Wagner Van Dorthman?" He smiled delightedly.

Camille placed her suitcase on the floor next to her big canopy bed trimmed in sheer white fabric. She sprawled out on a roomy loveseat in the corner under an expansive window. The sun was beaming through. "Oh, stop pretending you had nothing to do with it."

Pierson teased her some more. "*Moi?* What makes you say that? I'll have you know I'm a firm believer in keeping a positive attitude and paying it forward."

Camille grunted. "Oh, please, Harry. You certainly believe in paying people back, but that's quite different from paying it forward. Everyone within the Beltway knows you owe Beck a swift kick in the oompa loompas. And believe me, there are a lot of people lined up behind you waiting for their turn."

"Be careful, my dear. That kind of talk really turns me on."

"Easy there, big fella. At your age, having sex is like playing Russian roulette. But don't try spinning this stitching like you had nothing to do with it. Wagner's op-ed had your fingerprints all over it. I wouldn't be surprised if you wrote it yourself."

Pierson sat back and admired the ring of smoke he just blew. "You say that as if you didn't love every word of it."

He was right, of course. She had to admit she really enjoyed seeing Beck roasted in front of the entire world. She wanted nothing more than to grab her popcorn, kick back and watch Beck crash and burn. She forced herself to stay positive, though, and took no satisfaction in what Van Dorthman and Pierson did. This dimension was characterized by too much negativity as it was. She firmly believed in the Law of Attraction . . . negativity is like a magnet attracting more and more negative energy, more and more negative people, more and more negative events until one finds oneself crushed beneath the weight of darkness.

Conversely, the power of positivity never escaped Camille. She built her life into a monument to the spirit of humanity and interconnectedness. She never second-guessed her commitment to living in the flow of positive energy she could see radiating like a corona around the many good people whom she had met in this lifetime. She gravitated toward good people and did her best to avoid people that were "energy vampires"—negative or otherwise needy people who could suck the life right out of her. She put up walls to keep energy vampires at bay. Sometimes, however, they managed to sneak in. Other times, as with Beck, she allowed them to walk right through the door into her heart.

Having been First Lady, Camille knew Harry Pierson was far worse than an energy vampire. Never mind tapping energy; he could suck the blood right out of you. When Camille first met with Kofi in the Bahamas, Harry Pierson immediately jumped to mind as the one man who could help those poor women on Koulfoua Island who were about to be slaughtered. But it was with a bit of a heavy heart that she sought Pierson's assistance. His help was critical if the refugees were to be saved. If Harry Pierson wasn't on board, there was little Camille and Kofi could do on their own.

This put her in a strange position. It was critical that Camille used all her powers of persuasion on the vice president. Without Pierson, the refugees were as good as dead. At the same time, she distrusted him and had serious spiritual misgivings about enlisting a man like him. Her cause was just and good, but her hands would be dirty. There was no telling what he would do to "help" those women. Van Dorthman's apostasy made it clear—she would have to tread carefully around Harry Pierson lest she get dragged down in a whirlpool of dark energy. Of this she was certain.

"I have to admit it, Harry. A part of me took delight in Wagner's hatchet job."

"Then I guess you're calling to congratulate me, Red."

"God, Harry. Beck used to call me Red. You just made my skin crawl."

Pierson laughed as he polished off his Scotch. "Yes, well, I've always had a way with the ladies. You should see the look on the good Mrs. Pierson's face when it's time for our monthly relations, if you know what I mean."

Camille cringed. "Please, Harry. I think I just threw up a little in my mouth."

He ashed his cigar. "So then, to what do I owe the pleasure of your call if not to congratulate me on getting Beck out of the way?"

ANGLE OF ATTACK

Camille bit her lip. This was her moment of truth. So much was riding on this, so many lives. Even Pierson's dark side wasn't enough to dissuade her. She simply couldn't turn her back on all those women and girls, not after she'd come so far. In this sense, Camille O'Keefe was as determined as Harry Pierson to succeed.

She sat up. The whimsy left her voice. "I know you're not one to beat around the bush, Harry."

"Whoa, whoa," said Pierson. "The last guy around here who was beating bushes is about to lose his job because of it."

"This is serious, Harry. For once in your life, can you stop being a flippant ass and listen to what I have to say?" She exhaled loudly when she was done. Her sudden outburst surprised her. She wasn't aware she was holding in that much pent-up frustration. She chalked it up to all the lives at stake. She felt responsible for each of those five thousand souls.

Pierson was curious at Camille's newfound vigor. "Wow . . . were you this feisty with the Beckster?"

Camille was still feeling her power. It felt invigorating. "Don't patronize me, Harry. I may have been naïve when I first took up with the president—and he is still the president—but I'm not some passive chippie, even if Beck treated me that way. It just so happens that I have very pressing business to discuss with you. The matter is of the greatest spiritual importance. The world is in need of goodness, and that's why I need you. Yes, I said it. I need you."

Pierson laughed, just as Camille had predicted.

"As funny as that sounds," she added in a flat tone.

It suddenly all came back to Harry Pierson . . . how annoying Camille was, how she always tried to steer the president in some sort of freaky New Age direction. The staffers found her just as tiresome . . . the way she would suddenly blurt out weird stuff about the universe or past lives, or something like that . . . just like she was doing with him right there on the phone. He was beginning to regret taking her call in the first place.

"Boy, you don't change, do you?" he asked, with a tinge of sarcasm.

"Everything changes, Harry. What I have to tell you may change you in ways you never expected. When we change the way we see things, the things we see totally change. Sometimes we change along with them. It can be a good thing."

It was Pierson's turn to sigh now. He could really use a refill. He shook his head and wished his glass could automatically refill itself so he wouldn't have to get up. He stood up and headed back to the bar. He was not amused, either. "Speaking of change, I need to change my number so this doesn't happen again. I am very busy right now." He clinked a few rocks into his glass. "Very busy."

Camille sat up. She was concerned. It wasn't going well, and Pierson's help was the linchpin. Failure was not an option here. Five thousand helpless lives lay in the balance. She corrected her posture, cleared the din of negative self-talk from her mind, refocused her positive energies.

"I think you will change your opinion when you hear what I have to say."

Pierson wished he was busier. Most of his time was spent on dodging reporters and avoiding the fallout. He and Beck hadn't met face-to-face since their visit in Cooperstown. Pierson figured it best, considering Beck's slash-and-burn approach to handling the media and his political adversaries alike. He was going down with the grace and aplomb of a dinosaur facing extinction. That's exactly what Beck had become. Camille's book was tantamount to a meteor striking the Earth and marking the beginning of the end for the prehistoric beasts.

It was a bit early to hit the sauce, but being a probable lame duck was beginning to get to him. He needed to vent it somehow. Lately he'd been spending most of his time in his offices in the Eisenhower Executive Office Building rather than his office in the West Wing of the White House. It was easier to lie low there. And once word got out that Pierson had something to do with Van Dorthman's public obliteration of the president, it would be unlikely that the partnership he and Beck once shared could ever function normally again.

This office had other benefits, as well. He loved his view of the Washington Monument. He was going to miss it. His office in the

EEOB was only a stone's throw from the West Wing, but he felt more independent. He needed some breathing room. This whole business with Beck stressed him out. He had the party players on one side leaning on him to get Beck out. His wife was on the other side, busting his balls every night about the end of his career looming near. He used Wagner Van Dorthman like a Thai hooker. Somewhere in the whole damned business he'd lost a say in his own life. It made him bitter and vengeful. He was looking for another way.

Annoy him as she did, Camille O'Keefe had an undeniable knack for thinking outside the box. For all he knew, fortune might be smiling on him. "I'm listening," he said.

Camille perked up. There was something in Pierson's voice that gave her hope. Maybe there was a foothold? Maybe he would let her in just long enough to listen in earnest to what she had to say? "It's, um. . . ." She struggled with the moment.

"Camille," said Pierson, sternly. The alcohol made him snippy. "You have thirty seconds to sell me on whatever scheme you're cooking up. The clock is running, so some meaningful words better start coming out of your mouth."

Camille set herself straight and just let it fly. "I have come across some sensitive information. There are lives at stake . . . a lot of lives."

She knew this setup would surely pique Pierson's interest, given his insatiable appetite for clandestine intrigue and dark implications. A lot of people were depending on her being right.

Pierson watched dark storm clouds work their way toward the capitol. He liked how the Washington Monument stood out in the foreground, its unwavering yet simple fortitude juxtaposed against the ominous sky. "I like the sound of it so far, Camille. What else can you tell me in the twenty-five seconds you have remaining?"

Camille racked her brain to come up with one or two hot buttons to push. "There's a situation brewing in Chad."

The mention of Africa caught Pierson's ear. A good humanitarian crisis could be just the thing he needed to reclaim his image. "Really? Are civilians involved?"

Camille rode the momentum. "Yes, five thousand women, many of them young girls. They may not survive the week."

Pierson stroked his chin. The potential appealed to him. After so many years in intelligence, his brain was a highly efficient, razor-sharp analytical tool, an Occam's razor that Pierson could wield with steely precision. His mind instantly raced through the myriad ways he could spin the thing to his advantage. Yes . . . he definitely liked where this was headed. Maybe it was a good thing he took her call after all?

"That sounds like something we would call a tragedy," he surmised.

Camille somehow managed to keep her disgust hidden. It was so like him, so easy for him to turn human beings into an agenda. Camille reaffirmed her purpose. After all, that's why she had called him in the first place. It was now time to dangle a carrot she knew he couldn't resist chasing. "My people tell me *Boko Haram* is involved."

There was a moment of silence while Pierson contemplated the implications of the bomb Camille just dropped. "You have people, now?"

"In a matter of speaking. These women need you, Harry. You're the only person I can go to with this who can actually do something to prevent it."

She held her breath.

Pierson breathed deeply more from excitement than trepidation. This was exactly the kind of thing that could save his career. He turned from the window and sat down at his desk. He logged in to a restricted intelligence database that very few people in D.C. were authorized to access. He pulled up the central file on *Boko Haram*. There were thousands of entries. He opened the folder for Aliyu Adelabu. Aliyu's somber face filled Pierson's screen.

Pierson hated these two-bit arrogant bastards like Aliyu who fancied themselves global players. To Pierson, *Boko Haram* was nothing more than a gang of thugs like you would find in any U.S. city. Only in Africa, they could intimidate masses of people because there weren't enough resources to stop them.

"Do you mean *Boko Haram* out of Maiduguri, Nigeria?" He was testing her.

"Yes, that's the group. They are very nasty people."

Pierson eyeballed Aliyu's picture "Specifically, one Aliyu Adelabu. It doesn't surprise me that he's looking to wipe out a few thousand women. Of course, he's likely to take as many of them to sell as sex slaves before killing the rest. He's the sort of scum we need to be cleaning up. I'll give you that."

Camille was overcome with emotion. "I can't believe there are still men in the world who buy and sell girls for sex. My contact tells me there is even an entire underground internet for sex trafficking, child pornography, drugs. . . . I don't know what's wrong with people in this dimension, Harry."

"Trust me, Camille. We've had our eye on these so-called darknet filth for some time now. The same with *Boko Haram.*"

"So why do they both still exist?"

"Because nobody really cares. In the end, there has to be some sort of political benefit to it. The other thing is that you don't want to dig too deep lest you expose someone pretty high-ranking and influential. The same goes for the whole conflict-resource trade in Africa. If you follow the money too closely, you end up at the bank accounts of very wealthy, very powerful men, many of whom are actually in government. It's best not to look at all."

Camille let her disgust be known. "So you just let it go on? That's exactly what my contact told me. He said there's too much money and too much influence to upset the system. That's sad, Harry. It makes me cry."

Pierson had no comment. But he was thinking.

"Nothing to say about that, Mr. Vice President?"

Pierson cleared his throat. "Who's your contact on this?"

Camille was disconcerted by his response. At best, she felt it was too nonchalant, at worst it was sinister. She hadn't thought about that initially, but who knew what Harry Pierson would do if she gave up Kofi's name? Pierson said these matters often led to back very powerful men. What if some of those very men were affiliates of

Beck's or even connected somehow to Pierson himself? She had to walk a fine line here. She wanted to tell the world about these horrors blatantly going on right in front of everyone's eyes like she did when she wrote *This Soul's Journey through the Eye of the Storm*. And she might yet do that. But then she would blow things up with Pierson and that would cost five thousand innocent lives.

Pierson continued browsing through Aliyu's file. "Camille, you have to work with me here if you want my help. Of all the people in the world you know, you chose to call me. I can't help you if you don't work with me. Who's your contact?"

Once again, Camille found herself having to subordinate her values and bow down to the power of the phallus. "His name is Kofi Achebe. He's special envoy to the United Nations Council on Women and Families. I'm pretty sure he has a military background."

He quickly searched for Kofi in his database. A decent amount of information came back. There were some recent updates on Kofi's work with the United Nations. The majority of the intelligence, however, dealt with Kofi's dark past in the resource trade. "Did you say Council on Women and Families? I never heard of it."

"He travels all over sub-Saharan Africa bearing witness to the atrocities committed by these *Boko Haram* people. The stories and the pictures . . . Harry, they're terrible. I can literally feel the pain and suffering. It turns my stomach."

Pierson kept quickly scanning Kofi's dossier. "Okay, but this friend of yours is no angel. You know that, right?"

"He's seen a lot of terrible things, if that's what you mean," she answered hesitantly, afraid of what was coming next.

Pierson ran his forefinger along the rim of his glass. "Well, he's got quite a past . . . and a body count to go with it, although that's going back a bit. For the most part, he's what you say he is . . . a United Nations special envoy. It looks like he's trying to make new friends. I've seen it before. I can work with that."

Camille was nervous. "Does that mean you'll help, Harry? You'll be a hero to these women."

Pierson relit his cigar and puffed away. He just loved to tease Camille. That whole cat and mouse thing really did it for him. The more beautiful the woman, the more he liked to toy with her. The fact that Camille was the most popular woman in the world and the First Lady only made it sweeter for him.

"Maybe . . . I haven't decided yet."

He would like nothing more than to knock the piss out of *Boko Haram*. What he was weighing more intensely, however, was Camille's immense popularity and how she could help pull him out of the political abyss called Becket Rosemore. If he played his cards right, Pierson figured he might just resurrect himself by piggy-backing on Camille's appeal to save some helpless African women from some evil terrorists. The irony didn't escape him. Here was Beck's ex-wife saving his ass after he just hit Beck broadside with Van Dorthman's op-ed.

He slowly drew on his cigar. "You know I've always had a soft spot in my heart for you, Red. Even if you're the reason I will need to find a new job."

"Very funny, Harry. Many were the times you stood by while Beck's staffers mocked me for my spiritual beliefs. And if I really did some digging, I bet you knew all about Beck and his mistresses. But the plight of these African women is bigger than my ego, Harry. That's why I can reach out to you without getting offended when you say the things you do. I wish you could see past your ego, too. You're capable of doing some amazing things. I know you are. You have a very powerful spirit. I'll just leave it at that."

Pierson had made up his mind a few minutes earlier, but he really enjoyed listening to Camille stroke him. He certainly didn't get it at home. "I'll say two things in response, Camille. First, I will help you."

A wave of relief swept through Camille. She began crying softly. "Thank you so much, Harry. What's the second thing? I'm almost afraid to ask."

Pierson checked his watch. It was time for him to leave for his meeting with the Senate Majority Leader. Pierson planned on regaling him with the back story behind Van Dorthman's piece.

But now, it seemed like he could bring so much more to the table at the meeting . . . so much more. He recognized a window of opportunity he could pry open no matter how secure it appeared. Such was the moment now at hand.

"Don't sound so cynical, Camille. It's unbecoming for a woman as lovely as you."

Camille was busy throwing some last-minute items in her carry on. Now that she secured Pierson's help, she would let Kofi know. Time was of the essence. There was no telling when *Boko Haram* would strike. Judging from Kofi's opinion, the slaughter was imminent.

"I'm waiting," she said, as she tossed some extra clothes into her bag.

"Oh, yes. The second thing I want from you is a partnership going forward, something I can hang my name on in the public eye."

Camille grunted as she often did when scoffing at a naked attempt to use her. "You mean you want me to throw you a lifeline so you can climb out of the hole you're burying Beck in."

Pierson powered down his computer and extinguished his cigar. "I wouldn't put it exactly that way, Camille."

This time, it was Camille who enjoyed toying with Pierson. "Oh, then you simply want to latch on to my growing popularity in an attempt to regain some sort of respect in the public eye?"

"Okay, Camille. I get it. Let's lay our cards on the table then."

She threw a well-worn copy of Debbie Ford's *The Dark Side of Light Chasers* into the carry-on bag and zipped it up alongside her suitcase. "To be honest, I'm never really sure if you're shooting straight, Harry. I've always felt that way about you."

"Thank you. I consider that a compliment. So here's what I'm thinking. Dispatching of these *Boko Haram* scumbags is the easy part. They're nothing more than a bunch of third-world wannabes riding around in crappy white pick-ups firing shots into the air. They think they're tough, raping and murdering helpless people who barely have the strength to lift up a gun in self-defense."

He stood up and smoothed the pleats in his pants. He was on a roll now. "Believe me, Camille, when our boys are done working over this Aliyu Adelabu clown, this jack wad, he won't be praying to Allah. He'll be begging for one of our SEALs to finish him off and send him straight to hell with the rest of his band of buck-toothed savages. Yeah, I know this new generation of terrorist whackadoos like to display their college degrees. But believe me . . . they haven't been to school yet. Not the school our boys go to."

This was the stuff Camille preferred not to know about. She knew enlisting Pierson meant blood would be spilled. It was a trade-off . . . the terrorists for the refugees. She could live with that because her intentions were good. "I don't want to know about any of that stuff, Harry. You can save it for Kofi. You said he had a past, so I'm sure the two of you can yuck it up real good."

"Past? Who gives a shit about the past, Camille? Thanks to you, I may still have a future. It just so happens that I'm on my way to meet with the Senate Majority Leader. I'm going to tell him that the great Camille O'Keefe has asked me personally to assist in preventing the slaughter and enslavement of thousands of helpless African women. He'll eat it up. It's precisely what the party needs to regain its footing after you brought everything crashing down."

Camille waited for the second shoe to drop. "And in return?"

Pierson grinned. Why not think big? He was tired of hiding behind the curtain. He felt he deserved so much more. "Ah, now you're getting it, my dear. Maybe you did learn something about politics being First Lady after all. In return, I am going to run for president. I have the foreign-affairs experience. This little maneuver in Chad or whatever shit hole it is will solidify that for sure. I can run on something like that."

Camille laughed out loud. "Oh, come on, Harry. How stupid do you think the American public is?"

"You don't really want to know my answer, do you?"

It was almost too audacious for Camille to believe, even coming from Harry Pierson. "You forget that half of the voters are women. Do you think we're that pathetic?"

"Exactly!" pronounced Pierson, as if everything was a *fait accompli*. "That's why you're going to be my running mate. How does

Vice President O'Keefe sound? You have the popularity, you have the soft side I lack. That's what I mean by us forming a partnership."

Camille was frozen with disbelief. The way Pierson described it, it almost seemed possible. But how could it?

He poured it on hard. It was a spur-of-the-moment idea, but it sounded better and better the more he verbalized it. Why not shoot for the stars and ride her all the way to the top? "The world will love us. Think of the kick in the balls it will be to Beck. Come on, Red. You owe him one. His head will explode. He'll melt down. We'll see him on the *E Hollywood News* 'Where Are They Now' segment all fat and scruffy . . . half crazy and hanging out with toothless tweekers. That's just the icing on the cake. More importantly, there will be a woman—a real spiritual leader—in the White House for the first time. This is your destiny."

Camille had to sit down. She found the nearest chair. "I don't even know what to say. Everything you're saying is true, and yet I feel so . . . uneasy. I feel like you're trying to pick me up or something. You'll say anything to get me to go to bed with you."

Sensing he needed Camille as much as she needed him, he pressed hard. "Welcome to success, Camille. Look, forget I even mentioned all that revenge stuff with Beck. I know that's not your way. Make believe I never said it. Instead, focus on the amazing precedent you'd be setting. You stood up to injustice with Beck. And now you can do it again with *Boko Haram*. You can speak truth to injustice. Hell, write another book or something. Imagine having not one but *two* best sellers. Good God, woman, we'll both be heroes, just to different sorts of people."

He paused to gauge her. He felt he needed more. Disregarding any semblance of how he really felt, he went straight for her emotional center. "You see, Camille, I'm not like Beck. I'm different. I recognize your potential. Shit, I admire you. That's what a good team is all about. It's a partnership. We both help each other. Beck was a complete idiot for not taking advantage of a woman like you. I'm much smarter than that. I want to take advantage of that."

Camille rubbed her flushed face. "Oh, Beck sure took advantage of me."

Pierson cursed under his breath. He hated when she was a pain in the ass like this. "I mean politically, not sexually."

"Are they really that different? It's penis and ego any way you slice it."

Looking for another way in, Pierson tried to pass it off with a joke. "Please don't talk about slicing penises. It makes me uncomfortable. Let's talk about how we're going to save these women instead."

Camille was silent.

"Look," urged Pierson. "I have to go. I have this meeting, not to mention the fact that you've got me hitting the booze already. Do we have a deal or not? I need your word."

"Do I have yours, Harry? I think that's the bigger question."

"Of course you do. It's fate that we connected like this. Then it's a deal, Madame Vice President."

"I'm meeting Kofi Achebe this afternoon. We are meeting again in the Bahamas."

"Excellent. You understand that I can't get too close to this thing. I don't spill the blood anymore. But I can certainly facilitate everything from behind the scenes."

"Until it's time for you to step out from behind the curtain and take the credit," said Camille, sadly.

Pierson felt this, too, was a compliment. "Precisely. I think we have an excellent man in that theater. I'm pretty sure he's somewhere in the Caribbean right now getting some R&R, but that's his problem. Duty calls, right? His name is Harvey Guttman. At least that's what people call him . . . you know what I mean. I'll make sure he's briefed. Everyone will know this is coming from high up. That's me, by the way . . . I'm still the number two man until the American people throw my ass out. Then again, if things go according to plan, you and I will be enjoying the view from the White House for another eight years."

Camille was silent again.

"Hey," goaded Pierson, sensing Camille was wavering. "Let's get this thing done. First we save your women, then we save my ass. Along the way, you become a very prominent political figure, maybe the most powerful—change that, *influential*—woman in the world. Bingo! Let's do this."

Camille tapped her forehead trying to align it all. She just wasn't sure about any of it. Saving the refugees was the morally right thing to do, but even that course of action would be littered with dead bodies. For her, killing was killing, even if they were terrorists. Every action has an equal reaction. She knew there would be a spiritual price to pay.

This whole running for vice president thing sounded equally fraught with pitfalls. She'd just extricated herself from that world, and now she was supposed to leap back in with both feet . . . blindfolded? It sounded crazy to her. And yet, the last thing Pierson said stuck firmly in her mind. Camille O'Keefe had no interest in being powerful, but she felt it was her life's purpose to be the most influential woman in the world. That word Pierson used . . . *influential*. She had a view of the world and a plan for all people she felt must be heard. Harry Pierson's crazy plan may not have been so crazy after all. It gave her pause because it gave her opportunity. She felt she owed it to the universe and to the people of the world to explore the path.

She bit her lip before speaking. The one thing she learned hanging out with politicians is to get everyone's skin in the game. "Okay, Harry. But there are three conditions. There's no deal unless you agree. And by the way," she added from personal experience, "I want it in writing. No games. I want accountability on this. As you can see, I've learned a few things."

"Three? Jesus Christ, you must have learned how to bust balls from Beck. This whole 'putting it in writing' thing makes me uneasy, too."

Camille shrugged. It was plainly evident she was unwavering on her demands. "And that makes me uneasy. I'm sure you understand. It is what it is. Those are my conditions. Otherwise, you're free to go down with Beck tied around your neck like a noose or an albatross. I leave the choice or cliché to you."

At this point, Pierson was apt to agree to anything short of handing over both of his balls so long as he could drag Camille on board. "Let's have it, then. Give it to me straight."

Camille nodded. She was pleased. "First, I want to form a United Nations of Religions."

Pierson pursed his lips. "What the hell is that?"

"Think about it. The world we used to know is gone. We are leaving this cumbersome dimension and realizing our *I Am* being. We've entered a new period of cosmic change in which people will move faster than ever before toward their higher crystalline solar selves. At the same time, people will experience tremendous anxiety from the difficulties inherent in such unprecedented cosmic change."

Pierson pictured Camille. He was suddenly aware of a shooting pain in his frontal lobe. It's not about geographical boundaries any more. "I have no idea what the hell you are talking about."

Camille said to him sympathetically. "I know, Harry. That's part of the problem, but at least you try. Let me put it this way . . . there are dark energies rising up in resistance all around us, fighting to hold us down, even bringing us back to an earlier time of low vibrations. Geographical borders are no longer relevant. The EU doesn't even have them. More important is religion. It's the driving force behind humanity's best and worst behavior. We save people in the name of God, and we murder people in His name as well. Clearly, we need to establish some sort of governing body where all religions have representation but also accountability, a place where reward and punishment can be meted out."

Pierson smiled. "Now that I can get my head around. It sounds like you're describing these dirtbags in *Boko Haram* or some other terrorist group looking to take us back to the tenth century."

"There's plenty of good, religious people out there, too. In this new era of growth, we have transcended geographical borders. We don't have the Cold War anymore. We have religious wars."

Pierson scoffed. "Yeah, and look where not having borders got the EU. Terrorists and refugees by the masses are free to move around the entire continent as they see fit."

Camille nodded enthusiastically. "That's my point. The world is divided now by religious ideology that transcends territorial boundaries. As a result, we need to approach the relationship among people as the resonance of different religions."

"There's no accountability," said Pierson.

"That's right. That's what I said. Now there isn't. But if we establish something like a United Nations for Religions and set up Heads of Church, so to speak, we can at least establish central points of contact."

Pierson waved her off. "Good luck with that. You evidently haven't seen a Sunni go at it with a Shiite."

"It doesn't matter what religion or faction you believe in. The whole point is to allow for differences and freedom of choice while establishing a kind of chain of command . . . like the Pope."

Harry Pierson breathed deeply. It dawned on him that he could very well agree to such an endeavor for the sheer sake of appearances. If the thing had legs, so be it. If not, at least he could claim he was trying something different . . . and blame it on Camille.

"Sure," he said. "That sounds like a vice presidential project if I ever heard one. You run with it. What else do I have to agree to?"

"Okay, the second thing I want is more traditional, albeit just as unprecedented. When Beck first began his campaign for president, he promised me he would champion a fiscal plan put forth by a fellow named Johnny Long. As soon as he won, he abandoned it. I want you to promote that plan."

"You mean that corporate dividend thing?"

"That's the one. You know damn well what I'm talking about."

Pierson rubbed his forehead. She was giving him a headache with all this shit. "As I recall, this Johnny Long fellow wanted Beck to propose a bill mandating that large corporations pay a 25 percent dividend or something like that."

"Sort of. The point is that capitalism has become some sort of a mindless money machine generating vast wealth for a few people. There's too much inequality for a system so powerful. What Johnny Long thinks is that capitalism has grown stagnant. Money needs to be continually recirculated into the system so wealth generation spreads to more and more people. We don't need any more billionaires. We need more millionaires, more middle class and more opportunity. That can only come from moving capitalism forward . . . at least, that's what I think Johnny was pushing Beck toward. I'm not the expert, but I know one when I see one."

"It's a tough sell, Camille. You know that."

"Nothing is a tougher sell than you, Harry. Take it or leave it."

Pierson didn't like this requirement. He was afraid it would make him look like some sort of socialist even if this Johnny Long guy was right. It might cost him the election, but what choice did he have? Again, he resolved to agree and deal with it later. He would say just about anything right now to associate himself with Camille O'Keefe. It was his only way out.

"Fine, Camille. Whatever. It's a deal."

"Now, now . . . there's a third stipulation."

Pierson was beginning to sweat. Literally, there were wet spots under his arms. "You're killing me here. You know that, right?"

"It's all about killing, isn't it? You would think people would learn after thousands of years of war killing each other that this is not getting anyone anywhere. I know sometimes fate throws people together in such a way that violence is inevitable. Whatever you have in mind, I'm sure there will be as much killing as possible. You're a man's man, after all. Then there's all this police violence . . . cops shooting bullets into an unarmed black man already in handcuffs. We're all heading in the wrong direction."

Pierson responded aggressively to her wording. "Hey, cops have a tough job. We don't know what really goes on out there. What you see on some iPhone video isn't the whole story. A lot of times, these guys are resisting arrest."

Camille knew this was a delicate issue. But she also knew it was far bigger than race politics. "Generally speaking, we need to break out of this cycle where war creates new problems that eventually result in another war. It's the same with the police. The cops shoot two black men over the course of a summer weekend, and then the whackos come out looking to assassinate innocent cops in retaliation. It reminds me a whole lot of the Middle East. One killing begets another, which begets another, and so on. It's the same cycle of violence and desperation. It gets us nowhere. Actually, we regress. Do you get my point?"

"I do," agreed Pierson, surprising himself. "I'm a man of war, that's true. Like you say, it's sometimes inevitable. But it doesn't mean I don't think war is hell. It's terrible. And I certainly don't want a race war blowing up out there. If you're sitting on something I can campaign on, then I'm game to hear it. So what do you want from me?"

Camille rubbed her hands together while she struggled to find words Pierson would understand.

"For Christ's sake, Camille, just spit it out. I'm a big boy."

"Okay, here goes. I want you to take some prisoners. I don't want you to kill them all."

Pierson shot back a bitter, resentful laugh. "Let me get this straight, you want me to let some of these scum live? Do you think *Boko Haram* would do the same for you?"

"That's not the point. People in power shouldn't do right only to those who do right. We need to set the example for the world to follow."

"And what might that be, that we shouldn't kill the people who are trying to kill us?"

Camille understood where he was coming from. "Follow me with this, Harry. We've got to find an alternative to killing. You know perfectly well that I'm no friend of these murdering sex traffickers. We still need to catch bad guys and punish the people who do terrible things, especially terrorists who target innocent people. We still need to hold people accountable for the crimes they commit. At the same time, we need to draw the line at killing. If we remove that component, I think all humankind can at last move forward toward a brighter future."

Pierson was at his threshold. He couldn't imagine how he was going to sell this to the guys in the field he was planning to tap for the op. "So what the hell do you want me to do, invent some sort of stun gun? Come on, Camille. Give me something I can work with here. I can't go to a bunch of military guys and tell them not to kill the guys shooting at them."

Camille cleared her throat. "I know how you feel, Harry. But I think even soldiers will get the point. Beck used to talk about a new weapon that was like a stun gun or something. Is that a reality or something he was making up?"

Pierson was surprised. "Beck told you about that?"

Camille grunted. "Of course not. He barely spoke to me. I overheard him bragging about it with one of his chippie aides. It's like a new rifle or something like that?"

Pierson had to hand it to her. Despite all her rambling on about this and that dimension and crystalline bodies or whatever, she always seemed to have an ace in the hole. And she just played it. "It's actually a new type of ammunition . . . like a bullet. It's non-fatal. We were thinking about using snipers to deliver the shot. Anyway, inside the casing are these weird super-small nanoparticles or something . . . like a thousandth of a pinhead. It's like injecting a million microscopic spiders into the target. It's based on macrophage or some crap like that I don't understand. All I know is that the nanoparticles are like tiny spider robots that take over the target's brain in the time it takes for electrical signals to reach the head. It completely incapacitates the target, but they remain totally conscious."

This was exactly what Camille was banking on. "So instead of killing the person, this new nano-bullet knocks them out so we can take them prisoner?"

"No, it renders them incapacitated, but they are still conscious."

It was better than she could have hoped for. "Oh, wow. So the prisoners can hear and think?"

"Oh yeah," said Pierson. "They'll be conscious but totally unable to move. That's the whole point. It's the perfect weapon for taking high-value targets so we can pump them for intel. Think about it. It's the perfect weapon when you want to snatch an HVT who could have critical knowledge."

Camille smiled. Pierson made her point for her. "Or, Harry . . . the police could use this new technology instead of deadly force. The applications extend well beyond the battlefield."

Pierson wasn't inclined to accommodate Camille's checkmate. "Or, as I would say, we have a war going on here at home, too. The battlefield has moved to our inner cities."

Camille laughed. "So say it . . . I'm right. Go on, I dare you."

Pierson took a deep breath and swallowed his castor oil. "Fine, you are right. We might be able to introduce this technology here at home as well. But this is assuming it even works. I think we scrapped the project. Not enough of a body count for Congress to fund it."

"Even so, this may indeed be another way besides killing people."

"I can't believe Beck discusses this stuff with people who don't have clearance."

"He'll do anything to get laid."

"Anyway," said Pierson, hoping to wrap this up and get her off the phone. "It's still in the experimental stages with Special Activities Division and the CIA. Jeez . . . what the hell else did he tell his women, the launch codes?"

Camille grimaced. "Eh, spare me. It makes me feel dirty just thinking about it. What I have in mind is different. I want you to take Aliyu Adelabu and some of his men captive so we can use them as examples of a non-lethal option. We can also turn them. We can't do that if they're dead."

That last bit caught Pierson's attention. "Turn them?"

"You know, like work on them to get them to see the light. We need to learn how to help these people rehabilitate themselves, or we are going to be stuck in a cycle of war and killing each other for the next two thousand years, assuming we survive that long, which I very much doubt. Plus, I'm sure they can provide invaluable information we could use to help stop other attacks. Just because we're not killing them doesn't mean we're not going to use them to our advantage."

Pierson's wheels were turning at a furious pace. At first it sounded crazy. But the more he thought about it, the more he loved it. The island rescue would provide the perfect opportunity to roll out this new weapon, completely amazing the American public. They would eat it up. More importantly, he figured he could turn the whole thing into some sort of spectacle to use during the election. It was brilliant. Of course, Special Activities Division would go ballistic, but he was still the vice president. He could strong-arm them if need be. Yes, he was beginning to see it . . . wipe out most of *Boko Haram* to make all the Rambo folks happy. But also unleash the latest weapons technology and take Aliyu and some of his men prisoner. This would placate Camille and all those softies who loved her. Once he had Aliyu in custody and hidden off somewhere nobody could find, they could test all sorts of psychological operations (PSYOPs) on him. By the time they were finished with him, he might very well wish he was dead.

He pictured Camille on the other end of the call and smiled. "It's a deal."

Camille nodded. "It's a deal . . . although I'm not quite sure what to make of your intentions. For all I know, you've already formulated a side plan. That would be very like you, Harry. I guess that's the risk I run."

"I take that as a compliment, Camille."

He hung up and hustled off to his meeting. Where Becket Rosemore shunned Camille O'Keefe, Harry Pierson was now mated to her for better and for worse. Whatever people said about her, she'd won an important ally in Harry Pierson, one who at least seemed willing to listen to what she said. Harry Pierson had the power necessary to save those refugees. He had the panache to land on his feet and even run for president in the wake of Beck's destruction. Things suddenly looked damned good for the old man.

As for Camille O'Keefe . . . she was now in bed with the devil.

Chapter 36

Sometimes the master was not always the commander. Despite his ambition, Harry Pierson wasn't the president yet. He was limited in what he could do as vice president and that put constraints on his ability to help Camille save the women. He couldn't go to Beck for help. First of all, Beck might usurp the plan for himself in a last-ditch effort to save his legacy. Or, if he was so inclined, he could simply forbid Pierson from taking any action at all. There was also the matter of the Constitution, international law, and all that bullshit that drove guys like Pierson bananas. Conventional approaches were closed off. He would have to work outside the box.

Harry Pierson never paid much mind to following the rules, and he certainly didn't intend to start now. That meant working his usual back channels to get his things done. No problems there. He whipped out his spinning wheel once again. This time, he tapped another buddy of his, a two-star Rear Admiral named Pete Flint, call sign "Stickman" back when he was jockeying an F/A-18 Hornet at almost twice the speed of sound in the early 90s. Rear Admiral Flint was well placed at Special Ops Command Central—SOCC—and knew how to get an action like this approved, manned and executed via Naval Special Warfare Command (affectionately known as WARCOM) out of Coronado, California. It was also the home of SEAL Team 3. Flint was essentially "Papa Seal," which was what Pierson affectionately called him. Flint was also Harry Pierson's Ollie North on numerous occasions when plausible deniability was needed. Should things go well this time around, Papa Seal would find himself in Harry Pierson's cabinet should he win the election.

Part of WARCOM Group One, Team 3, covered the West Pacific and the Middle East. Like all SEALs, these men were the best trained, the best equipped and the best prepared operators in the world. Currently deployed at Camp Lemonnier in Djibouti, part of the Combined Joint Task Force Horn of Africa, the platoon was the obvious choice for the mission. They would use Camp Lemonnier as their Tactical Operation Center. Djibouti was a critical TOC for U.S. operations in the Gulf region but would prove wonderfully useful to Pierson now that he needed to stage an operation in sub-Saharan African.

Team 3 was busy, very busy, during the years of Operation Enduring Freedom when it was responsible for covert operations in the Horn of Africa, largely in Somalia. Team 3 was the reason why the mass of Somali pirates who captured the media's attention disappeared just as suddenly one by one until . . . poof . . . they were all dead and forgotten. The Seals were sixteen deadly sons of bitches, all of whom were going to say goodbye to *Boko Haram*. Each of these sixteen men could kill Aliyu Adelabu a hundred different ways, and yet not one of them felt comfortable with accolades because they knew every other SEAL in the world would do the very same thing when needed.

They shared a unique bond forged by a hellish training and initiation that brought them to exhaustion and the brink of death time and time again. They held their loyalty to each other above all else, including their own lives. They all knew when they signed up to be a SEAL that they were agreeing to give up everything, including their lives. You never knew how they would arrive, but you always knew how they would leave . . . all together, the dead and the living. They never left a man behind. This was the code for all special operations teams.

When Pierson decided to move forward with the strike, Rear Admiral Flint turned to WARCOM, setting into motion an amazing array of manpower, firepower, tactical and logistical support platforms. Pierson's plan was complex, with lots of moving parts and danger at every critical juncture. His goals were clear, though, and he was willing to take the necessary risks with other people's lives. He would watch it all from his office via satellite uplink, making sure his grand vision came to fruition.

It was also critical that Camille make an appearance on the island. He needed her to make a stirring speech after the attack so he could record it and edit it for use during their political campaign. Thus, the first order of business was getting Camille into the theater securely. Pierson and Flint discussed a variety of options. But as Papa Seal pointed out, most of them would likely result in Camille being killed. That would be a bad thing. Pierson needed her alive not because he particularly liked her, but because losing her would spell disaster for his political ambitions. He couldn't just drop her directly onto some tiny island in the middle of Lake Chad. Instead, Pierson and Flint carefully constructed a complex, multifaceted game plan for an overwhelming win, culminating in a stirring victory speech.

They set the plan in motion quickly. Not long after she made her deal with Pierson, Camille was on board Air Force 2, headed for the Bahamas to collect Kofi. From there, it was on to Chad. She and Kofi were not going straight to Koulfoua Island. It was way too dangerous. Instead, they would be staged about 150 miles south in N'Djamena, the capitol of Chad and home to a half million people with a palpable distaste for Americans. It was less risky than dropping them on the island ahead of the assault. But it was in no way safe.

Kofi was used to this sort of thing. He lived life in the crosshairs. Not a month went by without shots being fired in his general vicinity. Back in the day, firefights had been an everyday part of his life. He'd come to expect a degree of risk in what he did. He lived inside a kind of carapace from which he stuck his head out occasionally. Like Beck and Harry Pierson, he was a man of conflict. That hard exterior shell protected him not only physically but also emotionally. He needed the world around him as it was. From that wellspring, he drew his purpose. He spoke with the dead in order to hear their stories and feel their pain, but he would be equally impacted were they never there at all. Kofi Achebe needed a world of pain and suffering in order to feel purposeful and necessary.

Camille enjoyed no violent interaction with the world at large. Unlike Kofi, she found the massive pain, suffering and inequality of the world disrupted her sense of equilibrium. She needed oneness. Yet she was headed straight into the belly of the beast, a world of death and violence unlike anything she'd ever seen. She had no idea what was waiting for her at N'Djamena or Koulfoua Island. She was certain it would be inhospitable, aggressive and violent. As much as she was a hero to some, she was a target to others. Such was the multiplicity of the world which she embraced.

Up to that point, Camille had her share of trouble. Aside from the emotional pain of being cheated on incessantly, she was involved in that suspicious car accident that left her scarred both physically and emotionally. Few people knew that before she became First Lady, she was attacked and beaten by a man seeking revenge against Beck. On another occasion, she had to be rushed to a safe house for fear that an international operative was trying to kill her. Her Secret Service bodyguard was killed in the process. She knew she had an inner strength Beck and his cohorts assumed she didn't possess. But this new phase marked a significant shift upward in risk. It was going to be sticky.

Chad was wide open. Government, army and police officials were often in cahoots with *Boko Haram* and had no problem killing off adversaries who grumbled too much. N'Djamena and Koulfoua Island were no place for a high-ranking U.S. dignitary to find herself, especially a woman, and especially a woman like Camille O'Keefe. The fragile changes she was trying to bring to the world could be halted instantly with a single shot to her head. She knew it, Kofi knew it and Harry Pierson knew it (although he accepted it as an acceptable risk given the potential reward). There was no way around it—Camille O'Keefe was a high-value target.

Millions of violent, deadly men like Aliyu also recognized Camille's value to the world. Theirs was the very patriarchy Camille threatened to bring down should they fail to bring her down first. Her ideas, her independence, everything she represented threatened the ancient, fossilized *Sharia* code by which they lived. This was the same code they fought to impose upon the entire world through *jihad*. The world of *Sharia* was completely incompatible with a woman like Camille O'Keefe not because Camille was intolerant but because she refused to be subjugated, enslaved or ensnared by a monolithic mode of being. If anything, Camille was too tolerant to coexist with *Sharia* hegemony. *Boko Haram* represented *Sharia Law*. *Sharia Law* represented a movement back to a centuries-old moral system.

Camille represented a future of new possibilities. As such, she was radical Islam's most wanted . . . dead, not alive. The ideological overtones enthralled Harry Pierson, who saw this as a classic story of Good versus Evil. Camille would not have seen it this way. She believed all people were free to make choices of faith and religion. If that led to harming others, the universe would act as judge. Pierson did not share her trust in divine reconciliation. Instead, he believed fully in himself. His rules and definitions were the only context necessary.

His plan was exact, and timing was everything. Given the tight timeline, coupled with Pierson's insatiable drive to turn the attack into a marketing extravaganza, the best course of action was to dispatch Camille and Kofi to N'Djamena as quickly as possible. Camille couldn't accompany the strike force, and she certainly couldn't land on the island unprotected ahead of the attack. Kofi would be with her, but what could one man do? Pierson wanted Kofi there to translate Camille's speech to the refugees, speak Arabic if necessary, and "give the whole thing a bit of an African feel." That would be important to African leaders as well as liberals here at home.

The risk was tremendous by any stretch of the imagination. Were Camille not on the outs as First Lady, it never would have been permitted. Then again, Camille O'Keefe was a risk taker. She was forged from a different ethereal plane. She was tough in ways that could easily go unnoticed. Her book made that perfectly clear.

She was going to do things differently, so Pierson figured why fight it? Instead, he played his hand with the cards he had. To facilitate her position in N'Djamena, Guttman orchestrated a sizeable "payout"—via the Swiss banking system—to the few key men running Chad. A few million dollars would hardly be missed by the U.S. government, but it went a hell of a long way in Africa. Pierson considered it a small price to pay to ensure Camille's safety. And if something went awry, if the players in Chad decided to double-cross him and kill Camille, he would figure out how to spin the thing to his advantage by martyring her or something. He'd figure something out.

Even though he was pulling all the strings, Harry Pierson wouldn't be anywhere near that island when the shit went down. He didn't need to be. That's what his Agency man Harvey Guttman was for. Pierson would be watching it all via drone from his office while Guttman and the SEALs did all the dirty work. He sent Guttman back to Maiduguri, only this time he wasn't Dr. Feelgood peddling drugs as part of his sting operation to sell red mercury to *Boko Haram*. No, this time Harvey Guttman was running point for the rescue mission, keeping eyes on Aliyu's movements, and preparing to trigger an overwhelming assault against *Boko Haram,* who would never see it coming.

Papa Seal planned to hit the terrorists by sea, air and land. Operation Woman and Child . . . that's what Pierson called it. A name like that would play brilliantly with the media. Who could challenge such a lofty sentiment? The nobility of it would obfuscate the bloodbath he was about to unleash. Once he had the raw footage back in Washington, he could have it edited to his exact liking. If it went according to plan, it would clear the way for him to run for president with or without Camille, although he preferred to have her as his running mate for many reasons. He was wary, though, not to leave bodies behind. That never played well. People liked the idea of SEALs kicking ass, but they didn't really want to see the corpses. Instead, he would focus the world's attention on the slaughter he prevented by saving all those women and children.

For the moment, Pierson wanted to send a message. He wanted to tell the world that he would bring the fight to the terrorists, he would strike fear in their hearts, he would have them worrying that once they went to sleep, they would never wake up again. He also intended to use Camille to further a message to the victimized of the world—the United States was back, he was the new sheriff in town, and he was bringing with him one bad-ass posse, point blank, end of story. It was all part of his plan to reinvent himself as the next great world leader. And from the looks of it, he could wear this rescue mission like a crown, including Camille O'Keefe as the premiere crown jewel.

With Camille, Kofi, Guttman and the SEALs en route, it was just a matter of waiting for Aliyu to make his move. Guttman was tasked with providing the recon on Aliyu's makeshift armada. From what Guttman could discern, Aliyu planned on sticking with his basic crew of about 50 men. Dr. Feelgood recognized them as the usual suspects whom he kept well-supplied with his deliveries of Valium, Oxycontin, Prozac and Captagon. "At least we'll send them to Allah with a smile on their face," he told the Rear Admiral. "There are worse ways to go."

After a quick bit of digging, Guttman discovered that Aliyu had staged his boats along Lake Chad in a rural town called Doro Gowon about 15 miles (25 clicks) due east from Koulfoua Island. Aliyu didn't even bother to hide the boats. Why should he? *Boko Haram* had already laid waste to the region. About a year earlier, *Boko Haram* had raided Doro Gowon and neighboring Baga. They had slaughtered over 2,000 innocent people. They had left the bodies rotting in the streets for days before Kofi could get there.

Of particular note in Kofi's report were the many pregnant women whose fetuses were cut from their bellies and left in a bloody heap next to their mothers' beheaded corpses. Aliyu was not inclined to allow non-Muslim babies into his *Sharia* world. Guttman happened to be in Nigeria at the time as well and visited the site shortly after it went down. The degree of savagery floored him. It was the only time he remembered puking at the site of inhumanity, even though it was the currency in which he most often traded.

Operation Woman and Child marked the first time he'd been back in Doro Gowon. There were still many ghosts for him there.

He didn't want to go, but he had to get eyes on the watercraft. He could almost smell the rank, putrefying bodies all over again. He remembered the bloated faces looking like they were going to explode or "pop" as the locals called it. He actually witnessed one popper. Being back in Doro Gowon made him want revenge in the worst way, and he was glad he had tossed a few more Valium than usual in his pocket before setting out.

What he saw was nothing special. Like all *Boko Haram* transports, the boats were rickety "water hoopties," as Guttman called them, except each boat was mounted with a .50 caliber machine gun. Makeshift as the transports were, the .50 cals made them deadly and not to be taken lightly, despite the ragtag nature of Aliyu's men. Guttman noted the addition of four large transport vessels. From the looks of them, they were converted barge-like ships, probably used for transporting animals. Guttman figured Aliyu was probably going to use the barges to transport the slave girls. Assuming he packed 250 girls on each barge like animals, Guttman determined that Aliyu intended to take about 1,000 girls as *sibya*. He assumed the other 4,000 were marked for execution and would never leave the island, but rather find the bottom of a few large mass-burial pits. Or maybe Aliyu would just leave the heaps of corpses where they fell. That would be typical of him.

What surprised Guttman was not Aliyu's disregard for hiding his equipment. Nor was he particularly taken aback that 4,000 people were marked for slaughter with no more thought than a farmer would give to putting down some old, feeble horses. No, what surprised Harvey Guttman was the fact that each boat, including the slave transports, was outfitted with bad-ass 557-horsepower outboards. As Guttman shot his surveillance video, streaming directly back to the Tactical Operations Center in Djibouti, everyone could see that the engines were brand new out-of-the-box.

A quick cross-reference of the brand name revealed Aliyu was powering his assault boats with the same state-of-the-art GM engines used in the Cadillac CTS-V. It was remarkable and summed up the irony of the entire fight against terrorism. Here was an avowed *jihadi* using run-down boats yet also relying on technology that was 100 percent made in America, with a price tag of about $70,000 per motor. That put the total cost at just under $1 million for the propulsion without taking into account their weapons. Once again, everyone was reminded how much money flowed into these terrorist organizations, even one as seemingly insignificant as *Boko Haram*.

There were millions and millions of dollars pouring into various terrorist factions to be distributed and invested in the worldwide *jihad*. *Boko Haram* was only a small part in the global terrorist network, but it was a microcosm nonetheless. Gone were the days when old, weathered *Al Qaeda* men hid out in caves and crept around in the shadows. Having been on the inside with Aliyu, Guttman saw the new face of terrorist leaders . . . young, college-educated, often from well-to-do families. They used social media and lived right out in the open just like their boats. The level of arrogance and blatant disregard for repercussions scared Guttman because the influential *jihadi* were now everywhere.

Guttman also knew that the infrastructure of this new terrorist world order, the backbone supporting the entire *corpus putridas*, was the Swiss banking system. His man on the inside, André Lamon in Geneva, was tracking massive amounts of dirty money moving through the system for anybody who cared to look. It was as obvious as a rat going through a python. It was all legally transacted, no matter how devious the intent. Money knew not from good and evil; that distinction was reserved for the men sending and spending it. Guttman was certain the money for those engines came through the Swiss banking system. It would be easy enough to trace a purchase like that, but that was for another time and another story.

Back in Maiduguri, Aliyu made no pretense of secrecy. During his surveillance, Guttman used a highly advanced laser listening device recently rolled out by the CIA. He could hear Aliyu and his men discussing their plans as casually as if ordering a meal. That's how it was with these guys. He had sat next to Aliyu on many occasions. It was always the same . . . Aliyu's house was rife with the stench of hypocrisy and betrayal. Guttman hated the way Aliyu surrounded himself with "yes" men willing to blow themselves up so long as they took innocent civilians with them, men who panted and salivated like wild animals each time they entered a young girl, even if she was a lifeless black ragdoll on the verge of death from being raped so many times. Nothing mattered to these guys.

But now came the time to turn the tables. The man Aliyu knew as Dr. Feelgood couldn't wait to bring the hurt down on those arrogant sons of bitches. He couldn't wait to remind the world terrorist network that the United States of America was back and coming on hard. He wanted the bad guys to know that special operators were coming to put an end to it all . . . their twitter accounts, their encrypted darknet recruiting sites, their money. They were toast. They were dead men walking.

Harvey Guttman could list a hundred despicable facts about Harry Pierson. Operation Woman and Child was not one of them.

Chapter 37

Aliyu's plan is pretty simple. He thinks it will be a cakewalk. They will land their boats, cut down thousands of helpless people, dump them in pits, grab the young girls and beat it back to Maiduguri. They will take some girls for themselves, pay off people with others and sell the rest on the darknet. Then it will be time to plan their Christmas attack on the marketplace. Little do they know that Harvey Guttman has been listening in on their briefings, and there will be a very different story to tell.

As Aliyu describes it, the *Boko Haram* convoy will head north to Monguno, continuing up to Kauwa. There, they will turn northeast and take the Kukuwa-Kaua Border Road leading to Doro Gowon where the boats are stashed, the same town they annihilated a year before. They will make *Al-Asr* afternoon prayer at the Doro Gowon Mosque. Then, *Boko Haram* will conduct their slaughter. Aliyu doesn't even care to wait for the cover of darkness. Failure never enters his mind. Nor does facing any resistance.

Phase 1 is already in motion with Camille and Kofi on the move to N'Djamena. The SEALs have been mobilized as well. The beauty and the beast were both on their way to deliver very different messages. Having bribed the right people to clear the way for Camille

in Chad before running his recon, it's now Guttman's job to notify
TOC when *Boko Haram* pops hot. Once Guttman calls it, Phase 2
will begin. The shit will go down pretty fast from there.

A drone out of Niger, one of six drone stations in the theater,
will keep eyes on the *Boko Haram* convoy as it makes its way from
Maiduguri to Doro Gowon. The drone will provide any other tactical
needs that might spring up and also send live satellite feedback to
Harry Pierson so he can watch the whole thing unfold, Scotch in
hand, from the comfort of his office. Once *Boko Haram* is on the
move and Phase 2 is fully under way, Camille and Kofi will hop a
Blackhawk accompanied by her usual Secret Service agents plus a
squad of ass kickers from the Army Third Special Forces Group.
Two Apache attack helicopters and two AH-6 "Killer Eggs" from
the elite Army 160th SOAR Knight Stalkers will provide close air
support for Camille and her team as they come in from the rear of
Koulfoua Island. After that, all five birds will leave the theater since
the fighting has not yet begun. Two other CIA operatives will have
already gathered the refugees in advance of the assault. There, toward
the rear of the island, is where Camille will address the women
directly, let them know there are people who care about them, people
who believe in their essential humanity. Kofi will translate for her.

During the second phase, the SEAL platoon will spring into action
as well. They have already been repositioned from Camp Lemonnier
in Djibouti to the drone base in remote Niger, off the N1 south about
50 miles, north up the coast of Lake Chad from Doro Gowan. When
drone surveillance has *Boko Haram* in their boats and actually on
the water, the SEAL attack group will come down the coast and light
up the flimsy armada. Accustomed to close combat against well-
armed enemy combatants, the American strike force can take steps to
mitigate and otherwise control the enemy's ability to respond. Their
most significant advantage, though, is the element of surprise. Aliyu's
arrogance is blinding. According to Guttman, the *Boko Haram* leader
expects no resistance at all. This, in itself, may be his fatal flaw. *Boko
Haram* may be armed, but when the Americans surprise them and
unleash devastating firepower, Aliyu's men will panic.

It seems easy enough. But no op is routine. Every plan changes when the bullets start flying for real. The fact that Aliyu's boats are outfitted with monster motors makes the timing much tighter. It also gives *Boko Haram* a tactical advantage in sheer speed. This may prove challenging. As Guttman noted in his recon report, Aliyu's boats are mounted with .50 caliber machine guns powerful enough to take out a SEAL boat or even a helo. Guttman did not report seeing any rocket-propelled grenades during his recon, but the team had to assume Aliyu had some. In this part of the world, buying an RPG is like adding a shake and fries at the drive thru. As with the .50 cals, an RPG could easily take out a boat or helo.

The SEALs are accustomed to all this. What they are not used to is working for Harry Pierson, whose personal agenda rivals Aliyu's in its lack of foresight. There are certain things Pierson needs to accomplish with Operation Woman and Child. Foremost among them is grabbing video footage of the attack as well as Camille's address to the refugees afterward. He can't do this at nighttime. His camera crew needs ambient light. He's unwilling to settle for night-vision footage. He wants the real thing. And so, at the vice president's insistence, this is to be a daylight op.

This was the one aspect of the plan that really bothered Rear Admiral Flint when Pierson laid out his objectives. If Papa Seal had his way, his boys would hit Aliyu and his lieutenants at his house in Maiduguri the night before and get the hell out. He was sure *Boko Haram* would collapse after suffering such a critical loss of leadership. At the very least, the terrorists would have to scuttle the raid on the island. Pierson's insistence on running the thing in broad daylight introduced significantly more risk. Even if Aliyu Adelabu were a high-value target, Flint argued, why not take him at night?

Never one to pull punches when his men's lives were on the line, Flint gave it straight to the vice president during the preliminary planning stage. "It makes no sense, Harry. Why not hit these guys at night. Take out the high-value target and some of his top guys and get the hell out. Or, if you want to use this new nano-bullet, just take them all into custody. The rest of those *Boko Haram* jokers will pack up shop and scramble like cockroaches. Then you can show up on the island with the UN, the First Lady or whoever the hell else you want and pull the refugees out. You'll look like a hero. That's what you want anyway, right?"

Pierson didn't want to hear it. Since he and Flint went way back, he at least offered some justification, however transparent. "That's the exact opposite of what I want, Pete. This is more than a rescue mission. There's a lot going on behind the scenes that you don't know."

"Let me guess . . . politics."

"Exactly. There are larger interests in play here."

This was the thing about Harry Pierson that had always pissed Flint off, even in college. Pierson could turn anything into gold for himself without any regard whatsoever for other people. "We own the night, Harry. You of all people should know that. Christ, there was a time when you wouldn't take a piss in the daylight. So what am I supposed to tell my guys when they ask why the hell they're running a daylight op? Should I tell them the vice president wants a good highlight film?"

"No, Pete. You don't associate my name with this. You just tell your guys to do what they're told. Leave the politics to me."

Being longtime friends was one thing. But supplanting his combat experience with a campaign agenda was a different matter altogether. Papa Seal was seriously pissed when he looked Pierson square in the eye and said, "If any of my guys go down, it's on you."

"No, Pete. I'm the vice president, you're a Rear Admiral. If any of your guys go down, it's on you." He laughed. "Anyway, stop worrying. It'll be like whack-a-mole. Your guys are the best in the world at swinging the mallet. Everything will be fine."

"Maybe you can run for Caesar next, Harry?"

Pierson liked the sound of it. "I take that as a compliment, Pete. Oh, and by the way . . . the two snipers who will fire the nano-bullets . . . I will provide them. Stay out of it."

There was no further debate. The mission parameters were set. Harry Pierson needed his footage, and so he needed a daylight op.

Chapter 38

When the team comes together in their pre-action meeting, they will detail the particulars of the op. It will be a joint effort. A Lockheed P-3, a complete airborne monitoring and engagement platform similar to an AWACS, will provide integrated command and control battle management from high above. If things escalate and the team needs some serious firepower, the P-3 can direct a JDAM straight up Aliyu's ass without so much as a drop of lube.

The SEAL platoon will be divided into two squads of eight men, plus two aerial snipers. Both snipers will remain on the Blackhawks doing what they do best . . . one shot, one kill. Eight men from each squad will man a rigid-hulled inflatable boat or RHIB. They look like a cross between a dingy and a small fishing boat . . . add weapons. Each RHIB will be commanded by a coxswain who, like the bass player in a rock band, doesn't get a lot of glory but keeps it all steady under fire.

The RHIBs themselves will arrive in spectacular fashion, being dropped from a C-130 cargo plane. Ordinarily, the SEALs would just jump out after their boats. Running out the back of a plane was all part of a day's work as far as they were concerned. But for this mission, Papa Seal wants more firepower. The last thing he wants is another

Somalia. So, insertion into the hot zone will be courtesy of two Black Hawks from the Army Knight Stalkers like Camille's escort. Two AH-6 choppers, also from the Knight Stalkers, will provide close air support. Equipped with two 7.62 mm mini-guns and two 7-shot Hydra rocket pods, the "killer eggs" have enough firepower to light it up like a Christmas tree.

Engaging *Boko Haram* is Phase 3 of the op. But Harry Pierson has his own sideshow planned. For this, Harvey Guttman will direct the video activities from a separate helicopter. Pierson intends to use the battle footage of America's elite Navy SEALs and Army Special Ops to sell his prowess as a tough son of a bitch when it comes to foreign policy. Once *Boko Haram* is destroyed, Guttman's video team will record Camille's speech. This will give his potential running mate the air of diplomacy she sorely lacks and also make him appear like a kindhearted and generous leader.

But the real icing on the cake, the real spectacular-spectacular, involves Camille's demand to leave Aliyu and some of his key personnel alive. Pierson and Papa Seal agreed that using snipers was the best bet for delivering the nano-bullet. Pierson made it clear, however, that he would provide the snipers. That personnel decision was his and his alone. Flint was to stay out of it.

There was nothing Flint could have said to dissuade Pierson anyway. The vice president's show was already set in stone. Now that it's about to go down, he's sure it will be the public-relations event of the decade. For this monumental occasion, Pierson had the Special Activities division assign two female snipers. Two women . . . it's almost too perfect. The SEALs are all men. But this third team, Pierson's two-women sniper team, will deliver the nano-bullets that will take down Aliyu. Put the combat, the nano-bullet and Camille's victory speech into his spinning wheel, and Rasputin can weave gold.

Only Harry Pierson and Harvey Guttman know the two snipers— Nancy Harper and Dana Daniels—are already on Koulfoua Island. The Agency positioned them several days before. Trained by the Army Special Forces under a special test protocol studying women's capabilities in combat, Harper and Daniels possess all the abilities of their male counterparts except brute power. Even so, they are both ripped and can bench-press any man in *Boko Haram* fifteen times.

Harper and Daniels are not simply two women plucked off the street. They were chosen out of thousands of candidates to be the first of their kind. They don't flirt. They don't date. They aren't married with children. They train . . . all the time. And when they aren't training, they're cleaning their weapons or blowing off steam at the gun range. They smell like the gun powder or CLP they use to maintain their Barrett rifles rather than Halston or Chanel. Occasionally, some unsuspecting dude tries to get with them, thinking he has to get his hands on a body like theirs. Needless to say, there is seldom a second attempt.

They call Nancy Harper "Death Finger." It's simple logic. When she squeezes her finger, people die. She can put a .50 cal round from her Barrett through Aliyu's brain from a thousand yards away. There aren't many men or women who can pull that off, even in ideal conditions. Nancy Harper . . . Death Finger. She likes the moniker. She jokes that her daddy would be proud. She also knows it wouldn't look too nice on a wedding invite so why bother with men in the first place? There's no marrying for her until she's done becoming her own woman.

Dana Daniels barely even jokes. They simply called her "the Bitch" or, as she likes to remind the men, "Lieutenant Bitch." Ball busting aside, the Bitch isn't a lesbian, and the Bitch isn't straight. If there is a term to describe a woman whose soul mate is her rifle, that term would describe her to a tee. Her Iowa farmland upbringing gives no hint of the cold blood that runs through her veins. Her daddy was a corn breeder who worked at the university developing new GMO stacks. He believed a productive balance between science and respect for the earth was the path to a prosperous future. Her mama is famous for her cornbread, made from scratch, and bakes the best peach cobbler in the entire congregation.

The Bitch is different. Dana is stealthy, a natural-born sniper. She'd just as soon put a round through your eyeball as buy you a Jameson. It surprises nobody that her first job was in a slaughterhouse.

She was seventeen. The funky, rank stench of death and gore didn't bother her, nor did the fact that almost all of her coworkers were Mexican. She took her lunch and shift breaks right along with everyone else and learned her corn was their maize. Her daddy paid it no mind, but her mama didn't like it. Dana was not swayed either way. As she liked to say, "a job's a job," whether it be lining up cattle in a slaughterhouse or taking out an enemy combatant.

Harper and Daniels were already positioned on Koulfoua Island. They were dropped from a helo into Lake Chad with an inflatable Zodiac and then made their way to Koulfoua Island with little more than their rifles, ammo, a supply of nano-bullets, a sidearm, Ghillie camouflage suits and some MREs. Drone intel identified a crop of trees about 300 yards from the shoreline. That's where they are now.

All the plans are set. All assets are in place. It's now time for everyone to wait. . . .

Chapter 39

Change . . . change was happening everywhere. Beck's power was waning while Camille's was ascending. He saw the writing on the wall and grew increasingly sullen and cantankerous. His staffers also saw their careers going under and tried desperately to distance themselves. And so Beck saw his people come and go with no particular conviction. He was a lame duck. It filled him with bitterness. He had no clear vision of his future. Fear and self-interest were the rule.

The exact opposite was happening with Camille. The more her story of suffering and humiliation came to light, the more she became a hero and a role model. For the most part, she was focused on helping those women on the island. This was her sole purpose for the moment. She didn't know exactly what Harry Pierson was planning, but she'd seen him at work before. There was no question he would devise a plan to crush *Boko Haram* and perhaps something magnanimous for the refugees. Still, she was acutely aware of something far bigger taking place, bigger even than saving those five thousand lives.

It wasn't all smooth sailing. Things got a bit tense after she and Kofi repositioned to Nigeria. For starters, their safe house in

N'Djamena was quite different from what she was accustomed to. There was no staff tending to her every need or five-star restaurants serving seafood so fresh it was still moving in the kitchen. Half a world away, she found herself holed up with Kofi in a small U.S. military office building eating only MREs and gut-bomb takeout Kofi described as some sort of goat. The building was located on Avenue Charles de Gaulle overlooking the *Hôpital de la mère et de l'enfant*, a women and children's hospital established by the French years before. Around the corner was the *Grand Mosquee*. Camille and Kofi were positioned almost directly in the middle. She noted the irony with delight. She felt as if a certain symmetry was in play.

The building itself was unassuming, drab and cracked with sunburned tan siding. The windows were filthy, and the gray metal desks mostly unused. It was a temporary workplace intended to support basic logistics in the fight against regional terrorism by the likes of *Al-Shabaab* in Chad and *Boko Haram* in neighboring Nigeria. In reality, the State Department set it up to satisfy demands from the UN that the United States do something—anything—about the alarming practices of these rapists, thugs and human traffickers. At most, it was a dog-and-pony show. It was never intended for the office to house anything more than a skeleton staff of State Department underlings assigned to the post in order to make appearances at select events hosted by the United Nations and the Chad government.

Likewise, the office was never meant to support actual military action. Any action taken against *Boko Haram*, *Al-Shabaab* and so on would be staged and executed exactly how Pierson and Flint set it up . . . small, covert and deadly. Nothing would ever be reported to the United Nations. They would have to read about it in the papers like everyone else. As for the Chad government, there was far too much corruption and far too little accountability to include them directly in any engagement planning.

This made it incredibly risky, sending Camille and Kofi into N'Djamena. At best, the politics were unpredictable. In a resource state like Nigeria or Chad, the money trail led to the very top of the power structure and branched out across the globe from there like veins through an immense, diseased body. Through those veins flowed the true lifeblood of the entire resource economy . . . money . . . money clawed from the earth, money forged into weapons and processed into drugs, money from the sale of people, money cleaned through the largest "legitimate" corporations or absconded from public scrutiny by a Swiss banking edifice built atop a dungeon of human pain and suffering, money wrenched from the people.

A man like Kofi Achebe had seen it all many times before. This makeshift office with its empty desks, unplugged fax machine and unused coffeemaker told a thousand tales about Africa in the eyes of the world. His people were invisible. The few occasions when the African people were recognized by the world at large, they were most often reduced to caricatures in a black-face cartoon animated by whatever Western needs were most expedient at the time. In a way, he walked a line between the two worlds. His story was a tale of two worlds, progress on the one side and depravity on the other. Here was the problem—the line blurred more and more with every passing day.

Such was the world in which Kofi operated. He'd seen all the sides of the rubric. There was a time when he was part of the system he now found abhorrent, a time when he did terrible things, ruined people to the point of suicide, a time when he could kill a child as easily as shooting a sparrow with a BB gun. Now, he fought to bring that system down as best he could. For him, that meant shining a light on the darkness, revealing the horror that goes on in the shadows all around us all over the world all of the time. The suffering was ongoing, a sort of perpetual motion requiring little more than greed and hatred to keep the gears of the mill churning human beings into grist.

If he were a writer like his uncle, he would use language to make people see what lies behind the curtain. He felt that was the highest purpose of language and of the novel—to pull away the veil of civilization and reveal the horrible truths by which it is all perpetuated. Writing was in Kofi's blood, in his ancestry, in his DNA. He knew the power of the word that can make a story metaphysical and tell us about ourselves, our problems, our victories and our failures.

But he did not allow himself the solace of writing. It was too removed for him. Instead he spoke with the dead right there where they dropped, listened to their tales and carried it inside himself, knowing it would inevitably overgrow and fester. He cannot resolve it. At the same time, he knew the ultimate truth was out there somewhere waiting for him . . . a bullet with his name on it. When that day finally comes, he will be released from it all . . . guilt, suffering, speaking truth to the façade. He welcomed that day with open arms.

Kofi sat on a high-backed wooden desk chair that he wheeled over so he could face Camille. Camille was sitting on a green couch that looked like it was right out of the surplus depot. It was. A chipped coffee table provided a place for them to set their things. He was thinking. Camille had seen so little of his world. In the end, would she be a help or a hindrance? He banked on her as the linchpin to saving those people, but for all he knew, she might crack. And what if something terrible went down? What if they took fire and she was killed? Kofi harbored a lot of guilt about the things he'd done in his life, but he could never live with himself should Camille O'Keefe become a casualty of his little war.

Time seemed to crawl. For two days they'd been milling around waiting for Guttman's call. Camille was visibly nervous. Violence was not her way, and she had grave misgivings from the start about bringing on a man like Harry Pierson. She hadn't even begun to contemplate the deal she made with him, their presumed run for the White House and the humiliation it would bring Beck. A lot of anger would ensue. She could read anger in Kofi, as well. She could feel his anticipation and his thirst for revenge. The darkness of *Boko Haram* seeped into every nook and cranny, and could poison a man's soul if he didn't watch out. Camille could see it like a black fog descending over the city. All of this raw, violent, masculine energy . . . it changed people. Or rather, it prompted people to revert to their basic selves.

As a result, Camille had her walls up to repel all this negative energy. But she knew she was alone in doing so. Everyone else was preparing for bloodshed. When she told Pierson how she felt, he told her it would be good training for her role as vice president should they be fortunate enough to actually pull it off. When she told Kofi that she feared he would be consumed by his need for vengeance, he laughed it off.

"Everyone in Africa has a death story," he told her. "There is no life here that does not come coupled with death. We live every day with that duality."

Camille reminded herself that there was a higher purpose to all this, that saving those five thousand women was, if nothing else, a mitigating factor. It was also morally important to her that Pierson agreed to her three demands. That the two of them would make a serious run for the White House based, at least in part, on her desire to form something like a United Nations of Religions made her feel like she was heard and respected by a man for the first time in a long, long time. She was certain that times were changing and new methods of communication were required if humanity was not to blow itself into oblivion.

She was also reassured by Pierson's promise to give Johnny Long's dividend plan a serious look. Beck had paid lip service to it until he won the election. After that, he dropped it almost as fast as he dropped Camille. Again, she was certain that there was more potential in the American financial system. She was just as certain that it had grown stagnant and long ago ceased working for all Americans. If Pierson was true to his word, the two of them could make history as the greatest economic visionaries in modern history.

And of course, there was Pierson's promise not to kill all the terrorists. She had many misgivings, coupled with many nightmares, about her complicity with violence on this kind of scale. Saving the refugees was important to her, and justified military intervention. Even so, she couldn't help feeling she would be held accountable in the court of Universal Law, the only venue that really mattered after all was said and done in this dimension. None of it put to rest the dissonance that rattled around in her soul. It challenged her core beliefs because she felt stuck in a catch-22. Whether she did nothing to help those poor people or intervened as she had done, a lot of people were going to die as a direct result. She didn't like this. For deep down, deep where her intuition lived, she knew there would be blood on her hands either way. Worse, she knew she would carry this karmic burden forward for many lives to come.

Many lives, many Masters . . . only time would tell.

There was no denying how convoluted it was. If Pierson stuck to his word, they would have a bunch of prisoners to rehabilitate in hope of finding a way of avoiding conflict through freedom of choice rather than through terrorism and violence. Camille hoped that these men—these avowed terrorists, rapists, drug dealers and sex traffickers—could be made to see the light, so to speak. In Camille's words, to "recognize in themselves an essential humanity they shared with all people defined by a divine covenant with the universe itself." Oddly enough, she trusted Pierson would keep his word. It sure as hell helped her sleep. Not much else did these days.

Camille checked her watch for the fifteenth time. 3:00 p.m. . . . 1500 hours. Soon, the call would come in, and she would be hauling ass 150 miles to Koulfoua Island in a Blackhawk. She contemplated the steaming cup of green tea one of the two Secret Service agents brought her from a nearby café called New World Order right there on Rue du Cherif next to the hospital. The name was fitting enough. The patrons were mostly affiliated with the hospital, young, worldly and educated, the new face of Africa that countries like Nigeria and Chad wanted to present to the world. This was good. These were the successful Africans who lived in the light, out in the open. Unfortunately, far more people lived in the darkness cast by the shadows cutting across the rest of the country and the continent as a whole. Chad, Nigeria, Somalia . . . the fight between good and evil waged on around the clock, independent of café society.

Camille sipped her tea and allowed her mind to flow freely like the steam rising up from the cup for the first time in a long time. Kofi sensed her misgivings.

"This must be done," he said. "You are doing a very great thing not just for these women but for all women in the world. You must believe that."

Camille smiled, but it was apathetic at best. "You're right about one thing. I *must* believe that. Otherwise, I couldn't bear to even sit here knowing what is about to happen."

Kofi nodded. "I understand how you feel. There was a time in my life, back when I was trying to clean up my life, when I believed all killing was bad. But now I think that we do not all come here as equals. There are some who deserve to die and others who deserve to live. Then there are people like me who deserve both."

"What about up there?" asked Camille, gently pointing to the sky.

"Yes, up there, as you say, we are all equals. But not here, not in this world. These men must be removed like any disease."

Camille sipped her tea and stared down at the table. "Ah . . . disease . . . disease is a sign that the patient is spiritually sick. Disease is the manifestation of spiritual illness. To cure disease, you must cure the spirit, the cause, not the symptom. If this disease, as you call it, exists, it is only because our society is spiritually sick. I trust you know that."

Kofi laughed. "That is easy for you to say, my dear. I do not mean to sound patronizing, but the women on that island . . . I think they would rather have the cancer removed now and worry about the cause later." He thought for a moment. "Yes, that much I can say for them with certainty."

Camille put her tea down on the worn table. "Well, let's hope that someday these women will speak for themselves."

"*Touché*. And I can only assume you will move all women of this world to speak more freely about their condition . . . whatever that may be. That is, after all, why I sought you out in the first place. You have the rare ability to touch all women and give them a voice."

Camille stretched her arms and blew a red curl from her face. "That's all I need, more spiritual contracts. I've been burdened with so much this last year. It seems like an eternity. That's how I know I need to work things out spiritually. My soul-time flow is out of whack."

Kofi said nothing. He just listened.

Camille stood up and started walking around the room. She peered out the window at the hospital. One of the agents shook his head, and she moved away from the window. She was growing exasperated.

"I mean, it's not like we're moving forward through all this, Kofi. Sure, we will save those women. Trust me, if I know Harry, there are some very nasty men getting ready to take down *Boko Haram*. But where does that get us spiritually? What happens in life is a series of tests. Is cutting down fifty terrorists going to change the world that much?"

Kofi squinted. He really couldn't understand what Camille was talking about. "What you say is all very strange to me. This is a small step, it is true. Five thousand lives is just a start. You will gain even greater notoriety and go on to bigger things . . . saving more lives, and so on. Who knows what heights you will reach? It's a process."

"Yes . . . me, me, me. And still children die in droves from disease and malnutrition. The pile of riches grows for the select few while most survive on a few dollars a month. They may be alive, but that's not living, if you know what I mean. Troops on the ground and planes in the air, staggering amounts of money moving from account to account, people coming, people going. . . . what really changes throughout the ages?"

Kofi stood up. He was getting antsy, too. "You can only make decisions in the present. You speak often of the spirit. Well, God gave each of us the greatest gift of all . . . free will. With it, we are free to do great good or great evil. We have no way of knowing how things will turn out. We can only do what we think is best."

Camille turned to him and smiled. "It is all about intentions, isn't it?"

"Exactly," said Kofi, emphatically. "Each of us is here to live life as free people, not as controlled objects or slaves or whatever other name you want to assign them. I often think that we come to know who we are as human beings only through fighting when we are sure of losing. What happens after that is called history."

Camille sighed. "Yes, his-story . . . not hers."

Kofi laughed. "A word of advice, Camille O'Keefe, not that you need it from me. You are a hero to women all over the world because of your book. But remember that sometimes, you're never more vilified than when you are being perfectly honest. And so this world goes."

Chapter 40

It's 4:00 in the afternoon. Finally, the phone on one of the desks rings. Kofi answers it, according to plan. It's Harvey Guttman. *Boko Haram* is on the move, heading out from Maiduguri east along the N3 toward Doro Gowon.

Kofi hangs up the phone. He turns to Camille. "It is time to save those women."

Camille nods to her Secret Service agents. One of the men mumbles into his cuff that the package is on the move. Within seconds, two armored Humvees with Camille's Special Forces detail pull up in front of the building. Each truck has a manned .50 cal gun mount.

It appears the millions Guttman paid out in bribes has staved off the dogs for the moment. Camille is shuttled into one Humvee and Kofi into the other. They speed off down Avenue Charles du Gaulle toward a discreet section of the international airport where Camille's Blackhawk and two AH-6 "Killer Eggs" are waiting. Their turbines fire and rotors begin turning. The crew triple-checks everything . . . weapons, coms, everything. They have a very special cargo onboard, the world's most precious woman. Two Apache attack helicopters appear overhead out of nowhere, as does a drone for broader visual tracking of the surrounding streets. The P-3 assigned to provide tactical support begins monitoring the operation from 30,000 feet above.

Normalcy quickly returns to that little strip of road. Two CIA operators quickly visit the rooms that Kofi and Camille occupied. They work their way through the area, chemically cleaning it to remove all traces of DNA. Camille O'Keefe and Kofi Achebe were never there.

Chapter 41

Harry Pierson is sitting in his office in the Eisenhower Executive Office Building half a planet away. He's five hours behind, so it's a little after 11 a.m. He has real-time coms with Papa Seal Pete Flint in Coronado Springs as well as mission coms via the P-3. He also has several televisions on his wall where he can watch multiple live feeds . . . the drone covering Camille, the drone covering the *Boko Haram* convoy, Guttman's video feeds that they will later edit for release to the press, and, of course, Camille's speech. For the first time since he took office, the vice president feels like he's in command, and he's loving it.

It's going to be an old-fashioned ass whooping. He pours himself a Scotch, lights a cigar, and orders a huge dinner from the White House kitchen. They'll deliver it from next door, and then he'll sit back and watch it all unfold before his eyes. He feels like God looking down from heaven seated in something he imagines to be like Lincoln's chair in his monument looking out over the Mall. This, he thinks to himself, is why a man aspires to be president.

After notifying Camille's team, Harvey Guttman "paints" Aliyu's truck with a laser as the *Boko Haram* convoy pulls out. High above, the P-3 locks onto the signal and guides a drone in to keep eyes on the convoy. The drone can unload Hellfire rockets and end things right then and there. Or Apaches and the SEALSs can hit the convoy. In both instances, the refugees will be saved with minimal risk to U.S. servicemen, even in daylight. But this doesn't suit Pierson's plan. He needs combat footage shot on a broad expanse like Lake Chad. More than anything else, he wants Camille's speech shot in the heat of the moment, not some canned shot 200 miles from the action. He needed the fighting dumped onto her lap to get the sort of raw emotion he is looking for.

Guttman doesn't give a crap either way. His next call is to Papa Seal. He notifies the Rear Admiral that *Boko Haram* has popped hot. "The weather has shifted. There's a storm front heading east."

That's the only information Papa Seal needs. "Roger that. There's rain in the forecast." That's all that needs to be said between the two.

Guttman's work on point is complete. He has executed his first mission flawlessly. Now it's on to his second mission, getting Pierson's video footage. When he gets confirmation that the drone has a visual on the convoy, he packs his things and heads to his truck. He is set to rendezvous with his camera team in thirty minutes. The crew includes a cinematographer. They will shoot footage from a helo on gear used for shooting Hollywood films. Guttman even hired a director, the same man who made *SEAL vs. Predator*, *Military Man from God* and *Win Now, Apocalypse Later*.

Papa Seal Pete Flint is good to go as well. He and his command team are set up in the WARCOM Battle Command Center, a state-of-the art mission-management platform that is fully integrated with all the moving parts for Operation Woman and Child. He is seated at a large oval table. Several other men join him. The perimeter of the room is full of support personnel and intel equipment. Like Pierson, they have all the coms and live feeds up and running. If something were to happen to the P-3, Flint can run the op from there.

Flint picks up a phone. It's his direct line to the vice president. "It's time."

"I've been waiting all day," replies Harry Pierson. "I just ordered a double porterhouse. A new era begins here, Pete. It's a new chapter in American history. Harry Pierson and Camille O'Keefe in the White House, and you as the Joint Chief. Things are going to be very different in the world once we're in charge." He puffed his cigar aggressively, sending a thick billow of smoke above his head.

Pete Flint laughs. "I don't know, Harry. I hear that woman really did a number on the president. How do you know you're not next?"

Pierson sips his Scotch. "Eh . . . no worries, Pete. God has yet to make a woman I can't keep in line. But remember, we're going to need a woman like Camille to soften our gruff demeanor, shall we say. It's funny . . . she will actually help us keep the women of the world in line."

"You know what they say, a soft pair of gloves makes the bloodiest hands beautiful."

Pierson pursed his lips. "Who said that?"

"I think it was O.J."

Chapter 42

The drone base in Niger usually houses about a hundred men. Today, it's got sixteen more by way of the SEAL platoon. The platoon will operate as two squads with an additional coxswain in charge of the two RHIBs. They're getting restless. They've been throwing weights around and hitting the range about as much as they can. They've cleaned their weapons enough to make their barracks smell like CLP. They need to go. They need to engage. They feel pent up. It's go time. They were told the op would likely go down sometime today, but time is dragging its ass on the ground so that every inch feels like a mile, every minute like an hour.

The men are grab-assing in the barracks, methodically working their dip into dark brown streams of spit to fire into empty coffee cups or bottles stuffed with napkins. Most of the guys like country music. The dualistic pull between painful loss and kickin' it up in the sticks reflects their lives. But today *Led Zeppelin IV* is playing from a beat-up iPod dock one of the men carries in his kit. *Battle of the Evermore* . . . even the rednecks like that one. Again, it reminds them of the dotted line they walk between living and dying. That's the real line they sign when they agree to become a Navy SEAL. They all believe—each of them to the man—that dying ain't so bad.

They can feel it's almost time. Their rucksacks are filled and sit atop each bunk. Once the mission is complete, they will return, conduct their After-Action Review, and get back to Djibouti where they will prep for their next op, a strike in Somalia on a group of *Al-Shabaab* leaders. Their gear for this mission is all laid out. Each man has his own personal kit, his weapons of the trade and the gear he feels are most suited to the job. If this were a night op as preferred, each man would wear black-on-black BDUs. But thanks to Pierson, they're going in daylight, so they opt for standard gray/green camos. They're free to make their own choice of footwear. They aren't planning on a visit, board, search and seizure, so slipping isn't a particular concern. If it were, the guys would choose something like Converse Chuck T's or something lightweight, non-slip and quick to dry. They have no intention of detailing any of Aliyu's ships, so Salomon Quest boots are the universal choice today.

The men know they're heading out with a single objective . . . EKIA, Enemy Killed In Action, complete annihilation except for Aliyu, whom they must leave to the women snipers. The two RHIBs are each equipped with a .50 cal up front to shred *Boko Haram's* boats along with the men inside each. Each man carries an M4 rifle and a Sig P226 sidearm, both pretty standard choices. Some of the men carry the Sig P226 barreled for a .357 brass round guaranteed to crack a grizzly's skull like it was a coconut. The guys will also carry a frag or two in case they get the opportunity to toss one in a boat and ice the entire *Boko Haram* crew.

The risk factors are high but not like going door to door in Kandahar or Fallujah. All in all, they're running pretty light. They likely won't wear helmets or NBGs, but they sure as hell will wear their body armor. Their equipment vests and armor weigh over fifty pounds. The vests are already on the RHIBs because they're jumping from the Black Hawks and don't want the extra weight. They'll put them on once they're safely onboard. *Boko Haram* may not be as highly trained as the SEALs, but they are no strangers to firing a weapon. Fire enough bullets, and one "lucky" shot may find its mark. None of the SEALs wants to be the guy who buys it from a *Boko Haram* skinny.

One of the two Squad Leaders, a guy they call Pokey, is fiddling with his helmet and removing the Night Optics Device. He catches shit for even considering a helmet for this op. "You really wearing that brain bucket, Poke?"

Pokey's from Arkansas. He spits a dark stream into an empty Snapple bottle. He's one of the few men who prefer a wad of loose-cut Red Man chaw to a lipper of long-cut Skoal. "Shit, yeah. Any one of these emaciated sons of bitches can squeeze off a lucky shot, even if they're nothing but a bunch of pimps. My wife's due in two months. I want to be around to coach his football team, ya know?" He rolls his wad of chaw against his bulging cheek and smiles. "Shit, how embarrassing would it be if one of these skinny bastards killed my ass?"

One of the other men, a guy they call Pig Man for obvious reasons, suggests that Pokey's kid probably ain't his anyway. "To tell you the truth, Poke, there's a good chance that son of yours gonna look a lot more like me." He smiles, revealing two missing teeth near his right cheek. He always has a glistening ball of dark dip spittle on his lip on account of those two missing teeth. That's where some crazy chick cracked him with a beer bottle after he grabbed her ass a bit too far up between her legs. The way he saw it, she put her ass on his hand, not the other way around.

"Look like you, Pig Man?" says one of the other guys, "I wouldn't wish that shit on anybody, let alone a child."

Pig Man shrugs. "Yeah, well the Pig Man needs to get the hell back to California. These Muslim women here don't dig pork, man." Pig Man snorts like a pig and flicks his tongue obscenely.

Just then, the Officer in Charge strides in, and the men immediately shut up. They know it's go time. The OIC doesn't need to say much. The men know he's terse to the point of being abrupt, but they don't care much for words anyway. He's a proven commodity, and the men trust him even if they bust his balls about his being the fifth in his family to attend the Academy. If his men are willing to die carrying out his orders, the least he can afford them is a bit of ribbing at his expense.

"Okay, the storm front is heading east," says the OIC, meaning Aliyu popped hot. "We're a go. Briefing room now." He turns and that's that.

"Hell, yeah," shouts Pig Man. "It's killing time."

"It works both ways, Pig," says Pokey, acting like a Squad Leader now that the op is officially under way.

"Let's make this a one-sided affair," adds the other Squad Leader. They call him Ripper, as in Jack the Ripper. Pig Man is part of his crew. "I don't know who these clowns are, but their ammo is the same as ours, know what I mean?"

The men gather their gear without speaking. A palpable seriousness has suddenly descended over the room. Rounds click into chambers. As they file out, each of the men tosses a $20 bill into a spare hat like they do before every mission. The money goes to the guy who KIAs Aliyu Adelabu, the op's high-value target, even if his boat is off limits. They have no idea about Pierson's plan to use the nano-bullets on Aliyu. All they know is that two female snipers, Nancy Harper and Dana Daniels, have the lead on disabling Adelabu and so the pot is irrelevant. But that won't stop the guys from following tradition. They'll just roll it over to the upcoming mission in Somalia. For now, they're totally dialed in on taking out the rest of *Boko Haram* as efficiently as possible and getting out casualty free. That's never, ever a given.

Aliyu Adelabu isn't aware of what's coming ahead. His gang of thugs exits the Doro Gowon Mosque having finished their prayers and immediately boards their trucks. They head south down a dusty road that intersects with the Kukawa-Kauwa Border Road. There, the convoy turns east and tears down a nameless road that runs a few miles to the shore of Lake Chad where Aliyu has his boats and equipment waiting. Everything is ready to go for their incursion.

Like the SEALs in their barracks before the op began, Aliyu's men are raucous with anticipation. They're yucking it up and grab-assing, too, as they clamor onto their trucks. Some of them are nervous, but not many. These are men born of death and suffering, and so they perpetuate an ongoing cycle of depravity that sucks Africa down like a vortex of evil. These men have known so much death that suffering and empathy no longer exist in their truncated lexicon of emotions. Men like Aliyu and his lieutenants, educated men from relatively well-to-do families, are motivated differently. For Aliyu, *Boko Haram* offers the fastest track to power, wealth and influence. He cares not that his so-called empire is built on fear, murder and human trafficking. He only cares for the end result . . . how much money and power can he amass. This, he learned from the Western world.

More than anything else, the men can't wait to get their hands on some girls, the younger the better so long as they are over eight years old. This is a cultural limit they may not violate. For these men, there is no such thing as rape or pedophilia. The ancient *Sharia* code they follow—the same code they wish to impose upon the world—allows for their male privilege so long as they do not render the girls unable to bear children in the future. Their world is built upon protecting and reinforcing their privilege. It underpins everything they do . . . every person they murder, every girl they rape and every slave they sell. It's all part of a larger plan to bring about a holy war against the Anti-Christ and bring about *Qiyamah,* the end of time, *Yawm ad-Din* . . . judgment day. In the end, it all boils down to one thing—power.

The trucks pull up at the staging area, spewing pebbles and dirt everywhere. The men have whipped themselves into a frenzy much like their trucks kick up a trail of dust behind the convoy. Their need to kill has swelled their egos; their need to rape has swelled their manhood. They need release. Aliyu takes notice. He gathers the men around him.

"Listen, you killers. I expect this to be a glorious day for Allah."

The men howl. They are chanting *Mon Gode Allah, on Sharia we stand . . . Mon Gode Allah, on Sharia we stand. . . .*

Aliyu silences them with a wave of his hand. "Yes, our God is Allah, and we carry His ancient laws forward into tomorrow. But listen to me . . . no one is to touch any girl without my permission. Not yet. These *sibya* we must keep pure for sale. They will fetch a tremendous price. Each of you will receive his fair share of the money. Each of you will be someone important in Maiduguri. So do not violate this rule. You do nothing without my permission."

The men start chanting again. *Mon Gode Allah, on Sharia we stand . . . Mon Gode Allah, on Sharia we stand. . . .*

Aliyu smiles. He can feel the power. He feeds off it, just as he will feed off of each life they take and each girl they sell.

He holds his hands up for silence. "Yes, we are men, very dangerous men. With every raid we launch, we take another step forward toward our destiny. It is our fate to spread the glorious law of *Sharia* and the divine will of Allah, just as it is our fate to take what we will from women and infidels. And so you will have your share of the money from selling the girls, and you will have your right to take any of the older women you see fit to take . . . but no more than three women each will you have. And as I said, you must wait for my permission. I am generous, but I am also serious about this rule. Do not test me."

Aliyu has elevated his men to a mass of throbbing bad intent with just a shred of self-restraint, enough to conduct a paramilitary mission. Many of the men are singing. Others are grabbing their crotches to show each other how manly they are. A few are already negotiating trades among themselves should they happen to get a woman they don't much care for. Others place side bets on a game they call "*Choke*," in which four men hold a woman down while a fifth takes her. While he is raping her, one of the other men chokes the woman. The men bet on whether or not their buddy will climax before they can strangle the woman to death. The men love playing *Choke*. It's good fun.

Aliyu has them exactly where he wants them. He points to some cargo containers that sit near the boats. They will off-load the girls from the barges into the shipping containers just like they would with cattle or goats. "Soon, we will fill those containers with our precious cargo. And we will take those girls with us back to Maiduguri on trucks. But hear me clearly. I will say it just this one last time. Any man caught having sex with a child will answer to me directly. I will kill that man where he stands. The young ones, the children . . . they are for sale, not for your taking. Other than that, you men may exercise your hard-earned privilege. Take what you will. Kill the rest."

Aliyu circles his fist in the air. That's the signal for the men to launch the boats. They descend on the staging area like jackals and fire up the beefy engines that came via rich Saudi supporters and their Swiss accounts. They load the .50 cals and test them, spraying rounds into the water. Everything looks good to go.

Aliyu slaps one of his lieutenants on the back proudly. "No *dulling*," he says. Let's not prolong things. "It is time to bring the will of Allah to Koulfoua Island."

"No *wahala*," says the lieutenant. No worries.

Chapter 43

At the same time, the drone base is hopping. It's time to unleash American fury. The SEALs seem like different guys now. The horsing around has been replaced with focus and determination. Each of the men is organizing in his mind what he needs to do to execute the battle plan. Like Olympic athletes, they've been trained to visualize, using their mind's eye, as Camille would say, going over every conceivable possibility and how they might respond. Of course, there is no predicting the unpredictable, and every one of the SEALs knows the mission plan becomes obsolete the instant they engage the enemy. No battle plan survives contact with the enemy, although contact with the enemy is the only certainty and survival the highest order.

"Whataya think, Poke?" asks one of the men, called Worm, in Squad One. They call him Worm as in bookworm because he is always quoting some book to make his point.

Worm scratches his scruffy beard and contemplates the question. He pulls out a pouch of Red Man and balls a big wad of loose cut in his hand. Popping a fresh wad before boarding is a nervous habit of his. He lifts his fist to his nose and smells the ball of tobacco. It focuses him. He crams the chaw into his cheek and spits.

"You never know with fools like this," Pokey says. "I call 'em boars . . . crazy-ass wannabes looking to make a name for themselves. You never know if they're gonna run away or charge right at ya."

Worm thought about Pokey's analogy. "No crazy pig is gonna scare me. Ever read *Lord of the Flies*? A bunch of kids spear this boar."

Pokey finds the comment equally amusing. "You love to quote books, Worm, because you ain't been torn up in the leg by one. It's not something you forget."

"Damn," says Worm.

"So the idea is simple. You don't wait to find out if that crazy-ass boar is gonna ditch or come right at ya squealin' and screamin'. You just shoot 'em on sight. It's easier that way."

Worm likes that. "In this case, they'll be squealing *Allahu Akbar*."

Pokey grunts. "Not if you shoot 'em first."

Both squads are lined up waiting to board. Two Black Hawks pull chokes and roar to life sending dust and sand everywhere. The two AH-6s come to life as well. The men climb aboard the Black Hawks and take their seats. The helos lift off. The C-130 is already inbound from Lemonnier. The orchestration is precise, with the crew of the P-3 directing the movements like a conductor leading a symphony. Airborne, the strike force heads east and then turns due south down the coast of Lake Chad.

Pokey's Squad One is always more laid-back. His men pack fresh dips and do a final check on their weapons. One of the men, a guy they call Lucky Jones, passes around a lucky key ring. It's a glass disk of dirt collected from Fenway Park when his Red Sox won their first world series in a long time back in 2004. Each guy knocks it against his gun before passing it on. The ritual always ends with Lou, who always says the same thing . . . "Screw you, I'm a Yankee fan." He knocks it against his gun anyway. The ritual is always the same, and they always laugh.

Pokey surveys his men. They seem a bit casual today, like they're taking *Boko Haram* a bit too lightly. "Hey, listen up," he says, his voice crackling over the coms. "I'm not sure what we're up against today. You never know with these crazy bastards. Some of 'em might be looking to become martyrs. So let's not take these guys lightly. Let's just send them to Allah and go home."

"We'll be alright," says one of the men. "They can't be half as bad as those freakin' Somalis a few months ago. That was like shootin' shadows."

"Yeah," jokes one of the others. "These *Boko Haram* guys are a bit fatter. They're easier to shoot."

Pokey just laughs and shakes his head. "Don't look ahead to the next job, even if it is back to Somalia. Let's just get this done and get the hell out of here."

Ripper's guys in Squad Two are more serious. They don't jaw much. No mission is safe. They know *Boko Haram* will fight to the last man. They aren't satisfied with the way the shit went down on their previous run in Somalia. They made some mistakes. They didn't lose anyone, but it wasn't clean. A few of the guys got winged. It serves as a constant reminder that any third-world son of a bitch with an AK-47 and some RPGs can tear a guy up or take a Black Hawk down. The birds fly low and slow on an operation like this. You just never know. They can't take anything for granted because a mistake could cost a life. When they make a mistake, guys die. That's the deal.

Like Pokey, Ripper also senses the danger in today. Maybe that's why they're in charge. "Yo," he blurts into his coms. "Listen up. I know I don't have to tell you this, but don't mess around with these bastards. They're missing a chip in their brains. They want to die or some martyr shit like that."

"That's fine by me, man," says one of the guys. "I like dead. Dead's good."

"I hear ya. But I'm not looking to join them, if you know what I mean. I'm just looking to help them on their way."

"We got good intel on this one? It seemed kinda general in pre-action review," asks one of the men.

Ripper shrugs. "Not too much. CIA."

The men groan in unison. "Aw shit, man. You didn't say they sent in schoolgirls."

The guys laugh, but they all get the point. They don't trust the Agency guys. They live by a totally different code. They call them schoolgirls because they feel spooks will turn on you at the drop of a hat if it behooves them. In contrast, the SEALs will take a bullet for their own.

Ripper cleans his glasses. "Like we went over in pre-action, they have fast boats . . . probably AKs. Agency guy says .50 caliber guns on the boats. Other than that, it's a crapshoot. RPGs weren't confirmed, but I would assume they got 'em. Whatever they can buy at the neighborhood weapons store, know what I'm saying?"

"They gonna whip out a Koran and throw it at us?" jokes one of the men.

Ripper doesn't find it funny. "I assume whatever they send our way can kill us, so cut the crap. Like I said, we gotta figure RPGs even if the schoolgirl didn't confirm it." He's referring to Guttman again. They laugh.

"The only easy day was yesterday," says one of the men. The others *hooyah*.

"Wait," says Pig Man out of the blue. "Did you say there's an island full of women?" He snorts like a wild animal in need of a meal.

Chapter 44

Meanwhile, Camille and Kofi are already on Koulfoua Island, having made the 150-mile hop from N'Djamena. They are set up nicely at the rear of the island where Camille plans to address the refugees after all is said and done. The two nano-snipers, Nancy Harper and Dana Daniels, arrived on the island a few days earlier. Dusk begins to settle over the lake. The *Boko Haram* war party is speeding across the water toward Koulfoua Island. The men can hardly wait for the killing to start. The faster they slaughter the non-valuables, the faster they can load the girls and other valuable women onto the barges and set out for home. Once safely back in Maiduguri, they can divide up what Aliyu has allotted them and the raping will begin. They don't see it as rape. They see it as their right. It's a matter of perspective.

The U.S. strike force turns due east and moves to come up behind the *Boko Haram* boats. The *Boko Haram* men have no idea there's a torrent of death gathering behind them. The choppers are still too far away, and the massive boat engines would drown out any audible clues anyway. Aliyu and his men have their sights set straight ahead. Out there in the distance of Lake Chad is their treasure island. That's all they're concerned with.

The Americans' timing is flawless as they head toward the lake. Sensors in the drone pick up the enemy armada and pass off the information to the Black Hawks. The men listen intently as their coms come alive.

"Okay, guys. We've got contact. We should have eyes on them in a few miles," says the co-pilot of Pokey's Black Hawk, call sign Hawk One. "The drone's got 'em heading due east. The P-3's got 'em, too. Ten small boats and four barge-type transports. Formation is horizontal and moving fast."

"Here we go," says Pokey. "Drone images show two men per barge and four or five per boat."

The P-3, call sign Eagle Eye, checks in with Ripper's bird. "Hawk Two, confirm contact. We can ID 2 fight-age males in each barge and four or five fighting aged males (FAMs) per boat."

The co-pilot of Ripper's bird, Hawk Two, confirms. "Understood, Eagle Eye. They're laid out for the picking."

The men in both squads sit up straight and take deep breaths. This is it. They're all going out, but they may not all come back. Stomachs are always a bit tight just before the melee. Pokey looks at each of his men and smiles. There's no more joking around now.

Pokey smiles at one of his guys. Ripper looks at each of his men and nods firmly.

The C-130 drops the RHIBS.

"Be advised," says Eagle Eye, "your package just dropped."

The men can see two parachutes billowing down over the water about sixty yards offshore. It's their RHIBs and equipment vests coming in like clockwork. By the time the RHIBs splash down, the C-130 is long gone into the distance. Its job is done for the day.

"Hell, yeah," says Pig Man. "Party time. I love taking a boat out on a lake for the day."

The men grunt and pack fresh, fat lippers. Their good-luck ritual is quite different from Pokey's. Pig Man methodically brushes his fingers along his wiry mustache. It's the same line every time.

"Hey, boss. My fingers smell like your wife."

Ripper's response is always the same, too. "Yeah? Tell her I said hello. I'll tell your mama the same."

The men love their rituals. They laugh and break the ice as they prepare to rappel down to their RHIB.

On board Hawk One, Pokey reminds his men of the one critical rule of engagement—no one is to kill Aliyu Adelabu. "That honor goes to those two chick snipers. So lay off. That goes for all of you. Nobody takes out the HVT unless it's the absolute last resort."

"And now that you've gone on record with that?" quips one of them.

Ripper smiles. "Well . . . you know how it can get out there. Sometimes mistakes happen. If a bullet happens to find Mr. Adelabu, well . . . worse things have happened is all I'm saying."

"Grab some rope, boys," says the co-pilot. "Time to get off your asses and to go to work." He's just busting balls. He still gets a few rounds of "kiss my ass" from the guys.

Hawks One and Two circle around and hover above the two RHIBs that sit waiting on the water below. Each coxswain takes his position at the helm and prepares to get under way while the rest of the men ball up the parachutes and snap on their vests. The two Black Hawks break off and take up a position covering the platoon's rear, ready should a hot extract be necessary. However, their primary role is to provide support should the Nigerian or Chad military go back on their word and try to interfere. Papa Seal is good at his job. He knows he can't trust anybody in Nigeria or Chad and planned for this distinct possibility early on.

The SEALs take their positions on each RHIB, the coxswains get them moving and, just like that, the assault is underway.

Chapter 45

Aliyu and his men never see it coming. The two AH-6's little birds, the "killer eggs," are tasked with taking out the four slave barges that are travelling side-by-side. The pilots fence in and switch over to full combat mode. Guttman's Black Hawk takes a position above and behind the two killer eggs as they drop down to 200 feet like angry birds of prey. They cross the fence to engage, going in balls to the wall about four hundred yards behind the four transports. They close in seconds and hover to hold their position.

The first bird, Sparrow One, lets two Hydra rockets fly at the barge on the far left. Both hit dead on. The explosion is tremendous, sending pieces of steel flying in all directions. The two *Boko Haram* men on board are incinerated instantly. Like that, they are gone, vanished, evaporated without a trace and nobody to remember them. In the blink of an eye, there are two fewer rapists and sex traffickers in the world.

The pilot coms-in to the rest of the group. "Sparrow One strike shack on. Two enemy killed. Repeat, two EKIA."

Within seconds, Sparrow Two joins in, sending a Hydra at the slave barge on the far right. The rocket blazes into the target. Another direct hit.

"Got another enemy transport down. Looks like two EKIA."
The two little birds begin pressing forward now. Both pilots are deadly serious, stone-faced. The amount of information they are processing is enough to paralyze the average brain, and the pressure of knowing they could be killed instantly is enough to rattle an otherwise brave man. They go about their work methodically, as if working on an assembly line processing one terrorist at a time. At a certain point, they step into a realm that is almost automatic. Neither pilot really stops to "think" about things. They are perfunctory in their execution. It's a matter of training. But it's not robotic. It's more like an attached form of fear.

The remaining two barges begin to veer off in opposite directions. Realizing they are under attack, the *Boko Haram* crew scrambles to man the big .50 caliber machine guns that are installed on the front of each barge. They pull the tarps off the deadly guns and take aim. It's difficult to fire back over the length of the barge. The problem for them is that the Americans are coming from behind for precisely this reason. Guttman's intel was valuable in this regard.

"Fifties . . . fifties . . . fifties," alerts one of the American pilots.

For the first time, there is emotion in his voice. It's tough going to fire those guns back over the stern, but he also knows those machine guns he's staring at can tear him up and kill him in seconds. His stomach tightens a bit. He has a wife and three kids. His mother lives with his brother and sister-in-law around the corner. She makes a big lunch every Sunday after church. Back home, his wife is probably food shopping or cooking lunch for the kids. Maybe Jimmy has baseball or Lauren's at school. Maybe they're doing homework. Whatever they're doing, none of them know how close to death their daddy operates. Had they known, they might have hugged him harder before he left. Jimmy might have kissed his daddy, even though he hates kissing.

While he fights in the middle of Africa to save a bunch of women he will never know, his own wife is back on the home front taking care of the family. She has a knot of dread in her stomach that never leaves until he comes home. Her greatest fear isn't him having an affair. Hell to her is that unmarked black car pulling up out front . . . that knock on the door . . . that soldier in dress uniform who regrets to inform her that her husband is dead. Daddy is gone.

None of this enters the pilot's mind. How could it? The only thing he's thinking about is his race against time as the *Boko Haram* machine gunner tries to send death his way. Everyone is pissed off. The *Boko Haram* gunner opens fire, sending deadly rounds tracing through the air at both helos.

"This is Sparrow One. Be advised we are taking .50 cal fire."

"Break, break, break," barks his co-pilot, realizing they are coming in dangerously close to the barges.

Both killer eggs break off in opposite directions and come back around at 400 yards. Both pilots are gaunt, their jaws tight. Their bad intent is evident. The men on the two remaining barges fire continuous streams of bullets toward the inbound American birds.

"Let's get this thing done," says one of the pilots. "These crazy bastards think they got something to die for."

The pilots open up with their mini-guns, sending a nasty hailstorm of 7.62 mm rounds at the barges. The *Boko Haram* men onboard are yelling. They are panicked. They weren't expecting the Americans to show up, let alone get the drop on them like this. This is not at all what they planned. It's their right to kill infidels. It's their right to take slaves. This is what Aliyu promised them. He said nothing to them about fighting Americans. To martyr themselves on their own terms as a glorious *jihadi* was one thing. But being slaughtered like dogs by American infidels where nobody would hear about it would be a humiliation unworthy of a legacy.

There is no time for their outrage. Their lives are at stake. "Keep shooting, *arro*," yells one of the barge captains to his gunner, whom he just called an idiot. He veers the barge suddenly, creating a large wake that rocks the other boat violently. The captain of the bouncing barge loses his footing and falls to his left, turning the rudder sharply to port in the process. The barge begins going in circles. The gunner stumbles, too. His machine gun is firing off in all directions. It's complete chaos.

Sparrow One sends two Hydras at the reeling boat but misses wide. Seeing the gunner out of sorts and the other barge now fleeing, the pilot decides to rush with his mini-guns blaring. The barrage of gunfire is relentless and completely overpowering. His barge still circling to port, the *Boko Haram* gunner manages to regain his balance and attempts to return fire. But it's too late. The American has won the race against time. A stream of bullets hits the gunner in the chest, virtually tearing him in half. His body erupts, and he bleeds out furiously. His intestines look like a big snake slithering out from inside him as they spill out in the blood on the deck.

There is still life in his eyes for just a moment longer. Those last few seconds seem like an eternity to him as time stands still. This is not what he was promised. He set out that morning to collect his fortune in the slave game. He is willing to die for Allah, but not like this. This day there is no glory for him. No fortune and no glory. He will not bring about *Qiyamah* and *Yawm ad-Din*, the end of time and the great apocalypse. He will not die a martyr or reap his heavenly reward of 72 virgins granted from Allah Himself. He neither gained the world nor saved his soul.

Life leaves him. His eyes are empty and his legs collapse, but his hands are still gripped to the machine gun and his nearly severed torso pulls the barrel of the gun up and around toward the bow. The gun shoots straight up in the air until the man's hands release the gun stock and fall to the deck with the rest of his tattered torso. He is no longer anything. He has left this world like he came in . . . a penniless nobody, just another third-world ghost who has both endured and caused so much suffering. His devastated remains bespeak the pain of his people outside of religion and political economy.

He is a smaller image of the whole. Like so many terrorists, he is a victim and a victimizer at one and the same time. Thus is the paradox of his life, an existence of double binds and no-win situations. His only aim in life was to feel like a big man. With nothing to lose, what value does life have . . . his life, a woman's life . . . any life? None, other than as a means to an end . . . becoming an *oga*. Terrorists— whether Aliyu's men or any one of the thousands of faceless *jihadists* roaming the earth—are unable to see the essential humanity in their victims. Instead, they see an opportunity to kill in the name of their own self-promotion. They have no other currency to trade except death. In death is value.

Where do they go, those who wander this wasteland? And how do they pay their way?

With the gunner dead, Sparrow Two can finish off the crippled barge. The pilot gets a good mark on the out-of-control boat and launches a rocket. It finds its target. The explosion sends shards of steel and fragments of body parts flying in all directions.

"Third transport down. Two EKIA."

Guttman catches it all on film. He always considered himself a bit theatrical. One of his teachers said what a big Broadway producer he should be . . . not a thespian, of course, and certainly not "flamboyant," but a famous producer for sure. His parents wanted him to be a doctor instead. And now, he is pretending to be both. How proud they would all be. Dr. Feelgood is not flamboyant, but he has an eye for the dramatic. He knows what the American public wants to see. He knows how to usher Harry Pierson into office.

Guttman does not see himself as a terrorist, even though most people in the Middle East do. He doesn't waste energy wondering why those he seeks to help resent America so much. The truth is, he doesn't care about right or wrong, about good or evil, about any of that bullshit. When it comes right down to it, Harvey Guttman only worries about one thing—Harvey Guttman. That's why the SEALs don't trust spooks. It's almost a game for guys like Guttman . . . deadly serious, but still a game. He's American, he's empowered, he has privilege. Truth does not matter to him. Only the production matters. Maybe his teachers were right? Maybe Harvey Guttman turned out to be a great producer after all, staging his own productions of *Something Wicked This Way Comes*.

Life is a commodity with a market value for him. In this regard, he is like Aliyu. Also like Aliyu, he has long since lost sight of himself. He is unable to distinguish his true self from his collection of covert personae. Sometimes he doesn't know which self will emerge or even when. Like when he spared the mugger in the park. He could have erased the man from existence. Instead, he gave him money . . . a lot of money to make up for a savage beating.

He has no such reprieve in mind for *Boko Haram* today. He's been waiting a hell of a long time for Aliyu Adelabu to go down in flames. He remembers all those times when he was undercover and had to take humiliating jibes and anti-Semitic bullshit from some scum-of-the-earth terrorist and his band of scrawny-ass African wannabes. Now it's his turn to help dish it out mercilessly with a little help from his friends in the Army and Navy.

He gives the thumbs up to his director, who also has a huge smile on his face. The footage thus far is terrific. "Coppola's got nothing on you, my man." He looks at the burning remains of a sinking barge. "Yeah . . . payback's a bitch."

The director sees himself as a great French master, maybe the André Gide of film. Yeah, that's it, man. He's like Gide revealing the naked truth in death. Or maybe the Georges Bataille of cinema? Yeah, with his merciless, penetrating eye revealing truth in violent contradiction . . . yeah, that's it. This footage will win him new friends in powerful places and powerful friends in new places. He smiles back at Guttman. That smile says it all . . . yeah, man, death brings with it opportunity.

Caught up in the moment, Guttman can't help himself. He yells out loud but it's completely obscured by the whirling cacophony of the Black Hawk. "How do you like this American now, you son of a bitch?"

Back in his office, Harry Pierson lets out a whoop and tosses some fries into his mouth. "Guttman, you'd better be getting this on film," he says out loud to himself. "This is gonna go viral."

Guttman's cameraman focuses in on the two killer eggs as they come around to chase down the last remaining barge. The *Boko Haram* captain has the throttle opened full in a frenzied attempt to escape to the south. He's looking over his shoulder yelling for one of his crew to hurry up. "Forget the gun! They are behind us. Forget it. One of you get the rocket! *Yalla! Yalla!*"

One of the crew runs to a green crate. He pops it open. Inside are two RPGs taken from the weapons cache in Aliyu's secret basement storeroom. Guttman never gained access to the storeroom, so he couldn't confirm *Boko Haram* had RPGs. He also could not confirm that Aliyu's men loaded them on the boats.

Ripper was spot on when he told his guys they'd better assume *Boko Haram* had the rockets because the game has just changed. Now that they know Aliyu's men are armed with RPGs, the timing becomes even more critical. It's a little like a duel at fifty paces. Who can get off the best shot the fastest? Neither speed nor accuracy alone will suffice. Both are required to score a hit. The risk level for the American helos also goes up significantly, given the tight range of engagement. The window for error just became much smaller.

Most of the Aircraft Survivability Equipment the American pilots rely upon is geared toward defeating or avoiding guided weapons that can lock onto them. Expendable countermeasures like chaff, decoys and flairs in conjunction with sophisticated jamming devices help pilots defeat guided-missile attacks. But RPGs are unguided weapons. Ironically, American ASE is ineffective in protecting the pilots. *Boko Haram*'s RPGs may be "dumb," but they can be deadly. The American pilots will have to depend on tactics, techniques and procedures to survive. Until America develops some sort of hard-kill measure to shoot down incoming RPGs, jab, bob and weave is the sum total of Helicopter Active RPG Protection. HARP isn't much to hang your hat on, and the American pilots know it.

The barge captain knows it, too. His clock is ticking. He grows more emphatic. "*Yalla! Yalla!*"

The crewman does his best to load the rocket-propelled grenade as the two killer eggs bear down on him. He is just a kid, twenty years old, but he has killed dozens of women and raped twice as many girls, some as young as ten years old. It is his birthright as a man and as a *Boko Haram*, but he is looking to prove himself as a man. That's why he signed on with *Boko Haram* in the first place. He wants to be more than another black face in a crowd of impoverished Africans. In this sense, he's a lot like an American gangbanger.

He wants to be a man of power, feared. Adelabu promises to give him that. In Allah, he feels he can find it.

But now that he's staring death in the face in the form of two American attack helicopters, Aliyu's promises ring hollow. Nobody told him this could happen. His hands are shaking as he fumbles around with the RPG. He has messed around with them many times, but he has never fired under the intense pressure of combat. Buildings and cars don't shoot back. Little girls aren't elite combat veterans. This is a totally different scenario.

He looks up and sees the two helicopters coming around and heading straight for his barge. He loads the RPG and raises it to his shoulder. He lines up Sparrow One in the RPG's crosshairs. The rocking of the boat makes it hard to keep the American chopper in his sights. He asks Allah to guide his rocket and blow one of the American helicopters out of the sky with His glorious might. If the second chopper kills him afterward, then he will gladly go to Allah having proved himself a man.

The American pilots see what's going on. Their hearts start pounding, but they've trained for this. They've spent years learning to discipline themselves, learning to disassociate themselves from their families and freeze their emotions. Their hands are steady. RPGs are nothing new. But precisely for that reason, there's cause for concern as well.

One of the men calls it out. "RPG . . . RPG . . . RPG. He's got a rocket on the deck."

TTP, tactics, techniques, and procedures. Sparrow Two pulls off in an urgent attempt to put 500 meters between him and the barge. That will put him out of range of the RPG. But Sparrow One holds fast. The pilot thinks there's no way a piss-ant *Boko Haram* terrorist can make a shot like that from a rocking barge.

"No hyper-jack! *Yalla! Yalla!*" screams the barge captain.

Three internal clocks are ticking away. The American pilot opens fire about the same time the *Boko Haram* gunner launches his RPG. A flash of light is the last thing the shooter sees before the bullets rip him up. His arm is torn off with such force that it hits the *Boko Haram* captain steering the barge. He is still alive, though. He is fixated on the rocket as if oblivious to his mangled body. His determination is that strong. He watches the trail of smoke as the RPG flies straight at Sparrow One. He knows he did his best to advance his name in the eyes of his one true God.

He smiles at one of his fellow crewmen. "*Katakata . . . katakata.*" Big trouble for the American infidels. Then he is gone.

It's the same for him as it is for Harvey Guttman, Harry Pierson or any of the SEALs. They believe in their mission and their right to impose their will on those they believe are lesser or simply in the way. It's a test of will. It's a matter of perspective all in the eye of the beholder. In the end, people are people. Some win while others die. For the *jihadists* as for the SEALs, even death can be a kind of personal victory.

"Break . . . break . . . break," yells the co-pilot when he sees the RPG airborne.

The pilot wrenches Sparrow One hard to the right, exposing the belly of the bird. Somewhere buried deep inside, he knows he took the terrorist too lightly and played his hand too aggressively. The RPG slams into the bottom of the chopper. Shards of flaming metal fly through the air in all directions as the killer egg is broken. It shatters into pieces. The cockpit with the pilot and co-pilot plummets into the water. In what seems like the blink of an eye, the cockpit immediately fills with water and sinks to the bottom of the lake, leaving behind a flaming slick of aviation fuel and a few tattered pieces of fuselage.

Already in pursuit of the other boats, the SEALs see what happened. The explosion thunders across the water and smacks the SEALs with the sharp backhand of reality. The 20-year-old *Boko Haram* fighter is dead. Nobody will remember the kid. Nobody loved him. He lost the birth lottery being born as he was and never had a chance. He died like he lived with the exception of this one glorious triumph. He should never have picked up that weapon or raped young girls. He should never have decided to join *Boko Haram* in the first place. At the same time, he should never have felt that he had no other option. There is no perfect answer.

Both Americans in Sparrow One are also dead. The Americans leave behind wives and children . . . five kids in all. Their worlds, once a world apart, have been forced together like atoms in a fusion bomb. The Americans will mourn their dead husbands. The kids will try their best to keep their chins up at Arlington as their daddies' coffins are lowered into the ground amid all the pomp and circumstance. Dead soldiers believe they gained glory, but the families left behind must bear the unbearable weight of loss.

"Be advised, Sparrow One is down. Repeat, Sparrow One is down. Both crew are gone."

Guttman has seen enough. He can't do anything with two dead Americans. He motions for the cameraman to kill the shot and refocus on the SEALs and their two RHIBs.

The coms are silent.

Chapter 46

Harry Pierson sits in his office watching it all unfold on his wall. His face is crimson, and a vein in his neck looks ready to pop. He throws his crystal rock glass across the room but not before emptying it. It shatters against the wall. He barks into the squawk box that he has set up for real-time coms with Papa Seal in Coronado Springs.

"Pete, what the hell just happened? Did those cassava-eating sons of bitches just shoot down one of *my* best birds?"

The squawk box crackles for a moment. "Not now, Harry. Please. . . ."

"I want fireworks, Pete. Do you hear me? I want the Fourth of July, bombs bursting in air, body count, Pete. The American public is gonna want a body count. Do you read me? I want dead African terrorists, or Muslims, or whatever they are."

Rear Admiral Pete "Papa Seal" Flint cleared his throat. "Can I get back to our guys in the field now, Harry?"

Pierson flips his squawk to mute and sits fuming in silence. He knows he has to watch his step lest he find himself in another Iran–Contra situation. But his anger is undeniable and wants its voice. Keeping it in only makes him angrier.

He flips off the mute. He speaks through gritted teeth. "Shove a damned Hellfire up their ass, Pete. I want dead men."

The battle wages on. Alone now, Sparrow Two swings around and re-orients on the last remaining barge. The pilot knows the *Boko Haram* gunner has been taken out. He has a clear path. In the wake of Sparrow One going down, Papa Seal orders in the "tin can," the drone that has been surveilling overhead the whole time. In addition to providing aerial footage and other logistical support, the drone is armed with a 100-pound Hellfire rocket, itself a laser-guided mini-aircraft capable of taking out heavily armored tanks if need be. This is the firepower Pierson called for, but the Rear Admiral already had it coming.

The drone is locked on to the fleeing barge. The P-3 checks in. "This is Eagle Eye. We've got your shooter heading southwest for land. Tin Can is locked on and clear to engage."

But the pilot from Sparrow Two isn't having it. "Negative, I want his ass."

He has only one thing on his mind. He wants revenge. He feels the pulse of the rotor as it vibrates through the fuselage. It's as if his hatred ticks up a little farther with each rotation. He didn't know the co-pilot very well. He was a new guy. But the pilot who was killed was his good friend. Their wives are besties. Both women will be devastated. The guy's son will never be the same again. There's only so far a folded flag can go to assuage the searing pain of growing up without a dad.

Even though it can't get more personal than this, Papa Seal knows that ego can get the best of a man when a brother in arms falls. He's not backing off the drone strike just to let one of the pilots have his revenge. The op is more important. Never screw the op.

"Eagle Eye, clear to fire," says Flint.

The drone releases the Hellfire. "Rifle, rifle, rifle, weapon away," calls the drone operator, indicating the air-to-ground missile launch.

Sparrow Two also fires. Night Stalkers don't quit. The pilot will not be denied his payback. He is icy as he sends two Hydras at the barge as well. A tremendous amount of firepower rains down on the remaining barge. The blast is overwhelming, incinerating the boat and its captain.

The pilot reports in. "The last transport is gone. Adios, mother."

"Damn it," snorts Papa Seal. He is not happy. He understands the pilot's rogue actions, but he demands more from his men. He shakes his head and pinches the bridge of his nose. In his mind, those are two Hydras that could have been used in the remaining fight. The bird's only carrying a single pod of seven rockets to begin with. There are too many mistakes being made. He can't do anything about it now, so he orders Sparrow Two to provide close air support for the SEAL RHIBs that are coming up fast behind Aliyu and the rest of *Boko Haram*.

"Be advised, I've got boats heading due east toward the island," reports the P-3.

Sparrow Two heads north and swings around on a strafing run across the entire *Boko Haram* line stretched out horizontally. Aliyu could not have chosen a worse formation. By now, he and his men realize they are under attack. He waves his arms frantically and points at the helo. His men scramble to their .50 caliber machine guns that have been mounted on each boat. But the killer egg gets the jump on them. The pilot launches a rocket into the closest boat. His eyes widen as he follows the vapor trail. He is feeding his appetite for destruction and his need to avenge his buddy.

He scores a direct hit, and the craft is obliterated. The explosion sends a powerful wake across the *Boko Haram* line. The boats jump, skip and pull a lot of trim. A dark plume of smoke rises into the air. Gasoline burns atop the water. The pilot takes advantage of the chaos and takes his bird on another strafing run across the enemy line of boats. He lets a steady stream of bullets loose as he passes over the remaining nine boats. His chopper screams over them as the *Boko Haram* men scramble for cover. It's an incredibly dangerous maneuver. He's in real close should the *Boko Haram* gunmen manage to return fire with a volley of their own.

The sheer speed of it all aids the American pilot, and Aliyu has not established good coms with his men. Confusion is the rule.

Before they can organize themselves, Sparrow Two has already unleashed another deadly hail of fire. Pieces of fiberglass and metal fly up everywhere. The rounds catch five *Boko Haram* fighters, cutting them down instantly. Dark pools of blood wash over the decks of their boats as water splashes up over the sides.

The deadly chopper swings back around from the other end of the flotilla this time. This time, the pilot sends his last rocket at the closest boat. He follows up with his mini-guns on another vessel. A few .50 cal rounds hit the bird, but not enough to cause much damage. The rocket, on the other hand, finds its mark on the first, and the rounds cut up the second. Two more *Boko Haram* boats burst into flames, leaving a burning trail of fuel in their wake as they quickly sink to the murky bottom.

Aliyu and the three other men in his boat plus a second boat with his best lieutenant and several other men hold their course for Koulfoua Island. At the sight of all the devastation, however, the other captains completely lose it. It seems dying an anonymous, fiery death is not for them. They scramble off in every direction in a frenzied attempt to save themselves. Aliyu sees his men abandon him. He is livid. He blames the Americans. They have humiliated him, made him seem incompetent enough that his men would turn and run.

Aliyu Adelabu cannot accept this. It's an outrage. He cannot live with the shame. He figures he can redeem himself by taking out a U.S. helicopter using a secret weapon of his own. He may be in the dark about the American plan to use a classified nano-bullet on him. But the Americans are equally unaware that Aliyu brought with him a deadly NATO SA-7 Grail surface-to-air missile. It's cheap, dependable and readily available to any scumbag for the right price. It's basically the AK-47 of the missile world.

The shoulder-fired MANPAD looks more like a bazooka than an RPG, but it's a hundred times more dangerous than both put together. Where the RPG is the unguided, doltish high-school dropout of the missile family, the SA-7 is the prodigy mad scientist. It's a deadly infra-red-guided weapon ideal for destroying low-and-slow flying aircraft like helicopters. Aliyu never mentioned anything that would have tipped Guttman off. And while Guttman knew Aliyu had to have a few RPGs lying around, he never figured Aliyu for the sort to pass up an opportunity to boast about his prowess.

Following the Arab Spring, military stockpiles of such weapons were compromised and got out to the streets. From there, black-market sales proliferated. Aliyu doesn't have an actual SA-7, however. Instead, he has a Chinese knockoff. He bought it through a black-market contact in Lagos. The proliferation of deadly weapons has skyrocketed in Nigeria and the rest of Africa. With the amassing of Chinese power and influence in Nigeria comes more than gated communities, factories and dumplings. The Chinese bring death and destruction with them as well.

Luckily for the Americans, Aliyu has only the one rocket on his boat. But he knows how valuable it is. He has to make it count. He has two men on the boat with him. One is manning the .50 cal. He instructs the other to activate the MANPAD. He gets the attention of one of his lieutenants, who is steering the boat across from his. He points toward the island. Aliyu is more determined than ever. He considers the American attack a personal affront and an insult. He wants vindication for being embarrassed in front of his men. He wants revenge for his dead comrades. Most of all, he wants his girls to sell as slaves, even if he considers them all *ashawo*, all African whores.

Alone, the remaining little bird would be seriously vulnerable. When fired, the 21 pound, heat-seeking SA-7 missile will attempt to lock on to the helo's exhaust. But the Americans are operating as a well-integrated support group. When Aliyu's man activates the rocket system, American weapons-detection systems go crazy. The P-3 picks up the infra-red guidance system instantly.

"This is Eagle Eye. Something went hot down there. We're picking up infra-red targeting."

Situational awareness becomes paramount as the SEALs realize their plan has holes. Battle plans always do. Originally, they figured *Boko Haram* to be a paper tiger capable of destroying a rural African village but certainly not an elite Navy strike force. They figured the terrorists would be armed with AKs and maybe a few .50 cals.

The RPGs were to be expected, too. But the introduction of a MANPAD really threw a wrench into things.

As it turns out, things aren't going to be so easy. Guttman should have done a better job with the recon. It was just another reason for the guys to hate spooks. Only minutes into the engagement, and they are down one chopper and two crew. *Boko Haram* boats are scrambling in all directions, and the SEALs have strict orders not to touch Aliyu. The problem is that there's an active heat-seeking missile system on his ship.

Originally, the best option was to pick off the retreating boats as best they could and leave Aliyu to the two chick snipers. Sparrow Two would keep pounding the *Boko Haram* boats, driving them toward the SEALs coming up from behind. That plan goes to shit with an infra-red missile in play.

"Repeat, we have a hot targeting system."

Sparrow Two is hung out to dry. They are in too close for comfort, so close the co-pilot can clearly see one of Aliyu's man hoisting the launcher to his shoulder.

"There it is," he calls. "SAM on the deck. SAM on the deck with the HVT."

"Did he pull that shit out of his ass?" says the pilot. "What in the world, man."

Papa Seal intervenes. Once again, he finds himself in a compromised position. "This is Honey Pot. Be advised, you cannot blow that boat with our high-value target on it."

Aliyu's man locks on to the little bird.

"They've got tone," warns the co-pilot as alarms sound in the cockpit.

The pilot pulls hard away and heads west straight toward the sun. He grunts hard and instructs his co-pilot to "engage countermeasures. Now, now! "

The co-pilot initiates the automated Directional Infra-Red Countermeasure System. The system detects the missile's UV emissions and instantly locates the inbound missile. Flares launch instantly to create multiple heat maps that confuse the missile's IR heat-seeking guidance system. A high-intensity gas-arc lamp fires a beam of infra-red energy at the missile's seeker. Combined with the pilot's ascent toward the sun, the beam "blinds" the missile with a blast of radiant energy, making the missile think it's off course and adjusting its trajectory repeatedly in an endless error loop until it misguides completely.

The entire process lasts only a few seconds. But for the crew of the little bird, it seems like forever. The co-pilot sees the launch over his shoulder as the helo brakes. The flares burst out around them.

"SAM's in the air, SAM's in the air," he says emphatically.

The pilot presses it to the envelope. "I'm climbing. I'm climbing."

Papa Seal is tense. He can't possibly lose two birds today. That's four men . . . completely unacceptable. "Come on, you son of a bitch," he says to himself. "Climb."

Down below, the SEALs follow the missile through the air. It begins to waver. The high-intensity-beam countermeasure is working. The missile attempts to reacquire its target, but the seeker is blind and can't correct itself. It soars low and wide of the helo. The crew of Sparrow Two has survived this time. Many chopper pilots don't.

The SEALs have to get their heads back in the game. So does the crew onboard Sparrow Two. The panicky *Boko Haram* gunners are spraying bullets in every direction as they bug out. Sparrow Two needs to re-engage and comes back in balls to the wall with a vengeance. The little bird is a killer egg again.

The pilot cuts across two boats trying to squirt away to the North. He rotates a bit. "Guns, guns, guns," he calls and then unloads a thunderous barrage of mini-gun rounds at both boats. Red hot, empty shells pour down into the water beneath the helicopter, sizzling upon impact. The pilot can feel the power pulse through his hand into his entire body. He likes it. After almost buying the farm, he needs to feel the raw force satisfy him on a cellular level.

One of the *Boko Haram* captains tries desperately to evade the rounds raining down on him. The boat hits a large wake. The gunner stumbles and accidentally sends .50 cal rounds into his own boat as well as the boat next to him. The captain and the rest of the four-man crew are killed instantly, as are all four men aboard the second vessel.

Everyone onboard is dead. The boat speeds off unattended. Sparrow Two takes care of the lone survivor and also sinks the second boat. The pilot surveys the two mangled bodies as the boat goes down. He wishes he could revive them and kill them all over again. He unloads another volley into the last remnants of the boat as it slips under. If he could, he would keep firing forever.

He reports in. "One boat down. The second is a ghost. Screw it. They're all dead on board."

The P-3 comes back. "Roger that, Sparrow Two. We've got three remaining boats plus the HVT and his escort. That's five total."

Aliyu is the HVT, the high-value target, and he is still making straight for Koulfoua Island with one of his lieutenants speeding his boat alongside. He had only the one SAM, and he is disconsolate that his incompetent recruit can't shoot straight.

"This is Honey Pot. Say again, leave the HVT," instructs Papa Seal. "His boat goes through to the island. Engage the remaining enemy combatants."

Sparrow Two begins to track down one of the boats as it speeds back to shore . . . right into the SEAL platoon. The co-pilot gestures to the fuel gauge. The unexpected maneuvering ate up more fuel than anticipated. He is only one level above the point of no return.

The pilot informs Command. "This is Sparrow Two. Be advised I am at Joker. Repeat, Sparrow Two calling Joker." A few minutes more and he will be at Bingo, the actual point of no return and will have to splash the helo.

Papa Seal curses. "Roger that, Sparrow Two. Return to base."

The pilot looks at his co-pilot. They both want to stay and finish off the other boats, but they know they can't. It makes them sick to their stomachs. They want to finish the job they started. The pilot shakes his head in disgust. "Roger, Sparrow Two RTB."

He veers off and heads home. As he passes Guttman's Black Hawk, he notices the camera and flips the bird. Harvey Guttman pays him no mind. Aside from the unfortunate incident with the downed chopper, he feels it's been going great. Pierson will have more than enough footage to cut up any way he chooses.

Momentum seems to be shifting back in the Americans favor. The two SEAL squads are now in range.

"Thanks for the help, bird man," says Pokey. "We'll take it from here."

The situation is growing more chaotic by the second. Reigning in the frenetic boats is like herding cats. The P-3 provides new intel to the SEAL squads who have been setting the trap. "Looks like we have enemy combatants heading back to shore. Two boats coming in shit hot. There's another boat heading south."

Pokey motions to his coxswain to swing the RHIB and come up on the flank of one of the boats. The *Boko Haram* captain doesn't realize he's stepped into an ambush. He thought he was home free when Sparrow Two pulled out and returned to base. He thought he was going to live to fight another day. In his mind, he will take it out on some defenseless villagers sometime in the future. Not so bad.

"No more *kata kata*," he says. No more trouble. "We will find other girls to satisfy us."

This is the life Providence has issued him. He is not some rich kid, some *ajebutter*, protected by his father's oil money. He has no father. His mother died . . . he can't remember when. He boasts faith in Allah because if not for His divine will, how else can he justify the atrocities he commits? If he deals death with a heavenly hand, at least he can see himself as a holy warrior carrying out God's will. His belief in Allah makes him feel better than some *ajebutter* or educated *I Know Too* from Lagos. He is deadly, and it gives him status in the world of shadows. His righteous cause is the only thing distinguishing him from a *mugu* fool, a common, jack-thug criminal.

"*Gbe ja . . . gbe ja*," he yells to the other three men onboard. Let's get the hell out of here. He has the throttle open full bore. The mammoth engines blare. But the SEALs have a different plan for him. Pokey's Squad has their angle of pursuit laid out perfectly. They come in at 45 degrees. One of the SEALs mans the .50 cal machine gun on the bow. He begins to lay down intense fire. The rounds strike the *Boko Haram* boat. The captain now realizes that he has run right into a trap and that his plans to get away unscathed may have been premature. He panics and turns the wheel as fast as he can. It's a big mistake. The boat turns too sharply, exposing him to the incoming wall of bullets. Several rounds strike his chest. His torso explodes as the rounds blow through him. The SEALs take out the rest of the crew, standing bewildered and helpless as they prepare to meet Allah in person.

"Four EKIA and another boat down."

Falcon One, one of the Black Hawks assigned to cover the group, moves to intercept the second boat making for shore. "Guns, going guns," calls the pilot before he begins spraying machine-gun fire into the boat. The boat captain flies back and writhes around on the deck. His left arm is gone. It's not even on the boat anymore. He is screaming and spraying blood everywhere like a geyser. His gunner witnesses the devastation and hits the deck. The two other men on the boat drop down, too. They are surprisingly calm, considering they're lying in a pool of their comrade's blood while his boat speeds off with no one at the helm.

Pokey calls it in. "We've got a ghost. One dead, three possible shooters still active down on the deck."

Collecting himself for his final act of glorious defiance, one of the *Boko Haram* crewmen crawls over to a crate of RPGs and opens it. The SEALs open fire on him. They're bouncing around pretty good, though, and can't get a clean shot. Plus he's pretty well hidden behind the hull.

The shooter seems far more experienced than any of the others so far. He's smooth. He knows what he's doing. He deftly loads a rocket, pops to his knees and fires the RPG.

Pokey's coxswain calls out. "RPG . . . RPG . . . RPG! Incoming!"

Pokey and his men hold tight and cover their heads as the coxswain cuts hard to starboard. The rocket sails past into the orange sunset behind them. The shooter drops back down to the bloody deck to load another rocket. His two comrades urge him on.

Pokey is really pissed now. "I've had about enough of this shit." He barks instructions to his men. "I want suppressing fire. Keep them pinned down. Do not let them up, do you understand?" His next instructions are to the Black Hawk who took out the other boat. "Falcon One, light that skinny up."

Pokey's men *hooyah* and do their job laying it down.

The Black Hawk hovers, rotates a bit, and prepares to finish things off. "Roger that." He calls to the P-3. "Hawk Eye, paint it."

The P-3 paints the boat with a laser so the Black Hawk's Hellfire laser seeker can acquire its target. "He's painted, Falcon One."

"Roger that. Target's hot. Got lock." The SEALs are in close proximity, so the pilot warns them the missile is airborne. "Rifle, rifle, rifle . . . weapon away. Watch your asses."

The men in the RHIB cover their heads as the missile decimates the boat. Shards fly everywhere. Some of them land near the RHIB.

"Shack-a-lacka-ding dong," calls Pokey. "Sayonara, psychos."

Two of the fleeing boats are down; one remains. After that, there's only two left—Aliyu's and his lieutenant's. What started out as a band of fifty *Boko Haram* men is down to twelve including Aliyu. The Black Hawk swings out to intercept the boat trying to escape to the south. The bird comes up on them with ease. The *Boko Haram* crew makes no attempt to shoot back. Two men drop to their knees and pray. A third crewman leaps from the speeding boat into the choppy waters of Lake Chad. The Black Hawk fires on the boat, killing the captain and the two praying crewmen instantly. Two hundred bullets reduce them to a lifeless mass of organs, limbs, the remainder rendered unidentifiable. The rounds blow the bow apart and the ship nose dives into the water. It sinks in seconds, engines blaring as the stern lifts out of the water before plunging under.

The chopper then hovers and rotates to finish the crewman who jumped off and is now flailing in the water. He obviously cannot swim and is barely keeping his head above water. The pilot is about to open fire. Then he pauses. His co-pilot looks at him and nods. They decide to let him suffer and drown instead.

"Boat down. Four EKIA."

What started out as a grand plan for power and riches has turned into a nightmare for Aliyu and his men. When he ascended to the top, he never considered taking on trouble with America. He loathes the bourgeois world he came from—his parents, the university snobs, the corrupt oil men—but his goals were more local . . . amassing wealth and influence while becoming the most feared man in Nigeria. He has never considered himself an insane sociopath. When he looks in the mirror, he sees a completely sane man, a revolutionary. What he does is the logical extension of his world view.

Now his forces have been decimated, and most of his men are dead. Only two boats remain. Aliyu is holding steady for the island. His most faithful lieutenant steers his own boat alongside his leader. The SEALs are hot on their tail. This time, it's Ripper's squad that takes the lead. Pig Man is on the .50 and trading fire with the *Boko Haram* gunners. The other SEALs add M4 rounds to the mix. It's a wonder anybody survives.

"Pig, keep those skinny bastards pinned down," instructs Ripper. "Don't let them get another SAM off, damn it."

Ripper looks back at the Black Hawk hovering behind. He checks in with Papa Seal.

"Honey Honey, Honey Pot, are we still non-engage on the HVT?"

"Affirmative," says the Rear admiral. "Non-engage."

Ripper is disgusted. This political bullshit is gonna get one of his men killed. He calls to the Black Hawk. "Falcon One, Falcon One, can you take out the starboard boat without chopping up the HVT in the other?"

"Roger that. No problem. Going guns."

With Pig Man providing suppressing fire, Aliyu's men can't get off another guided missile. This clears the way for the Black Hawk to move in and fire on the boat next to Aliyu's. It's captained by his best lieutenant. There are three other crewmen onboard as well. Two of them are killed instantly when the Black Hawk fires. The machine gunner is also hit. The impact throws him from the boat. Wounded, he cannot stay afloat. He goes under and swallows a mouthful of water. He can taste his own blood as he begins the anguish of drowning. The SEALs leave him to his own demise. He will not rape any more girls.

The skipper of the boat is Aliyu's right-hand man. He shuts off his engines and waves his hands in the air. "*Kpro . . . kpro*," he calls out. "Take it easy." He stands with his hands up. The two remaining crewmen do the same.

Aliyu speeds on alone with just his gunner. The coxswain pulls the RHIB alongside the boat.

"*Kpro . . . kpro.* Take it easy. I surrender."

Ripper quickly looks over the boat. He nods to two of his men to board, but Pig Man wants the glory.

"Shit yeah," says Pig Man. "I got me some bad childhood memories to take out on this scrawny mother."

Ripper is annoyed. "Damned, Pig. Get your ass back on that .50, or I swear—"

It's too late. Pig Man is already on board the *Boko Haram* boat. He walks up to the gaunt sex trafficker.

"Take it easy. No problems," says the man. He lowers his hands and pleads. "You are the boss, man."

Pig Man is unimpressed. "No shit. Get your hands up now, you piece of shit." He lands a dark stream of Skoal spit on the man's chest.

The man lowers his eyes respectfully. Pig Man likes that. "Yeah, that's right. Don't you eyeball me. Whataya have to say now, you bony bastard?"

The man is relaxed, almost languid. The Americans think he's surrendering like a coward. He has them right where he wants them. He is a proud *jihadi* and will prove them so very wrong. The man reaches into his cargo pocket and pulls out a grenade. Time seems to stand still as the striker lever pops up into the air. In a single, swift movement, he shoves the grenade into an open pocket on the front of Pig's vest.

"*Allahu Akbar!*" is what the man has to say. He looks Pig Man straight in the eye. "Screw you, American."

"Frag . . . frag . . . frag!" yell the SEALs. They hit the deck.

Pig Man has a moment of clarity. He knows he has made his last dirty joke about Ripper's wife. He knows he has porked his last hooker. He knows in about three seconds, he's a dead man. But his brothers . . . he can't let them take shrapnel.

Without thinking twice, Pig Man wraps up the terrorist with a tremendous, engulfing bear hug. Close enough to kiss, he smiles, and spits a stream of dip juice in the man's face. "My fingers smell like your mother."

In a single, powerful motion, Pig Man throws himself and Aliyu's man off the far side of the boat. The grenade detonates. Pig is wearing his body armor, but the frag tears his throat out and nearly severs his head. He is forever gone, but his brothers are safe.

"Damn it!" yells Ripper.

One of the men dives into the water to grab Pig Man's lifeless body before it sinks deep down to the bottom. They don't leave one of their own behind . . . not ever.

Up above, Harvey Guttman rubs his face. His stress is evident. That's another man down. He can only imagine what other shit storm lies ahead. He still has Aliyu to film as he lands on the island where the two female snipers are waiting with their nano-bullets. He knows that back in his office on the other side of the world, Harry Pierson, the man who would be president, is surely letting loose a string of obscenities that would make LBJ blush.

The only easy day was yesterday.

Chapter 47

Aliyu has no intentions of leaving Koulfoua Island empty-handed. The mission has been a disaster for him. Everyone but him and the two other men in his boat are dead. To hell with them, he thinks. They were cowards. He does not know his best lieutenant blew himself up, taking Pig Man with him. This is not his primary concern right now. Running through his head are thoughts of his own failure, even helplessness, at the hands of the American interventionists. He cannot tolerate this. He imagines his mother and father laughing at his downfall. He wishes he'd killed them already instead of leaving it for some time in the future when he has more power. His parents—his entire family—disgust him. They represent everything he has come to loathe, everything he learned at *madrasa* to be the manifestation of a corrupt, fetid Western infidel world.

He knows he cannot return the way he came. The Americans are coming up fast from behind. This is also a philosophical realization for him, as he would rather die on the island than return home to Maiduguri an abject failure. He is virtually alone save for the three other men with him. Everyone else is dead. There is only one way for him now . . . straight ahead. This, too, is a reckoning for him. If he cannot get help from his friends in Chad, he vows to go down taking as many people with him as possible.

He shuts down the screaming engines and glides in until his boat grounds on the shore. The four men jump out. Time is of the essence. Aliyu knows the Americans are closing in fast. His men are panicked. He needs to regain control of the situation.

"It must be the Americans," he tells them. "They are scum."

"What are we going to do now?" asks one of the men. "We are no match for them."

Aliyu is enraged at this cowardice. He feels it reflects upon him. He refuses to allow his last moments to be defined by shame and humiliation. This has been the source of his violence since he was a teen. He raises his AK-47 and puts two bullets into the man's head. He turns to the other two men, who dare not utter a word of dissent. One of them is a lieutenant.

"Do any of you have anything to say?"

"Of course not," says the lieutenant. "The man was a coward."

"If we are going to die today, then we should die like holy men with pride and honor," says Aliyu.

"Agreed," says his lieutenant. "What is your plan?"

"The only thing we can do is try for escape into Chad. And kill as many of the women as possible. We should not leave with bullets left in our guns."

The lieutenant nods. "Yes. What if there are more American soldiers waiting for us?"

"Then we die like holy martyrs standing up to the infidels. But we should still try to get help from our friends in Chad."

He takes out his cell phone and makes a quick call. "It is me. We have a problem. I will need you after all."

He listens to the man on the other end.

"As many men as you have. We cannot go back across the lake. We need you to get us to Chad immediately. We will take some girls with us, as well."

The man on the phone is yelling about not having enough time and about how expensive it will be to pay off everyone.

Aliyu yells back. "Just do what I say! I will move it through Switzerland as usual. You always get your money, don't you?" He ends the call and vehemently curses the man's greed.

"Who was that?" asks the lieutenant.

"It is a friend in the Chad police. They will come immediately to the far side of the island. The Americans won't dare follow us into mainland Chad. Look at them. They are afraid to come on the island because we are in Chad now."

"It is like the early days in Somalia," opines the third man. "When Mohamed Farrah Aidid stood tall and defied the Americans, knowing they were prohibited from attacking."

"Exactly," agrees Aliyu. "The people feared Aidid. They trembled when they heard his trucks coming because they knew his men would kill them without hesitation while the Americans could do nothing but stand by and watch it happen. Those cowards."

He points toward the lake where the SEALs have been ordered to take up a holding position. They are not to touch Aliyu. Instead, they sit frustrated, looking at Aliyu pointing at them mockingly. The Americans know the two female snipers are waiting for him on the island, but the politics still goad them. They would much rather kill the men themselves.

"We have to hurry," Aliyu urges. "Let's go."

One of the men runs to the boats and returns with as much ammunition as he can carry. He also has a suicide belt packed with explosives and loose screws. He passes out the ammo. With the SEALs holding offshore, they are revitalized, thinking they have yet again won the battle of politics against America. They mock and curse the SEALs. They grab themselves and make other obscene gestures toward the Americans.

Aliyu takes his ammo. He orders the man to put on the suicide belt. "If need be, martyr yourself and take many people with you." He addresses his lieutenant as well, now. "Kill anyone you can. Grab a few girls as we escape to the other side of the island. Take no girl over fifteen years old."

He tosses out a sack of handcuffs. "Cuff them together. We will drag them along the ground if we have to. If any of the little bitches gives you trouble, kill her and take another. The whores are all the same to me. Just make sure they are young. We need to make as much money as possible now, and the police will want at least five girls for helping us."

The men scramble up the beach ready to gun down anyone they see en route to their escape into mainland Chad. Kill first, take slaves later. This is their focus. When they reach the refugee camp about fifty yards up the beach, they are prepared to initiate the slaughter. They descend upon the tattered and vulnerable makeshift tents. It is impossible to imagine five thousand women and girls finding shelter enough there. A few fires smoke and smolder. A few dogs scrounge about a large rubbish pit dug in the sand in which the remnants of what little aid and relief supplies the refugees received are deposited. It also serves as a latrine, but there is nowhere near enough lye to do the job.

Aliyu and his men are downwind from the pit. It reeks of piss and shit. The *Boko Haram* men are disgusted. "See," says Aliyu. "They live like animals. We are doing them a favor by killing them. They are human waste. They should be thrown into that pit with their own shit. The girls we are taking . . . we are *saving* them from their disgusting lives."

The men see Aliyu's point. "Yes," says the guy strapping on his suicide belt. "I knew we should have made an entire vest. This belt is good, but it is not powerful enough to kill many. We really should kill them all. It is the right thing to do. The Americans have interfered with the natural order once again, and bring shame upon those they claim to help."

Aliyu nods. He knows they could have used more explosives. The belt has some explosives and is packed with loose screws that actually cause most of the lethality. It is, more or less, a homemade claymore mine. But it is unfortunate he did not bring a vest packed full of C-4. "Quickly, with that belt," he commands. "Enough talk. We do not have anything stronger. *Yallah, yallah.*"

The men rush forward. They fire indiscriminately into the tents. One of the men cuts down the dogs and then joins the others as they empty their first clips. There is an eerie silence as they reload. There is no screaming. There are no refugees running for their lives to use as target practice. There is nothing . . . nobody. The camp is empty.

The men are furious. "What is going on?" demands the lieutenant. "Where is everyone?"

They violently rip down tent after tent. Again . . . nothing . . . nobody. They cannot fathom what has happened. They don't know that the refugees have already been relocated and are gathered at the back of the island with Camille, Kofi and their armed detail. There are, however, two women who remain behind . . . Nancy Harper and Dana Daniels are positioned in the tree line a few hundred yards away.

Aliyu's men realize they have been fooled again, but they are afraid to say anything. There is still hope of escaping with the Chad police, and they don't want to set Aliyu off again.

"This cannot be," says Aliyu. He begins thinking about the shame and humiliation. Nobody in Maiduguri will fear him if word gets out. He can't help calculating all the money he will lose. He begins sprinting up a hill toward the part of the island where Camille and Kofi are waiting with the women. He's heading straight for the two snipers.

Harvey Guttman doesn't miss a trick. He radios down to his remote camera crew he has positioned with the refugees in order to capture Camille's big speech. They begin rolling to get some footage of the refugees who have, at best, only a very general idea about what's happening. All in all, they seem aloof, resigned to their fate, like cattle waiting to be slaughtered.

Nancy Harper raises her rifle and clears her sinuses. It won't be long before Aliyu and his two men come up over the hill. She exhales slowly, methodically. In the hands of Nancy "Death Finger" Harper, her highly specialized Barrett rifle is like a laser at 1,000 yards. She is lethal. She and Dana are nothing like Camille. They're not looking for a better path to human enlightenment or to elevate the world to a higher frequency of vibration. They are not concerned with five solar strands of Godly DNA running through their spiritual core or becoming crystalline solar-bodily beings as the Third Dimension suddenly transforms. They're just trying to stave off the tide of terrorist troglodytes they see growing every day. That, and not get killed.

Unlike Camille, they're both young women. They don't know the difference between Fascists, Commies or Gooks. Their world is populated by Hajis, Towel Heads, Camel Jockeys and these three Nigerian Skinnies . . . but it's all the same trash to them. Dropping Aliyu is no different than dropping one of them critters they grew up shooting with their granddaddies. Their lives are so different from Camille's. And yet, when they met her for the first time on the island, they were both struck by the First Lady's radiant energy. "She has IT," as Harper said to Daniels afterward.

Both female soldiers feel an ineffable bond with Camille, suggesting something far greater than some newfangled nano-bullet in play. They both respect Camille for her desire to move the world forward, even if their job as elite killers doesn't fit into that plan. Dana put it perfectly in her journal after meeting Camille. "The First Lady's desire to move the world past killing and thousands of years of an 'eye for an eye' is a feeling I don't share, but I feel like I ought to. As for this nano-bullet shit, I would rather kill these dirtbags a thousand times over for what they do to women."

They take their job of keeping her safe with the utmost seriousness, perhaps more than they would if it were Becket Rosemore standing before the refugees. Camille O'Keefe can feel the power of the Community of Heaven flowing through her always. Nancy Harper can feel the nano-bullet sitting in the chamber ready to fire. Each woman has her own intuition. But for the moment, they are working for the same cause . . . breaking the cycle of killing by taking prisoners instead of killing them. Prisoners can provide invaluable information. Prisoners can save lives. Prisoners can be turned to the light.

Five years of research went into developing the nano-bullet. Originally, the primary goal was to develop a weapon capable of delivering a time-release dose of toxin via a nano-delivery system smaller than a pinhead. Outside of the jarring impact akin to being hit with a rubber bullet, the target would feel little more than a pin prick. The CIA intended to use it as an assassination platform that would be untraceable back to them in part because the nanotechnology was undetectable.

The plan was eventually scrapped, but the idea of using nanotechnology in combat lived on. When Camille demanded things be handled differently before agreeing to partner up with Pierson, a new use for the bullet came to light. With it came a new rationale—what if masses of enemy combatants could be immediately incapacitated, taken into custody and "reoriented?" There were clear implications for law enforcement, given all the controversy about police killing black men. Pierson saw it as a perfect fit, an ideal way to get Camille on board while also taking possession of a valuable asset . . . namely, Aliyu Adelabu. It was interesting, to say the least.

And so it came to be. The snipers use their usual Barrett with a powerful .50 caliber round for the stopping power, only it's a rubber bullet like the Israelis use in crowd control. Upon impact, the head of the bullet flattens enough to allow a needle inside to penetrate the clothing, skin and muscle tissue of the target. From there, nano-particles very much like microscopic robots go to the brain and incapacitate the target, leaving him completely unable to move albeit fully conscious and aware of what's going on around him.

In this way, high-value targets like Aliyu can be captured without risk of his detonating himself or otherwise resisting capture. More importantly—and keeping with Camille's demand—the shot is not to be fatal. Rather, the HVT will be rendered helpless, completely paralyzed, but fully conscious and aware. The Americans will have Aliyu as their prisoner, Harry Pierson will have his footage and Camille O'Keefe will have her wish for the beginning of the end of killing to achieve peace which, for her, is the only way to save the world from annihilating itself.

The shot will be no problem for either Harper or Daniels. Both can drop a man from over a thousand yards. If they were so inclined, they could probably put one through Aliyu's eye at 500 yards. In close at 200 yards like this, however, the women need to make a few adjustments to their sights.

"How are you looking on your come up?" asks Daniels.

Harper dials in her 500-yard dope. "Dead men walking," says 'Death Finger' coolly. "Well . . . I guess I should say 'they will be stunned shitless.'"

"Hope he brought toilet paper." Daniels' tone is dry. Neither woman laughs, but the joke is funny as hell. They know Aliyu will crap his pants the instant his nervous system seizes. It happened every time in testing on volunteers.

Nancy can't resist. "So . . . like . . . are we gonna have enlisted guys wiping asses every time when we start using this nano-bullet shit?"

Dana finally cracks a smile. "Nice pun. How long did it take you to come up with that 'nano-bullet shit' line?"

Nancy feigns thought. "About as long as it took me to beat your ass on the range last week."

Enough now, it's time to get to work. They need to make sure nothing happens to Camille O'Keefe. That would be bad . . . very, very bad.

The P-3 updates the women on Aliyu's position. "Wonder Woman, this is Eagle Eye. Be advised you have three fighting age males coming up over the hill now. Range about 215 yards. We have positive biometric ID. Your HVT is in the middle. There is one FAM on either side of him."

Nancy confirms. "Roger that, Eagle Eye."

Aliyu and his men reach the top of the hill. The women have them in their sights. Dana adjusts her scope. "You take the HVT. I'll take the guy on his right."

"What about the third guy?" asks Nancy. "I guess we'll have to knock the crap out of him, too."

Dana grunts. "Fine. You take the third guy. By the way, that joke is old now. Get some new material."

"Yeah," says Daniels. "We've got eyes on three FAMs heading straight toward us at about 200 yards now. Not a problem." She looks at her partner. "Hey, Harp. These skinnies kinda look like zombies, don't they? Real *Walking Dead* shit."

As they come up over the hill, Aliyu and his men finally catch sight of the mass of refugees. "There!" yells one of his men.

It's time to put the women and their new nano-technology to the test. This is Camille's doing. It's her plan, her insistence on using a non-lethal alternative to show the world they can break the cycle of killing that spawns more and more terrorists. She needs this. It's part of her mission. She believes there is light in all people. Some have allowed shadow to overtake the light, but another thousand years of killing will not solve the problem. Aliyu and his men see things differently. They want revenge in the worst way now that they have lost everything.

The women make a few final adjustments. They epitomize cool. In contrast, Aliyu and his two men are rabid and burst into a sprint toward the area where Camille, Kofi and the refugees are positioned.

"Let's kill dem bitches," yells one man with the suicide belt on. "I want to chop *kpomo* today, oy!" Yes, he wants to skin the herd of cows. He begins firing at the women. The crowd of five thousand gets panicky. But they don't bolt or scatter. Instead, they bunch up into a large mass, looking to Camille for guidance.

Nancy Harper steps in. "This is Wonder Woman One. Shots fired toward our friendlies."

From above, a drone sends a real-time feedback to Command. It has one Hellfire rocket left. Papa Seal steps in before anyone tries to use that last missile. "This is Honey Pot. This is Honey Pot. Be advised, Tin Can is *no go* for engagement. I repeat, Tin Can is *on hold.*"

Nancy Harper and Dana Daniels don't have time to worry about politics. They know their job and fully intend to execute the plan, and they have Aliyu and his men in their sights.

The P-3 updates the situation. "Wonder Woman, Wonder Woman, this is Eagle Eye. Be advised, three Fighting Age Males moving toward your position. Muzzle flashes visible."

"No shit," confirms Harper. "Welcome to thirty seconds ago. Bullets are flying everywhere. It's a good thing these skinnies can't shoot worth a damn."

Aliyu's sudden charge forward surprises the snipers a bit. "Damn," says Nancy. "Now theses skinnies decide to move fast?"

She traces Aliyu as he and the two other men begin firing again toward the crowd. The refugees scatter this time. They are screaming. Complete chaos is about to break out. Nancy Harper fires and hits Aliyu in the right thigh. Dana Daniels fires immediately after. She hits Aliyu's lieutenant in the thigh as well. Both men stumble from the sudden impact of the .50 caliber rubber bullet. They try to pick themselves up but are immediately paralyzed. Neither man can move. Neither man can speak. They are completely aware of their surroundings but totally helpless.

Aliyu struggles in vain to move his arms. He tries to kick his legs, to regain his feet . . . nothing. He tries to speak, tries to proclaim Allah's wrath will rain down upon America . . . nothing. He has no idea what has happened to him. His body is frozen, but his mind is racing. He is aware of everything happening to him, and yet he is powerless, incapable of striking out. His brain is alive and processing the possibilities only to settle upon one.

It is a fate far worse than hell for him. He has been rendered incapable of resistance, left to the mercy of those whom he vowed to destroy. And still he struggles. But it is futile. Aliyu Adelabu is powerless, broken and about to be taken prisoner by the Americans who have killed all his men and totally kicked his ass. A million thoughts run through his head . . . it's a strange sensation. He is fully aware of what's happening around him, and yet he has no idea what's happening *to him*. One second, he's charging up a beach to murder and pillage. The next thing he knows, he's flat on his back, unable to move or utter a word. The same goes for his lieutenant, who lies sprawled out beside him contemplating the very same fate.

Chapter 48

Camille's wisdom finally begins to shine clearly, as if the island were a portal through which divine radiance passes. Aliyu Adelabu is denied a martyr's death. He will not become a hero of the people. Nor will his name go down in history as the ruthless leader of the most feared African terrorist organization. He will not be remembered as the defiant *jihadi* who swiped his girls out from under the American military while they stood by and watched. Instead, he will be taken into custody where he will disappear from the world. His sympathizers will never hear from him again unless it serves a greater purpose, the will of light rather than the machinations of darkness.

The moment Nancy Harper shot him with the nano-bullet, Aliyu Adelabu ceased to be a feared terrorist and sex trafficker. He became instead the subject of Camille's divine will. He will not murder any more women. He will not rape any more girls or sell them into slavery where they will be kept as wives or strung out on smack and used for kiddie porn and prostitution. He will not blow up any public markets, killing scores of innocents, or even detonate himself in one final act of martyrdom.

The moment Aliyu Adelabu was shot with that nano-bullet was the moment he became karma's bitch. And now he knows it. It dawns on him what has occurred. It's all a trap. All of it . . . a setup. The Americans are not standing to the side helpless to engage. They are watching their prey ensnare itself. The Americans are watching him become a zombie and vanish from history.

He musters every ounce of strength he can in order to put his gun to his head and end his life. But it's futile. He cannot move. He can only stare up at the sky and wonder why Allah has forsaken him so. If he could speak, he would curse Allah Himself. He wonders, though . . . has Allah cursed him first?

The last remaining terrorist hugs the sand when Aliyu and his lieutenant go down. He's got the suicide belt on, and he feels for the detonator. He has no idea what's happening, but he knows this is probably the end of the line for him. He looks over at Aliyu lying motionless next to him.

"We are finished," says the man. "You have killed us all. Every one of us. You have killed us."

Aliyu's face is blank, frozen. About the only thing Aliyu can do at this point is move his eyes. He shows no visible sign of the disgust tearing him up inside. He looks at his last remaining man. He keeps gesturing with his eyes for him to continue the charge up the beach, to detonate his belt and kill anyone he can. Better his man die gloriously than become the third American prisoner.

The man realizes now what is happening. "They shot you with something," he says.

Aliyu just keeps gesturing with his eyes for the man to continue the attack. It makes for exquisite footage. Guttman is ecstatic as he watches from his chopper, imagining the ludicrous monologue that must be taking place. "Jesus Christ, this is fantastic. Zoom in as tight as you can."

Once an obedient soldier in the ranks of *Boko Haram,* the man is now bitter and resentful. His voice is filled with vitriol. "I will not become an American slave like you, Aliyu. We take slaves, we do not become them. You promised us wealth and power, you have given us nothing. Instead, you have gotten us all killed . . . except for yourself and that pig of a lieutenant lying next to you. You will rot in an American prison where they will train you like a dog. And so you are."

He reaches into his pocket and takes out the detonator. "But not me, *sagba*. If they shoot me with one of those bullets, my belt will detonate. I will martyr myself and go to Allah in glory, unlike you. You will lie here waiting for your new American masters to come and take you to your dog cage."

A myriad of insults and invectives are rifling through Aliyu's brain right now, but he can only stare back in silence. The man is so enraged, he leans in and bites Aliyu's earlobe clean off and spits back in his face. "I should have sold *agati* instead." Yes, selling a little weed would have been a much safer bet.

He reloads his weapon, jumps to his feet and makes a mad dash for the refugees about 100 hundred yards away. He has the detonator gripped firmly in one hand. With the other, he wildly fires his freshly reloaded AK-47 everywhere he sees a scrambling horde of refugees. He is yelling wildly that he is coming to skin the cows.

"Great," remarks Nancy dryly. "A death blossom." It's a term she picked up in Iraq, referring to the way Iraqi security forces panic easily and spray fire indiscriminately whenever they take a little bit of fire. "What a piece of shit."

There's another problem. Now that he's less than 100 yards, the women see he's wearing a suicide belt.

"Shit, shit, shit," says Dana. She coms in. "Be advised, the last FAM is wearing what looks like a belt IED. Repeat, he's hot to pop. He's hot to pop."

Nancy Harper remains perfectly calm and lines him up. "Okay, scumbag. It's your turn . . . easy peasy."

As she is about to fire, Harvey Guttman's Black Hawk swoops in to get a close-up of her taking down the last *Boko Haram* terrorist in Nigeria. The rotor sends sand and dirt flying everywhere. Harper loses her line of sight. She fires and misses. Daniels curses and hurries off a round. She, too, misses.

The women are beyond angry. "Get that damned helo out of here!" barks Harper in her coms. "What the hell is wrong with that asshole?"

Papa Seal is ready to kill Guttman himself. "Get those Hollywood pricks out of my theater before I blow them up myself." He bangs the table.

Dana updates the situation. "Okay, okay, listen up. We've got one skinny heading straight for the First Lady. He's wearing a belt and he's gonna pop. Repeat, he's headed for the First Lady."

Both women try to get a bead on the last terrorist. But now there's even more dust as the Black Hawk pushes urgently to get out of the way. Reacting on instinct, the two women jump to their feet and begin sprinting in a desperate attempt to take the man down. The distance between them is too great. Five thousand refugees are scrambling every which way, screaming and crying. People are running into each other. It's mayhem. Camille stands tall a mere fifty yards away. Kofi is standing at her side, pistol drawn.

The shooter keeps spraying his death blossom, pumping in every direction. Some of the rounds find their mark. Women and children collapse by the dozens. Some are dead, killed instantly by a stray bullet. This seems like their life's theme—in the wrong place at the wrong time. Why does one woman catch a slug to the back of the head while the woman standing next to her escapes unscathed? Why does one little girl, struggling to wrest an infant from its dead mother's arms, make it to safety with the baby, while another girl less than five feet away is gunned down?

Nobody has time to think of such things when life and death seem divided by apparent caprice. They're too busy dying. Things are on the verge of going terribly wrong. Camille is horrified by the death as it unfolds around her. She has never seen anything like it, at least not in this lifetime. One of her Secret Service agents is cut down by a bullet to the face. The other agent puts his arm around Camille and begins returning fire. She does not understand why any of this is happening.

What is for us to know, we who wander and roam this vast wasteland, the realm of man and his will to power, his will to truth? The answer perhaps lies within an arm's reach of ourselves, within the wisdom of Camille O'Keefe, the woman who is the microcosm of the macrocosm. Even as bullets fly all around her, even as frightened as she is, she is not afraid of dying. It's only a transition to another form of energy for her. The effect is startling. She stands tall and unwavering amid the chaos. It is quite a vision, this fiery redhead with soft, white skin standing between a Secret Service agent wearing a blue suit in sweltering weather in the middle of a firefight and a giant of an African, dark as night and grizzled from too much death and destruction.

Camille, Kofi and her surviving agent are in a double bind. If they shoot the crazed attacker, his thumb will release the detonator, and the explosion might kill Camille. But if they don't kill him, he will surely detonate his belt and likely kill her anyway. Once again, Harry Pierson's need for self-promoting video put people in harm's way. Beck, Van Dorthman, the soldiers, the agents, the refugees, Kofi and, of course, Camille herself are just pawns in his game. He keeps getting away with it, though, because people need what he has . . . information and the position to use it.

The maniacal *Boko Haram* gunman is about 20 yards from Camille now. At last, his magazine is empty. He's killed thirteen women, eight young girls, and left many more writhing in pain. He's pointing his weapon right at Camille, pulling the trigger mindlessly. The AK-47 just click, click, clicks. He has no time to reload, nor does he care to. One way or the other, he's a dead man. His only goal now is to become a holy martyr, a hero of the Islamic people, a beacon for *jihadists* the world over.

He sees Camille's Secret Service agent and Kofi both draw a bead on him. He holds up his hand with the detonator. "Big boom," he says smiling. He finds the Secret Service agent very funny all dressed up in a big-man's blue suit on an unknown island in the middle of African hell.

"So now what?" he says.

Kofi takes the lead. He motions for the Secret Service agent to ease off. He deals with shitheads like this all the time. True, they aren't usually wearing suicide belts, but he figures when in Rome. . . . "Easy, *oga*. Easy. You are in charge, *oga*. We can make a deal. There are many girls you can have. We can make a bargain. You're a businessman. You fancy a bargain, right. I can get you a planeload of *agati,* so much weed, you will be the most *bolo, no wahala, oga.* "

For a minute, Kofi almost has him. The man would very much like to walk away from the whole thing with a planeload of government weed and a few girls to sell. He knows that could set him up for life. He also knows it's Camille O'Keefe standing completely vulnerable only twenty yards away. Her pale skin, her blazing mane . . . who else could it be? The sight of Camille pushes him to find one last reserve of strength. He digs down into the wellspring of hatred boiling deep inside. He cannot tolerate the idea that a woman like Camille exists. She threatens everything he fights to destroy . . . freedom, equality, sexuality, female empowerment. A woman like Camille O'Keefe can upend his extremist world order with a simple smile or a few heartfelt words. He cannot allow her to live. His only regret is that he did not pack enough explosives. The screws will probably kill her, but it is not a foregone conclusion.

Kofi senses he's losing the guy. He's seen that look before. It's never good. The Secret Service agent also recognizes that look. But he's never been in a standoff like this before. Camille intuits what's about to happen and turns to the agent.

"No!" she yells.

It's too late. The man whose sole purpose it is to protect her makes a tragic mistake and fires several rounds. The bomber's stomach ruptures. His femoral artery is blown open as well. From his knees, he holds out his arm and loosens his grip on the detonator. This is the moment he has been waiting for, the moment when he achieves one with the almighty Allah and dies like a man. This is the moment the life of a great woman, Camille O'Keefe, and all the promise she holds for the world is snuffed out.

In seconds, Camille O'Keefe will be dead, and *Boko Haram* will have scored their greatest victory ever, even in their final defeat. This is exactly what the nano-bullet is supposed to prevent.

"Allahu Akbar!"

Kofi Achebe understands what Camille's death would mean, the setback for the world that would result should she die at the hands of these terrorists. He understands the fragility of the world at this moment. She is the savior he can never be. He knew this before he reached out to her. The world needs her, not him. It's his time to move on.

He spits his last stream of dip juice and launches his mammoth black body onto Camille's. She is buried beneath him when the belt detonates.

His last thought . . . *I am redeemed at last.* He dies as he always imagined it—with a fat dip, his gun on his hip and a smile on his lips.

The shrapnel from the screws in the bomb kills the second Secret Service Agent and about two dozen refugees. Many others are screaming in pain with serious injuries, including mangled limbs and serious head wounds. Many of them will soon die.

Many men sacrificed themselves this day. They all believed in their own salvation and redemption through their final deeds. What, then, makes them so different? Meanwhile, the men responsible for all the death and suffering, Aliyu Adelabu and Harry Pierson, are spared death and suffering. Bathed in irony, the great juxtaposition of it all escapes even Harvey Guttman's eye in the sky, for some things can only be captured in the web of words born from human suffering to expose the truth of everything we'd rather not know.

This is why great novels are written about events that reflect the core of who we are.

Chapter 49

It's hard to imagine polishing up a world as bleak and depraved as this in order to reveal something precious. But that's Camille O'Keefe's greatest gift. In constant communication with ethereal energies, she connects to a multitude of planes. She understands intuitively that we are all energy, and so we must all interconnect to raise ourselves up out of the muck and mire. Camille O'Keefe believes the physical world is "boot camp," where people must prove themselves capable of putting love in motion with so much inertia that the power of light builds critical mass and simply overwhelms the world of shadow.

Aliyu Adelabu and the rest of *Boko Haram* symbolize the great darkness that has enveloped this world since the Enlightenment. We are in a new Dark Age, but not to Camille O'Keefe. She sees opportunity in loss. She sees awakening in death, a life plan in misfortune. These are the thoughts filling her head as she stands stunned before the mass of frightened refugees who are looking to her for guidance now that the fighting is over.

The refugees have gathered around Camille. Guttman's guy with the handheld camera pushes his way in. It's exactly as Pierson schemed. When he started planning the whole thing, he felt in his bones that "these Mandingos" would naturally gravitate to Camille "like bugs to a bright, white light." As he once explained to Guttman, "These people don't know right from wrong. They're almost like savages in that way. It's tribal. When they see our beautiful Camille with her exotic red hair and pure white skin, they'll be treating her like a Goddess."

Camille has no such pretenses. The SEALs have landed on the island, taken Aliyu and his lieutenant into custody, and are now trying to corral her into a Black Hawk and get her the hell out of there.

"Madam First Lady," says Pokey. "We need to get you out of here right now."

Camille pushes him away.

Pokey respectfully tries again to persuade her. "Ma'am, we are in Chad. Who knows what's coming next? For all we know, the Chad military is on their way. This is no place for you."

Camille turns to him suddenly. "Look around you. This is exactly the place for me. This is exactly where I need to be right now."

She walks over to Kofi's body. His back was blown apart by a handful of deadly screws. But one of the refugees had the presence of mind to cover his body for some dignity in a place where there is so little. Camille is not that naïve, though. She sees the dark dirt around him where the earth has swallowed his blood.

She kneels down, pulls the tarp back from his face, and touches his shoulder. "Thank you. I will see you in the next life, my friend. I'm sure of it."

She re-covers his face and stands up. She notices his trademark aviator shades a few feet away. She takes them and starts for the crowd.

It's Ripper's turn to talk some sense into her. He grabs her arm. "Ma'am, we need to go." Camille holds up her hand. "No, young man. I'm tired of people telling me what I need to do. Now if you'll excuse me, it's time for me to address these people who have been through hell."

She puts on Kofi's glasses and walks to the crowd of refugees.